Best American Gay Fiction

1996

Edited by BRIAN BOULDREY

LITTLE, BROWN AND COMPANY
Boston New York Toronto London

First Edition

The characters and events in this book are fictitious. Any similarity to real persons, living or dead, is coincidental and not intended by the author.

Copyright Acknowledgments appear on pp. 316–318.

ISBN 0-316-10320-9 (hc)
ISBN 0-316-10317-9 (pb)
ISSN 1088-5501

HC: 10 9 8 7 6 5 4 3 2 1
PB: 10 9 8 7 6 5 4 3 2 1

MV-NY

Published simultaneously in Canada by Little, Brown & Company (Canada) Limited

Printed in the United States of America

THIS BOOK IS FOR

Hugh Rowland, ENTHUSIAST.

Contents

Contents

Acknowledgments

Several people were helpful in the creation of this book. The editor wishes to thank the following people for their help with this project: Mark Chimsky, Peter Ginsberg, Hugh Rowland, Don Osborne, and Catherine Crawford. A very special thanks to Judith Rees, who provided the quiet and space to work and entertained with the *Wahkiakum County Eagle* sheriff's report: She "do the police in different voices."

Introduction

I am a restless reader. When friends come visit me at home and inspect my bookcase, I watch their eyes narrow as they try to peg my tastes, only to come away puzzled: What do *The Wooings of Jezebel Pettyfer* and *How to Make Your Own Stradivarius Violin* have in common? My peripatetic reading agenda is satisfied by anthologies, which are plentiful these days. The nature of the anthology is restless because it is a patchwork of different voices and moods. Some of the pieces of that patchwork clash, some harmonize; one story's theme will augment and inform another's and create a new, more complicated theme. Contributors to an anthology find themselves under one cover because they share a subject or the writers share a certain background — but after that there are more differences than similarities in style, substance, mood, length, and effect.

The mutual restlessness of an anthology and a reader like me creates an exciting energy. Stories speak of each other, leading me on a search for other, similar stories or authors investigating a certain trend. I explore anthologies the way I rummage through the refrigerator looking for a midnight snack — sampling salty pickles, hot salsa, sweet ice cream — waiting for something to please my taste, sate my appetite.

That's how I put this book together. It was created not to be an exclusive club that leaves many deserving writers out in the cold, but as an inclusive, enthusiastic gathering, a party.

I aimed for breadth and I hope that it shows in the collection: Michael Lowenthal and Rick Barrett write about AIDS, but one story is erotic while the other is told from the point of view of a middle-aged, middle-American father. Bernard Cooper and Jim Grimsley explore the coming-of-age genre, but one story is brainy and imagistic while the other is a mythic fantasy sunk in a too-real world. There are stories of transsexuals, drag queens, call boys, porn stars, and political dissidents. There are also stories about parents, closeted rock stars, and teenage girls.

Tapping into this restlessness is also a way to contemplate diversity. In an age when political correctness has become little more than bean counting, it's time to look at quality over a breadth of subject matter, individual aspirations, and experiments. This doesn't mean, however, that the same criteria should be applied to every story. Each one has to be judged on its own terms and by its own goals for success.

In my restless search for the stories that make up *Best American Gay Fiction 1996*, I sought variety. I pored over shelves full of novels and short story collections, haunted the 'zine racks in alternative magazine shops, quizzed other avid readers about their discoveries, even flipped desperately through my in-flight magazine on plane trips, hoping to stumble on that perfect story in the most unlikely place.

A friend calls with an urgent message: "Have you looked at this new Caribbean anthology? There's a story by Gil Cuadro, the Cuban who wrote *Strawberry and Chocolate*."

"Yes, it's great," I say, "but it was published six years ago in Spanish and there's nothing particularly fictional about his memoir of his relationship with his father."

"Have you got Mark Merlis in there? Don't forget Mark Merlis," another friend chides me.

"But Merlis's novel was published in 1994, not 1995," I lament. "I'll have to catch him on the rebound."

"*Best American Gay Fiction?*" an acquaintance sounds it out for himself when I explain the new book I'm editing. "Great; will you put in some of Anne Rice's new novel?"

My answering machine was full of recommendations, like clues to a treasure hunt:

"There's this great book, but it's only published in England, and there are only three hundred copies, and they won't ship it because of obscenity laws, but you'd be stupid not to publish it in your anthology." *Beep.*

"My boyfriend has a perfect story, but it hasn't been published yet, but maybe you could get some magazine to print it before the deadline?" *Beep.*

"Did you check out the *National Review?* Seems to me I remember something that might have been fiction in an issue back in February. Or was it March?" *Beep.*

"There's an on-line magazine that has the best drag-queen story I've ever read, but you'd better download it fast, because their web site is disappearing tomorrow." *Beep.*

I hope my own rovings and treasure hunting have made it more convenient for readers to see the wide range of work — and methods of publishing — that are appearing in greater volume every year. And you can trust me on this one: There was very little good gay fiction published by the *National Review* in 1995.

How can I be so sure? What sort of standards must a story live up to in order to qualify for a book called *Best American Gay Fiction 1996?* Who would have the nerve to be the arbiter of taste for the rest of the reading world? It's important to set the tone and discuss the criteria for a book that promises to appear once a year. Excellence, as I see it, comes from individual genius. That an individual voice rings clear in each of these stories is more important than a perfect yet slavish imitation of other writers.

Loving an individual voice does not mean loving smallness. These stories, even the shortest ones, have a large presence, a fullness, an ambitiousness. Individual voices take big chances.

If my construction of this book came from a restless mind with a restless task, then my taste in writers goes, too, toward the ambitious, the adventurous, and the energetic. And gay writers *are* energetic, if quantity is any marker: The 1996 Lambda Book Award nominations for fiction alone were drawn from forty-eight books, many from large mainstream publishing houses. There are several representatives from large publishers in this book. But there are also plenty of examples from small presses, 'zines, and obscure gallery catalogs, the places where the great writers of tomorrow are showing themselves for the first time.

Consider the freedom, energy, and possibility offered by smaller publishers: Back before the profitable possibilities of gay writing caught the eye of mainstream publishing, there existed a handful of small publishers like Alyson, Cleis, and Alamo Square who were largely responsible for putting out gay writing. Because gay writing was already in the margins — "weird," to the mainstream — it didn't matter that writers like John Rechy, Dennis Cooper, or Robert Glück got even weirder.

That initial unsettled adventurousness continues today, and you can find in gay men's fiction a spirit of innovation that is at the vanguard of all writing.

If my goal is to uncover innovation in this collection, what is at the heart of the innovative trends? Look at the examples in this book. One of the themes that binds together this patchwork quilt is nostalgia, a look back at a time "before the fall." Time can be divided into before and after AIDS. Perhaps even the gay male obsession with recycling styles of the past, like those flimsy disco shirts filling fashionable boutiques these days, comes out of this looking backward with a wistful need to sort it all out.

That looking backward, that recycling the past, is explicated beautifully by Matthew Stadler in "Allan Stein": "Childhood can only be seen by those for whom it has ended," he writes. "It is conjured into existence, it becomes visible only by its disappearance. When it is finally seen, childhood has a trajectory, a countdown aimed toward zero. This is the sickness of nostalgia."

The transformation, the fall, the disappearance of childhood as it is apparent in the body, mind, and spirit, is the focus of much of the writing offered in this anthology The body's transformation (from health to sickness, from child to adolescent, from man to woman) is at once erotic and terrifying to us, as R. S. Jones's dying character testifies in "I Am Making a Mistake."

The body and its changing state is the preoccupation of plenty of the *Best* stories. Just look at some of the titles: *Mysterious Skin, Flesh and Blood.* Edmund White's story comes from his collection *Skinned Alive.* "The Medicine Burns" has a narrator whose skin is ravaged by acne. A split lip is all-important to the story of that title. What's changed in "After the Change" is a matter of the flesh. Gay men's writing in many cases begins with the objectification of the body and moves deeper from there.

One of the most exciting things going on in much of this fiction is an examination of the retreat from the body and this world, the transcendence into the next. Of course, this exploration is often prompted by the way the AIDS epidemic has entered our lives. But I think this factor cannot be isolated; it works together with many other aspects of gay male experience.

For example, gay men usually spend a lot of time closeted in their early years, pretending to be something they're not, indulging in fantasy and theater. Jim Grimsley's "On the Mound," from his novel *Dream Boy* — an almost mythological depiction of two boys falling in love in an old-time religious southern town complete with haunted mansion and ghosts — is filled with magic, theater, and the impossible. Similarly, Jason K. Friedman's "The Wedding Dress" offers at its end a mysterious moment of grace that is not exactly of this earth. And the narrator of Rick Barrett's "Running Shoes" speaks from some heavenly place where the mute can speak: A father reacquaints himself with a son who has mystified him in every possible way. Why doesn't he like football? Why would he move away from me? Why has he become an artist? Why is he gay? And why is he dying?

Barrett's, Grimsley's, and Friedman's stories are almost parables (or fairy tales?), with lessons not at once clear, like morality plays in which the morals they want to teach us have long since become extinct.

Those old morality plays came out of medieval thought and its expression in the art of the time. Like the iconography of stained glass or the Desert Fathers' renunciation of worldly things in favor of self-mortification, in many of these selections there is a backing away from matters of this world, including the body, toward a place in paradise (either the heavenly one or the disco of the seventies) where AIDS doesn't ravage our lives anymore.

Consider other ancient examples with which you can compare contemporary gay literature. In the *Song of Roland* (in which Charlemagne's favorite boy is ambushed by the Moors), the *Bhagavadgita* (incidentally, I went to my bookshelf to find my copy of that Hindu religious work and discovered that it was translated by

Christopher Isherwood; more than coincidence?), Dante's *Divine Comedy*, and even the Bible, the narrative is not really about life in this world but the search for transformation. They're not told like tales about a lust for life. They don't happen in ordinary time. Roland can't wait to die for his Christianity, and for Charlemagne. Arjuna is directed to battle by Krishna because his life on earth has one purpose: to transcend life on earth.

Like contemporary gay writers, medieval writers ignored most of the Aristotelian unities of character development, plot, and pace in order to pursue transcendence. Every liberty that can be taken with time has been taken by gay writers, and that is where the most interesting work is being done. They pursue that transcendent moment by suspending time (Stephen Beachy's filmmaker looks frame by frame for that perfect image of his subject), repeating things (Ernesto Mestre's contortionist narrator is constantly reminding us how he escaped from a prison camp), invocation (Jim Provenzano's "Split Lip" is a litany of directives), cheating time (the dead lover in Michael Lowenthal's "Going Away" speaks again through a tape recorder), or even going backward (Matthew Stadler's countdown). There are many methods by which these writers explore the way time has its effects on our bodies, and on our work.

By putting this anthology together, I hope I've saved readers time. And time can work to our advantage. After all, in our own lifetime we've witnessed an explosion in the amount of gay writing being published, creating more and more to choose from. Widespread publishing has given us the opportunity to be more discriminating and name for ourselves what is "best." I hope you find this book is a good start.

So as you read restlessly on, discovering stories by the names you love and hopefully discovering some new names, think about what binds these stories together. It's not just glue and stitching, but quality, community, transcendence, redemption, and not a little imagination.

Brian Bouldrey
April 1996

Best American Gay Fiction

1996

HIS BIOGRAPHER

He had traveled so much that, paradoxically, the few authentic places left in the world looked especially fake to him, as though where Nantucket had once been, a real whaling village built by hardworking Quakers, now there was only a theme park that contained or embalmed it, as a ceramic crown reproduces in a dead material the still-living but whittled-down tooth it sheathes. In the same way the Ile Saint-Louis was no longer a place where people lived, shopped for food and worked but rather an ensemble of stately, empty investment flats that stood dark and untenanted eleven months out of twelve, the seventeenth-century façades concealing luxury twentieth-century interiors rarely visited by their owners, who were groups of American or Saudi — well, not even people but corporations. Key West — famous for its decrepitude, Cuban cigar makers, shrimpers and destitute artists — was now glistening with hasty but radical restorations perpetrated by retired tax accountants growing their gray hair long.

No, all that was real in the world was its despised, interchangeable platitudes, the suburban shopping malls, the millions of vernacular miles of California strip architecture or, on a lower level still, the sprawling concrete apartment buildings outside Cairo or Istanbul fissuring and rusting even before completed, open sewers between them seeping through the red mud.

From an airplane that's all you could see no matter where you flew over the globe and anything that could be described as charming or picturesque — the snow-topped red barn in Vermont, the historic heart of Basel — was either a guest house or a neighborhood of psychiatrists' offices, a self-conscious reference to itself, words between quotation marks, a boutique or about to become one. From an airplane Greenwich Village wasn't visible, just miles and miles of Lefrak City. From a plane you couldn't see Bourges, which in any event was composed of polyurethane half-timbering out of a kit tacked onto fresh stucco and new car-free cobblestones reflecting like fish scales the lights bouncing off the cathedral *son et lumière;* no, all that was visible from a plane was industrialized wheat farms and drizzle-flecked 1960s public housing, regular as tombstones in a military cemetery.

Worse, he had the same bleak view of himself, the feeling that the only parts that were genuine were those that had never been remarked on precisely because they were unremarkable. For a long time he'd told himself he was tough and unsentimental, but for the last two years he'd admitted he was simply numb and empty of sentiments, a hive that looked normal and functioning until closer inspection revealed it had long ago been burned out and abandoned. Two years ago his nephew had said to him, "There was a study in which all these women complained their husbands were incapable of showing their feelings, and then after lots of therapy it turned out the men just didn't have any feelings."

Charles said to his nephew, "I'm like that. I don't feel anything." He wanted to see if his nephew would protest or if some inner bell would start clanging to warn him he was plunging into deep nonsense. But nothing happened. His nephew flickered into a half smile. The words just hung there in the air, like the devastating truth a stand-up comic tells about himself, funny exactly to the degree that no one before had ever admitted so simply and with such chipper panache to something so sordid.

That's why Charles could tolerate only the malls and council flats of his soul, the parts that functioned routinely, that were no better than or even different from comparable parts in everyone else. He doggedly admired the part that could watch four hours of CNN at a stretch or eat heavily sugared cornflakes at midnight as he stood half-nude and half-awake by the cryptic light of the fridge or talk about the weather to the grocer. Even those actions were too "typical," too "revealing." The person who filled out a registration form when checking into a hotel, who poked a hemorrhoid back into his arse after a shit, who ironed a shirt, that person was perhaps possible.

Perhaps that was also why he wobbled on the balance between equal weights of vanity and irritation at the idea of someone writing his biography. Charles "was the author of" (i.e., had somehow stumbled, both panicked and exhausted, to the end of) biographies of three twentieth-century French writers (Cocteau, Jouhandeau and Stuart Merrill) and he knew that no matter how diligent a biographer might be in sorting out the chronology and uncovering unpublished manuscripts and letters, no matter how skeptical in discounting the special claims the living might have on their dead subject, no matter how subtle he might be in tracing out the indirect, even reciprocal, links between the life and the work, what readers expected and publishers demanded was, quite simply, the *key*, or at least a *scoop*. The key was almost always sexual and inserted into the nursery door; Virginia Woolf's incestuous brush with her older half brother had been a capital moment in the locksmith's art. Ideally the scoop, also sexual, would be the discovery of a previously hidden document that would confirm that Cocteau's father had indeed committed suicide because he was a homosexual or that Jouhandeau's wife had denounced her ex-lovers as Jews to the Gestapo or that Stuart Merrill had contracted syphilis during his brief return to the United States to attend a university (his American parents, long settled in Paris, had been horrified to discover that their son, who at seventeen was one of the original Symbolist poets, could scarcely speak English, but their plans to educate this exquisite dandy in the rough and tumble of Columbia University resulted only in his publishing a single slim volume in English, *Pastels in Prose*, before he sailed back to France, despite the pleas of America's most eminent novelist, William Dean Howells, to stay in the New World, where his talent was much more needed than in a France already surfeited with genius).

But what would this Mr. Tremble dig up on him, Charles? What keys would he insert, one after another, into the frozen lock? Perhaps the most obvious theme to develop would be how he, Charles, who'd written about two homosexuals and one aesthete, was, in spite of his small stature, soft voice and diplomatic ways, an insatiable and improbably successful womanizer. (But he hoped Mr. Tremble wouldn't dwell on that too much; after all, his wife, Catherine, even after thirty years of marriage, was still jealous and, above all, *pudique* about what strangers might say and think).

Or Mr. Tremble might build up the paradox that Charles, a Jew from Lebanon born to an Egyptian father and Turkish mother, had moved to France after the fall of Beirut and devoted himself entirely to — well, to what? Here the lines of the design became tangled, since Cocteau (the plural of "cocktail") had played host to modernism, whereas Jouhandeau, that dreadful little clown who couldn't stop writing and had penned almost a hundred books, had ignored the present entirely and harnessed the pure language of Racine to his own petit bourgeois mixture of Catholicism and sexual slumming (*Don Juan's Breviary*, the subtitle of one of his books, said it all). If Cocteau and Jouhandeau were major writers, Merrill was just a curiosity, although the late poems he wrote in Versailles about the Great War achieved a certain marmoreal (the English would say "Georgian") grandeur. No, one could always propose that Charles the eternal outsider had a fine psychological take on Cocteau, who was at once the very heart of Paris *frivole* for five decades and almost carelessly despised all the men who mattered most to him (Gide, Picasso, Stravinsky). Or Mr. Tremble could play up, rather crudely, Charles's heterosexual Don Juanism as the basis of his grasp of Jouhandeau's "abjection" amongst butcher boys (this prospect made Charles bristle). Or Merrill the Marginal — but then, who didn't consider himself to be marginal? In France, every *vieux con* conservative government minister, born in Saint-Germain-en-Laye and graduated from Sciences Po, dressed in Sulka suits and Weston shoes, would smile, show his palms and declare during a long television interview that he was something of a "dreamer" and "misfit," despite his rich wife and his own aristocratic parents and his teenage daughter off riding to hounds in Ireland. Oh, no, everyone was "marginal," just as everyone was "passionate" about his work. It was all part of the aristocratization of everyday French life; no one could dare admit he worked to get rich or out of habit or just to eat. No, work had to be a "passion." . . .

He'd have to pretend, no doubt, to Mr. Tremble that passion had driven him to write his autobiography and his three biographies, though in fact he'd become a writer to escape the drudgery of door-to-door canvassing for an electronics firm, the job he'd landed when he was washed up on the coast of Brittany after he'd escaped from Beirut. He'd never been a good worker or student. In fact he'd never been a good adult. He'd been happiest as a boy when he'd lived amongst his mother and sisters and girl cousins, something like the pasha's son in the harem, the only other intact male. He despised work and if he were a millionaire he'd never write another line.

What he did like — what he was passionate about, if to be passionate meant you couldn't stop doing it — was research. He wanted to know everything, not because he was vain of his knowledge. No, he'd never been after honors or even passing admiration and had nearly flunked out of school, though he did like it when a woman would smile at him because he'd murmured the name or word or title all the big, important men had been vainly seeking. No, his research was linked to his sexuality, though to say so sounded like biographical key-rattling. He wanted to see the insides of dossiers, bedrooms, bodies, he wanted access to archives and intimate secrets, and the first "No," far from discouraging him, only made his eventual conquest more piquant. Difficult people, even impossible people, fascinated him.

His very success in all domains made the going harder now, since in the past, before he was known to be a Don Juan, each woman had thought she must be the first to take pity on him, so uncomely was he with his gap teeth, frail body, balding head, just as each doddering French book collector had thought there could be no harm in showing an *inédit* to such a diplomatic little Lebanese Jew who skirted so cleverly all Parisian literary feuds and belonged to no *chapelle*.

Now things were closing in on him, at least in Paris, precisely because of his all-too-conspicuous literary and amorous successes. To be sure, now that he was infamous certain women wanted to know what all the fuss was about, just as certain collectors were charmed to be seduced by the man who'd already deflowered libraries long thought to be beyond approach. *The*

Seducer in Letters and Love — would that be the subtitle of Mr. Tremble's clumsy little effort?

He'd been delighted to accept this yearlong appointment in New England, because he thought it would give him a breather. To tell the truth, he wasn't the least bit like Don Juan, since he, Charles, never dropped anyone, loved everyone and remained true to them all after his fashion. *Tant pis*, since that meant he had to listen to a lot of weeping and had to run frantically from one rendezvous to another all day every day. Now his women would have a year to cool off.

Although Catherine, as tiny as he, was stunning and always elegant, in his extracurricular romances he specialized in women who were a bit . . . "homely," to use the cozy, domestic American word, as well as those who were just a bit "over the hill" (his English was improving; he kept long lists of expressions that amused him or "caught his fancy" and he eschewed any more diligent approach to the language). Cocteau and Jouhandeau worshiped their lovers (Cocteau thought of them as gods, Jouhandeau as God) and needed them to be beautiful (for Cocteau they were gleaming, well-carved chessmen the Poet advanced in his brilliant but losing game with Death; for Jouhandeau they were altars before which he knelt, at once defiled and exalted by these boys). Charles didn't worship his women. He made them laugh. He was tender with them. He liked knowing where a woman was vulnerable. In Beirut he'd once even made love to a woman with a wooden leg and he'd finally convinced her to let him unharness her.

One of his women now was Jade, a Chinese stockbroker in her fifties who'd not been touched once in the last ten years by her handsome, scholarly husband, head of a now-discredited cultural organization founded by the Chinese Nationalists that had attempted to "regild its coat of arms" (*redorer son blason*) by offering courses in computer science to unemployed Chinese hooligans in the fifteenth arrondissement. Jade had clearly given up on love and had been astonished when Charles, whom she'd met at a dinner given by the grandson of Stuart Merrill's best childhood friend, had invited her to lunch. She'd assured him she wasn't that kind of broker, she only handled corporate portfolios, but he'd persisted. By the end of the lunch she'd already told him she'd long ago been a tennis champion as a teenager in Singapore — and she'd given him her private number at the office. At the Bibliothèque Doucet he'd met other women, young and old, intelligent and not. As he'd grown more successful with each biography, he'd become more handsome — better dressed, better coiffed, more confident.

But he resented the way Catherine had slowly domesticated him. They'd lived together a long time before they married. That had been the exhilarating time when they'd met in Beirut where she, a proper Breton girl, had come in search of adventure. His father was still rich then with his Renault dealership and Charles had worked freelance in advertising only very occasionally. He'd sometimes gone to his family's seaside house for weeks on end with Catherine, each of them outfitted with a suitcase full of books. Hers were English comic novels in French translation (Austen, Waugh, Lodge) and his were detective stories in any language at all. But then after his father had lost his money (the bit that he hadn't gambled away at the Beirut casino just days before they'd been forced to evacuate the city) Charles had had to work full-time in Brittany, where they'd taken refuge with Catherine's parents. His idle, bohemian existence had come to an end. In the Breton drizzle he'd had to go from apartment building to building in Rennes ringing doorbells and subjecting those who responded to questionnaires that took an hour to fill out. Fortunately, the

French were complacent, pedantic and bored — a combination that made them wonderfully susceptible to such imbecile bureaucratic exercises. Whereas they would have bridled if they'd been asked personal questions, their vanity tweaked to a probing of their least significant habits. Far from brushing him aside or rushing through the form, his respondents made a substantial meal out of the absurdly detailed interviews. One of his first respondents had been Milan Kundera, newly arrived from Czechoslovakia to teach literature at Rennes. He assumed the questionnaire must have been issued by a government agency and accordingly answered each question with dogged application. Later Charles liked to joke that he had in his possession a long interview of Kundera that had never been published and that showed him in an unusual light.

His spies had told him Tremble already had three hours of interviews with Charles's estranged Mexican-Jewish researcher, Tom Smith, as he blithely called himself, though his real name was Tomăs Weingarten Smith, the appropriated "Smith," in accordance with Spanish custom, indicating his English mother's surname, whereas his real "last name" in the Anglo-Saxon sense was Weingarten, the family name of his father, a Russian-Jewish immigrant. Tomăs, a Paris acquaintance who'd worked fitfully on the Cocteau research (he'd mainly dined out on his expense account with Jean Marais, Cocteau's actor-lover), was a balding, self-hating, overweight homosexual; he systematically turned on everyone who'd ever helped him and following his system was now filling in missing mischievous misinformation about Charles in interviews granted to the American press. Tom Smith had undoubtedly told Tremble all about Catherine, Jade, the Bibliothèque Doucet harem and so on.

Tremble was due to arrive in half an hour on the train from Boston. Charles could walk to the station from his office, in the

French Department's luxurious quarters, in just fifteen minutes. He had time to give a few more teasing instructions to the department secretary, a *sympathique* roly-poly widow in her sixties from the intriguingly named town of Tallahassee — an Indian name, she'd explained. He was going to ask her if she had some Seminole blood. Could that explain why her white hair had taken on such a mysterious blue tint? Would she let him look at her palm just a moment? He knew something about how to read the palms of Occidentals and Orientals, but he had no experience at all with *les Peaux Rouges*, not that her skin could possibly be whiter — or softer, he might add.

He hurried down the hill past the white wooden church everyone here swooned over but that he'd found most unappealing at first, though now he could just begin to understand the frozen spiritual yearning the steeple expressed — or was it a finger accusing heaven of not conforming to the strictest political correctness? The fruit trees were all in flower, which made Charles gasp and wheeze. A bed of daffodils wavered in the cool breeze. It was a late April day, the sun's warmth was concealing a treacherously cold *fond de l'air*. After the bleak winter the students with their small features and big bottoms were all lolling on the grass in shorts. The "women" (i.e., *filles*) sometimes wore sweatpants over their immense *po-pos*. The pock-pock of a distant tennis ball sounded at irregular intervals, then disconcertingly stopped altogether. Two jocks (or was that word "Jacques"?) trudged toward each other like moonwalkers, their baseball caps turned front to back. They said in loud, uninflected voices, "Hey, dude." Luckily these robots wrote "personal essays" in French class, which revealed cultured, ironic minds dartingly at work, completely at odds with their inflated spacesuit bodies and idiot conversation.

Charles had scrupulously left his door open during private conferences with "female" students (he had a hard time making

Americans understand that in French *femelle* could apply only to an animal). Eventually Charles became wary even with boys, since intergenerational sodomy was also much on everyone's mind. He gave everyone A's, partly because he had been hostile to grades ever since his own student days, when he'd sounded such low notes, and partly because he'd learned that in the States a B could provoke accusations of rape. It appeared some old professorial "goats" actually did flunk those "kids" who wouldn't "put out" (these infernal English prepositions — was it "put *in*"?). Students considered an A (*vingt sur vingt*) to be their birthright and Charles was delighted to cooperate in this amusing fantasy. Never in history had there been a culture less coquettish, less seductive. On the streets no one looked at anyone. On a date there was no teasing, no flirting, no courting. Apparently one passed directly from indifference to safe sex or from copious yawns to rape.

The university was feeling him out to see if he might like a full-time appointment in the French Department. Charles doubted if he could stay away so long from Paris, but he did like the option and he was sure Tremble's meddling wouldn't help, not on a campus where feminism, two decades after it had died out in France, was still in full cry ("A lesbian is the condensed rage of all women" announced a poster Charles had put up in his bathroom. "Be the bomb you throw").

So far Charles had not had the least problem, since he'd remained studiously neutral, even neutered, on every "gender-related issue" and had won a few extra points by proposing a course on Luce Irigary, Hélène Cixous and Monique Wittig, three forgotten Frog frauds whom only American feminists still mentioned. No, but if Biographer Tremble used Don Juanism as a *key*, then Charles would never receive tenure (Charles pictured Tremble as a matronly *châtelaine* with a heavy bunch of cumbersome keys dangling from his waist).

Of course Tremble would probably not deliver the bio (*Lebanese Lothario*) until five years from now. Tremble was forty and had never published a book. He was an itinerant instructor in the Chinese language who had never received tenure anywhere because he'd never produced a book. Charles had done a bit of counter-research and discovered Tremble had been married once. Despite his unusual surname (French for "aspen") apparently it was just an open fan, a flickering subterfuge, masking a German-Jewish visage and a long name of all consonants like a bad Scrabble hand. Even though his paternal grandparents had been German, Tremble had been raised in Toronto.

What would a Canadian Jew make of his family's complex heritage? Charles wondered as he traversed a bridge that had recently been flung across the dirty, rusty river, paved over for decades but liberated in the last six months as part of a hopeless program to "beautify" the center city, a melancholy ensemble of baby skyscrapers from the 1920s, boarded-up storefronts and a vast windswept, deserted square. The only center of animation was an all-night diner frequented by bikers and "home boys" (one word or two?) who would surround a car waiting at a stoplight and beat drunkenly on its roof with their fists, even start to rock it and threaten to overturn it. Charles and Catherine had been subjected to this initiation on their very first night in town.

The question about Charles's Jewish heritage wasn't an idle one, since he knew perfectly well that if Doubleday had commissioned this biography it was to follow up the sweet, windfall success of Charles's own memoirs, *Passports*, which had become a bestseller against all odds. Apparently the only people who bought books in America were Jews, or rather Jewish women, and these *âmes soeurs* had been intrigued by the English translation of his book (a nonevent in France). *Passports* had delightfully jumbled all their preconceptions.

Charles's mother's ancestors had been Spanish Jews who'd been welcomed by the Ottoman Sultan at the time of the Spanish Inquisition. In fact Charles's mother spoke Ladino, an ancient Romance language that had been preserved from the fifteenth century down to the present. His maternal great-grandfather, a Turkish merchant, had happened to be traveling in Algeria at the very moment when the French government was offering French citizenship to Algerian Jews. He wasn't an Algerian, but he fudged his papers and obtained the citizenship anyway. After that, every generation of his family was duly registered at the French consulate in Istanbul and attended the French *lycée* there, though not one person in the family ever lived in France or had even visited it. When Charles's mother met and married his father, an Egyptian Jew, the only language they had in common was French; their children, raised in Beirut, were duly registered in the French embassy, attended a French Jesuit school and spoke French (and of course Arabic).

Charles's father's passport was Egyptian until Farouk fell. He then bought an Iranian passport — valid until the Shah was driven out. Next he purchased a Panamanian passport, but a new dictator canceled all his predecessor's deals. When Beirut went up in flames and down in rubble, Charles and his brother and mother had no problem finding refuge in France, since they were all French citizens, but Charles's father was still stateless and was allowed to settle in Paris provisionally only because the other members of his family were French. For the first time this "French" family saw France.

The story didn't end there. Charles's older brother, while growing up, had always played with Muslim children and had despised Maronite Christians and Zionists — and in France he'd become a professor of Arabic, converted to Islam and had even married a woman of North African heritage who did not herself speak

Arabic, so it was he who had to teach their children the language. His parents were distraught and flareups occurred at every family reunion. As though to compensate for his brother's apostasy, Charles was studying Ladino (so that the language would not die out in their family with his mother) and he and Catherine spent their holidays in Turkey in the Istanbul Jewish summer colony of Büyükada. Catherine had never been happier than during her four years in Beirut, and Charles missed it too. They both found Istanbul to be the closest approximation to Beirut, though Istanbul was dirtier and poorer, more dour and more majestic with its palaces and mosques stepping away from the Golden Horn and its melancholy cemeteries, the tombs of virgins covered with a carved marble veil and those of notables topped with a stone turban.

Nothing could be more distant from Istanbul than this New England town with its freshly painted eighteenth-century yellow wood houses and their dark green shutters or the empty, snow-swept streets with their strange names. Charles, who was used to eating bouquets of fresh mint and raw lamb brains, sweet gazelle horns and fluffy, sugary puddings of creamed chicken, lamb brochettes and parsley-pungent tabbouleh, now sat down to meat loaf and mashed potatoes and brown Betty at the Faculty Club. He could almost picture this "Betty," *une métisse bien en chair.* . . .

Charles stood at the top of the stairs as passengers who'd just arrived on the train ascended the escalator. A husky man with smudged glasses, gliding up, caught sight of Charles and gave a weary, ironic smile and raised his eyebrows high, higher; Charles saw what he thought was a New World expression compounded of embarrassment and humor, as though to say, "Yes, here we are, after all, and we must greet each other just as everyone always does." Except even the greeting turned out to be awkward. Charles put out a hand to be pumped in the American fashion, whereas Tremble bent down to kiss his cheek *à la française* — only it wasn't French after all, it was a New World one-cheek-only-peck, which Charles, going for the second cheek, realized too late: their glasses collided and Tremble's went askew.

As they walked up the hill, Charles offered to take one handle of Tremble's suitcase in order to share the weight, but apparently Canadian he-men of a certain age (even such a downtrodden example from Toronto) couldn't be seen admitting physical weakness any more than they could be observed wearing a silk foulard or a cologne other than one based on bracing lemons or virile limes.

"So here we are!" Tremble exclaimed.

"Yes," Charles hastened to interject, "but you'll see that the part around the university is much more beautiful."

"Clean air!" Tremble said, winded, with that trace of faint contempt residents of big cities adopt to praise the provinces, the city mouse's pink-eyed, sparse-whiskered disdain for the dowdy country mouse's dull and healthy habitat.

"Hope you don't pass out from the oxygen intake," Charles murmured, his deadpan delivery making Tremble's glance swerve covertly in his direction: Subject Has Unexpected Wry Sense of Humor, the mental note undoubtedly read.

As they climbed the long hill up toward Benefit, Charles wheezing from an asthma attack provoked by all the flowering trees, Tremble ashen and exhausted, his glasses making his eyes look extinct, like capped wells, the Canadian made a remark about "vigorous Wasp exercise" not quite being his "thing."

"You'd be surprised," Charles replied, testy about Tremble's bid for automatic Jewish complicity, "half of these Jacques or jocks are Jews. See that blond *boeuf* on roller blades? Trevor (if you please) Goldenberg."

Catherine had prepared them tea, which Tremble drank but dubiously, examining the pretty tea service, which had been part of the furnishings of the house, with that same smile, the one that seemed to say, "Nothing in this world is real but woes and grief. How curious that we should be pretending to be people who drink tea." Charles thought such heavy-handed inauthenticity was rather puerile — but perhaps he was misinterpreting the smile.

Well into the conversation Charles realized that Tremble wasn't taping anything or taking notes — or even asking pertinent questions. When Catherine slipped out of the room in search of more cookies, Charles said, "You know, Catherine is typically French in that she thinks a biography of anyone alive who's not a rock star is slightly absurd."

Tremble had gone sterile behind his glasses; no paramecia were squirming in those stolid petri dishes.

Since one has to be excruciatingly direct with North Americans, Charles added, "I doubt if Catherine would give you a real interview but you might slip in a question or two during the evening."

"And you? What do you tell people when they find out I'm writing your biography?"

"I always say my life is so dull — which it *is* as you're no doubt discovering to your dismay — that I can't imagine it would make substantial reading ('That winter he deliberated long and hard whether to give Suzy an A or B' or 'His step quickened that morning as he headed toward the archives'). Not just dull but a full treatment is undeserved, unmerited. But I always add that I had so much trouble getting people to cooperate when I was writing biographies that I wouldn't dream of standing in your way."

Tremble nodded as though Charles's words were a tempting but treacherous food, like foie gras, that takes a long time to digest. Or was Tremble silently despising every pompous thing Charles said but suppressing his objections in favor of objectivity? "Yeah, but all the attention must be flattering, huh?" Tremble asked, a half-mocking glance penetrating considerable eyebrow and eyeglass.

Catherine came back in with a bottle of airport whiskey. Charles bit his tongue. An English Cocteau scholar was planning a monograph on Charles's life and works and suddenly Charles thought he'd give each of his two biographers different, conflicting versions of all the same events. There was something entirely despicable about being the subject of a biography. The subject alternately preened and cowered, the most deplorable grandiosity in him responding to the promise of an immortal portrait while his cowardice told him he was about to undergo the worst of all possible fates — to have his fleshly body copied in granite, to have all of his past faults, which he excused because they were redeemed by future aspirations, quarried out of a strong eternal present: nothing but the pitiful facts.

And yet, after all, writing a biography was a métier. Tremble would need to establish a chronology, put together a bibliography, interview friends and colleagues from each period, each intellectual domain, each country. But when Charles gingerly touched on these professional matters, Tremble said, "I've got my own method, the Tremble System. I don't research, I don't take notes, no Xeroxes — I just absorb, absorb, absorb, and then one day I start writing, it all comes out."

Charles nodded, frowning seriously out of respect for the Tremble System, though he hazarded that such an approach might be more appropriate to an article than a book, even the slimmest — unless, of course, the writer had a prodigious memory (something he, Charles, was renowned for, though even he'd found that details dropped out after a few weeks unless he took notes, especially during a period of heavy interviewing).

Charles said, "I'm curious how you're going to reconstruct the Beirut years — how pretentious that sounds, to refer to one's own idle, haphazard life as though it represented a meaningful sequence."

Tremble had found a yellow spot on his trouser leg that he started scratching furiously. "You're the biographer — how would you go about it?"

"If I were Canadian and didn't speak Arabic or French?" Charles asked.

"Oh, that's easy, I can always hire translators. I suppose I'll just go there, to Beirut."

"A visit could always provide a certain sense of . . . atmosphere, although our house is rubble and my father's office was leveled and all our friends and family members are dead or have emigrated."

Catherine apparently had decided Tremble was hopeless; she changed the subject to Asia, which she knew interested him. She asked him constant questions about his years as a teacher in Hong Kong and his interlude leading tourists to Tun Huang. Tremble kept pouring himself large tumblers of Scotch; after the third full glass he'd brightened up, undone his tie and taken off his jacket to reveal a very old white shirt stained yellow under the arms.

Catherine expressed her ideas on the Far East, which were idiotic since she knew next to nothing about that part of the world. She, too, was drinking more red wine than usual; her English, sketchy at best, sometimes gave out altogether, but Tremble, fully awake and on his way to enthusiasm, assured her, as all North Americans do, that he knew exactly what she was saying and that her way of saying it was delightful. After every compliment he cast his eyes balefully, like a spavined workhorse, toward Charles, as though these compliments might be annoying the Master. Charles had spent his life siding with women and children against authoritarian men; he'd been the Artful Dodger, yet now he was being treated as the witless tyrant.

For Catherine it was all a game; she even said, "I hope Charles

isn't *vexé* that we speak on other subjects, not only his *life*." She
laughed merrily; she had a Gallic disregard for the American language and American pursuits — such as a biography of a living
man, virtually unknown and not even sixty years old. Like many
French tourists in the States she liked to collect examples of
American madness to exhibit later, colorful snaps of "typical" de-
formities. She chortled over gay studies, guidelines for politically
correct usage on all university publications, student evaluations
of, if you please, professors; she smiled with curatorial glee when
she learned that a local lesbian powwow had gone unattended
since no map of the rural location had been provided lest it favor
the seeing over those who were visually challenged and thus be
guilty of sightism. She rubbed her hands together over the sol-
emn, heavy-handed way young Americans were systematizing
only now the whimsical provocations tossed off so long ago by
Barthes, Derrida and that impenetrable, illogical Lacan.

Now she was trying to draw Tremble out in order to isolate
another amusing curiosity. "But aren't you afraid that Hong Kong
will be destroyed by the Chinese?" she asked.

"No, no!" Tremble shouted, though twenty minutes later he
lapsed, as Anglophones always do, into anecdotes, which were so
complicated he lost his point, if he'd ever had one other than the
desire to show his expertise.

Charles the professional biographer was conscious of a mental
clock ticking away. He'd told Tremble that he'd be able to see him
just two or three times altogether; he'd explained that whereas he
in no way opposed the book he thought it would be fatuous to
collaborate on it with too much lip-smacking self-regard.

After the cheese, the dessert, the coffee and the chocolate
truffes (sent in a CARE package from Brittany), Catherine discovered she had a migraine and went to bed with Elizabeth Taylor
(the English comic novelist, not the American activist).

Charles found a dusty half bottle of brandy that belonged to the owner of the house. He'd have to replace it before the proprietor returned. Tremble proceeded to toss the brandy back. He was raving intermittently about Singapore for some reason (Charles hadn't followed every twist and turn in his monologue). He was sitting on a rag rug in front of the small fire Catherine had lit before retiring. His shirttail had come out on one side and the earpieces of his glasses had worked their way up his scalp so that the lenses were tilting down toward the blue flames emitted by the chemical log.

"She's great, Catherine," Tremble shouted. "What a lovely lady. What class! I've never been entertained so royally. Her English is impeccable. And her knowledge of Asia is encyclopedic."

"Yes," Charles concurred. "Living with such an *érudite* can be a humbling experience."

"And a looker, too, though that may sound sexist."

"Not to our Old World ears," Charles assured his biographer.

"You're a lucky man, Charles, though — " He suddenly lowered his voice. "Do you think your wife can hear us?"

"No, her room is on another floor. You were saying?"

"Well, one of my informants," Tremble said conspiratorially, "has suggested you're not indifferent to the attractions of other women."

His informant must be that infernal Tom Smith, Charles thought. He murmured, "An elegant periphrasis for adultery." He despised Tremble and recognized that the book, in the unlikely event it would ever be finished, would *soil* a life, several lives, which seemed all the more precious now that they were about to be desecrated.

"Of course," Tremble admitted, pouring himself another brandy and making a cursory effort to serve Charles, who didn't even have a glass, "in Canada and the States there's a saying bachelors always use against marriage, 'Why buy a cow when you can get milk through a fence?'"

"Charming," Charles said, going over to his desk and jotting it down. "You're helping me improve my English by leaps and bonds."

"Bounds. It's 'leaps and bounds.'"

"*D'accord.* But tell me, frankly, why you took up this thankless project?" Charles came back to his stool next to Tremble, who was now soggily propped up on one elbow on the floor.

"You really want to know? The real bottom-line reason?"

Charles nodded vigorously.

"Well, maybe I shouldn't tell you, you might be hurt, 'cause I never was especially interested in you and it does sound like a lot of work, I mean what with all these exotic locales, Lebanon and France, whereas I'm really an Orientalist, but I met a young editor at Doubleday who'd read that *Vogue* profile somebody did on you after *Passports* hit the list and they asked me if I knew someone who could write a bio on you and I said, 'What would the advance be?' and they said, 'Roughly fifty thousand, with twenty-five grand on signing,' and I said, 'Done! I'll do it,' because that was exactly the sum I owed American Express. I'd never even read a word by you till then, though now I'm plowing through that book on, how do you say it, Jew-Hand-Do?"

"How did your bill get to be so high?" Charles was now mentally sneering not only at this grubby hack sprawling on the floor beside him but at his own vanity in wondering, earlier in the day, how he would present himself to a biographer he had ridiculously assumed would be at least an admirer.

"Gee, I don't know if I can tell you." Tremble writhed on the rag rug and — could it be? — looked as though he were actually blushing.

"Have you forgotten where you spent the money?" Charles ventured.

"Not at all. You see, I kind of fell for this one dominatrix, I guess you could say I'm sort of a masochist, and — that's why I think I'm good at understanding and forgiving your sexual excesses, Charles, you know, all the banging you're doing on the side? Anyway, I became a complete slave to Mistress Quickly and she did some amazing things to me, I've still got the scars to show for it, but of course that doesn't come cheap, the old meter was ticking on and on and after twenty-five thousand dollars Amex cut me off."

Tremble launched into a discourse about his estranged wife, who'd been "unbelievably cruel," although Charles couldn't sort out whether cruelty in her case had been a desirable or deplorable attribute.

Suddenly Tremble began to heave with sobs, strange hyena yelps that were so immoderate and convulsive that Charles assumed he must never have wept before in front of another human being, unless that person might be a Venus in Furs. Charles, who was always lamenting that he no longer felt anything, was reminded now of the inconvenience of emotion. Did he really want to go back to these humiliating sounds and writhings? For some reason he remembered the ancient metaphor of the poet as a flute played on by the breath of a god, so seized was Tremble by an outside force, an inspiration that flowed from his eyes and barked out of his mouth. Together perhaps Tremble and Charles could make one whole man.

Charles disliked touching men but he knelt beside Tremble and patted him comfortingly on the shoulder.

Charles thought, Tremble will never finish this biography but if by some chance he does he'll make me pay dearly for this sympathy I'm showing him.

After Charles had helped an excessively grateful Tremble into a taxi bound for the train station, he laughed out loud and said to himself, "Perfect! I can't think of a better biographer for me and my absurd life." But he was trying to convince himself that he found this bizarre coupling of subject and biographer "amusing" (that word Parisians always resorted to in order to cool down their irritability and to aestheticize their indignation).

Until today Charles had thought his life was banal and would make dull reading but suddenly, confronted with this drunk, incurious incompetent, Charles sighed, remembered Lebanon and thought of his family's destiny, at once so idiosyncratic and so emblematic of the comic, tragic last days of the Diaspora. He found a cabalistic symbolism in his need to seduce women other men had forgotten and "put out to pasture" (the cruelty of the English language!) because they were getting "long in the tooth."

As he made himself a chamomile tea in the kitchen, Charles thought how tiresome it would be, though, if his biographer were an intelligent, sensitive man capable of understanding his life from within. If the real materials of his life, expertly ferreted out and felt, were to be forced into the mold of a traditional biography, a form in search of a trajectory, an imperative that produced a destiny — well, that would be truly intolerable. He was an elusive man, a seducer, a diplomat, an artist in reticence, a genius of the vague. No, Tremble was perfect; he'd found his ideal biographer.

SPLIT LIP

You never forget the moment when you did nothing. You never forget how his skull would have looked had you owned a gun. You never forget the glint of joy in his eyes as the blood flowed from your lips.

You're surprised at how the plainclothes police are oddly polite. They drive you around the neighborhood looking for their faces. You know they ducked into a straight bar or down the hole to the PATH train. The police won't follow up too hard. After all, you fought back. You got a few punches in. They like you for that.

The surgeon at St Vincent's, where you expected to be treated cruelly, is tall, Asian, handsome and gay. He jabs your mouth with a needle full of anaesthetic, covers your face with surgical paper, and sews into your lip. You remember an episode of *M*A*S*H*.

You go to work on Monday, rationalizing that the reason you spent the entire weekend in bed was simply because you were tired. At your desk, you run your tongue over your stitches about four hundred times. The plastic thread juts up from your skin.

You remember little details in your nightmares. One had an earring. Another's sneakers were red. The third wore a Georgetown baseball cap. The dreams make you lose sleep. You snap at everyone at work. You even cause a guy to quit his job. His desk is cleared in a week.

No one knows how much hate got into your veins.

You try to be nice to your sort-of boyfriend later that week. He holds you and strokes your head. He can't kiss you because your lip is still swollen. You can't suck his cock because your mouth is puffy and raw. They have succeeded in preventing you from making the soft form of male-to-male contact they so despise. Three weeks later your boyfriend starts cancelling dates because you've been so *negative* these days.

You go shopping for weapons with your straight cousin who lives in the Bronx and got shot on the subway. He gives you his *nunchackus* and suggests you buy a hunting knife. Switchblades are too tricky. Instead you get Mace and a whistle — maybe you'll go back and get the knife. The *nunchackus* hang on a wall, becoming more decorative than functional.

You walk by the bar where it happened. You see the sidewalk where your bloodstains have been trampled away. You see the boys inside watching video clips of Joan Rivers. They stand in their J. Crew slacks and Perry Ellis sweater vests. You remember how they shrivelled out of sight when the fighting started, how you shouted back, defending this bar and your right to stand in front of it, the look on the gay men's faces, stunned at the blood spattered over your Read My Lips T-shirt and black leather jacket, being suddenly embarrassed for looking like such a clone, then more angry at the simpering manager who gave you a paper towel. Your friend, when he asked to call the cops, was told to use the pay phone outside.

Looking around at the silent drinking men, you wonder what you thought was worth defending.

In the morning, weeks later, while getting dressed, you think through your day's plans: "Do I wear the Doc Martens (for kicking back) or the Reeboks (for running away)?"

You walk the streets, wary of every corner. Your hands grip whatever pocket weapon you brought today. You see the crazy people on the street and now know how they got that way. You wonder how long it will take before you act like them.

Wearing a whistle on a chain around your neck, you feel safe, sort of, trying not to think that blowing a whistle might merely call attention to your beating, inviting not assistance, just an audience.

You become extremely comfortable with your heterophobia. You learn to admire drag queens and prostitutes. You begin to travel exclusively in packs of large, muscular men.

You break into tears for no apparent reason. You spend hundreds of dollars on cabs. You no longer have second thoughts about the execution of certain criminals.

I AM MAKING A MISTAKE

William's hospital room was in a corridor shared by patients who all had poisoned blood. Red plastic garbage bags were draped over every door to announce the peril. Placed in the corner by every bed were red plastic boxes in which orderlies carted the refuse away, as gingerly as a man might carry plutonium. William's food was served by nice, gloved ladies who volunteered their services five days a week. Except for Henry and Susan, he never felt the naked touch of another's skin. Even his doctor now prodded his glands with hands sealed in sheer latex that had the color of flesh, but was cold and stiff as a cadaver. Although Henry railed at the staff's caution, William didn't care. He had come to like his dangerous body. Sometimes he felt a kind of irradiated glow emanating from his skin, like an aura, that kept all others one step removed. Sometimes he stroked the contours of a vein, feeling the blood pulsing within, the way a hunter might caress the barrel of a gun. The hospital workers were often so afraid of contamination that they treated him with respect, as they would a murderous don who could turn vicious without warning.

William pushed the button by his bed and adjusted the

mattress until his legs were lifted even with his neck. He groaned as he propped a pillow under them, trying to ease the pressure on his back. He pulled open his robe to examine the crisscrossed scars, thick as a bramble of thorns, slashed across his stomach. He remembered nothing of his operation but surrendering to the anesthesia like a little death. After he awoke, some memory of the days before was restored to him: his head smashed against the bathroom tiles; a cold wind; deafening crowds; painted faces; a giddy feeling as if he were lifted high above the street by someone's hand; then a blank until consciousness returned in waves of nausea, every face and object in the recovery room spinning before his eyes.

As he gently touched his incisions, he tried to imagine how the knives had loosened the outer layer of his flesh. He did not know what his body looked like underneath, but somewhere there were muscles, tissues, veins, that had to be cut through before the surgeon could find the mass of tumors coiled around his intestines like a colony of worms. She had cut them out, but without promising there wasn't other damage that couldn't be repaired.

William closed his robe and gripped the bed rail. A bullet of pain shot from his arm to his neck, then to his lung, before it was buried in the beating of his heart. It felt different from the constant flames that flickered from his tattered nerves: heavier, thicker, as if clots ran through his blood like stones.

After so long being ill, he had familiarized himself with the nuance of every twitch as his disease progressed out of anyone's control. He barely glanced at the x-rays his doctor hung over light boxes for his inspection. He didn't need them. He could feel things growing within him from the most solitary cell until they collected together like magnets, weeks before they became visible and hard. He believed he could describe every aberrant cell and flourishing germ, and the malfunctions that had not yet appeared on any screen.

He tried to view the ruin of each part of his body dispassionately. Since his operation, he had made mental lists of those organs he was willing to lose, in order of preference. A leg, a lung, an arm, seemed less important to him now than they might have the month before, but still he clung to those parts he couldn't live without. He cherished his brain, his ears, his remaining good eye, like remnants of a family fortune, for what would become of him if he couldn't think or hear or see?

When he felt most sorry for himself, he made lists of things he had done for the last time: had sex, had a drink; gone to work, to the movies, a restaurant, the gym, a museum; taken a run in the park, driven a car, left the country, flown in a plane. Even a trip to the lobby to buy a newspaper had attained a significance he couldn't explain to a person who did it without thinking. His world grew smaller, minute by minute, yet there was so much room for it to grow smaller still. The moment would come when he would leave his apartment for the last time, then the hospital, his room, finally his bed. Before too long he would be ticking off friends he would never see again. He was obsessed with knowing who the last person would be. He didn't want it to be a doctor or nurse. He didn't want the eyes of his corpse to be closed by a stranger, but lovingly, regretfully, by a friend.

Henry.

Time and again he told himself, *This is no life*, but despite his multitude of afflictions, he still didn't know how to decide when he'd had enough. He had always hoped that some clear sign of resignation, some peaceful feeling of surrender, would overtake his mind and show him the way out. It hadn't happened.

From the first day of his diagnosis, he had promised himself that he would not die a lingering death. He had often read of

people who killed themselves before their suffering became unbearable. He remembered a newspaper headline from years before about two lovers who bound their wrists and ankles together
and leaped off a roof after being told they shared a terminal disease. And a doomed woman who killed herself in a van with a
doctor's assistance while her husband held her hand. William assumed his own doctor helped his most miserable patients to die,
but not until they had suffered longer than he believed it was rea-
sonable to do.

I could bear feeling worse, he told himself as he took stock of what
was left, ticking off things he could still do that others couldn't:
walk, wash, dress, read, feed himself. He had learned to bear the
itches, the labored breath, the gray fatigue, the cloudy vision, the
cramps that ambushed different parts of his body at will. He didn't
know anymore if what he endured on ordinary days would be in-
sufferable to the healthy, or if every moment marked a compromise with his disease that he wasn't fully aware he was making. A
few years before he would have found just one of his symptoms
intolerable; now pain had become a part of him in ways he
couldn't explain to those who didn't share it. Bearing it took no
tricks of bravery or courage. He had no choice once he surren-
dered to the fact that it was never going away. But how much
more could he stand?

So many horrors existed within his body, dangers he had never
dreamed possible. What frightened him most was the quickness
with which new symptoms appeared. In the beginning his decline
had kept a gradual pace. Now sores were born in the middle of
the night — bloody, gaping pockets worn into his skin as deeply
as if cut with a knife. He had seen patients struck dumb with brain
seizures that flashed out of nowhere like electrical storms. No
minute was safe, despite his vigilance. Every second he stayed
alive only increased the odds of losing to a catastrophe.

"You have to have hope," his doctor told him, as if hope were the miracle that would save him. But hadn't he noticed the patients William saw every day in the hospital ward, dying in pieces? Hadn't he watched them endure months of useless treatments, pricked and poked and poisoned with no observable effect? Often William shared the treatment room with a man named Juan. Over recent weeks he had watched Juan's eyes overtake his face, growing hugely black and round. The last time Juan had come there, spittle thick and yellow as yoke was dried on his chin. He had mouthed "hello" silently, terror pinching his face, as in photographs William had seen of prisoners in cattle cars. William was too smart not to know that he was on the way to becoming just like Juan, but each time he had given up, hope would creep up on him again, like the germ of another disease.

Still, he was plagued by fears of waiting until he was too weak or feeble to find the means to take his life. Already he felt so unreal sometimes that he forgot where he was; often in the middle of the afternoon, he couldn't tell the difference between waking and sleeping. What he dreaded most was his body hooked to a respirator: gagging on tubes, listening to the steady *whoosh whoosh whoosh* as each breath was forced out, while he lay speechless, locked in the machine's embrace more tightly than in a strangler's hands.

Months before, he had looked up the best ways to kill himself in a book. He knew he could never use a knife or a gun, or throw his body in front of a speeding train. As miserable as he felt, he was still too accustomed to comfort to choose a painful death. The book claimed the sweetest way for him to die was to swallow a lethal combination of pills, then tie a plastic bag around his head. The bag should be loose at the face but tight at the neck, secured with two rubber bands. The instructions included the required number of pills, more than enough for a good night's sleep, but not so many that he would awake vomiting, brain-damaged and still alive. So far William had endured his suffering with the knowledge that he had ten times the number of pills he needed, hidden in the nightstand by his bed, a secret pharmacy he had made Henry bring from his stash at home. William liked to have them near because the nurses were often grudging about doping his misery or letting him escape into a dreamless sleep.

He leaned down and pulled the plastic liner from the wastebasket. He poured a glass of water and selected a bottle of sleepers from the drawer. It was midnight by the clock on the wall, hours before an aide would come to draw the morning's blood, even longer before Henry stopped by on his way to school. All he needed to do was swallow two fistfuls of pills, and soon it would be too late to save him. For years he had taken more vitamins than that during a normal day. Before he grew too groggy, he would wrap the bag around his face and settle into the pillows. He imagined waves of a familiar, drowsy blackness, almost a giddiness, as unconsciousness slammed upon him. Only this time, somewhere between night and morning, the sleep would drift away to death.

He swung his feet off the bed and raised himself up by leaning on the IV pole. Although his stomach cramped violently, he struggled to the window and rested on the arm of the chair. His sight was best at closer range, so the opposite towers of the hospital building were as indistinct as mountaintops in fog. Up so high, the lights from the street split and shattered in his kaleidoscope eye.

He stared at the pills, shiny as marbles in his hand, and began to drop them into his mouth, first one, another, then three, four, until they rattled against his tongue. He raised the cup of water to his lips and sipped.

Do it, he told himself, but his throat seemed to seize and close by instinct, as if his muscles were beyond his control. He tried to force himself to keep the liquid in by imagining something irrevocable: either aiming the barrel of a gun at his head or stepping off the roof of a skyscraper into midair, but still he coughed and retched. Scattered sounds blew up at him — an accelerating engine, an isolated shout — but mostly the peculiar silence of the city filled his ears, a static buzz like the hum of high-tension wires. He closed his eyes, mesmerized, and in that instant he knew he would trade anything to feel his feet touch those streets again, even just to lie in bed and imagine the life below as it had once existed, with him still part of it, if only in a dream.

He spit the pills into his lap, their blue coating melted in places by his saliva. *I am making a mistake*, he thought in despair, but still he drowned their bitter taste with gulps of water. When he had first considered killing himself, he recalled the night he heard his parents whisper about a cousin who had thrown herself off an overpass into the path of an oncoming truck. During his months of careful planning, William had marveled at her courage to run headlong and never stop. Now he wondered if it wasn't courage at all, but a kind of indifference he didn't share. Despite everything that had happened, he still cared deeply about his life. It was just possible that one day soon the doctors would discover the proper combination of pills to save him. After all, most discoveries were accidents. Or maybe one morning his body would awaken to a remission that would buy some extra time. It had happened to others before.

That day in the waiting room when he had watched Juan being wheeled past, William heard a man whisper to his companion, "Promise me you'll kill me before I ever get that bad." At the time, William had silently agreed. He had always believed he would rather be dead than crippled from a car crash or maimed by an explosion. When he saw photographs of men charred in fires, their features melted, he never understood why their doctors hadn't let them die. Even when he heard stories of families killed in burning houses, four children and a father dead, he always believed that the measure of the mother's heartbreak would outweigh any reason to survive. The choice had seemed simple when he still was blessed with the mind and body of a healthy man, but now he understood how a person could cling preposterously to life without ever wanting to let go.

He turned away from the window and struggled to the bed. He placed the bottle of pills in the drawer and wadded the plastic bag into a ball. As he slipped between the sheets, he reassured himself that the same way out would still be available the next day, or the day after, whenever his hope or his energy ran out, whichever came first. At the very least, he didn't want to die in the hospital, but back at home, where he belonged.

He waved his hand over his stitches, trying to ease their burn. The nurses had told him that itching in his incisions was a sign of healing, so he savored the sensation as it sparked across his stomach, then traveled back repeatedly, as if he were pricking his pores with hot pins, wanting to believe his body was still fixable.

A few weeks before, he had heard a story on the news about a graveyard excavated beneath the foundation of a building in the heart of the financial district: a cemetery of slaves, the poor, the bleakest cases, dumped into a mass grave in what had once been beyond the farthest borders of the city. The archaeologists discovered that all of the bodies, stripped of any adornment but buttons and bouquets of desiccated flowers, were pointed east so that they might sit up and face the morning sun on Judgment Day. If hope remained even within the most hopeless lives, maybe William, too, might join that clatter of skeletons with rough sockets of bone for eyes, rising up again on Judgment Day to be blinded by the light of the Lord.

THE WEDDING DRESS

One Saturday afternoon, as he was crossing Route 12 on his way to the station, Junior came upon a wedding dress in the middle of the road. It was zipped up in a see-through plastic bag and straddled the double yellow line as if it had been set there deliberately. Before he had time to wonder, he saw a red pickup rounding the curve toward him, so he threw the dress over his arm and darted across the road. He eased down the grassy embankment, jumped the ditch, then headed up the incline on the other side. He crossed the cement plaza between pumps number three and four and went inside the food mart part of the gas station. His mother was ringing up a customer, so she could not see him cross the store behind her and go into the back room, where he put the dress down on top of two stacked cases of cherry bombs.

Except for finding the dress, Junior's routine was no different than it had been every Saturday afternoon for the past year. On the day his father died, struck by a truck carrying chickens into town as he crossed Route 12 on his way to work one miasmic morning eight years before, Junior's mother had told her son, "You and I are going to build your daddy's business into something he can be proud of, wherever he may be." He was named John James Grumley, Jr., but from that day on his mother called him Junior and began taking him to the station with her or having him meet her there after school. For his fifteenth birthday present she gave him his very own shift, and the following Saturday he came in to relieve her at two and remained there until ten, when Eddie Hawkins came in for the night shift.

Junior did not mind working at the station. Even as a kid he ended up covering for his mother and Eddie so often that he knew he should be getting paid more than free candy bars and Cokes, though he never said anything about it. So it was only fair when he started to get paid, even if it was his mother signing the checks. The Saturday shift was all right. On Saturday nights the other kids from Thomaston High went to parties he did not know about or drove to secret clearings in the woods to drink, so he wouldn't have had anything to do anyway. At some point in the evening they came in to play the machines in the back or put gas in their cars or buy cigarettes or even rubbers. At first he was shy to wait on them, but he got used to it.

And when they were gone, when the store was silent except for the humming of the refrigerated case and the surge of the air conditioner, he walked over to the magazine rack. He stared at the covers as he listened for the sound of a car or truck turning off the road. On the covers there were usually girls with lots of curly blond hair, and his heart beat faster as he ran his hands along the plastic wrap covering their faces and breasts. Anyone could have walked in and caught him. Sometimes his heart beat so loudly and quickly that the beating was in his ears and he couldn't hear cars turning off the road. Sometimes when he was looking at the magazine covers kids on foot or bicycle came in to buy candy, and when that happened he fumbled at rearranging the display, then returned to the cash register.

It was a miracle his mother had never caught him. Although they lived in a two-bedroom block bungalow in the woods directly across from the station, his mother refused to cross the road on foot. Instead she drove their yellow seventy-nine Plymouth Valiant twenty yards down the old Cohoochee Highway, turned right onto Route 12 until she came to its intersection with Route 13, then made a U-turn at the crossroads and doubled back to the station. If she had walked in while he was looking at the magazines, his heart certainly would have exploded in his chest and in his ears and he would have dropped dead at the magazine rack.

Sometimes he took one of the magazines and put it on the shelf under the cash register. Back home in his room, he ripped off the plastic and turned the pages so quickly he could hardly see the blond girls, only smell the magazine's gluey chemical smell. He would turn and turn until he found a man with one or more of the girls, and then he would stare, feeling his heart now in his crotch as well. He would scrutinize the picture, imagining he was in it as well, but not a willing participant, forced. He did not even want to look at the picture, but he could not put it down, and in his confusion and mounting panic he sometimes tore at his hair and clawed at his cheeks, though he could not say why he did these things either. By the time his mother knocked at the door to remind him about supper, there were tears in his eyes, and he threw the magazine under the bed and said, "I'm coming, Mama," having first rehearsed quietly to monitor his voice for signs of weakness, of distress.

"That you?" she called out from the cash register.

"Yes, ma'am." He arranged the dress bag so that it hung evenly over both sides of the top crate of fireworks.

"What are you doing back there?"

"Nothing." He came out front and kissed her. "I just found something in the road."

"In the road? What were you doing looking down at the road? I told you to be careful crossing that road."

He stood opposite her with his palms on the counter as if he were a customer. "I am careful. I just couldn't help seeing it."

She squinted through glasses with square red frames. Her hair was newly curled. "What was it you found, then?"

"A dress," he said, looking down, as if the word itself shamed him.

"A dress! Why, how could there be a dress in the road? Who would have dropped a dress in the road?"

"I don't know. There just was."

"Well, what did you do with it?" she asked, winking. "I could use me a new dress."

"I'll go get it," he said.

When he came back out his mother was reaching up for a pack of cigarettes for a woman in flip-flops. After the woman had left, he set down the dress bag and he and his mother stared at it in silence. Someone called from the fireworks aisle and Junior went over to help him.

When he got back to the register his mother whispered, "Did you know this was a wedding dress?"

"I guess," he said. "I mean, not really."

"That's what it is. And an expensive one too. Where'd you say you found this?"

"Right out front in the road."

"Route Twelve?"

He nodded.

"Over the last thirteen years I have seen more than my share of things in that road, but they usually run to the roadkill side of things." She ran her hand along the bag. "I'm going to take this home for you so it doesn't get all wrinkled."

"All right."

"I mean if that's all right with you. This dress is your responsibility now, and far be it for me to presume."

"Oh, Mama," he said, looking down.

"I mean it."

When he looked up, his mother was holding the dress, sprung from its transparent cocoon, in front of her. "It sure is nice," he remarked.

"I'm not completely washed up yet, am I?" she asked, stealthily slipping the dress back into its bag. Then she took off her name tag and stuck it into the pocket of her sweatpants. "I mean, I know I'm no spring chicken."

Before Junior could respond, the young guy from the fireworks aisle made his way over to the counter and set down a box of Red Devils next to the wedding gown. "Somebody getting married?" he asked.

Junior could feel the hot blood in his face. His mother picked up the dress and said, "Not at this rate they ain't."

The following Wednesday, the main headline on the front page of the *Thomaston Town Crier*'s Round the Town section read, "Teenage Boy Finds Wedding Dress in Middle of Route 12." There was a picture of Junior sullenly contemplating the cover of *Bride's* magazine. His mother, who was standing off to the side at the photography shoot and urging him to smile, was responsible for the story. After telling Junior her plan, she had called Ed Sanders, the editor of the paper and a regular customer of the station's, and told him the story while he jotted down notes. The bride, she explained, was advised to drop by Grumley's Amoco service station on Route 12. The gown's exact description was purposely kept obscure.

On the day the story came out, Junior's math teacher called him over after class and said, "I see you're a local hero now." Nobody else said a word. But the next day his homeroom greeted him with a mixture of backhanded congratulations and sly taunts. "I see you found yourself a wedding dress," said Bobby Bryson, who played basketball and had a pale scar over one eye and had never before even looked at Junior. "Now all you need to do is find yourself a bride." Everybody but Junior laughed, and then the bell rang and Mr. Fowler walked in.

There were two kinds of women who responded to the newspaper story. It got to the point that whenever Junior was helping his mother out at the station or working his own shift, he could spot them as soon as they walked through the door.

The first group that Junior came to recognize were the down-on-their-lucks. These were the girls whose wedding gowns really had been lost or stolen. They usually tried to enter the food mart by pulling instead of pushing on the left door, then, thinking they had figured it out, decided to push, but on the right door, which opened by being pulled. And when they had made it to the cash register they held out a ragged clipping of the newspaper story and said, without much hope, "You the people that found a wedding dress?" They told their stories flatly and succinctly, then surveyed the store from the counter as if they had come for something more mundane. When asked, they would describe the dress to Junior's mother, their words trailing off before they had really begun. And when Junior's mother told them how sorry she was but that the dress she had wasn't theirs, they nodded, as if the verdict could not have been otherwise. They usually picked up a cold drink on the way out.

The other group were the lonelyhearts. These women had been unlucky in love — either jilted at the altar or some unspecified time before reaching it. Some of them came to talk, pouring out their troubles to Junior's mother as other customers looked on uneasily and the older woman passed across the counter miniature packets of Kleenex.

Those lonelyhearts who did not come to talk came for the specific purpose of meeting Junior. When they showed up during the week they asked for him, and when Junior's mother asked if they had come about the dress, they would reply that if she didn't mind, they'd rather just speak with Junior himself. Junior's mother soon confessed that if they weren't too trashy looking or too old, she told them when his shift was.

So they showed up Saturday nights. They were easy to spot. They didn't smile much. He watched them walk past the counter with their eyes down, circle the store until it had emptied out some, then stand in front of the cash register staring at the floor. They were as skittish looking as he probably was when he examined the magazines.

"Can I help you, ma'am?" he asked one of these girls one Saturday night. Bones jutted out from the top part of her chest, where her lacy white blouse was unbuttoned. Her lips were smeared with Vaseline or clear lip gloss.

She looked up. "Oh, am I next?"

When he said yes she replied, "I mean, you can go ahead and wait on somebody else first if you need to." Finally she said, "Were you the one that found a wedding dress in the middle of the road?"

"I did," he said, silently cursing his mother for sending her here tonight. She insisted on interviewing the girls herself, so there was no reason for him even to be talking to her.

"I saw your picture in the paper."

He smiled.

"You don't really look like that."

"Like what?"

"Like your picture in the paper."

He didn't know what to say. He wished he could be easy and charming like Bobby Bryson and most of the other kids at school, but he couldn't. He didn't know how. In the chill air-conditioned store he began to sweat, and he grabbed a napkin and wiped his forehead. He could end it here. All he had to do was ask if she'd come about the dress. He'd expose her in her folly, and she'd leave with her head hung low.

"You don't look worse or anything, you just look . . . different. Taller."

"Well." And then he resorted to something he'd read in the paper, in a column about manners. It was bad manners to ask someone what they did, but it was good manners to ask them where they were from. "Are you from around here?" he asked.

"No. I'm from Brookletville. Have you ever been there?"

"Naw."

A bearded man with a package of baloney, a loaf of white bread, and a jar of mustard was standing behind the girl and staring with his lips set at the ceiling. When Junior gestured for him to come forward, the girl moved aside. She stood perfectly still and stared at her feet.

When the bearded man had gone she came to life again. "There's nothing in Brookletville," she said. "There really isn't a damn thing there at all."

That night, at the end of his shift, he crossed the two-lane highway without looking both ways, without even listening. It would serve his mother right if he got hit. His family had never been religious, but he knew that thinking this way was a sin. He couldn't help it. He trudged through the underbrush as slowly as he could, choosing his path so that the porch light was hidden by the greatest number of trees.

Inside she leapt up off the couch and met him in the kitchen. "You'd think that by now I could hear you coming," she said. "I guess I must have the TV on too loud. Old ladies tend to be hard of hearing."

He kissed her brusquely, then went to his room.

"How was work tonight?" she called from the other side of the locked door.

He took off his pants and folded them across his chair.

"Nobody give you any problems, did they?"

"No, ma'am," he said, taking off his shirt. He removed his underpants and socks and stood before the full-length mirror on the door.

"Did bachelorette number one come by to claim the dress?"

"Uh-uh." He ran his fingers down his cheeks. He didn't think he looked so bad in the paper. That was what he looked like, at least in black and white. Longish light-colored hair, wide face, big eyes, a few soft hairs above his mouth, droopy lower lip. What did that girl really mean when she said he looked "different"?

His mother knocked four times. "Baby, what are you doing in there? Ain't you going to wash up for dinner?"

"I'm not hungry."

"You're not hung— You haven't been eating those nasty hot dogs again, have you?"

"Naw."

"Well then, I can't understand why you're not hungry." She knocked again. The knob turned one way, then the other. "Unless you're not feeling a hundred percent. Baby, are you feeling all right?"

"I'm fine." He ran his hand over his skinny white body, pressing his fingers into his ribs, his breastbone. "I'm just going to lie down for a second."

The TV boomed from the living room. "All right, but I fried you some fish, and it'll get too dried up if it sits in the oven too long. I put your plate in the oven to keep warm."

He examined the sparse brown hairs at the bottom of his chest, the soft trail of them leading down to his crotch. He did not want to lie down. He did not want to look at his magazines. His fingers slid along his what's-it, cupping the end of it, then sliding along it again. He thought of that girl who came in tonight. She was skinny like he was, and if she just smiled, she might almost be pretty. He imagined her taking off her white blouse and her bra too. Imagined himself cupping his hands over the little mounds of her breasts. He closed his eyes and rubbed himself so hard that his what's-it began to hurt. He imagined her taking off her jeans too, but now Bobby Bryson was in his head. It was Bobby Bryson taking off his jeans the way he did before PE, then snapping on his jockstrap. The hair on Bobby's legs was blond and thick.

Junior tried to picture the girl from the station again, but it was hopeless. When he opened his eyes the side of his what's-it was the color of a ripe tomato. He bent humbly to examine himself and almost cried out when his sweaty finger touched broken skin.

His mother's footsteps trailed away on the carpeting.

Because the gown was so expensive-looking, it occurred to Junior's mother that it might belong to someone in Hilton Head or Savannah. The Amoco station was in the country exactly halfway between the two, and perhaps some wealthy Savannah family had been transporting the dress out to Hilton Head for the wedding. "I hear that's the in thing to do these days," she told Junior. "Getting married on a beach. That sounds awfully uncomfortable to me."

A month after Junior had found the dress, his mother told him she was going to phone the papers in Hilton Head and Savannah. "Can't we just forget about it?" Junior asked. His mother looked up from the hot-dog broiler, which she was wiping with soda water. "No, we can't just forget about it. Do you think that dress will just disappear?" "We could sell it," Junior offered, but his mother kept wiping and did not reply. When she had cleaned the broiler to her satisfaction, she stood back and appraised it. "In my heart I promised your father I'd show you the right path in this life, and until now I thought I'd set you on it."

The following week a story about the dress appeared in the Local section of the *Savannah Morning News and Evening Press*. "Thomaston Teen Finds Wedding Dress in Route 12," read the headline. "Cinderella Search Is On." Because Junior had refused to be photographed, the Savannah paper used the same picture that had appeared in the *Town Crier*; the story was skimpy because he had refused to be interviewed. "My son's just modest," his mother had explained to the reporter.

One Saturday night in early June, Junior was straightening up the counter displays when a thin, good-looking man walked in and said hello. He had short brown curly hair and a mustache. Junior said hey and asked if he could help him. "Yes, I think you might be able to help me," the man said. He pulled out a card from his wallet and handed it across the counter. The card read, "The Bridal Boutique/Savannah, Georgia/Richard Kersey, Bridal Consultant." By now Junior had thought he could spot just about anybody with any interest in or claim to the dress. In addition to the merely curious, the latest newspaper stories had attracted several crooks, whom Junior could identify chiefly because they seemed resentful rather than grateful he had found the dress. He felt he had gotten pretty good at hearing them out, then sending them away. But a man! How could he possibly figure out a man who came to claim a wedding dress? What would he say to him? He stared at the card until he had it memorized.

"Now don't go ripping my business card into shreds." The man stuck out a hand. "Hi, my name's Rick Kersey."

Junior put down the card and shook the man's hand. His own hand was cold and damp.

"As you can see, I run a bridal shop over in Savannah, and I think you might have found my dress. Tell me, is it in good condition?"

"When I found it it was in a bag and it's still in it."

"Thank goodness. I try to take extra care when I'm delivering a dress to a client, but you know, you can't take every variable into account."

Junior nodded. The man's shirt was unbuttoned three buttons, and soft hair massed at his neck.

"Do you think I might have a look at the dress?"

"My mother has it." He wanted to keep standing here across from the man, but now there was not much more to say.

"Oh, yes. From the article. Where might I find her at?"

Junior looked down and said, "Well, she likes me to kind of ask people who come in a question or two, if you don't mind."

"Of course."

"Well," said Junior slowly, searching for the right words. "Do you think, I mean, would you mind describing it to me?"

And without hesitation the man began talking about lacework and beaded trim and a hoop skirt. The dress, he said, was one of a kind; its color was ivory cream, he said, pronouncing *cream* as "crem."

For all Junior knew, this man might be the true owner of the dress. His description sounded good enough, and Junior just couldn't place him in a category as easily as he could the women.

But what did Junior care? It was his mother who was so interested in the dress, in returning the dress — not him. That dress could have burned up in a big fire and he wouldn't have cared. He just wanted to stand here and talk to this man, not send him away. But it was no use. "We live just across the way," he said, pointing to the street lamp broken up by trees rising from the lowland.

"Thanks a lot, buddy," the man said, and Junior met his eyes and tried to smile. His heart beat in his throat. He stared at the man as he walked out the door.

Junior thought about the man for the rest of his shift, and he kept thinking about him as he crossed the highway and made his way through the woods and up to the house. He thought of the way the man had winked at him — so subtly that most people would not have been able to catch it. He thought of the way he walked — with determination but lightly, as if he were better suited to move through the air than other people were.

Junior let himself in and said hello to his mother in the living room. He could not remember when, but sometime recently he had stopped kissing her when he came in and she had stopped jumping up from the television. "Thank goodness you're home," she said. "Or am I not supposed to say that?"

He started for the bathroom.

His mother said, "Your friend came by tonight."

For a second he had the crazy idea she was talking about Bobby Bryson. But it was even crazier for his mother's voice to be saying the same thing that his mind's voice could not keep quiet about. He stopped, reached for the remote on the coffee table, and asked, "Can I turn this down?"

"Do what?"

He pressed the Mute button. "I said can I turn this down."

"Well of course you can turn it down, but you don't have to

turn it off. Now I missed that." She snatched up the remote and the set blared again.

"So what happened?" Junior shouted. His mother looked different. She looked like she wasn't there.

"You can imagine how frightened I was at first, this strange man coming to my door in the middle of the night. Honestly, Junior, you really should know better."

He sat down before the television.

"Oh, now don't go worrying yourself over it. Your old mother can take care of herself, I guess. Especially around a man that's that way."

Junior turned back to his mother, who was holding up both hands limply at her chest, as if parodying an obedient dog. From somewhere he heard familiar laughter, then realized it was coming from himself.

"What are you laughing about?"

Then all at once the laughter stopped. Nothing seemed funny anymore. "Nothing."

"Nothing, huh." She stared at the television, then picked up the remote and turned it off. "You know, I'm trying my best, but I just don't think I can take much more of this."

Junior stared at the blank screen and listened to the air conditioner pulse.

"I mean," she went on, "every child goes through a rebellious phase, but that doesn't mean every mother has to play along. I always thought we had a different relationship."

"Different to what?" he asked, still staring at the screen.

"You know what I mean." She tore off her glasses, then pulled out a clump of shredded yellow tissue and dabbed at her eyes. "Just different. Closer. I've tried to play along with you, I really have. When I saw you stopped wanting to kiss me it felt like a knife through my heart. But I kept all that to myself. Did you know I cry myself to sleep every night?"

He didn't reply.

"Well, I do. And then to have you go and send a strange man over in the middle of the night to your father's house. I just don't know what you're trying to do to me anymore."

"Oh, Mama." He turned in her direction but did not meet her eyes. Lately the house had become so tiny and close that sometimes he couldn't breathe. Now he took in breath after breath, then let them all out at once. "So did that dress belong to him?"

"What were you even doing having a conversation with a fellow like that?" she blurted. "He said he had such a nice 'chat' with you. He didn't try to do anything to you, did he?"

His ears burned with shame.

"Did he?"

"I don't know what you're talking about."

"Did he!" Her face reddened, the veins in her neck lay in relief against the loose skin.

He stood up and went to his room and locked the door. She pounded on it and said, "I wish your father was here. He'd know what to do about all this."

He pressed himself against the mirror and shut his eyes tight.

"I sure do wish he was."

Area papers ran brief stories on the return of the wedding gown to its rightful owner. "Wedding Dress Saga Ends," announced the *Thomaston Town Crier.* The *Beaufort Bugle* ran a picture of Richard Kersey with the dress on a rack behind him. This time, Junior had not been the only one who refused to be interviewed. "There's nothing that I have to say on the matter," his mother told the reporters. "Case closed."

Overnight the dress seemed to disappear from the local imagination. No one came to the station to claim the dress or talk about
it. The bungalow across from the station grew quiet. Now when
Junior came home from work his mother let him take his supper
out of the oven himself. Sometimes she got up from the couch
and joined him, but she never said much, and when she did it was
only about what she had been watching on TV. For Junior, it was
a relief.

The wedding dress used to pop into his head at odd times —
when he was crossing Route 12, for example, or swimming in the
lake. Now it was the man who appeared in Junior's thoughts. He
had clipped the man's picture and tucked it between the stiff pages
of one of the magazines. In Junior's fantasy, the man walked in
staring at Junior, as if he had not come for the dress at all. Behind
his bedroom door Junior set down the man's picture, closed his
eyes, and stared at the hairy V below his neck. Afterward, he lay
sweating on the bed, tracing cum around his navel. From the
other room, television voices sounded evenly. For nearly an hour,
he made no effort to rise from the sour-smelling bed. He lay there
and waited.

One Saturday night toward the end of summer, the Bridal Boutique van pulled alongside the gas pumps and Richard Kersey got
out and walked into the food mart. Junior had rehearsed this en-
trance so often in his head that at first he was neither surprised
nor thrilled. Then Kersey met his eyes and seemed to be smiling — in the fantasy the man did not smile, only stared gravely —
and at that moment Junior's heart began to thud in his chest
and he felt as if he had been punched in the gut. "Hey there,
buddy," Kersey said, removing a credit card from his wallet. "Remember me?"

Junior smiled shyly and said yes.

Kersey handed over the card. "I'll fill 'er up with silver on number three."

Did Junior imagine Kersey wink at him as he turned to go out? Could there have been any sense in what his mother was ranting about that night? Junior turned on the pump, and when Kersey was out of sight of the cash register Junior picked up an orange-plastic-framed pocket mirror from a box on the counter and checked the cracks between his teeth for traces of hot dog. He put the mirror back and from another box withdrew a mint sprayer and sprayed.

Junior took care of two customers, and then Kersey was standing at the counter. Junior pressed the total button on the keyboard: $4.39. It was too low. No one filled up a van — or even a car — with a credit card and then put in only $4.39 worth of gas. Junior fumbled with the card and did not look up.

"I tell you," Kersey said as they were waiting for the receipt to print out, "I had no idea they'd be doing a write-up on me. I guess I should have expected it, but when the phone started ringing that kind of caught me off guard."

"I bet," Junior said.

"Not that I mind it." Kersey's eyes were so pale blue they were almost white. "I am a businessman after all, and every little bit helps."

The receipt pushed out like a tongue, and Junior handed it over.

Kersey removed a silver pen from his shirt pocket. "So how's your mother?"

"Oh, she's fine. The same."

"Good. That's good to hear. Because I think I gave her a little bit of a fright."

"Aw, she's all right," Junior said, then suddenly emboldened added, "She can be a little high strung."

Kersey laughed. "She can? I'm glad to hear you say that. I thought it was just me."

Their transaction was complete. Now Kersey held Junior's eyes with that grave look Junior had imagined as characteristic of him. Just then Bobby Bryson came in and pretended not to notice the man with the mustache stepping back from the counter. He threw down five dollars on the counter and said, "Hey, Junior." Bobby's mouth curved up in a half-smile, a smirk. Junior took down a hard pack of Marlboros and handed them over. Now he had no choice but to go through with whatever Kersey had in mind, no choice but to make his humiliation complete — and worth something.

"You know," Kersey said after Bobby had left, "I really appreciate you finding my dress and keeping it so nice till I could come claim it."

"Well."

"No, really, I mean it. There's a lot of snakes out in the world these days. I'd like to give you a little reward."

"That isn't necessary."

"No, I insist upon it. Do you ever come into Savannah?"

Junior looked down. What could he be besides a disappointment to this man? "Not much."

"You don't?" Kersey did not look surprised. "It's so close and all, I'd expect you to be out every night there with your girl-friends."

"I don't really have any girlfriends," Junior said, knowing full well what he was saying, knowing his fate was sealed.

A week later, he drove the yellow Valiant through the dark countryside, past the trailer park, then the scrap-metal factory, and then a lone bungalow or two before the pine woods closed in on both sides of the narrow road. Then the trees ended, and he was

Jason K. Friedman

driving across the marsh. In the distance to his right, lights from the paper mill twinkled and a fat coil of smoke rose into the unreal glare. Now he could see the bridge set like a great jeweled bracelet against velvet, and the low buildings of the Savannah skyline beyond it. On one side of the road squatted a pink-fronted trailer with a pair of big green neon dice in constant tumble, and a single yellow street lamp shone over three cars in a dirt lot. There was a similar establishment across the street. He could remember when these were fruit stands, then firecracker stands. He could remember when Grumley's Amoco service station had two pumps and no food mart and his daddy held him on his lap.

Junior was meeting Richard Kersey at the Pirate's House, a famous old restaurant near the river where Junior had been once, with the Cub Scouts. He remembered being taken on a tour of the place, its tiny candlelit rooms and narrow passageways. In one corner, he recalled, an iron gate blocked off a stone stairway leading down to a tunnel, and a dummy pirate slumped across the torch-lit landing began to speak: *Shanghaied. I was shanghaied, ye mateys. Down to the river and onto a boat. Down to the river and onto a boat.*

They have great desserts there, Kersey had said that night at the station. You do like dessert, don't you? Isn't that how you got to be so tall?

"Did you have any trouble getting here?" Kersey asked once they were seated, at a table by a cold fireplace.

"Naw. I just told Mama I was going to a party."

They sat without speaking. Then Junior asked after the dress, and Kersey told him it had walked down the aisle the day before yesterday and was probably in an attic somewhere by now.

After they had ordered, Kersey grinned, revealing dimples, and said, "You look nervous."

"Naw." Junior stared at the fireplace. "I mean, I reckon I am."

· 55 ·

*   *   *

Junior and Kersey had walked into the gay bar together, and Kersey had greeted the big man just inside the door by name, and as far as Junior could tell, no money had changed hands, though he had spotted a sign reading, "NON-MEMBER TEN-DOLLAR COVER CHARGE." Junior was six-foot-one, but surely no one believed he was old enough to be here. Rick Kersey seemed to know everyone, and Junior was sure he was talking about him with his friends as they stood near the bar and laughed into one another's ears and touched one another more than men usually did. Junior stood slightly apart from Kersey and his friends, smiling as brightly as he could. Kersey did not speak to him but brought him one beer and then another. When the two men walked out into the night a hot breeze blew over the river, and Junior knew that he was not going to be home by midnight, as he had promised, and that he did not care.

Kersey lived in a townhouse on a square two blocks from the bar. Junior was led by the hand to the third floor and into a high-ceilinged apartment with round tables draped in lace and covered with figurines. On the walls were old-fashioned pictures of rich-looking people Junior knew Kersey had never met. By the bed the top half of a sightless naked-woman mannequin sprouted from a pole with a round base.

They sat on the bed and Kersey said, "You don't look so damn nervous anymore. I guess you must be used to me already."

"What?" Junior felt suddenly dizzy from sitting down. "Yeah, I'm all right."

"But you still have that distant look on your face."

"Well." Junior put his hand over Kersey's. In the window of the bungalow he saw his mother's face, the lines on her forehead and the furrow between her eyes. "I was just thinking how weird my mother is."

Kersey withdrew his hand. "Now let's not bring her along on this ride."

Junior's laughter enlarged into a resounding burp. "Excuse me," he said and fell back laughing.

Kersey stood up and walked to the end of the bed. Then he removed his clothes, revealing his body in sections — first the milky chest with a nest of brown fuzz rising up from the center, then the muscular thighs and calves, and finally his dick, which emerged fully erect and with such momentousness that Junior could only say, "It's so big."

"Bigger than yours, I bet," Kersey said. He sat down next to Junior and placed his hand on his crotch.

Junior closed his eyes and the darkness turned and he remembered how he thought it would be. That was just a year ago, and in a sudden access of memory he remembered what he had not thought of since then, since he got started with the magazines. Surely, he had thought, his legs would rub against another man's and that would be it, the shame of it coming over him in Rick Kersey's bedroom as it had come over him in his own in those mad weeks when he walked around and around in his room with an erection and touched himself every now and then, hoping for something to happen. Then he had begun working in the station and discovered the magazines and his fantasies had grown more complicated. In his own way he had become experienced, he had become dirty, and he hoped Kersey could see that.

In bed, Kersey loomed over him like a statue, as beautiful as a god, and said, "I just want to fuck you a little. Your smooth white ass, I can tell it's tight."

It was all Junior had ever wanted. But suddenly he was in such pain that he cried out, and Kersey, inclined over him, clutched Junior's hair and whispered, "Your tight white ass. I bet you never had your ass fucked before." Then he drew back and spat on Junior's chest, whispering with a lover's tenderness, "Motherfucker. You goddamned motherfucker."

Junior, tapping a reserve of will he did not know he possessed, pushed Kersey backward. He had wanted to continue, he was simply in too much pain. "Hey, what the hell?" Kersey said, tottering on his knees to avoid falling onto the Oriental rug. Junior, to redeem himself, lunged forward and slipped his mouth around Kersey's penis with its rubber dangling like a nightcap, sucking it with artless frenzy until Kersey pushed him away.

"I've never seen *that* before," Kersey said, and for a moment Junior thought he had proven himself. He thought he had done something good.

DON'T OR STOP

Neil McCormick was a scruffy, moody stick of a boy. I developed a crush the same day I set eyes on him. It didn't take long to discover my crush was doomed: he was one of those queers.

The kids at Sherman Middle School realized this fact during an afternoon recess séance. It was September 1983; at twelve, I'd begun to slip into the antisocial skin I've never slipped out of. The trends my Hutchinson classmates followed seemed foolish: neon rubber bracelets, nicknames in iron-on lettering on T-shirt backs, or illegal lollipops made with tequila and an authentic, crystallized dead worm. But when some other sixth graders became interested in the occult, I joined them. "Finally," I told Mom, "they're into something cool." Groups of us traipsed through graveyards on dares. We bought Tarot decks; magazines devoted to telekinesis or out-of-body experiences. We gathered at recess, waiting for some small miracle to happen.

My mom claimed she was observing a change in me. For my upcoming birthday, I'd requested albums by bands whose names sounded especially disturbing or violent: The Dead Boys, Suicide,

Throbbing Gristle. I longed for the world that existed beyond Hutchinson, Kansas. "You, Wendy Peterson, are looking for trouble with a capital T," Mom had started to warn.

In my eyes, that trouble equalled Neil. I'd noticed him, but I doubted anyone else had. He always seemed to be alone. He was in fifth grade, not sixth, and he didn't participate in the daily half-hour soccer games — two disqualifications from what most everyone considered cool.

That afternoon, though, he fearlessly broke the séance circle. Two popular girls, Vicky and Rochelle, were attempting to summon a blond TV star from the dead. Sebastian So-and-so's BMW had recently crashed into a Hollywood brick wall, and my classmates were determined to disclose whatever heaven he now hovered through. "Aaahhhmmm," the girls moaned. Hands levitated in midair, attempting to catch this or that spiritual vibration.

When Neil interrupted, his sneakered foot stomped squarely on a Ouija board someone had brought. "Watch it, fucker," a séance attendee said.

"You shitheads know nothing about contacting ghosts," Neil said. "What you need is a professional." His voice sounded vaguely grandfatherlike, as if his brain were crowded with knowledge: Eyes opened, concentrations broke. Someone gasped.

A few tall boys' heads blocked my view. I tried to peek above their shoulders; saw a mop of thick black hair. A breeze blew it. To touch it would be like touching corduroy.

Neil picked up the valentine-shaped beige plastic disk from the Ouija board. It looked like a tiny, three-legged table, a gold pin poking through its center. Sun glinted off the pinpoint. Only moments before, Vicky and Rochelle had placed their polished fingernails on the disk to ask about the coming apocalypse.

"My father's a hypnotist," Neil said. He waved the disk in front of his face like a Smith & Wesson. "He's taught me all the tricks.

I could show you shitheads a fucking thing or two." From Neil, all those *fucks* and *shits* were more than just throwaway cuss words. They adopted some special meaning.

Neil slipped off his shoes, sat on them, and pretzeled his legs into a configuration only someone that skinny could have managed. The crowd blocked the sun and shadowed Neil. The air felt chilly, and I wished I'd worn a jacket. From somewhere behind us, a teacher's whistle shrieked. Some classmates chanted a brainless song, its words confused by the wind.

"Who wants to be first?" Neil asked. He excited me to no end. Maybe he'd expose their infinite foolishness.

Vicky volunteered. "No way," Neil said. "Only a boy will work for the kind of hypnotizing I'm going to do." Vicky pouted, planted her tequila pop back on her tongue, and stood aside.

Neil pointed toward Robert P., a kid whose last initial stuck because two other sixth graders shared the same first name. Robert P. could speak Spanish and sometimes wore an eye patch. I'd heard him bragging about his first wet dream. Some girls thought him "debonair." Like most everyone else in school, he seemed stupid to me.

People made room, and my view improved. Under Neil's direction, Robert lay on his back. Random hands smoothed the grass, sweeping aside pebbles and sandburs, and someone's wadded-up windbreaker served as a pillow. Roly-poly bugs coiled into themselves. The more nervous kids stayed on the circle's outer edge, watching for teachers, unsure of what would happen.

Neil sat beside his volunteer. He said, "Everyone, to their knees." We obeyed. From where I knelt, I could see into Robert P.'s nostrils. His eyes were shut. His mouth had opened slightly, flaunting teeth that needed braces. I wished for a spot at the opposite side of the circle. Being near Neil McCormick would have satisfied me.

Neil touched his middle and index fingers to Robert P.'s temples. "Breathe deeply." The fingers rubbed and massaged. I would die, I thought, to be that volunteer. Neil's voice lowered: "In your mind, begin counting backward. Start at one hundred. One hundred, ninety-nine. Keep going, counting backward, slowly." Everyone else's mouths moved in synch. Could he hypnotize an entire crowd?

"Eighty, seventy-nine, seventy-eight . . ." His voice softened, nearly a whisper. My eyes darted from Robert P.'s face to the back of Neil's head. I was so close to him. "Sixty," pause, "nine . . ."

By the time Neil reached sixty-two, Robert P. looked zombieish. His chest moved with each breath, but all else remained motionless. I figured he was faking it, but wondered what Neil would make him do or say. I hoped for something humiliating, like a piss on Miss Timmons's shoes or a brick demolishing a school window.

A girl said "Wow," which Neil seemed to take as a signal. He crawled atop Robert P., straddling his stomach. Belt buckles clicked together. "Fifty," Neil said. Robert didn't move. Neil gripped his wrists; pinned his hands above his head. The circle of kids tightened. I could feel fingers against my skin, shoulders brushing mine. I didn't look at any of them. My gaze fixed on Robert and Neil, locked there as if I were stuck in a theater's front row, its screen sparkling with some beautiful film.

Neil's body flattened. He stretched out on Robert. The buckles clicked again.

Clouds crawled across the sun. For a few seconds, everything went dark. Another whistle blared. "Recess over," Miss Timmons screamed, but no one budged. We couldn't care less about the whistle. The silence grew, blooming like a fleecy gray flower. A little voice inside me kept counting: thirty-three, thirty-two.

Then it happened. The lower half of Neil's body began grinding into Robert's. I watched Neil's ass move against him. By that time in my life, I'd seen some R-rated movies, so I knew what fucking looked like. Only these were boys, and their clothes were on.

Neil positioned his face directly over his subject's. Robert's eyes opened. They blinked twice, as beady and inquisitive as a hen's. A thick line of drool spilled from Neil's mouth. It lingered there, glittered, then trailed between Robert's lips. Robert coughed, swallowed, coughed again. Neil continued drooling, and as he did, he moved his face closer to Robert's. At last their mouths touched.

Vicky screamed, and everyone jumped back. Kids shouted things like "gross" and "sick." They sprinted for Miss Timmons and the classroom, their sneaker colors blurring together. I stood and stared at the separated pair of boys. Robert P. wriggled on the grass like a rattlesnake smashed by a semi. A chocolatey blob stuck to his chin: dirt, suffused with Neil's spit.

One of Robert's buddies kicked Neil's ribs, then hustled away with the others. Neil didn't wince, accepting the kick as he might accept a handshake.

"Queer," Robert P. said, plus something in Spanish. He was crying. He kicked Neil, too, his foot connecting with the identical spot his friend had chosen. Then he ran for the school's glass doors.

Neil sprawled there a while, smiling, his arms spread as if he'd been crucified to the earth. He struggled to get up. He and I were alone on the playground. I wanted to touch his arm, his shoulder, his face. I offered my hand, and he took it.

"That was great," Neil said. He squeezed my fingers and shuffled toward the school.

Something important had happened, and I had witnessed it. And I had touched Neil McCormick. I waited until he departed earshot. Then I pretended I was a character in a movie. I said, "There's no turning back now." A small spit bubble lay on the dirt at my feet like a toad's gleaming eye. I bent down and popped it. If I could make Neil my friend, I figured I wouldn't need anyone else.

The séances vanished. By the end of that week, the kids who'd brought their Ouija boards and magic eight balls had jumped back to four-square and soccer. I watched them and wanted to scream. I longed to approach Neil again, this boy I saw as my doorway from the boredom I wanted to escape.

That Friday, a team of bullies gathered on the soccer field. They found Neil standing by a tree and cornered him. "You're one of those queers," a kid named Alastair yelled. Neil flew at him. A crowd formed, and I joined it. Arms and legs darted and windmilled, and the ivory crescent of Neil's fingernail sliced Alastair's chin. There were tears and a few drops of blood, all of which turned out to be Alastair's. At twelve, I'd seen more tornadoes than blood. Its red looked magnificent and sacred, as if rubies had been shattered.

When the fight was history, Neil stood beside the same oak. He wore a hot rod T-shirt, a real leather coat with zippers like rows of teeth, and matching boots. Animals had died for those clothes, I thought. He would be perfect holding a switchblade in one hand, and me in the other.

I took a deep breath, collected the gumption, and tiptoed over. I tilted my head heavenward to look cool. The sun rebounded off the steel plates of Sherman Middle School to reveal the roof's slant. It had been littered with toilet paper, a yellow ball some vandal had sliced from its tether, and random graffiti. GO STRAIGHT TO HELL was all someone could think to spray paint. I stared at the jagged red letters and kept walking. Around me, brown five-pointed leaves fell like the severed hands of babies. I moved through them. Neil heard the crunch, crunch and glanced up.

I leaned against another tree, feigning nonchalance. "You *are* a queer, aren't you?" I said the *Q*-word as if it were synonymous with *movie star* or *deity*. There was something wonderful about the word, something that set him apart from everyone else, something I wanted to identify with.

"Yeah," said Neil.

I felt as if I were falling in love. Not so much with him, though, as with the aura of him. It didn't matter that he was a year younger than me. It didn't matter, all the distaste I detected in teachers' voices when they called his name during recess. Neil McCormick, they barked, the fence is there for a reason, don't cross it. Neil McCormick, put down that stick. I had eavesdropped on Miss Timmons in her office, as she whispered to the school nurse how she dreaded getting the McCormick boy in her class next year. "He's simply evil," etcetera.

To me, "evil" didn't seem all that bad.

Neil's long hair frayed in the breeze, as shiny black as the lenses in the spectacles of the creepy blind girl who sat behind me on the morning bus. His eyebrows met ominously in his forehead's middle. Up close, I could smell him. The odor swelled, like something hot. If I weren't so eager to touch him again, I would have shrunk from it.

I breathed again, as if it were something I did once a day. "But you're a tough queer, right?"

"Yeah." He examined the blood smear on the back of his hand. He made certain I was watching, then licked it off.

In my room, I fantasized miniature movies starring Neil and me. My parents had okayed my staying up to watch *Bonnie and Clyde* on the late-late, and in my Neil hallucinations I assumed bloodred lipstick and a platinum bob that swirled in the wind, à la Faye Dunaway. I clung to his side. We wielded guns the size of our arms. We blew away bank tellers and other boring innocents, their blood spattering the air in slow-mo. Newspapers tumble-weeded through deserted streets. MCCORMICK AND PETERSON STRIKE AGAIN, their headlines read.

In these dreams, we never kissed. I was content to stand beside him. Nights, I fell asleep with clenched fists.

Weeks passed. Neil spent most recesses just standing there, feeling everyone else's fear. I wasn't afraid, but I couldn't approach him again. He was like the electric wire that separated my uncle's farm from the neighbors'. Touch it, Wendy, my little brother Kurt would say. It won't hurt. But I couldn't move toward it. Surely a sliver of blue electricity would jet from the wire and strike me dead. I felt the same way about Neil: I didn't dare go near him. Not yet.

Zelda Beringer, a girl who wore a headpiece attached to her braces and who wouldn't remain my friend much longer, teased me about Neil. "How in the world can you think a queer is cute? I mean, you can tell he's a freak. You can just tell." I advised Zelda that if she didn't shut up, I'd gouge out her eyes and force her to swallow them. The resulting look on her face wouldn't leave my mind for days.

For Columbus Day the cafeteria cooks served the school's favorite lunch. They fixed potato boats: a bologna slice fried until its edges curled, a scoop of mashed potatoes stuck in its center, watery cheese melted on top. They made home fries, and provided three squirt bottles of ketchup per table. For dessert, banana halves, rolled in a mucusy marriage of powdered gelatin and water.

Fifth graders sat on the cafeteria's opposite end, but that day I was blessed with a great view of Neil. He scooped the boat into one hand and devoured it in a single bite. If I'd had binoculars, I could have watched his puffy lips in close-up.

I remember that day as near perfect, and not just because of potato boats. The yearly sex-ed filmstrips arrived. All afternoon, teachers glanced at clocks and avoided our gazes. We knew what was happening. We'd been through it before. Now we could view those films again, together in the room with the virgin fifth graders. "We're going to see cartoon tits and ass," Alastair said, the slightest hint of a scratch still on his chin.

Grade five lumbered in. Neil stood at the back of the line. For the first half of the process, the principal, Mr. Fili, separated boys from girls. The boys left, and Miss Timmons dimmed the lights. The room felt stifling, as if some killer had snuck in to poison our air with a noxious nerve gas. I rested my elbows on my desk; planted my chin on my fists.

Miss Timmons hesitated before reading the film's captions. "Sometimes, at this age, young men will want to touch certain places on a young lady's body." She bit her lip like the section of an orange.

When the filmstrip was over, Miss Timmons handed out free Kotex pads. Most girls popped theirs into purses or the back shadows of desk drawers. I examined mine. It resembled something I would hold over a campfire or take a chomp from.

After ten minutes, the boys returned. "Find a seat, men, somewhere on the floor," Mr. Fili told them. "This time, try to keep quiet. If you feel the urge to make some capricious outburst, please hold your breath. And no commentaries. This is serious stuff." When he said that, he scowled at Neil.

Neil moved toward me, as if following a dotted line to my desk. I swallowed hard. He sat, his knee touching my calf.

Part two of the birds-and-bees rigamarole was special: a film instead of filmstrip. Kids oohed and aahed when they heard the projector's buzzes and clicks. Perhaps this meant we would see real, live sex action.

Some fool of a filmmaker had dreamed up the idea that humor was the best way to teach sex. Tiny cartoon sperm wriggled and roller coastered toward a bulging, rouged egg. The egg licked its lips, as eager and lewd as an old whore. The music — *The 1812 Overture* — swelled, and the quickest and most virile sperm punctured the egg. "Bull's-eye!" the voice-over cackled.

Some kids clapped and cheered. "Shhh," said Miss Timmons.

Neil looked up at me. I swore I could smell bologna on him. A smear of ketchup had dried on his shirt front. He smiled, and I smiled back. He mouthed the words, "This is total bullshit," moving to lean against my legs. When he shifted, I felt his backbone move. No one was watching us.

On screen, drawings of a penis and the inside of a vagina flashed on and off. A couple of fifth graders giggled. Penis entered vagina, and white junk gushed forth like mist from a geyser. More giggles. Miss Timmons shhed again.

"Ridiculous," Neil whispered. "Not everyone fucks like that." Some kids heard him, glared and sneered. "Some people take it up the ass." One girl's face reddened, as if scratched.

As the credits rolled, Neil's hand rested on my sneaker, resulting in a goose bumpy feeling that lasted three tiny seconds. I wiggled my toes. Lights clicked on, and his hand moved away. "Let's go, fifth grade," Mr. Fili said.

"How fucked up," Neil said to me. He was speaking to no one else now. "Why don't they teach us something we don't already know?" Disappointment amended his face.

Neil waved as they filed out. Kids' heads turned to stare at me, and I felt as though it were Neil and me versus everyone else. It was a good feeling. I let my classmates gawk awhile, then shook my middle finger at them.

That evening, I upped the volume on the stereo to drown out the TV my parents and brother were fixed in front of. Even with the bedroom door closed, I could hear televised trumpets blaring "America the Beautiful." A newscaster said, "Happy Columbus Day." I lifted the needle from my Blondie album and started side one over again: "Dreaming," my favorite song.

My geography book toppled off my bed. I was just beginning to effectively imagine myself as a singer onstage, a cluster of punks bouncing below me, when Mom rapped at the door. "Can you hear in there?" she asked. "You'll shake the house off its foundation. Anyway, you've got a phone call. It's some boy."

I ran to the kitchen's extension. Mom had just finished drying dishes, and her set of knives lined a black towel on the table. By that time in the fall, it was starting to grow dark by six o'clock, so the room looked like some kind of torture dungeon. I left the light off.

The music on the phone's other end sounded cool. I listened for three, four, five seconds. "This is Wendy."

Someone stuttered a hello. Then, "You might not know me. My name's Stephen Zepherelli."

My eyes widened. Everyone knew the notorious Stephen Zepherelli. He attended class in the adjoining building at school, one of the Learning Disabilities trio we occasionally saw delivering messages to Mr. Fili or bending over water faucets in the hall. The LDs, we called them. Stephen Zepherelli was the most severe of the three LDs. He wasn't retarded, but he was close. He drooled, and he smelled like an old pond.

Then I realized the absurdity of him calling me. I'd heard

Zepherelli's voice before, and this wasn't it. "Okay," I said. "Not funny. Someone's got to have at least half a brain to know how to dial a telephone. Who is this really?"

A laugh. The new-wave song paused, then began blasting a guitar solo. "Hey Wendy, this is Neil McCormick." I couldn't believe it. "I've called three Petersons in the phone book already, and I finally found the right one. What are you doing?"

I forgave Neil for the Zepherelli joke. "Nothing," I said. "As usual. How about that film today?"

We chatted for ten minutes about people we despised most at school. While Neil spoke, I handled the knives, arranging them on the table from longest to shortest. "I'd like to stab all those fools," I said, my back turned from the direction of the den and my parents. "Make it hurt. Stab them in the gut, then twist the knife real slow. I've read it really hurts that way. Or I'd cut their heads right off."

When I said that, Neil laughed. I pictured him throwing his head back, his mouth open, his teeth gleaming like an animal's.

By Halloween I stopped riding the bus home and began walking with Neil. His house was only four blocks from mine. Sometimes we carried each other's books. We tried alternate ways home. Once we even went the opposite direction, heading toward the prison on Hutchinson's east side. Neil stood at its gate, his shoe-laces clotted with sandburs, breathing in the wistful smells of the rain-soaked hay and mud, the raked piles of leaves. "Kansas State Industrial Reformatory," he read. "Maybe I'll end up here some-day." A guard watched us from the stone tower. We waved, but he didn't wave back.

Neil lived with his mother, and had no bratty brothers or sis-ters to deal with. And his father wasn't a hypnotist at all. He was dead. "Killed in a war," Neil said. "He's nothing but a corpse now. I know him from one picture, and one picture only. He looks nothing like me, either. What should I care about the guy?"

Mrs. McCormick drank gin straight from the bottle. On the label, a bearded man was dressed in a plaid skirt. The first time I visited Neil's, his mom slid the bottle aside and took my hand in hers. "Hello, Wendy," she said. "It's not often I see a friend of Neil's. And such vibrant blond hair." Her own hair was as black as her son's. She had pinned it back with green pickle-shaped barrettes.

A bookshelf in Neil's house was piled with paperbacks with damaged or missing covers. Neil explained that his mother had a job at a grocery store, and her boss allowed her to keep whatever books the customers vandalized. Many concerned true kidnappings and murders. Mrs. McCormick saw me eyeing them. "You can borrow whatever you like," she told me. Soon I stopped reading about the tedious exploits of that ignoramus Nancy Drew. Within days I knew all there was to know about Charles Starkweather and Caril Ann Fugate, two teenage fugitives who blazed a trail of murder and mayhem across the Midwest a few decades ago. They weren't that much older than Neil and me. They even hailed from Nebraska, our border state. In two grainy mug shots, their grimaces couldn't have been more severe if their mouths had been clogged with thumbtacks. If I thought hard enough, Neil and I almost resembled them.

I had decided that '83 would be my last year as a trick-or-treater, and I wanted to dress as something special. I considered a gypsy, a freshly murdered corpse, an evil nun with a knife beneath her habit. Then I decided Neil and I should go as Charles and Caril. On Halloween night, I stared at the criminals' pictures and tried to change my looks.

Neil stretched out on his bed. "It's not working," he said. He tossed a baseball into the air, caught it. "No one will get it, so why bother?"

I wiped the lipstick on a Kleenex and watched him watching me in his bedroom mirror. When I peeled off the fake eyelash, my lid made a popping noise.

Mrs. McCormick dragged two spider costumes from her closet. She and a date, Neil claimed, had gone as "Daddy and Mommy Longlegs" to a party last year. "She lost that boyfriend around the same time," he said. "Sometimes she can't handle anything. But she's my mom."

We mascaraed circles around our eyes and thumbed black blobs across our mouths. Before we left the house, Neil gave me three yellow pills. "Swallow these." The box in his hand read DOZ-AWAY. I wasn't sure if that meant we'd grow sleepy or stay perky, but the box's cover pictured a pair of wide-awake eyes.

By that point I would have done anything Neil told me. I popped the pills in my mouth, swallowing without water.

Neil handed me the telephone beside his bed. He told me to call my parents and claim his mom would be escorting us. When I lied to Mom, it didn't feel so scandalous. "I'll take Kurt around the neighborhood without you, then," she said. "Call back when you want me to drive over and get you. Don't stay out too late, and remember what I told you about those perverts who prey on kids on Halloween." She laughed nervously. I thought of her stories of razor blades wedged into apples, stories that never ceased to thrill me.

Two hours came and went. We wandered around Hutchinson as spiders, our extra four legs bobbing at our sides. The rows of our eyes gleamed from our headpieces. The shadows we cast gave me the creeps, so we shied away from streetlights. Neil hissed when doors opened. One wrinkly lady touched my nose with a counterfeit black fingernail. She asked, "Aren't you two a little old for this?" Still, our shopping bags filled to the top. I stomped a Granny Smith into mush on the sidewalk. No hidden razor.

Neil traded his Bit-O-Honeys for anything I had with peanuts. "I'm allergic to nuts," I said. That was a lie, but I wanted to make him happy.

At Twenty-third and Adams, a group of seven kids walked toward us. I recognized the younger ones from school under their guises of pirate, fat lady, and something that resembled a beaver. "Hey, it's you-know-who from school," Neil said, and pointed to a green dragon in the crowd's center.

I couldn't tell who it was. "It's that retardo," Neil told me. He was right. Even under the tied-on snout and green pointy ears, I could make out Stephen Zepherelli.

"Hey," Neil said. Their heads turned. "Hey, snotnoses, where're your parents?"

The beaver-thing pointed west. "Back there," it said. The words garbled behind its fake buck teeth.

Zepherelli smiled. The dragon snout shifted on his face. He carried a plastic pumpkin, chock-full with candy. "Let's kidnap him," Neil said to me.

I'd witnessed Neil's damage to Robert P. and Alastair. Now, some dire section of my brain longed to find out what twisted things Neil could do to this nimrod, this Stephen Zepherelli. Neil checked the sidewalk for adults. When none materialized, he grabbed the kid's left hand. "He's supposed to come with us," Neil said to the rest of the trick-or-treaters. "His mom said so. She doesn't want him out too late."

Zepherelli whined at first, but Neil said we were leading him to a house that was giving away "enough candy for three thousand starving kids." Zepherelli didn't seem to mind the kidnapping after that. We stood on each side of him, gripped his scrawny wrists, and pulled him along. Mahogany-colored leaves spun around our rushing feet. "Slow down," he said at one point. We just moved faster. He stopped once to retrieve a handful of candy corn from his plastic pumpkin, and once to find a Zero candy bar. His painted-on dragon's teeth shone under street lamps, as white as piano keys.

We arrived at Neil's. "Is this the house with the candy?" Zepherelli asked. He rummaged through his pumpkin, making room.

"Good guess."

Neil's mom snoozed on the living room couch. Nearly every light in the house had been left on. Neil pushed Zepherelli toward me. "Hold this little bastard while I'm gone." He trotted from room to room, flicking switches. In seconds, darkness had lowered around us. Neil slid aside a record by a band called Bow Wow Wow and slipped another LP on the turntable. Scary sound effects drifted through the house at a volume soft enough to keep his mom sleeping. On the record, a cat hissed, chains rattled, crazed banshees wailed.

"Neat," Zepherelli said. His snout showed a smudge of white chocolate from the Zero. He nibbled the tip from a piece of candy corn.

I heard Neil pissing. I suddenly felt embarrassed, standing there with our victim. Neil returned, carrying a flashlight and a paper sack. He opened the latter. Inside were firecrackers and bottle rockets. "Left over from Fourth of July," Neil said. He winked. "Let's take him out behind the house."

The McCormick backyard consisted of overgrown weeds, an apricot tree, and a dilapidated slippery slide-swing set. Behind the swings was a cement-filled hole someone had once meant for a cellar. We walked toward it. The rotten apricot odor permeated the autumn air. Stars glittered in the sky. Down the block, kids yelled "trick or treat" from a doorstep.

Neil pushed Zepherelli toward the stretch of cement. "Lie on your back," he said.

The yellow pills had done something to me. My skin tingled like I'd taken a bath in ice. I was a hundred percent awake, and prepared for anything. I adjusted a loose arm and stood above the victim; Neil spilled the bag's contents onto the cement. "Bottle rockets," the dragon said, as if they were hundred-dollar bills. I could smell Zepherelli's breath, even over all those apricots.

Neil told him to shut up. He pulled off the dragon's snout. The string snapped against Zepherelli's face. "Ouch."

I watched as Neil took three bottle rockets and placed their wooden ends in Zepherelli's mouth. He pinched Zepherelli's lips shut. He moved briskly, as if he'd done it all a thousand times. Then he straddled the kid. I remembered that séance, Robert P.'s still face. Stephen Zepherelli's resembled it. It looked drugged, almost as if it really were hypnotized. It didn't register any emotion. Its cheeks had been smeared with green makeup. Its eyes were cold and blank, not unlike the peeled grapes we had passed around during the inane Haunted Hall setup at school that day. "These are the dead man's eyes," Miss Timmons had told us in her best Vincent Price voice.

"Keep these in your mouth," Neil instructed the LD boy. "Do what we say, or we'll kill you." I thought of Charles and Caril Ann. Neil's extra eyes caught the moonlight and sparkled.

From the effects record inside the house, a girl screamed, a monstrous voice laughed. Neil turned to me, smiling. "Matches are in the bottom of the sack," he said. "Hand them over."

I fished out a book of matches. The cover showed a beaming woman's face over a steamy piece of pie and the words "Eat at McGillicuddy's." I tossed the matches to Neil. "Be careful," I said. I tried not to sound scared. "Someone could see the fireworks." I still thought this was all a big joke.

"Tonight is just another holiday," Neil said. "No one's going to care." He lit the first match. The flame turned Zepherelli's face a weird orange. In the glow, the rockets jutted from his lips like sticks of spaghetti. His eyes were huge. He squirmed a little, and I sat on his legs. I felt as though we were offering a sacrifice to some special god.

Zepherelli didn't spit the rockets out. He made a noise that could have been "Don't" or "Stop."

Neil touched the match to the fuses. One, two, three. He shielded me with one of his real arms. We skittered back like crabs. I held my breath as tiny sputters of fire trailed up the fuses and entered the rockets. Zepherelli didn't budge. He was paralyzed. The bottle rockets zoomed from his head, made perfect arcs over the McCormick home, and exploded in feeble gold bursts.

The following silence seemed to last hours. I expected sirens to wail toward the house, but nothing happened. Finally, Neil and I snuck toward Zepherelli. "Shine the flashlight on him," Neil said.

The oval of light landed on our victim's face. For a second, I almost laughed. Zepherelli resembled the villain in a cartoon after the bomb goes off. The explosives' dust covered his dragon snout, his cheeks, his chin. His eyes had widened farther, and they darted here and there, as if he'd been blinded. We leaned in closer. Zepherelli licked his lips and winced. Then I saw what we'd done. It wasn't funny at all. His mouth was bleeding. Little red splinters stuck through Zepherelli's lips, jammed there from the wooden rocket sticks. Bubbles of blood dotted the lips.

The victim's eyes kept widening. I remembered thinking blood beautiful when Neil had punched Alastair. Now, from Zepherelli, it looked horrible, poisonous. I turned away.

Zepherelli made a mewling noise, softer than a kitten's. My

heart felt like a hand curling into a fist. He whimpered again, and the fist clenched. "Neil," I said. "He's going to tattle on us. We're going to get it." I wondered if my parents would discover what we'd done. For the first time, I wanted to slap Neil.

A look spread across Neil's face, one I'd never seen there. He bit his bottom lip, and his eyes glassed over. Then he shook his head. The glassiness left his eyes. "No," he said. "He won't tell. There's things we can do." He spoke as if Zepherelli weren't lying beside us. "We'll get him on our side. Help me."

I didn't know what to do. I gripped the flashlight until my palm hurt. Neil wiped dust from Zepherelli's cheek. When their skins touched, Zepherelli trembled and sighed. Neil said, "Shhh," like a mother comforting a baby. His left hand remained on the kid's face. His right moved from Zepherelli's chest, down his stomach, and started untying the sweatpants dyed green for Halloween. He squirmed a finger inside, then his entire hand.

"When I was little," Neil said, "a man used to do this to me." He spoke toward the empty air, as if his words were the lines of a play he'd just memorized. He pulled the front of Zepherelli's pants down. The kid's dick stuck straight out. I swung the flashlight beam across it.

"Sometimes I wanted to tell everyone what was going on. Then he'd do this to me again, and I knew how badly he really wanted it. He did it to some other kids, but I knew they didn't matter as much to him, I was the only one whose photo he kept in his wallet. Every time he'd do it he'd roll up a five-dollar bill, brand-new so I could even hear it snap, and he'd slip it into the back pocket of my jeans or my baseball pants or whatever. It was like getting an allowance. I knew how much it meant to him, in a way, and after a while, it kept going further and further. There was no way I could tattle on him. I looked forward to it, for a while it was every week that summer, before the baseball games.

It was great, he was waiting there, for me, like that was all he ever wanted."

Neil's voice sounded lower, older. It wasn't spouting nasty words or giggling between sentences. Then Neil shut up and leaned beside Zepherelli.

Neil buried his head in the kid's crotch. The dick disappeared in Neil's mouth. I watched the spider arms bob as Neil hovered over him. I slid back. The flashlight flipped from my hand. Its column of white illuminated the apricot tree's branches. Up there, a squirrel or something equally small and insignificant was scampering around. Already-dead fruit tumbled to the ground.

Stephen Zepherelli moaned. His breathing deepened. He didn't sound scared anymore.

The shadow of Neil's head lifted. "That feels nice, right?" The shadow moved back down, and I heard noises that sounded like a vampire sucking blood from a neck. I wanted to cry. I tried to fold myself into my dream of Charles and Caril Ann, those teenage fugitives. What would the blond murderess do in this situation, I wondered. Neil and I were nothing like them. I heard another chorus of "trick or treat"s, this time closer than before, maybe right there on the McCormicks' doorstep. I thought of Neil's mom, sleeping through it all. Where had she been when the man from Neil's past had put his mouth on her son like this?

I lay on my back until the noises stopped. Neil retied Zepherelli's sweat bottoms and handed him the dragon snout. "It's okay."

When Zepherelli stood, his eyes had resumed their normal luster. He was drooling. A comma-shaped trickle of blood had dried on his mouth. I got up, carefully pulled a splinter from his upper lip, and dabbed the blood with my black sleeve.

Neil patted the kid's butt like a coach. "I'll walk him home," Neil said. He smiled at me, but he was looking over my shoulder, not at my face.

We tiptoed through the McCormick house. In Neil's bedroom, I could see his tousled sheets, his schoolbooks, his baseball trophies. The scary record had ended, but the needle was stuck on the final groove. "Scratch, scratch, scratch," Zepherelli said. I faked a laugh.

Neil's mother was still sleeping. She snored louder than my father. I shone the flashlight on the bookshelves above her, making out titles like *Monsters and Madmen, Ghoulish and Ghastly, All the Worst Ways to Die.* Only days ago, I'd wanted to read those. Now I didn't care.

"I know the direction home," Stephen Zepherelli told Neil. He seemed anxious to lead the way. "I can show you where to go."

We left the house. The cool air smelled like mosquito repellent, barbecue sauce, harmless little fires. When the air hit my face, I ripped my headpiece off. A single beady spider's eye fell to the sidewalk. I bent to get it. In the weak street light, that eye stared back at me. I saw my reflection in its black glass. Instead of picking it up, I stood and ground it beneath my shoe.

"See you later, Stephen," I said. It was the first time I'd said his name, and my voice cracked on the word. "And you too, Neil. Tomorrow."

And I knew I would see him tomorrow, and the next day, and the day after that. Neil had shown a part of himself I knew he'd shown no one else. I reckoned I had asked for it. Now I was bound to him.

Neil led Zepherelli down the block. I watched them shuffle through the dead leaves, moving farther away, until the shadows swallowed them up.

BANKING HOURS

I'd never had what my father called a real job in a real office, but now that I was a high school graduate, he insisted I earn some real money to put toward my tuition at the University of Maryland, so he got me a job at the bank. I had worked in a theatre since I was thirteen, selling tickets, ushering, one summer even acting. I wanted to study drama in New York City, at Juilliard or NYU, but my father felt that seventeen was too young to leave home.

"Two years at Maryland and we'll talk about New York," he told me, puffing on a thick cigar. "After all, Freddy, you're the one who wanted to graduate a year early."

My parents took my early graduation personally, as though I was trying to get away from them. I was the last child left, and spent most of my time in my room while they poured themselves "one more drink before dinner" long after I'd made myself a meal, soup and a sandwich. The next morning when I carried my dinner tray downstairs to exchange it for breakfast, my parents would be passed out on perpendicular sofas, wearing last night's clothes.

The living room reeked of stale cigar smoke, and their half-drunk glasses of scotch looked like urine samples.

He was the man with the money, though, a successful attorney, and if I wanted to get to New York City it would be he who paid for it, just as he paid for my three brothers' and one sister's college educations before mine. If it meant working at a bank and spending two years at a university whose most famous theatrical alumnus was Ernest Borgnine, that's what I would do.

I told myself this as my father drove me to the bank that first day. He was meticulously dressed in a silver-gray summer suit, the color of his hair, the color of his cigar smoke in the morning sun. He never looked hung over, though he must have been. We rode in silence as we had during the single season I played Little League football as a favor to my father. Although my mother drove me to singing lessons and play rehearsals, it was my father who took me to football practice on chilly autumn mornings, my shoulder pads, helmet, and cleats in my lap, cumbersome and cold, like chunks of ice. The heater in the station wagon never worked, and my breath was as visible as the smoke from his cigar.

I was a better bank teller than a football player. The job lacked the glamour of theatre, but to my surprise, I enjoyed getting paid to work with numbers. There was one right and many wrong answers for each transaction, and all employees were bonded, insured, so if I chose a wrong answer, no matter how wrong, the bank would be reimbursed. Though the days were sometimes dull, the bank was comfortable, its temperature controlled, its walls freshly painted, its floors covered in emerald green carpet, plush compared to the cold sterility of my high school and the shabby disrepair of my parents' once-impressive home. Even the little compartments on the counters where the deposit and withdrawal slips were kept appealed to me: everything had its place, including me, but it wasn't a place I wanted to stay in for long.

From the beginning I was a big hit at the bank, though I had nothing in common with the other tellers: I was the youngest "on the line," as they called it. Charles, only two years older, already spoke of his high school wistfully, the best years of his life, and his long fingernails were stained yellow from chain-smoking. Next on the line was Happy Ho, a Vietnamese woman, barely as tall as the counter we worked behind. She moonlighted at a nearby 7-Eleven, selling a cherry-flavored ice drink called a "Slurpee." Happy was serious, and Dixie, our head teller and my biggest fan, told me they'd never seen Happy smile till I started working there.

"Personality-plus," Dixie used to call me, rolling her big, brown, blue-eyeshadowed eyes and coating her bleached coif with hairspray. She was my immediate supervisor, the one I reported to every morning, always late, no matter how early I'd tried to rouse my father off the couch.

Dixie never docked me for my tardiness: I made her laugh. Stepping out of the silence of my father's smoke-filled car and into the bank was like stepping onto a sitcom, security cameras hidden in the ceiling to film my show. I'd do imitations of angry customers, of Mr. Mulgrew, the bank president with a thick Irish brogue though he grew up near Pittsburgh. My most popular impression was of our branch manager, Nelva, who came from rural Maryland and spent all day on the phone telling her husband, Big Kenny, that he couldn't go to the cockfights.

"Life's been a ball since Freddy bounced into this bank," Dixie would say, her cigarette waving up and down between her painted pink lips like a conductor's baton as we counted stacks of crisp new bills, called "clean" money though it coated our fingertips with black ink.

My show ended when my father picked me up from work. I would wait for him long after the bank closed, glad the other tellers weren't there to see me sitting on the curb, watching for his big blue car, like a furloughed prisoner waiting to return to jail. My driver's license had been suspended after four speeding tickets and one failure-to-yield-right-of-way. At the Traffic Court hearing, my father refused to defend me.

"Maybe now you won't be in such a hurry," he said.

Hurry or not, I had no license until September, though sometimes I drove home from the bank if my father had had too many "drinks before dinner" at lunch, weaving his way through the parking lot, turning the wheel over to me. I never asked him about his work: he always asked about mine.

"How was the bank today, Freddy?"

"Don't ask how the bank is," I told him. "The bank isn't."

"Isn't what?" he asked.

"Isn't anywhere I want to be."

I was afraid if he knew I liked the bank, he'd never pay for New York, so I didn't discuss the tellers, or do my bubble-blowing Dixie bit, or imitate Nelva screaming into the phone, "Naw, Big Kinny, ya cain't go ta dem cockfights." Nor did I tell my father I'd been named "Teller of the Month" for June, a monthly award given to the teller whose drawer came closest to balancing, which mine did every day, to the penny, making Dixie nervous.

"They expect you to make mistakes," she warned me, "a few cents here and there. It looks unnatural if you don't."

Still, she cried when Mr. Mulgrew announced my name, rolling the "r" in Freddy. I expected applause, but instead, I got snapping fingers, a bank tradition. Everyone snapped, even the bank

officers in their dark suits, and it sounded like a roomful of popping popcorn as Mr. Mulgrew handed me a small badge, which
Dixie made me wear under my name tag, proud that someone on
her line had a perfect record. Mulgrew was a friend of my father's,
the connection that got me the job, but he never told my father I
was "Teller of the Month," and I kept the badge in my pocket
during the silent rides to and from the bank.

I'd been at the bank for over a month when Mandy came back.
She'd spent three years on the line without missing a day until
her miscarriage before I started. She hadn't wanted to come back:
she was embarrassed because she didn't know who the father was,
Dixie told me. Dixie told everybody everything.

I assumed it was Mandy when I walked into the employees'
lounge, for once on time, and saw her talking with Charles
and Happy Ho. She had pale blonde hair that rested in soft
curls on her shoulders, and her face was round and flat, with a
button nose and Kewpie-doll lips. Only two of her features were
sharp: her green, almond-shaped eyes, and her fingernails, long
and blood red, a shocking end to her delicate, porcelain white
hands.

Charles introduced us.

"Teller of the Month." Happy pointed to my badge.

"The first celebrity I've had the honor of working with," said
Mandy, snapping her fingers.

Mandy's drawer was next to mine, and whenever a customer
commented on my button, I would hear her snapping and giggling, so I started to snap when the regulars welcomed her back.
Soon we were snapping when Charles talked about his beloved
high school, or Dixie displayed another Avon product, or Happy
Ho said anything at all. We kept our hands at our sides, snapping
quietly so no one noticed, trying not to laugh as I performed for

Mandy, capturing the customers' accents, their odd methods of handling money. When it was slow, we turned our chairs toward each other and talked.

"Why are you working at a bank?" she asked me during a lull between the lunchtime lines and the rush before closing. "I love having you here, but there are so many things you could be doing."

"You too," I said.

"I guess," said Mandy. "I just don't know what they are yet."

"I know what I want to do," I said. Charles stared at the clock and smoked, Dixie studied a Mary Kay Cosmetics catalogue, and Happy concentrated on a Vietnamese crossword puzzle while I told Mandy my plan to move to New York to be an actor.

"Not an actor," she said. "A comedian. That's what you should be. What are you waiting for?"

Mandy hadn't waited for anything. She'd left home after high school, saying good-bye to West Virginia and her family's trailer home and renting a small apartment in Rockville. She was saving money for her uncertain future and dating a few men when one of them got her pregnant. I sensed none of the embarrassment Dixie had described: Mandy seemed proud as she talked about the doctor's visits, the daily changes in her body, the decision not to have an abortion. Looking at her tiny waist, it was hard to imagine her six months pregnant, working on the line in maternity clothes, as she had been the day she collapsed.

Dixie was right: Mandy hadn't wanted to come back to the bank. She hated the way the customers looked at her, relieved that she'd lost the baby, as if a child might have ruined her life. The future she'd been saving for hadn't included a miscarriage, and Mandy ran out of money. She still had doctors' bills that insurance wouldn't cover, several hundred dollars' worth.

Mandy and I gossiped as much as Dixie did, whispering to each other as we set up our drawers in the morning, counting the coins and speculating about Dixie's real hair color, Happy's out-of-work husband, Charles's sexuality.

"He's been wondering about yours, too," Mandy told me. "I overheard him talking to Dixie."

I wasn't sure about myself, though my high school classmates were convinced I was gay. They cornered me in the locker room and slapped me with wet towels that sounded like cracking whips and left red marks on my skin. Other men had cornered me too: older men in mall bathrooms, an actor in a backstage dressing room. The only sound then was my zipper being pulled down as he slid his hand into my pants, my heart pounding when he made me feel him, bigger and harder than I was.

These were things I never discussed, especially not with Mandy, the first woman I'd felt sexually attracted to. Working next to her, I could smell her floral-scented shampoo, as though she'd just stepped out of the shower, and I imagined running my fingers through her wet, golden hair, and kissing her delicate neck as she giggled in my ear.

I didn't want her wondering about me, so I told her, "I hope you set Charles straight."

"I don't think that's possible," she said, and we laughed.

"Pay attention to your money and save the coffee klatch for later," Dixie would say every morning. "That's how mistakes happen."

Most mornings I was too late to talk, and once I arrived almost an hour after opening, angry at my father for sleeping so late and holding him responsible for every red light and stop sign along the way.

"Nelva wants to see you as soon she's off the phone with Big Kenny," Dixie said.

Mandy helped me set up my drawer, which she wasn't supposed

to do. I told her why I was late, and told her about my parents' drinking.

"So move to New York," she told me. "You don't want to go to the University of Maryland anyway."

"On what?" I asked, waving a wad of fives. "A bank loan?"

"Start saving, Freddy. You don't need much."

"Do you know what Juilliard's tuition is?" I said.

"You don't have to go to college," said Mandy.

"And what would I do when I got to New York City?"

"Go there first and then find out."

I looked at Charles, already on his third cup of coffee and seventh cigarette at nine a.m., and Happy, cashing paychecks for people who made more in a week than she did in a month working two jobs. Even Mandy, whose eyes always flashed with new ideas, had nothing to fall back on but the bank. I had my father: if Nelva fired me for being late, my father could get Mulgrew to rehire me, or get me another job. I felt the protection of my father's prestige and my father's money as I knocked on Nelva's door, though I soon realized she wasn't going to fire me for being late, merely lecturing me on punctuality, a lecture I performed for everyone on the line, complete with her speaker-phone refusal to let Big Kenny go to the cockfights.

The "Teller of the Month" ceremony was held at the previous winner's branch, so we hosted the July meeting. Happy Ho had left to sell Slurpees, but the rest of us sat together like the home team at a high school football game as tellers from six other branches filled the folding chairs. Mr. Mulgrew started his speech with "Top of the afternoon to you," and I took off my badge, ready to turn it over to the next winner.

"It's yours to keep," Dixie told me. "You'll always have been 'Teller of the Month' for June."

The snapping started when Mulgrew announced the winning name, an older woman wearing a gold brooch with the bank's logo, surrounded by three "Teller of the Month" buttons.

"I don't know where to put it," she said as Mulgrew handed her the badge.

"I have a suggestion," I whispered to Mandy, and we laughed as clicking fingers swelled to an ovation.

At the reception afterwards, with store-bought cookies and canned punch, the employees were supposed to mingle, but each branch formed its own group, seven tiny circles scattered throughout the room. I introduced Mandy to Mr. Mulgrew, who'd never known her name.

"Nice to meet you, lassie," he said, winking at me man-to-man.

Mandy and I had agreed to be the cleanup committee, collecting empty glasses and half-eaten cookies. We took our time folding up chairs, stacking them in the storage closet, but I still had over an hour's wait before my father picked me up.

"I'll drive you home," Mandy offered.

"You live in the opposite direction," I said.

"Yeah," she giggled, "the other side of the tracks."

I left word with my father's secretary, then followed Mandy to her car, an orange VW filled with mismatched shoes and last month's magazines. She was used to driving alone: the passenger's seat was cluttered with soda cans and candy wrappers, which she tossed onto the floor, clearing a place for me. It was an adventure for both of us, me riding too fast in her funky car and her driving through increasingly exclusive neighborhoods, but as the homes got bigger, the gardens well kept, Mandy grew quiet, as if the gap between us was as wide as the space between the houses we were passing. By the time she pulled into my circular driveway, we were silent. She kept the motor running as she stared at my parents' huge white house set back amidst hundreds of trees.

"You live here?"

"Until I move to New York," I said. "I'd ask you in, but . . ."

"I understand," she said.

As she drove away, I wondered if she understood that it was I who was embarrassed, by the stack of unwashed breakfast dishes, the empty bourbon bottles on my father's bar, my mother sitting drunk in the darkened living room.

The sun set outside my bedroom window, replaced by a bright moon that shone on the trees below, and in my mind I turned those tall trees into tall buildings, all glass and steel, lit up at night like the New York skyline. I remembered Mandy telling me that her one-room apartment faced a brick wall, and I wanted to knock that wall down for her, to take her someplace expensive, le Lion D'or or Tiberios, and treat her to a little luxury.

The bank's air conditioner blasted air so cold it gave Mandy goosebumps, but I was sweating while I counted my drawer the next morning, waiting for the right moment to ask Mandy out.

"Maybe we could have dinner together on Saturday," I said softly as Nelva unlocked the front door and let the first customer in. "Someplace downtown . . . a French restaurant."

She smiled. "Sorry, Freddy. Can't afford it."

"Leave that to me. I've hardly spent any money this summer."

"How much have you saved?" she asked.

"Over eight hundred dollars," I whispered.

"But you need that money," said Mandy.

"I'd rather spend it on you than on the University of Maryland."

"Spend it on yourself, go to New York. That's what I would do. Not New York, but somewhere."

A woman came to my window to pay her phone bill, and Mandy got busy with a cashier's check. It was payday, a strange day at the bank because we cashed people's paychecks all day long, yet we didn't get one. The money was deposited directly into our accounts, more like an allowance than a salary. Payday also meant staggered lunch hours and a long line of customers. Mandy and I didn't have a chance to talk until the doors had been locked and I was balancing my drawer.

"You still haven't answered me," I said, tallying my coins. Happy had already changed into her 7-Eleven uniform, hurriedly counting her money so she wouldn't be late for her second job.

"About?" asked Mandy, bundling her cash, her drawer seventeen cents over.

"Saturday night. Dinner." I took the one-dollar bills out of my drawer and counted them quickly and rhythmically, the way Dixie had trained me.

Mandy stood so close to me I could feel her breath. It made me shiver. I kept my eyes on my money, but could see her cherry-lacquered nails drumming on the table next to me.

She stopped tapping. "It would be wonderful to have dinner with you at an elegant restaurant," she said.

I lost track of the fives and had to start again. Dixie was getting impatient, waiting for my balance sheet, but I was imagining the soft glow of candlelight illuminating Mandy's face. As I totaled the fives and moved onto the tens, Mandy watched me, the same way I'd been watching her for the past month.

"I'm going to miss you when you leave," she said.

I stopped adding my twenties and looked at her.

"That's weeks away," I said. "Besides, it's not like I'm leaving town. I'm not going to New York yet, remember?"

She didn't say anything. I continued counting my twenties, but something was wrong with my drawer. I was short. A thousand dollars short. A cold sweat started along my hairline, and the chilled air made the sweat feel like icicles.

Mandy counted the money. A thousand dollars short. Dixie counted it. Still a thousand dollars short. Nelva got the same total.

"I'm sure I locked my drawer when I went to lunch," I told Nelva, sitting in her office. "It's never unlocked."

"Even when you turn around to check a signature card or type a money order?" she asked. She seemed calm, but I knew she was upset, because she'd refused one of Big Kenny's calls.

"That only takes a few seconds."

"Someone on the line could easily have grabbed a pack of twenties while your back was turned. Especially during payday pandemonium."

Dixie knocked on the door and stuck her head in.

"He's here," she told Nelva.

Nelva stood up. "A policeman will be in to see you in a minute . . ."

"Policeman?"

"I'm sorry, Freddy. It's procedure. You wait here in my office, okay?" she said softly, winking as she left. I wondered if she was ever this nice to Big Kenny.

She left the door open so I could see him, a tall man with sunglasses wearing a brownish gray uniform. After talking to Nelva for a few minutes, he stood by one of the counters, and each employee was asked to empty their pockets and purses as they exited. Happy had left for the Slurpee machine before the money was discovered missing, but the others lined up, Charles first, with two packs of cigarettes and a Bic lighter. He waved good-bye to me after passing inspection, the first time he'd ever looked me in the eye.

Mandy was next. Her purse was bright red and very small, barely big enough for the nail file, hairbrush, and wallet she kept inside, a little girl's purse in the policeman's large hands, but Mandy paid no attention to him as he rifled through her bag. She looked at me, snapping her fingers. She stopped by the door to Nelva's office on her way out and blew me a kiss.

Tortoiseshell containers of eyeshadow and rouge poured out of Dixie's purse, along with several kinds of lipstick, lip liner, lip gloss, and various brands of hairspray, aerosol and non. It looked like a cosmetics counter and it made me smile, though she looked about to cry when she said, "You keep that 'Teller of the Month' badge on, you hear?"

The policeman came into the office and shut the door.

"Where's the money, son?" he said in an accent not unlike Nelva's, dropped an octave.

"I don't know. I didn't take it." My voice sounded too loud, like I was lying. I felt as if I'd stolen the money.

He asked me to tell him everything I'd done since arriving at work that morning, jotting notes on a little pad he pulled from his shirt pocket. He smiled when I told him about asking Mandy out, as though ready to dispense fatherly advice. After I finished, he took off his sunglasses and rubbed his eyes, which were too small and too dark for his fat, sunburned face, tiny black buttons glued onto a pumpkin.

"Young man, you have a choice. Either you give me the money, or I book charges."

"No, I don't have a choice," I said, "because I don't have the money. If you book charges, I still won't have the money."

He stood up.

"Do you know a good lawyer, Fred?" he asked.

I thought of my father passed out on the couch, his pants undone, his mouth open.

"No," I answered, "I do not."

Mandy called me late that night.

"Did I wake the entire house?" she whispered into the phone.

"A large explosion wouldn't wake my parents," I said. "They're too drunk. And I'm too hot to sleep."

"Crank up the air conditioner," she suggested.

"My father won't let me use it," I said. "He prides himself on keeping the windows open and the air conditioner off no matter how hot the heat wave."

"What did he say about the missing money?" Mandy asked.

"I didn't tell him. He's a lawyer, not a detective."

I told Mandy that Nelva suspected someone on the line.

"Dixie wouldn't jeopardize fourteen years at the bank for a thousand dollars," I said, "and I know you need money, but if you were going to steal, it wouldn't be from me."

"Charles?" said Mandy.

"He doesn't have the guts."

"That leaves Happy."

"She'd left the bank by the time I counted my drawer," I said. "Did she take the pack of twenties with her?"

After we said good night, all I could think of was the theft. I pictured Happy Ho in her brown-and-orange 7-Eleven uniform, standing by a Slurpee machine till midnight, then getting up early the next morning to go work at the bank, her eyes weary, her feet throbbing, her hands reaching into my drawer, and I was still awake when the sun began to rise, casting its harsh morning light across my pillow. I showered and dressed for work an hour early, but the heat made it harder for my father to wake up. It would look bad to be late this morning, so I took his car keys off his dresser and drove myself to work, expecting every police car I passed to pull me over for robbing a bank, or stealing a car, or both.

Dixie was the only one who beat me to the bank.

"Listen, Freddy, you can't handle any money today. Company policy," she told me. "I'll find something for you to do, like organizing signature cards."

I had expected this, taking a box of poorly alphabetized cards and sitting at the desk nearest the front door. Outside, Nelva stepped out of the passenger's side of a pickup truck, giving me a glimpse of why she called him "Big" Kenny as the truck squealed out of the parking lot. I started sorting through the A's, setting aside accounts that had been closed.

Charles's soft voice took me by surprise.

"I thought you could use this," he said, handing me a button that read, "Don't let the turkeys get you down!" He pinned it onto my shirt, below my name tag and the "Teller of the Month" badge, and I waited for Mandy to walk through the door and laugh at my being decorated like a war hero.

But Happy Ho was next.

"Sorry I'm late," she said, rushing into the bank. "The Slurpee machine break down last night and I didn't get home until two a.m." She wondered why I was sitting at the front desk, and when I told her about the missing money, she seemed to know nothing about it.

"Where's Mandy?" she asked. Nelva tried calling Mandy's number, but her phone had been shut off.

"Probably didn't pay her bill," said Dixie, and I wondered where Mandy had called me from the night before.

The bank opened at nine o'clock, two tellers short. I looked at the closed teller windows, side by side, and tried to imagine Mandy stealing from my drawer. At first I couldn't picture it, but as the hours passed and Mandy didn't appear, my disbelief turned into anger. I could see her committing the crime, though my vision of it remained blurry and unfocused, like the film of a bank robbery captured on hidden camera. I wished the movie had a different ending: me turning around and catching her in the act, slamming my drawer shut, and bruising her tapered fingers, breaking a glossy nail.

Everyone on the line wanted Mandy caught, but when the policeman showed up in the late afternoon, he told us Mandy had fled, taking her clothes and leaving behind what little furniture she owned.

"You're out of the hot seat, Fred," he said, smiling at me, his teeth as yellow as Charles's fingernails.

I was also out of a job.

"We have to cash in *your* bond to replace the money, because the only proof against Mandy is circumstantial," Nelva explained, "and if we cash in your bond, we have to fire you. The insurance company insists."

She didn't seem rural when she shook my hand, acting on behalf of the bank. Dixie hugged me, blue mascara running down her cheeks, and Charles gave me a surprisingly firm handshake, his nails digging into my palm. Happy smiled, saying, "You come to 7-Eleven anytime. I give you free Slurpee."

"Forget the Slurpee," I said. "I'll just stop by and visit with you."

Nelva offered to keep my account open, but I closed it, not sure when I'd be ready to step inside the bank without feeling the humiliation of having trusted the wrong person.

"Large bills or small?" asked Dixie, always the pro, counting out $873.46, my total savings for the summer.

I drove along the loop of highway that surrounded the city, again and again passing the exit to my parents' house, the exit to Mandy's, the exit to the University of Maryland, and the big green sign promising, "New York, 250 miles." I wondered if Mandy had turned off there, fleeing as far as she could on one thousand dollars, farther than New York. She'd probably made her escape the night before, as soon as she'd left the bank, stopping at her apartment to throw some clothes into the car. She could have been hundreds of miles away when she called me to find out if her plan was working, if her friendship with me would keep her above suspicion until she didn't show up at the bank.

It was dark when I got home, returning my father's car. I was ready for his drunken wrath, but it wasn't the car he was angry about. My mother gave me a tearful look and left the room as my father started to pace, lips clamped around his cigar.

"Patrick Mulgrew called this evening," he said. "He wanted to say how sorry he was about what happened. Imagine his surprise when he discovered I didn't know. You weren't man enough to tell me yourself?"

"I didn't take the money."

"Mulgrew explained that," my father said evenly. "He told me about that girl, the one who got herself pregnant. The bank takes her back and this is how she repays them . . ."

"Them?" I said. "It was me she stole from, my drawer she robbed."

"Why didn't you tell me?" asked my father, a lawyer posing the key question.

"What could you have done?" I asked.

"I'm an attorney," he shouted.

"So what could you have done?"

"I'm your father," he said quietly, and I realized he was sober.

I climbed the stairs to my room.

"You're on your own," he yelled after me. "I'm not getting you another job, and you won't get one yourself with this on your record. They've cashed in your bond, mister."

At the top of the stairs I turned and tossed his keys down to him. He caught them, shouting, "You pull that car stunt again and I'll have you arrested. Driving without a license, automobile theft . . ."

My father was still screaming after I closed my bedroom door.

"You can forget college for this year. You're obviously not mature enough. Just forget University of Maryland."

I already had forgotten it. I took off my name tag, the button

Charles gave me, my "Teller of the Month" badge. The sky outside my window was filled with stars, the same stars that shine over New York City, and I realized I'd never know why Mandy stole the money from my drawer. Perhaps she wanted me to close my account, take the money, and run. I pulled the $873.46 out of my pocket and counted it like a bank teller. I didn't know where Mandy had gone, but I knew where I was going.

THE EARLY WORM

I know for sure when the actual thief enters. I'm still asleep, but there's no mistaking the rattling lock, the dash of cold air on my lips and forehead. A scraping and a clicking — what's that?

When I hear footsteps in the hall a thin wave weakens me. But I'm already collapsed, far back in the apartment, with my ankles crossed and my head wedged against the wooden headboard. After looking at something painful I close my eyes; now that small nightfall extends into a second kind of night. I don't want to be lying down; I ease into a sitting position, open my mouth wide so my thick breath can pass in silence. The back of my throat cools with each breath. The knot of tension in my back turns out to be my glasses; I was sleeping on them.

I can't hide myself without making noise. Besides, I'm wearing only a T-shirt. I hear the scraping again, but now the air seems jammed — the boom and groan of cars, thudding heart, purr of shuffling cards, my breath, a siren, the low drone and high, frosty whine of room air. I hold my hands up as though conducting this orchestra.

So now I must relate to someone — how can I do that? I find

my glasses to defend myself with sight, but there is nothing to see. My glasses seem pathetic, their owner already dead. The lump of fear in my throat teaches me how to speak. I call out, "Who's there?" My voice is so shocking that I realize the intruder could have a simple explanation, so I repeat the question.

Something like my will supports this experience in order to keep it from contracting into nothing. That is, contact with others becomes remote and threadbare, always has. Always I begin to live in daydreams; the gist of these dreams is that contact is a prize given to some, withheld from others. It's a psychological problem, or a religious one — you could say evil holds my family in its clutches, if you call evil the lack of relation to the world's taking place.

After a silence that seems surprised, a deep, silvery voice replies, "Your father told me to stop by." It's a bizarre statement. I inform myself, the man in the hall says my father sent him.

My father is, what, easy to guess, sleeping in his recliner in front of *M*A*S*H* reruns and appalling newsbreaks and special reports — Archduke Ferdinand is assassinated, Khmer Rouge seizes power, Dresden is firebombed, China invades Tibet. His swollen legs are raised. He's rather deaf, so shocking blasts of laugh track are fired at the motionless old man in a white terry cloth robe tinted blue by the tube. The century is done with him. The scene is almost Egyptian in its rigid symmetry and lack of substance.

But I'm not in my home in San Francisco, I'm staying at Sally's, so probably the intruder does not even mean my father, and Sally's died in a minute three years ago of a brain aneurysm. I want to correct the thief, I want to say, "No, Ed sent you," since the thief claims to come from the dead.

The reflected light — his flashlight. The scraping sounds — a frame lifted from the wall. The clicks — wires being cut. I know

what that is: a large framed photo of an upside-down pawn floating amid the thick trunks of a redwood forest. The thief has offered me a lie to see us through a violent moment. I feel a jolt of
passionate interest; we need a fiction.

"This is mine," he says, as though I can see what he's holding.
My mind drifts through my ears; I try to read his voice. He sounds
"college educated" about his trade, like an unoppressed prostitute
who calls his business sex work. I take his side. After all, they
could be his in some way I have yet to understand. It's my job to
continue his story in order to show respect for life.

"Did my father send a message?"

"Nothing," he says, suddenly cautious, "nothing at all."

My father has nothing to tell me, but my conversation with the
thief seems to keep my father alive. Since my dad is already living,
I wish this lifesaving technique were applied to Ed. Ed would have
sent a message.

"And the key?" Exalted communication, it opens a starlit emptiness I enter to be recognized. He starts to whistle — whistling
while he works. A sharp buzz and the smell of sawdust. I'm confident the question of killing me is behind us. He is depriving
Sally of certain important choices she has made. I'm sorry that I
can't send the thief to my mother to make her feel less lonely and
to relieve her of certain choices. If I organize myself around a false
premise, does that mean other premises are true?

"Oh yes, your dad gave me the key." I hear a heavy object slide
against the wall, the far wall, so that would be the painting on
OSB of a weightless spaceman in his suit — beyond the spaceman
a naked "pinup" rotates in his mind or ours. Sharp, expressive
lines skid across slick, deserted worlds. I'm surprised to feel a wel-
ling up of love, because in the thief's lie I find more contact with
my dad than I can remember having. In space, no one can hear
you make comparisons. It's a social problem, or a linguistic one.

*   *   *

My dad expects Wall Street to collapse and the Armenians to be slaughtered. If he did send the thief, what lie is being upheld? I beam from one plot level down to another, bearing my imperfect desires as though intensity were just a trick of perspective. I'm naked as One at the limit of this story. My feet hurt as though I've been walking on cracked bones. I smell peanut butter, and the aroma leads me to a plastic bag of cookies that Sally left on the nightstand. Taking a bite, I mash toasty brittleness into sweet, salty goo. I'm not afraid, but the room is and the building — what — a sort of negative space of feeling. The air fizzles, lightly carbonated.

"What time is it?" I ask, urgent to know.

"Four-twenty," he replies.

"Well, the early bird catches the worm," I observe.

"And the early worm gets caught by the bird!" His beam in my eyes makes me teary. Why not confect an escape into the normal, because feeling pleasure normalizes even this creeping strangeness — the vaporous skirt a ghost trails above the ground — a failure of belief so deep it becomes its own mysticism, detaching electron from nucleus and dissolving every kind of relation.

Pleasure makes everything normal. If I write the word *pleasure* I must have sex on paper, because this is pornography's cat burglar with his spidery touch and baggy pants. (Young men wear them to hide their boners.) The mattress dips, he's sitting on the edge, he doesn't weigh much. Now he's naked and deathy as a garden god.

"Best if you don't see my face," he advises, switching off the beam. He muses for a minute on his own words, then slides his hand along my thigh. Blood streams beneath the skin. I palpate my thigh, probing the flesh he touched. He believes in the excitement he causes there. He adds, "You're a handsome man."

Since it's pitch-black, this strikes me as a pure compliment. "Handsome, yes," I drawl. "Next time you should bring your camera."

"You're touchy! It's the sweet ones who're grouchy at home."

A pressure in my chest could be lust. I would not have sex with just anyone, but as I think this I'm already shedding the blanket. The distance between untouched skin and touched skin is the unimaginable leap; the rest speeds by without transition. He has a long torso, slender and childish. He has a scar on his ass — a bite taken out of it. If I steal some flesh, will my face always lift and tilt as though in darkness? The thief's paintings and photographs lean against the front door. "And the box with the star chart and wine glass?"

"The Cornell? Totally awesome-blage!"

I'm in a woman's bed, my scent is light, floral. What phylogenic stage does *he* come from with his skinny arms and his sweet and salty flavor? I'm not in my own home, but I offer some hospitality.

That is, I welcome his spidery touch, narrow chest; his breath smells like steaming pavement after hot rain. What to do with his cock, blunt and knobby as a Bavarian nutcracker? He pushes it into me like newsbreaks and special reports: Two hundred thousand perish. His voice is reedy and his limbs are fragile and pliant as a tadpole's — he's dividing into the rigid and the weak. He's a child, weightless, his movements tentative, his head lolling on my chest, while a heavy weight drags me deep into the mattress. A pot of water set on a fire never gets colder, yet I'm freezing up — it's the reverse of a natural process. When I'm certain he's feeling pleasure, I let bits of circumstance slip out: "This is not my apartment." "My dad lives in Escondido." "The art is insured." By then it's too late for these airy facts to convince either of us or to redefine the calamity. Thanks, Dad, I think, communication at long last.

I blaze for a moment and subside. The perilous century turns away in the night and the latch clicks shut. My skin touches strange pillows and blankets, and the feeling of being alive displays itself like a ghost in the darkness.

MONOLOGUE OF TRISTE
THE CONTORTIONIST

No me crees. I see it in your eyes. You don't believe me. How else does a fugitive like me, un negrón tan jandango, get to see the most famous dissident in the Island. I took off from Playa Girón, walked into the waters, desnudito, así salí, y así llegué y te asusté.

Gracias. Gracias. The blanket is good. I was getting cold.

How else? I swam. The longest stretch was over thirty miles. No me crees . . . I see it. You don't believe me. But one day (when we're both free), I'll show you. It *is* thirty miles from Playa Girón to the most northern point of Cayo Largo. Me llamo Pedro Ovarín. But no one has called me that in a long time. I've been known as Triste all my life. Every since I was a kid, ever since I first put my left foot behind my right ear (like this), ever since I could graze parts of me with the tip of my tongue, in my abuelita's bed under the mosquitero, that other children dared not even touch with their hands (*that* I won't show you . . . I'm sorry. Perdóname if I am vulgar). I am a contortionist, a famous one who once loved one that you once loved. My abuelita said that I was a happy child till I started twisting myself into odd shapes. No me acuerdo. I have no memories of happiness.

¿Cómo? I swam. How else?

You are beginning to believe me. Your eyes are beginning to know who it is that I am. I promised him that I once loved that you once loved I would see you. So now you see me.

And it *is* thirty miles, though you don't believe me.

Gracias. Gracias. The soup is good. I was getting cold. I love garbanzo stew. What a great sense of humor Fidel has, ¿no crees? — imprisoning you near a town called La Fe, where the gods shit colored stone, in a hole full of nightingales, surrounded by forests where they mine for nickel and tungsten.

Do you know what tungsten is? It's a metal that most fires can't melt. You can't bend it like this or like this (don't be so amazed, that's only my fingers, you should see what I do with the rest of my body); tungsten is not a contortionist, it won't bend, even in the fires that flow in the hidden underground rivers of the earth. It would make the best prisoner — tungsten is immune to torture.

He too was imprisoned on this island that's the eye of the Island. So he was once you. He that murdered the ones you love was as you are now, inside the eye, trapped in a hole from where you can't see ni puta mierda. Perdóname, my tongue is dirty.

He was a good swimmer too — Fidel. ¿No me crees? But he never tried to escape from this island prison. I swam *in*. You believe me now. Yes, I'm tired.

Gracias. Gracias. The cafecito is good, better than the blanket, better than the stew.

I told you and you believed me. I promised him — not Fidel, but the one that I once loved that you once loved, and *he* believed me. I could see it in his eyes. So I had to swim in; and I'll swim out when the time comes, because I am a better swimmer than

Fidel. He never dared swim out. He was pardoned, as a child is pardoned.

The one that I once loved that you once loved that his men murdered, do you remember his name? Is that why I have no memories of happiness?

Don't tell me!

I swam. Water gets in my ears. It drowns all my memories.

¡Ay! Gracias. Gracias. The rum is good. Me encanta el ron, more than the blanket, more than the stew, more than the cafecito. I'll remember now. And then I can tell you why I came here. How I swam.

Give me a hint. What was his hair like? The one that I once loved that you once loved.

Don't tell me. I swam. I'll remember.

It was like wool, like tufts of black wool before it is woven into yarn. Vez, I remembered. My abuelita is wrong. I do remember happiness, even if sometimes it is twisted out of shape, like the ringlets of his hair (once, he let it grow long — he did not shear it until they made him — and just like his hair was then, wild and dark brown and twisted and twirled into all shapes, such was my happiness). That's what I had chosen. Do you remember happiness? Do you remember brushing your cheeks against his hair till they were scratched with joy?

You are beginning to believe me. What was his name? Do you know?

Don't tell me!

I swam. The water gets in my eyes. But if I can just have a bit more, maybe things will clear up.

Gracias. Gracias. Yes, that's good. It is no longer cold. I love rum. It heats me up inside, better than the blankets, better than the stew, better than the cafecito, mucho mejor. I swam. The longest stretch was over thirty miles. I walked into the waters of

Playa Girón, con los huevos colgando, y llegaron así, todos es-
cogeditos. Coño perdóname, Señora Alicia, I do not mean to be
vulgar.

You are beginning to see him, the one that I once loved that
you once loved. His eyes? What color were they? Give me a hint.

Don't . . . don't tell me! I remember. My abuelita was wrong
when she nicknamed me Triste.

His eyes were sometimes the color of a long-aged cognac or
sometimes the color of boiling honey. And I did not like it when
I loved him and I did not see them, for when I loved him, the one
that I once loved that you once loved's eyes closed, and just from
under the lids, light-droplets the color that was the color of his
eyes seeped out and clung desperately to his curled thick eyelashes
like water on a dolphin's back and then were blown out into the
air and dispersed and disintegrated as stars that have lost their
course. This was the wilderness in him, that clung to his eyelashes
in ochre dewdrops, that was my happiness, that my abuelita will
never know. She called me Triste. And now they all do, and it is
who I am.

You are beginning to remember happiness. I believe you. What
did your abuelita call *you?* Do you remember his name?

Don't tell me!

I swam. Why else wouldn't I remember? I swallowed too much
seawater. It changes me on the inside. It blanches my memories.
His mouth? His lips?

Era mulatico, pues claro entonces his lips were full, as if three
or four extra layers of flesh had been stretched there and softened
and colored over time by his breath, like the flow of the warm
undersea shapes a coral reef. I remember. Sometimes too they
were salty and when I tasted them I thought of the seawater. But
we were far from the sea. We could not swim. Yet his lips were
salty.

Gracias, pero no. Gracias, no. No more rum. Not yet. Not now. Not while I'm remembering what his breath tasted like.

Don't tell me! I'll remember. I was not Triste, though everyone called me that.

Like a late spring breeze peppered with pollen, yes, flowing with invisible nectars, not too warm, though warm enough; breath I could taste and swirl in my mouth and feel its heat in my chest when I let it in me, and much, much more intoxicating than this rum. I'd be drunk for weeks and I'm still hungover to this day, even though I swam, and the sea with all its galvanic stings should have cured me.

You believe me. You know. That's good. Now I'll take some more.

Gracias. Gracias. The rum is good. But it is a poor man's moonshine compared to his breath.

And when I loved him, the one that I once loved that you once loved's breath stuck to me and I did not bathe till I knew I could touch him again, and my skin, all of it, smelled of him, because his breath had sunk into my pores and spread throughout so that I was him, and when the guards would separate us, for weeks sometimes, sometimes longer, and I loved myself, it was him I loved and I called his name from my tiny cell where my head would bump if I stood up and where I defecated and urinated in one corner and crouched in the opposite corner, my head turned, to avoid the stench and *then* my abuelita was right.

What was it that I screamed when I loved myself as I was loving him? Give me a hint. Do you even know?

What did your abuelita name you?

Don't tell me! I'll remember. I swam. The longest stretch was over thirty miles. I walked into the waters at Playa Girón, and the three girls that were the girlfriends of the soldiers were alone on the beach — the soldiers were in the cabana for the third time that day; I had been with them and done things with them that they did not dare do with their girlfriends — and as I walked into the waters afterward, their girlfriends stared, porque estaba desnudito, así como llegué y te asusté. They stood and shielded their eyes from the sun with their hands as if saluting me (like their soldiers had taught them, seguro), and they followed me, they waded in as if they smelled their soldiers' sweat and their soldiers' spit on me. But the seawater is harsh and it washes quick, ridding the skin of its memories, so the girls waded back to wait for their soldiers who were still with each other. I swam long (thirty miles was the longest stretch, from Playa Girón to the most northern point of Cayo Largo), and my encounter with the soldiers left me empty, so on the white-sand beaches of Cayo Largo I loved myself and he was not there, the one that I once loved that you once loved. His breath was not in me. And what's the use of loving yourself if you're only loving yourself, if there's no one's breath seeping through your pores, if there is not a trace of what it was like to once have your arms around him so that his smell was yours, not yours to keep, but yours as your own body is yours and will not be yours at the day of reckoning?

His body. I remember. My abuelita was wrong. Por favor, por favor, don't tell me. I remember.

Holding him was like handling a caged bird. In every muscle, even the tiny ones that wiggled his monkey toes, there twitched the hollow-boned urge to fly, so that it felt as if I would let go, he would take off from me, like the magic balloons abuelita bought me at the circus the first time we went, and soar into the boundless blue sky and become a speck and then vanish, as if he had found a portal to another world. How could I let him go then, even after I had loved him three or four times a day, hidden by the tall gray-green stalks in some unshaven lot of the cane field, even though the dagger leaves were stabbing at us, even though we knew that the guards knew we were missing, and even though he could not really fly away, for he would have done it a long time ago and abandoned all his tormentors, those heartless bestias that also professed to love him, but in the end murdered him.

Don't stir. It is not something you don't already know and have not known for a long time. You would not be here in this island that is the eye of the Island, trapped in a hole from where you cannot see ni puta mierda.

I'll have some more rum. You should have some yourself.

Gracias. Gracias. This at least numbs the brain, dulls what I remember. It is almost as strong as the seawater.

Though when I wake, I always remember. My abuelita was wrong.

We were lovers almost from the start, and though he was very young, sixteen then, he was not innocent. He had been a lover before. This I knew from the first night, when after a performance, he came to my sleeping cart with a bottle of bourbon. I could not stand the bitter taste of it. *He* drank it without grimacing. He said his master had taught him.

What was his name? The master? The one that taught the one that I once loved that you once loved how to drink bourbon and how to fly?

Don't tell me.

He talked at length about him. There was not much room inside my cart, so he sat on my bed and swigged the bourbon straight from the bottle, and he pushed closer to me, letting his hand wander up my thigh, saying how great I looked all twisted and bent on the St. Peter cross *(Chévere, your arms and your legs looked like black serpents choking a young tree! And your long white nails were the twenty fangs with which the devil ate the baby Jesus).* He'd had too much. I took the bottle from him and he fell back and passed out in my arms. I leaned my face close to his and his breath smelled like freshly cut pinewood. I kissed him on the cheeks, tucked him in my bed, and left my sleeping cart. I finished what was left in the bottle, growing more and more accustomed to the tongue-pricking taste of the liquid that was the color of his eyes in the gas-lamp light. I remember. My abuelita was wrong. Although I was not sure if the great pity I felt was for him or for me. In the morning, when I returned to my cart, he was gone. Four nights later, he came back and he did not pass out and I did not leave.

What did your abuelita nickname you?

What was his name?

Don't tell me! I'm swimming in rum and I'll remember.

Much later, after the liberators came down from the mountains, bearded and thin, but not thin like the one that I once loved that you once loved was thin, not lithe like him, but thin like starved, so you could count their ribs, even the little tiny one that's no longer than the thumb at either side of the belly, after they had decided who would share in their liberty, and after they had excluded us and hunted us down and forced us to learn the process of love again, taught us like children what was right and what was wrong, o mejor dicho, forced us to unlearn what was wrong, to forget everything back to the first time when that uncle who is only three years older takes me to a barren field on the edge of his father's finca, and forces me to pull down my work pants — they are stained and sticky with the sweet syrup of the cane stalks, so a lo mejor he just wants to wash them in the river — and I am tired and do as my uncle says, and even though my skin is black-black-brown, darker than the darkest cup of cafecito, de negro puro, as my abuelita says, I can see a patch on my lower legs, from where my work pants were rolled up to where my boots cover the ankle, where my skin is impossibly darker from the mud-spatter of the felled stalks; my uncle likes this, and when my

ankles are resting on his shoulders in that barren field at the edge
of his father's finca, he passes his tongue over that darker part of
my legs, and I concentrate on his rosy tongue as it too blackens
from the mud of the cane fields. I'll never let my uncle know how
much it hurts because he sees it in my eyes watching his tongue,
sees that beneath the riptide of pain passing over my body, there
runs a more powerful undertow of pleasure, a lightning current
of joy, which I won't forget, long after my uncle who is only three
years older than me has disappeared and a brigade of other men
has taken his place. I remember; no matter what the liberators
who came down from the mountain and decided who will share
in their liberty did, no matter what my abuelita named me.

*   *   *

Gracias. Gracias. The rum is good. It frees my tongue. Sí, sí
¿cómo no? — have some yourself.

When they had rounded us up and put us in their work camps,
they pretended to make us soldiers. They called the camps Military Units to Aid Production. We were sent to the same camp,
the one that I once loved that you once loved and I. I thanked
Changó and all the saints for that, but cursed them in the next
breath because they had let me become a slave again. Monday
through Friday we were out in the fields. Fidel had promised the
world the world's weight in sugar. And though every year he falls
far short of the goal, he promises even more for the following
year and sends his henchmen out to gather more slaves. Saturday
was conscript relaxation day, which meant that families that
worked all week at the factories or at the mills were forced to
volunteer time in the fields while we got to play fútbol games with
the warden's team. Changó forbid we were to win, though we did
once or twice, no matter how tired we were from our labor in the
fields, and paid for it on Sunday.

*   *   *

Sunday was conscript education day.

Aside from a few intellectuals and artists, mostly poets, who Fidel had begun to gather up early on, almost as soon as he took power (though Fidel's real attacks on the intelligentsia hadn't begun, that would come later, when *they* who were supposed to be the forefront thinkers of our land finally dared to question the sacredness of la Revolución), most of us were maricas, as we were always reminded, for every sentence the guards uttered to us either began or ended with gran cacho de maricón, even to the poets, many who weren't really maricas, but who had always sympathized with us. Now, as a reward, they were lumped in with us, addressed with same insults.

I remember. Sunday was conscript education day.

There was the room with the magazines and the green projector and the machine with the four levers, each one with a different colored plastic cap, one red, one yellow, one black, one green, a four-note pianito with an infinite number of chords. I was the only one, it seemed, who could concentrate hard enough, keep my mind enough away from the pain, to discover which lever corresponded to which wire. I told the one that I once loved that you once loved in the fields the following Monday. He said he did not care, that he did not want to know, as did most of our other camp mates. Why did I imagine that they *would* want to know? That if the bearded pianito player on the other side of the long wobbly table spread with open magazines and black-and-white glossies pushed the green lever all the way down, then the electric current would not flow through the wire attached to the folds of your anus (that was the black lever), nor through the one attached to your right testicle (that was the red one), nor through the one attached to your left testicle (that was the yellow one), the current would flow through the one attached to the underside of your penis, to the fleshy triangle where the head meets the shaft, that Sunday after Sunday had become scabbed and scarred and the numbness that lasted for weeks and spread to the other points of their unholy sign of the cross emanated from its apex. The green lever was the pianito player's favorite. The others did not want to know. But I remembered.

Sunday was conscript education day.

After breakfast we would wait and see who was selected. A doctor checked us, made sure the burns from any previous sessions were properly healed. On Saturday nights, some picked at the scabs and scrubbed them raw to make them seem worse, but no one ever went more than three weeks without visiting the pianito player. After they had selected us, we sat on the floor in a room next to the pianito room. We heard the shouts of who was weak and who had not learned the last lesson; and if the screams were constant, if even the older men fell into their traps, or some of the poets who weren't maricas (for they too were made to go through this), then we knew they had some good material, that they had found a new film or taken a new set of glossies in the barrack showers.

Sunday is conscript education day.

When they call me in, I strip down in front of the others, but I know that they will not look. If they do, then it is noted, and it is a sin paid for not much later. I walk into the room with the four-note pianito. There are three men in there, all in uniform, their crotches bulging and trembling as if some tiny field mouse has been stuffed in there and is struggling to get out. Every time I visit, it is three different men. From the look on their faces, this assignment is obviously a reward. There is a long wooden table on which lie closed magazines wrapped in brown paper. The four-note pianito, a simple metal box that someone buffs and shines every Saturday night, is set at the far left end of the table. In its corners I can see my broken reflection. Long wires, all the same color, a ghastly gray, sprout from under it like roots. At the end, three of the wires are shaved and welded to a thin metal plate, square and thinner than a coin; one wire is thicker and is shaved longer than all the others, and the silver filaments at the end are opened and spread out like a spider with many legs. I know why. There are three finger-long pieces of medical tape dangling on my side of the long table. There is another longer piece of tape, which dangles just short of the floor. There is an empty chair on each side of the table. The one on my side is fitted with three leather straps on each arm and on each leg and another thicker strap around the seat. It is bolted to the concrete floor. Behind my chair is another smaller table, on which is mounted a green crank-by-hand movie projector. A film is reeled in and set to go.

"No me mires la cara, negrón, maricón," one of the men says. I obey him. I lower my eyes. But I remember his face. Its skin is the color of wet sand. I remember his eyes. They are yellow, sprinkled with coffee dust. "Have you forgotten your place, negrón, maricón?"

I have not. I remember. I know exactly what to do. I have been in here too many Sundays. I give my back to the three men and bend down and rest my torso on the long wooden table. I feel four hands on my back, pressing down. I feel the field mouse bulge of one of the men brush against my right thigh. I try not to imagine who it belongs to. I hear him wet his finger in his mouth. He reaches into me and prods around with his wet finger till he finds what he is looking for, then he pushes his finger into me and leaves it in a moment and plucks it out. He grabs the thicker wire, the one I know is connected to the black lever on the four-note pianito. He wraps the shaved end of the thick wire around his finger and pushes into me again. When he pulls out, I feel some of the silver filaments stay in, and some spread out over the soft flesh around my anus. He rips a piece of the medical tape off the end of the long table and fixes the wire in place.

"Your asshole stinks, negrón, maricón." He spanks me softly, like a reluctant parent disciplining a child.

Sunday is conscript education day.

My eyes are still closed. The four hands on my back ease their pressure and they lift me and throw me back into the seat with the straps. Before I am strapped in, my bare feet are hoisted up and a shallow steel pan half full of water is slid under them. My feet are lowered into it. The water is cold. The straps are buckled. The field mouse bulge of the man who stuck his finger in me is brushing against my right shoulder. Then it is not. I hear two more pieces of tape ripped off the end of the table and the man's fingers (they are still moist) lift my sac and affix two thin cold plates underneath it on each side, making an "X" with two pieces of the medical tape, plates connected to wires connected to the red lever and to the yellow lever. Then he lifts my penis and lifts the head and pulls the skin back and rubs the head between index finger and thumb and he lets my penis drop. I hear him smell his fingers, sniffing deeply as if having walked into a kitchen where his abuelita is preparing arroz con pollo.

"You are still not washing like we showed you, negrón, maricón."

He pulls the skin back again and affixes the last wire to the underside at the bottom of the head and wraps the longest piece of medical tape all the way around so that the skin remains pulled back. Then, with the loose ends of the tape he affixes my penis up against my lower belly. He goes back to my right side and I feel the field mouse grazing me again. I try not to think about it. If my penis becomes aroused, it will peel off my belly and want to stand on its own. I tell myself that I will not let this happen. But the pianito player is good, much better than the guards with the field mouse bulges. Aside from the magazines and the glossies and the films, he has at his command (depending on how far he presses down each lever and at what angle) the full range of chords of his instrument. He can please just as masterly as he can hurt. He keeps a proper balance. He tickles. He stabs.

I hear the pianito player enter the room. I hear him sit down and slide his chair in. I hear him tap the thumb of his right hand on the table. I know the other four fingers are hovering over the four levers of the pianito, the index finger over the green, the middle finger over the red, the ring finger over the yellow and the pinky over the black. He is waiting for me to open my eyes.

Sunday is conscript education day.

The pianito player is a simple-faced man with warm hazel eyes and a heavy peasant beard. He wears a sergeant's stripes, but his military jacket is three sizes too large on him and he is obviously not a military man. He wears also around his neck, dangling from a leather necklace, a cross whittled from the shell of a coconut. Because of this, because we have never known his name, because we only see him on certain Sundays and because he looks like a pastor, we call the pianito player Father. He approves of this.

"What is your name?" Father says when my eyes open. His voice is gentle.

He remembers, but I must repeat it. We must have the same conversation every Sunday like a litany.

"Triste."

"Triste. What a beautiful name. Who named you that?"

"My abuelita."

"Triste, do you know the story of the angels of the Lord who came to stay at Lot's house."

"Yes, I do."

"What did the men of Sodom want at Lot's door?"

"The men at Lot's door wanted to fuck the angels of the Lord."

"And what did Lot do?"

"He offered them his two virgin daughters instead."

"And what did the men say?"

"The men said no. They wanted to fuck the angels of the Lord."

"And what did the Lord do to the men of Sodom through the power of his beautiful angels?"

"The Lord struck the men of Sodom blind, struck them all blind, both great and small."

"Triste, since your last visit, in either thought or act, have you been at Lot's door?"

With his left hand, Father has begun leafing through the magazines with the brown covers. I do not lie to Father. It is no use. He plays the pianito too well. I can feel the current before his fingers even touch the levers. I can taste blood on my lips when there is none there.

I tell Father the name of the one that I once loved that you once loved, the name that I now cannot remember; then Father knows that I have confessed my sins and my education may begin again.

ON THE MOUND

In the morning, a heavy mist has settled onto the yard, and Nathan can hardly see the bus as he heads into the cloud zipping his jacket. His own books and Roy's are crooked in his arm. The idling motor guides him to the haze of the yellow bus. Roy straddles the driver's seat gazing out the window at the dismal morning. He says nothing, closes the door and turns on the headlights.

The rutted road tosses Nathan from side to side on the seat. The inside of the bus is like the sky this morning, a silence condensing around every sleepy face. Everyone says good morning to Roy pleasantly, distantly. No hello is returned by Roy with any sign of hidden feeling. Nathan searches but finds no evidence of a girlfriend in these faces. But this thought hardly brings any peace. Nathan already knows Roy has a girlfriend at his church, and Roy goes out with her all the time.

At school Nathan leaves the bus with the first wave this time, letting Roy sit like a boulder. His coldness seems oddly expected. But Nathan remembers lying on their clothes in the cemetery, his hand on Roy's naked belly in the shadow of the obelisk. Roy will treat Nathan as he pleases, and Nathan expects the coldness. In the daylight Nathan will be invisible.

So at lunchtime Nathan sits away from Roy and his friends, at a table by the southern wall of windows, among the black kids. He drinks his milk and chews his macaroni and cheese. His mind, as he eats, is a perfect wash, free of any stray imagining. He avoids the smoking patio, after lunch, in favor of the lawn in front of the school, sheltered by the brick sign announcing FORRESTER COUNTY HIGH SCHOOL to the fields beyond. He sits in the shadow, hidden, and hums a hymn from church about the peace that passes understanding.

A new friend crosses the yard beyond, Hannah from Nathan's civics class. Hannah visits briefly, asking if Nathan is ready for the test on the American Constitution next week. Yes, Nathan answers. Hannah is pimpled and pleasant and talks for a while, idle and mundane chatter, but while she is there, Roy passes. His posture radiates anxiety, hands jammed into pants pockets, shoulders rigid. He sees Nathan and stands watching. He scowls and shoves his hands deeper.

Even now, even from this distance, his body draws Nathan toward it, and Nathan stands to join him; but suddenly Roy storms away, shoulders hunched, frowning.

The afternoon chokes Nathan, sitting in hot, dark classrooms with windows no teacher will open. He sits through advanced math with his Venus pencil poised, paper glaring at him from the desktop. Mr. Ferrette crumbles chalk against the chalkboard. When the final bell rings and everyone hurries toward the buses, Nathan walks toward his own bus with a small fear inside.

Roy straddles his vinyl saddle watching the accelerator pedal on the floor, books loose in one arm. Others enter before Nathan does; he nods to them; Nathan is too far away to read Roy's expression; but when Roy sees Nathan he turns, making a production of settling his books into the basket beside the seat. Momentum carries Nathan to the back of the bus, where he sits, quietly watching the top of Roy's head in the rearview mirror.

The drive home is tedious and tense at the same time, the bus a senseless rattling contraption that sends up a cloud of stinking exhaust, vapid voices, and vacant laughter. Nathan props his knees against the seat in front, glaring at the ridged rubber mat that runs the length of the aisle. No matter where he looks, he can feel Roy's sullen anger at the front of the bus. Roy scans the highway with lips set in a line. Nathan clutches his books against his stomach, remembering the softness of Roy's cheek, the taste of his mouth.

The bus makes its usual stops, the bodies thinning among the seats. Soon there are only a few voices between Nathan and Roy. Again soon, Nathan sits alone in the back of the bus and Roy alone in front; Roy stares forward and Nathan stares downward, each with equal stubbornness. Roy turns the bus down the dirt road through the Kennicutt Woods. Nathan cannot help but watch the strong arms turn the wide steering wheel, while Roy remains oblivious and shifts gears with precise violence. But, past the first few curves of the road, he pulls the bus to the side and stops.

Nathan watches in surprise. Roy sags back against his seat, arms falling limp at his side. His deep breathing is audible. "I got a question for you."

Nathan's voice sounds timid, small in the empty bus. "What is it?"

"What were you doing with that girl in the front of the school?"

Studying the back of Roy's head for a clue. The mirror is empty. "Nothing. I was just sitting there and she came up."

"Oh sure," Roy says.

"She's in my civics class. She was asking me about this test we got."

"What's her name?"

"Hannah something."

"Do you like her?"

"She's all right."

Roy's voice trembles a little. "Do you like her the way you like me?"

The question echoes into silence.

"No."

Roy sits still. Nathan's heart pounds and calm is hard to find. Roy stands. He stares at the rubber mat as he walks down the aisle. He is shaking as he kneels beside Nathan's seat. "I don't know if I believe you or not."

"I'm telling the truth."

"Touch me," Roy says, and Nathan embraces him. He leans against Nathan, who caresses the thick hair at the nape of his neck. He opens his shirt slowly and Nathan feels the strong upsurge of breath and desire, same as the night before; only in the daylight the rich color of his flesh glows, blinding, and when Nathan touches the curves and planes, the sudden rush of heat engulfs them both.

For Nathan it is a moment of poise, in which he must balance between what he knows and what he should not know. The fact of Roy makes a difference. Here it is easy to be held. Nathan's body has never felt so safe. They are touching each other in intimate places with a feeling of perfection. Their breaths, as they fumble and mingle, come faster; they cling and press until they finish. Nathan holds his eyes closed, aware of Roy against him and glad of the clean curved lines of Roy's body. Glad to lay his hands on Roy's firm shoulders and flat waist. The trembling of a vein in Roy's neck draws Nathan's fingers. The clean lines of Roy are a relief and Nathan focuses on that. Without reason, in Nathan's inner seeing, the vision of Preacher John Roberts arises, telling again how at the Last Supper John lay his head tenderly on Jesus' breast. Nathan ends that way, with Roy's fingers in his hair. Roy asks, "Did you ever do this before with anybody?"

Nathan shakes his head, unable to speak. He has never liked it before. That much is true.

"Do you promise?" Roy asks, and the fear is plain on his face when Nathan looks at him.

"I promise. I never did it with anybody." Hoarse, almost inaudible. Feeling hollow inside.

"Because it's okay as long as it's just you and me." Roy's face is suddenly very sad. Nathan reaches for the face, pulls Roy close. Roy settles, sighing, against Nathan's smaller shoulder. "I never did this much before. Not even with a girl."

Nathan holds him as if he has diminished. Nathan becomes the shelter, the protection. He touches Roy's chest with the tip of his tongue and Roy shudders; inside, his heart is regularly bursting. Stillness settles over the bus. Roy sighs and loops an arm around Nathan, keeping close to him through the aftermath, as the sinking sun caresses them through the windows.

When they can move again, Roy leads Nathan to the front of the bus, drives home down the twisting road with the shadows of the trees passing across his shoulders. He parks the bus in the usual spot in the yard and turns in the seat. "Don't go in yet."

"All right. I won't."

Roy studies his own hands, gripping the steel frame of his seat, smooth nail against smooth rivet. "I can't come to see you tonight. We have prayer meeting."

"At church?"

He nods. "Every Wednesday." He will not look up.

"Do you like to go?"

"Yes."

"I have a lot of homework to do anyway. I have a test. I told you."

But Roy has heard only his own thoughts. Lips parted, as if words are close, Roy glances toward his house. He leans to Nathan, kisses him quickly. Pulling on his shirt, he says he will see Nathan later and hurries away without a backward glance.

The night is long and Roy moves restlessly in Nathan's thoughts. Nathan studies mathematics slowly, solving his tedious, nonalgebraic problems with an indolent air. Later he walks to the pond, though not as far as the abandoned cemetery. He can see the distant outline of the tombstones against the black backdrop of trees.

He has gone to bed when Roy finally arrives at home again, driving his parents' car into the yard, letting it idle a moment. Nathan leaps out of the blankets. He stands back from the window to make sure Roy cannot see him. Roy steps out of the car, illuminated by the yard light atop its creosote pole. His figure is handsome in white shirt and tie, his face in shadow. Judging from his stance, he might be watching Nathan's window. But still Nathan hangs back, listening to the muted creakings of the house around him, the syncopated drip of water in the downstairs bathroom. Wind rattles the upstairs windows in their frames. Roy presently heads into the deeper gloom beneath trees, walking with his mother, who moves slowly due to her size. Nathan hovers in the dark over them both.

Soon a dim light burns in the bedroom above the hedge. As before, Roy's shadow slides across the visible wall. Tonight he avoids the window, and Nathan watches his shadow undress.

When that room goes dark, Nathan stands dumbly before his own window, reluctant to turn. When he returns to bed, a small fear seizes him. He replays in his head every moment of Roy's arrival, his stepping out of the car, his standing in the shadow, his undressing out of sight of the window. Nathan lies in bed and examines each of these images over and over. Something in the sequence of events frightens him.

Yet the following day proves to be all Nathan could have wished. In the morning he sits in the seat behind Roy again, and on the way to school Roy talks to him in an almost intimate way. At lunch Roy sits with Nathan and afterward takes Nathan to the smoking patio. No friend takes precedence over Nathan, and no girl excites his attention.

Only once, when Nathan asks about prayer meeting, does the little fear return. Roy says the meeting was fine but refuses to look at him. All further questions about Roy's church stick in Nathan's throat.

That afternoon, when Roy parks the bus under the pecan trees, he tells Nathan to hurry inside and change clothes, he wants them to go for a hike in the woods while there's still light. To an Indian mound, he says, beyond the pond and the cemetery. He grins and lets the bus motor die. The door hardly swings open before Nathan dashes for his house.

In the kitchen his mother stands at the sink washing a cake pan and icing bowl. The room shimmers with afternoon light, filtered through red-checked curtains, adding color to her face and hands. "I'm making a coconut cake. Do you want a little piece of layer?"

"No, ma'am. I'm not hungry."

"It's still warm out of the oven, it would be good."

"I'm not hungry for cake right now."

This disappoints her a little, but she goes on smiling warmly. "Well, did you have a good day at school?"

"Yes, ma'am."

"Well, sit down and talk to me about it. What are you in such a hurry for?"

"Roy wants me to change clothes and come out to the woods with him."

She studies her dishes and frowns. Her glistening hands move deliberately. "What does he want you to go in the woods for?"

"To see this Indian mound."

"What do you want with an Indian mound?"

"I never saw one before."

She looks out the window. "There he is, too, waiting on you."

"Can I go? Is it all right?"

She goes on watching Roy, her face filling with worry. "I guess you can. But I don't want you to go too far."

"Yes, ma'am, I won't."

"Remember, he's bigger than you are. You don't have to do everything he does."

"Yes, ma'am, I know."

She dries her hands and kisses Nathan's forehead without looking at him. "Put on your everyday clothes. I'll tell him you're coming."

Nathan rushes upstairs, furiously erasing his mother's sadness from his mind. When, school clothes exchanged for everyday, he returns to the porch, she is fussing with her plants, pinching a dead leaf off the ivy, wiping the leaves of a snake plant with a cloth. She says to be careful in the woods, don't stay gone too long. Nathan answers, yes ma'am, yes ma'am, and bursts into the yard. Roy awaits beyond the hedge. The two boys run side by side through the apple orchard.

The rhythm of running carries them a long way, beyond the meadow. They crash through underbrush but make no other sound. Leaves strike the skin of Nathan's arms, stinging and caressing. Roy leads him west of the pond and cemetery; he lopes deeper into the woods, glancing back to make sure Nathan is keeping up. Roy laughs at the glory of motion, a bright, incomprehensible sound that echoes through the woodland. He leaps across a narrow stream where drooping ferns make elegant green arches, and Nathan follows, light, running as if he will never tire.

The forest is something other than a neighbor now; it becomes a new world. As the density of growth increases, the pace of their running slows. Soon it is easier to walk than to run, and Nathan draws abreast of Roy. Roy gives a look that instructs, that says he is pleased. The Indian mound is pretty close once they cross the creek, he says. The land is rising. Nathan climbs past bent saplings and red-leafed dogwood; Roy has run up the hill a little faster than Nathan and pauses, breathless.

The forest thins and light spills into the lower tiers of growth. Beyond a glade of trees, on a flat of land, a long mound rises. Only green grass grows on the mound, as if all other kinds of plants have been magically forbidden. Golden sunlight tumbles along the gentle slope.

Roy hangs his shirt from his belt loops. When Nathan does not follow suit of his own volition, Roy reaches for his shirt buttons.

The air, Roy's hands, light spilling down.

Roy offers Nathan the shirt, tenderness in his expression, then runs down the long slope. Nathan threads the sleeves through the belt loops of his pants and follows. Roy vanishes momentarily, but Nathan, heart pounding from the run, finds him. Roy is a strong silhouette against the bright mound, walking toward it. Nathan overtakes him halfway up the mound.

Nathan draws near shyly and Roy refuses to turn. Roy's back muscles shift in a rhythm that seems strong and good. The warm brown skin invites Nathan's hands, but he refuses to reach. They are still climbing. A curious fact, Roy's breath labors more than Nathan's. When on the crest of the mound Roy turns, his ribs are beating open and closed like wings.

Nathan lays his hand against the pounding in the cleft of Roy's chest.

Roy watches his hand, watches Nathan.

Their two fleshes are bright together, the two boys, warm like the colors of the late sky. The sun still has some descending to do, and they watch it and the clouds for a while. Roy settles along the ground, spreading out his shirt, and Nathan does the same. Soon they are layered against each other. Roy says the movement of the treetops is like the ocean. Nathan knows nothing about the ocean; he listens to the murmuring of Roy's insides, the ferocious heartbeat that shakes through them both. Roy is murmuring in Nathan's ear, a hymn from church, "There is a place of quiet rest, near to the heart of God." Nathan sings too, kissing Roy's soft throat, his collarbones, the underside of his chin. He can smell Roy's body, he can taste it with the tip of his tongue. Roy grips the back of Nathan's head as if afraid he will escape. He need not worry. Nathan knows the nakedness Roy wants, and soon achieves it. Roy arches with his body toward Nathan, a curve of yearning. He lies bare in the grass with a look on his face as if Nathan is making him sing through every cell.

They lie still while the sun settles into the green bath of leaves. Roy says nothing but Nathan can feel how his spirit darkens. The banded sky begins to drain of color as they dress. Roy stands with his hands in his pockets. He calls, "Nathan," in a strangled voice and Nathan walks close; he brings Nathan's ear to his mouth and says, "Please don't say anything about this to anybody. Okay? Please."

"I won't." For a moment, just a little, Nathan is afraid.

Roy has frozen with one leg in his pants, the other not.

"Is something wrong?"

"You just can't say anything about it. That's all." A bitter whiteness sheathing his expression. "It's near dark. We better get home."

But even then they linger in the forest. At first Roy holds Nathan's hand but later is ashamed or shy. Yet he refuses to hurry, walking slowly, never straying far. He brags that he knows all the land around his father's farm, he could find his way home in the pitch dark if he had to. Soon Nathan glimpses the cemetery through the trees, and then the pond, and they are walking along the tangled shore within sight of the backs of both houses. They slow their walking even more, and each reaches for ways to manage nearness to the other without seeming responsible for it. In back of the barn, Roy takes Nathan next to him, again furiously, as if the act makes him angry. "You can't do this with anybody but me. Do you hear what I'm telling you?"

Nathan's heart suddenly batters at them both. "I don't want to do it with anybody else."

"Just remember." Red-faced, Roy is already rushing toward his house.

Nathan wanders toward his own kitchen, hearing the sounds that indicate supper heading to the table. Already he is calculating the turns of the cycle, that tonight he will not see Roy, that tomorrow Roy will not say much on the bus. None of that makes him afraid, exactly. Nathan has no words for what does make him afraid. But he feels the chill of it as he descends into the house, where his mother has prepared a meal carefully but will hardly look him in the eye, where his father brings the Bible and a tumbler of whiskey to the dinner table, mumbling verses under his breath as he takes his seat. In the submersion of home, Nathan returns again and again to the image of Roy's body on the Indian mound, lost and bewildered under the power of Nathan's mouth.

THE MEDICINE BURNS

I see my pitted skin reflected in the tinted window of the airport limousine. Outside, the flat, white fields appear endless; my reflection is an overlay of holes. The landscape has other blemishes, dead trees here and there, an old farmhouse half sunk in the snow. Beneath the snow, I can just make out the dead, wiry stalks of corn combed back across the land, parted, it seems, like frozen hair.

We enter town as the lights of Old Capital are turned on. I see its gold dome from a distance. The driver points out the English and Philosophy building from his window. It is an old brownstone and unlike anything I've known in Miami. We drive up to the front of Stonecourt Apartments; I am overwhelmed with disappointment. The building is far from the campus, off the side of the highway. It looks like a dorm; less attractive than the dorms he'd pointed out on the way over here. I want to ask him to keep driving.

There's an information area near the banks of elevators. The attendant greets me eagerly, as though he's hemmed in by the counter.

"You're very lucky," he tells me as he slides the rental

agreement over the counter. "The tenant before you mirrored one of his walls so you have the only different apartment in the building."

As I sign my name to several sheets of paper, he leans over and whispers, "The guy who lived there was kind of kinky, I think."

I look at him, disinterested, and return the papers to him. There is nothing outstanding about his face; it is as common as the faces coming off the elevators. I find it both pathetic and enviable. Some people look like they belong, even in places like this.

"I live here, too," he says, and I notice his braces for the first time. They don't surprise me on children, but on him they're shocking.

"Maybe I'll check up on you later," he warns, "just to make sure you've got everything you need."

The mirrors are cheap tiles affixed to the wall next to the bed. My first instinct is to pull the bed away from the wall. I can't imagine rolling over in the morning and seeing myself right away.

I turn away from the mirrors as I make my way around the foot of the bed, but I detect an image from the corner of my eye, a presence I can never completely obliterate, hunched over, almost hiding, and wearing a blue shirt.

I meet Lawrence on the first day of class. He's smoking in the hallway, dressed beautifully, sure of himself. I ask him if this is where Theory and History of the Avant Garde will be taught. He nods. I look out the window at the slick walkways and I can feel his eyes on me.

"Is this your first semester?" he asks, more curious than the question permits. My face can do that sometimes, encourage curiosity. He has the striking beauty of a face you see in a magazine, looks, I am sure, that enable him to have whatever he wants.

We sit together in class, in the last row so we can talk while the professor shows slides. He asks me where I'm staying and when I mention the Stonecourt Apartments he whispers, "I'm sorry. There's a suicide there every winter." Then, "If I had to live there, I'd jump too, but from the penthouse."

When the lights are off, he seems relieved and leans back in his seat. He leans in toward me and whispers, "Brancusi's *The New Born*." The projected sculpture is perfectly smooth. The professor extracts a long, silver pointer from what looks like a pen. He cannot resist its surface and absently traces it while he lectures.

"He's passionate about his subject," Lawrence says, sounding ironic, jealous even of that work of art.

"You must have had him before?" I ask.

"Oh, yes," he says, "too often."

I look closely at the professor. He is thin but distinguished with a shock of gray hair at the front of his part, which someone, my mother probably, told me had to do with kidney dysfunction. Between him and Lawrence, I begin to suspect a conspiracy of elegant, wealthy men sprinkled throughout the general population of students, but the function of this secret fraternity is difficult to discern.

On the break, Lawrence tells me his full name, Lawrence Coolidge III. He must be joking, but I don't question it; there is something about him that makes me think, cynically, of the word *breeding*. He tells me that he is a painter and that his family lives in Chicago; he has been a student here in Iowa for two years. I've never been to Chicago; all my images of it are derived from *Sister Carrie*.

"I'm in the English Department," I mention. I decide not to tell him about my own failed attempts at painting. Even simple figure or perspective drawing is profoundly difficult for me. I don't trust my eye enough; I am always embellishing.

Maybe the secret club of beautiful men casts light on the ugly ones. I can imagine Lawrence and the professor shrunk down and in a glowing halo at the corner of my room watching me slide out of bed after I'd attempted sex with the information-booth attendant.

He looks so haggard under the standing lamp near my bed. He sits on the edge of my bed in discolored underwear and nylon socks, his brittle yellow body slumped with a shame I cannot rid him of.

I suppose that is what I am trying to do. I continue to disgrace myself in making him feel wanted. I'll often beg him to deliver his tongue to me through his wired mouth. He obliges me with a power he is unaware of. He is even more powerful when he doesn't oblige.

He is a codeine addict, and I've spent the afternoon driving around with him filling forged cough medicine prescriptions. There are three sticky bottles in the garbage can, one half-full on the night table. When I look at the red ring on the table, I can practically feel it on my skin. It feels like his presence, but though I'd like to be rid of him, I have my own addictions.

He flicks off the light, and until my eyes adjust, there is only the sound of him scratching his skin. He does this obsessively. My only relief is not seeing it.

"I wish you'd let me play my Hank Williams, Jr., record for you," he says sleepily. "I think you'd like it."

"How many times have I told you I hate country music and country people?" I am rigid in the dark.

I see his hand sliding from the side of the bed, searching out his guitar lying on the floor. The first two nights he spent with me, I had mistakenly told him I liked his playing. He told me he liked to sing me to sleep, and so I'd pretended with my eyes closed. But he could go on singing for an hour at least.

I grab his hand and twist it until I hear him whimpering. "No playing tonight," I say through clenched teeth.

He finally falls asleep while I sit propped against the opposite wall. I'm so tense I can't sleep. I concentrate on matching my breathing to his so that I can forget he's there.

I vow that I won't sleep with him again, and stretch out on the floor without cover or pillow. But my vow does not dispel my closet of skeletons, ugly burdensome men I've broken every taboo to meet. They hang there, as patient without me as they were with me. I am a bad medicine, I think. I do not heal them, and they discard me even when they are terminal cases and there's nothing else.

They hang there: the old ones, the amputees, the mentally retarded. I'd like to cut their ropes so they could fall with all the suicides of this building. I imagine them in a sordid heap at the lobby doors of the Stonecourt Apartments, their bodies like a barricade against the doors.

Lawrence invites me to his apartment, which is a large one-bedroom in a wooded area behind the campus. It's a quaint setting with a wooden bridge which crosses a landscaped ravine. We stop for a moment on the bridge, and look down at the thin brook trickling over black stones.

"Almost like wilderness," he says, "but they can trip floodlights and light up the whole set." He points out some of the lights, discreetly positioned behind trees. "A woman was raped here a few years ago. Now the place is like a laid trap."

"I'll watch where I step," I assure him.

I distrust the moonlight that makes his features take on the strange, alien quality of the man-made brook. It makes the thought of touching him seem odd and cold.

He opens the door to his apartment and ushers me inside.

There is an awkward feeling as we stand, hesitant, in the doorway, as though he were housesitting with instructions not to bring in guests. He takes my coat and the warmth of the room envelops me.

"Have a seat," he says, aware of my awkwardness. I sit down on an elegant, forest green couch. He tells me he'll get coffee and turns the radio on before he leaves the room. It's the classical music station playing softly Vaughan Williams's "Fantasia On A Theme."

"Do you know this piece?" I ask him.

"No," he calls out from the kitchen. "I don't really like classical music."

This is the apartment of someone established, I think, not a student. The room is rosy and wood-rich, too designed, too considered even for a student with wealthy parents. When he returns with coffee, I can't help but admire the way he moves around the place so comfortably, like an impostor.

"There's a man I've been seeing since I first moved here. He pays the rent on this place. I had him over last weekend. This is the radio station he likes to listen to. I don't listen to the radio when I'm here alone," he says nonchalantly. I notice, though, that he seems to be looking for a response, either shock or forgiveness.

For a moment, I don't know what I feel. Maybe envy.

"Do you love him?" I ask.

Lawrence looks at me as though I'm insane. Then his eyes soften a little. "I respect him," he says.

Lawrence insists on taking me by his studio. "It's on your way home." He gathers his coat.

He is one of the few students with his own studio in the painting building. The others stand in a large, open area at easels.

There is a padlock on the door and his initials, minus the III, painted on the wall. Inside, the space is crowded with canvases. Two of them are hanging on the wall, illuminated by a clamp light. I walk up close to them, surprised both by their accuracy and their beauty. They are self-portraits, simply and elegantly rendered. In one of the portraits he is looking into a mirror the way I never could, searching it as though it held the truth.

I turn to him. "They're beautiful," I tell him, and it's easier than admitting he is.

I stand at the center of my apartment in disbelief. Practically nothing has been opened or arranged. I begin cutting the tape on an earlier life comprehensively packed and already musty smelling and foreign.

I am uncomfortable putting out the books and records and posters. They seem frighteningly self-conscious now, as though I had gone out of my way to compensate, by way of taste, for a lack in appearance. The whole life is made up. I'm afraid that Lawrence will see through my obsession with the grotesque in film, my collections of criticism and philosophy. He will see just an ugly person filling in the holes.

I leave the boxes packed, the clothes neatly folded. I stand before the mirror tiles, stretching out my skin until it looks almost smooth. My hands move section by section over my face; I cover it all except for my eyes, peering out between my fingers.

I remember when I couldn't touch my face. It was two years after I had discontinued a violent dermatological therapy. My face was so red and disturbed I had grown afraid to touch it. The last doctor I saw, at the tearful request of my mother, was an old, Jewish hunchback who had an office in downtown Miami.

He took me into the bathroom and stood behind me and taught me how to wash my face. He held onto my hands and gently guided them over my cheeks and forehead. All along, I made him promise not to inject anything into my skin, not to use chemical peels. He stood behind me whispering, "Only pills, no pain."

In my room, the ghosts rise from the boxes like dust. I feel my parents' hands on my throat and feet. They, too, are pleading.

"Can't you do something about your face?" my mother asks disdainfully. "Wash it again," she insists, "you've got time."

"But I have washed it." I want her to notice that I'm wearing my new blazer and tie. But she only sees my face, stinging and burning from the medicine that puts holes in the pillowcase.

I close the boxes and start to pack them away in the closet. I sit down with the last box, though. It's packed with books. I draw one out and open it on my lap. It is a poem by Rupert Brooke, and I begin to recite it quietly to myself.

> And I knew
> That this was the hour of knowing,
> And the night and the woods and you
> Were one together, and I should find
> Soon in the silence the hidden key
> Of all that had hurt and puzzled me —
> Why you were you, and the night was kind,
> And the woods were part of the heart of me.
> And there I waited breathlessly,
> Alone; and slowly the holy three,
> The three that I loved, together grew
> One, in the hour of knowing,
> Night, and the woods, and you —

Lawrence is at the door. I tell him to come in quickly, fearful the attendant might be loitering in the hall.

"I think I've been drinking," he says. I have him sit on one of the two rotating chairs that the apartment came furnished with.

The chairs are covered in loud, flower-printed vinyl and look like hotel liquidation from the seventies. "Don't you have any chairs that sit still?" he asks.

I offer him coffee, and by the time I bring out a mug, he has found his way to the mirrored wall.

He opens up to me recklessly, "I'm sleeping with our professor, you know."

"Really? Is he good?" I ask.

"Lousy," he says. "He treats me like a work of art, touches me with a white glove, centers me on the bed and asks me not to move."

"He asks you not to move and doesn't have the decency to tie you up?"

"No way," he laughs. "He won't even use a collar on his dog."

"And he's not the one who pays your rent?" I ask.

"No," he says, becoming more serious. "That's Ray." He swoons a little, the alcohol showing. "I'm starting to worry about their paths crossing. Last weekend, while Ray was over, the professor kept calling, saying he knew I was there."

"Boy," I say, my voice sounding surprisingly mocking, "what a mess."

"I was counting on your understanding," he says conspiratorially.

"Shall I seduce him?" I ask.

Lawrence laughs. "He goes for the pretty boys," he says in a way that makes me think I shouldn't feel hurt.

It dawns on me suddenly that he sees me as clearly as he does himself. He is beautiful and I am ugly. How could I have ever imagined those lines between us blurring?

"What do you want me to do?" I ask, knowing his answer. He wants me to play the ugly role.

*   *   *

Just then I hear knocking at my door. "Oh God," I say under my breath.

"Please let me in," the attendant says through the chain.

"Get lost," I say bitterly.

"I know you have someone over. I just need to come in for a minute," he croaks.

"What for?" I ask, reddening.

"I need to get my cough medicine," he says.

"I'll get it."

I pick up the gluey bottle from the night table and uncap it. I stick my hand out of the crack of the door and pour the red liquid over his hands and on the rug. He stands there startled as though it were blood. When I look back at Lawrence, he is laughing.

I'm freezing out here, crouched in the shadow of the bridge. I see the professor's car driving slowly up the path and sink lower into the brush, pulling it over me like a blanket. I do this carefully, suddenly remembering the banks of lights trained on me. I imagine tripping the system and the ravine flooding with light, but there are only two beams quickly extinguished when he pulls into the driveway. My breathing seems to me too loud, and even though I try to calm myself, it is all I hear in the woods. And then I hear his door open, his feet on the gravel and up on the wooden porch. I crawl up closer to see him under the porch light. He stands there looking down at his feet after he rings the bell. He looks so gentle and patient and in love, I think, waiting to be let inside.

He steps into the doorway and it is as if a meter begins to tick away. I recognize it then as my heart. Lawrence pulls the shade down, and as we agreed, I begin to move toward the door, opening it quietly and letting myself in. I feel them instantly with the acute senses of an animal. Lawrence spots me from the bedroom (did he see me too soon?). I begin talking over the chaos.

"Oh my God," I say shocked. "I can't believe this."

Lawrence looks at me stunned (it is not very convincing, but the professor isn't looking at him. It is my moment).

Lawrence asks, "Why didn't you knock?"

"I just didn't," I say, beginning to feel real agitation. "I didn't expect to catch you in a private tutorial."

The professor is in his pants already, sliding on his glasses. He looks at me with wide, frightened eyes. It is our hope that he'll recognize me from class, but I don't see any recognition in his eyes. Only fear, as though I am a monster, some Bigfoot that lives in the ravine.

"I have to go," he says nervously. He is still looking at me when he says it. He starts to leave without his tan jacket. I hand it to him at the door. I am feeling so powerful, I give him a little push from behind. He turns angrily toward me.

"You've got nothing on me," he says, voice trembling, looking into my eyes. Then he must have seen something there that made him turn and go.

I think my face has changed. Not healed, but settled. Reinforced. Lawrence calls my face scary. He says there is something intimidating about it, and he loves to recall the way I looked on the night with the professor. "It was almost like a jealous lover had walked in," he says.

"It's been a week since you've heard from him," I say, "so I guess it worked."

"It worked beautifully," he says. "I wasn't complaining." But he looks at me sharply, and it seems for a moment that instead of me, he's looking at a small flaw on the couch.

"Ray's wife is leaving town for the next month," he says, "and Ray's asked me to stay at his place to help him work on the nursery. Rosemary's pregnant and Ray's already acting like a proud father."

"What's he grooming you for? A nanny position?" I sound like that scary person Lawrence finds amusing. "Why is he moving you in?" I ask, grasping.

He talks to me with his back turned, going into the kitchen. "He has a big, beautiful house. While she's gone, we're going to use it." His words sound so simple; it is like he is explaining it to a child.

"I wonder what it's like to have someone take care of you."

Lawrence calls out casually from the kitchen, "I didn't think you were the romantic type."

Why, then, do I feel excluded from him? Why do I feel left out of the happy family — Lawrence, Ray, and his pregnant wife?

But he emerges from the kitchen with a bottle of sherry and two glasses. Either to calm the panic he hears rising in me, or in genuine appreciation, he toasts to our friendship. I look into his eyes. Strangely, the closer he gets to me, the more remote I find him. I wonder if that is how it works with Ray.

It's gotten so that I can't think of Lawrence without Ray somewhere in the background. It's like when someone you know has cancer, how it's always there. It's not like Lawrence talks about him, about what they do, or how they feel about each other. It's just his name with a time and place written next to it under a magnet on the refrigerator, or his voice coming from the phone machine in Lawrence's bedroom. Whenever the phone rings, I always ask "who's that?" as though I'm waiting for his call.

Lawrence explains that I can leave messages for him and he'll call me from Ray's house. "I'll just be a few blocks away," he says, comforting me. But I can't seem to rid myself of the chill of that ravine, knowing this time I'll be locked out without a plan.

It is by chance that I've spotted him and Ray tonight coming out of The Mill. I would walk up to them and shake Ray's hand if they weren't so engaged in talk. Lawrence just keeps looking over to him, as though he is never going to see him again, as though he is trying to memorize his face.

I follow at a great distance. They walk together without touching until they start over the railroad bridge; then Ray takes Lawrence's gloved hand and guides him across, and it seems as natural as a father and child.

I am terrified of heights, and the bridge is no easy feat for me. It is not a footpath, merely an old railroad track that runs over some reinforcing beams. There is nothing to hold onto, except the track itself. I cross it on all fours. Far below, the water is frozen, certain death if I slip.

It takes me so long to cross the bridge, I feel certain I've lost them. Then, cutting across College Green Park, I see them again entering a sky blue, wooden house on the corner. The snow is lightly falling, and the perfect little house looks like a Christmas card.

I wonder what it is like to be pursued by an admirer, to be watched, investigated, loved.

Did Lawrence have to pursue anyone? Lawrence doesn't need to do anything, I tell myself, but I need to do everything.

Suddenly, the front door opens. Ray comes off the porch and looks up momentarily. I'm leaning against the oak, in the snow, with my ski hat on. I stand there casually turning a stick in my hands. He locates my eyes and glances away.

He pulls up the door of the garage and opens the passenger door of his truck. I see him removing a large roll of paper from the seat, then he takes a plastic bucket out of the back of the truck and carries them back into the house.

The garage is wide open. I stand there for a while looking at it. I am already walking out of the park and crossing the street. I've done crazier things, I assure myself, and I conjure up the feeling of power I felt pushing the professor out into the cold.

I glance over all the windows of the house, no movements, no one looking out. I hurriedly walk up to the garage. I feel safe once I'm inside, and begin to look over his things: his work table and saw, his toolbox, and the coils of extension cords hanging from hooks in the wall. It's a regular shop in here, I think, wondering if there is anything small I can take. I turn my attention to his truck, and there, as though he were offering them to me, are his keys dangling from the lock in the passenger door.

The moment they're in my hands I feel spooked and have to leave.

Lawrence calls. He's been at Ray's for two weeks, but he's alone tonight. He talks about the snow and how it makes him feel like a child, the one that felt trapped in his parents' house, an old Chicago house full of rugs and clocks and his father's pipe smoke. While he talks, I look out my window at the highway stretching north and the snow passing over all of it, the kind of lonely sight that makes people jump every winter, and I say, "It sounds safe and warm in your old house."

"That's why I never left," he answers.

We've come to Pete's, a small bar with pool tables and wooden booths, where it's not hard to be anonymous. There are just Pete and the two of us.

He's wearing jeans and a down jacket that is obviously not his. I remember us laughing about down jackets and how they looked like potholders. I don't mention it.

"It's difficult spending so much time at Ray's," he says thoughtfully, pouring beer from the pitcher. "I'm afraid I might get used to it."

"He wouldn't want that, that's for sure," I say. "Not with Rosemary coming back in two weeks."

There's a brief look of hurt in his face, and I wonder what it would be like to reach over the table and touch him. I am thinking that he does not want this to go on, and I know what he is asking me to do. I know what he is afraid to ask me to do, and I reach my hand into my pocket and feel the keys there like a charm.

"I understand how you feel."

"How could you possibly understand?" he asks, as though he's the most miserable person alive.

Tonight I saw Ray and Lawrence go to the Bijou for a screening of Fassbinder's *In the Year of Thirteen Moons.* If I could have, I would have warned them about it. I don't know how they could sit through that movie without feeling very uncomfortable; the lead character has a sex change to satisfy a rich, straight man who doesn't care about her. It's no wonder she tells her life story in a slaughterhouse.

It helps to know where they are and how long they'll be gone. I could probably turn on the lights. But I know this house by heart already, and besides, I like the feeling of being a shadow here, keeping away from the windows, touching everything with these gloves, Rosemary's gloves, which I'm now sure I made the right decision in taking the first night I came here.

There are two places I always have to check for clues: the bedroom and the nursery. I don't know what it is that I'm looking for. I guess I'm just interested in whatever it is they leave behind. I've felt compelled to take only a few things out of here, but they are inexplicable treasures to me.

At first, I touch the heavy draperies on the windows, the thick spreads on the bed. Then, like a neoclassical bedroom to which the wicked son is always returning, I sit on the edge of the bed and draw the cold, white sheets up to my face, with more than a sense of ownership. It really is, for a moment, like I've entered a painting, feeling so completely where I should be, as though I were positioned there by an artist.

Ray and Lawrence would feel it too, the limiting, perfecting structure of our interaction.

It was no surprise when Lawrence, five days before Rosemary's return, called to inform me that Ray had asked him not to stay at the house any longer. Time itself was conspiring to that end, but I was surprised by Lawrence's breathless weeping, which made it hard to comfort him. I asked him over.

I look around the apartment and it seems as though I have moved in at last. The boxes are unpacked; some of my favorite postcards are taped to the wall behind my desk. I've taken down the mirror tiles and stacked them inside the closet. The room and the fixtures themselves are ugly, but there is the feeling that someone lives here now, that someone is making do.

When Lawrence arrives, he concurs. "I feel more at home here than even at my own apartment," he says. He looks exhausted.

"Well, I guess so," I say. "Ray pays your rent."

He sits there drinking, silent.

"I don't know what happened," Lawrence says. "He started accusing me of things that I don't know anything about. Little things were missing, that he couldn't turn up — some of Rosemary's jewelry, which I'd never take." He looks so humiliated, as though he is accusing himself.

"Why would he think you did that?" I ask him.

"I don't know," he says angrily. "But he kept asking me if I was angry about Rosemary, and how I felt about them having a baby. I told him none of that mattered, and it didn't. But I think Rosemary took those things with her, or nothing's really gone and he's just finding a way to get rid of me."

"Maybe he doesn't find you compatible with his new family?"

"I didn't ask to stay at his house," Lawrence says. "I would have been content to have kept things the way they were."

"Well, that's how things are now, right? Back to the way they were?"

"No," he says. "He hates me now. He's politely asked me out of his life. Not even politely."

"He's afraid of you."

"I don't know why he thinks I would ever steal from him or try to disrupt his family."

"That comes with being the lover on the side," I remind him.

I don't know which one of us introduced the idea of mischief. Our desires seemed to cross then and run concurrently. By the end of the evening, we were sitting on the floor with a bottle of wine between us, laughing and crying, imagining ways to terrorize Ray.

"Let's make a baby," I suggest. I am thinking of the boxed baby clothes and the baby bounce swing I have in my closet.

"What are you talking about?" he asks.

"I found these baby clothes at the Salvation Army drop box. I can't imagine what else to do with them but make a little baby for him. It will be the one you couldn't have."

"Rosemary's Baby!" he shouts. We both roar.

We tear the plastic wrap from the boxes. On the collar of the little pink nightie Lawrence writes "Rosemary's Baby" in black magic marker. We stuff the clothes with an old gray pillow, leaving it bursting from the collar as a head. I draw in two weeping eyes.

I think how excited Ray must be about his family's return. He has come so far with the nursery. The wallpaper has cheery yellow balloons; the seams are perfect. The whole house smells like glue.

I wonder how he will feel about these stolen baby clothes showing up again.

Lawrence is busy drawing in the mouth.

"Cut it in," I say, our prank becoming a mad kind of voodoo. I hand him a knife I'd lifted.

He cuts through the pillowcase and pulls the dirty stuffing up out of the lips.

"Let's make them red," he suggests.

I don't have any paint, so we stain them with Mercurochrome.

Lawrence suggests we keep the knife buried in its head. We sit it up in the bounce swing like that. We hang it from a nail and stare at it. I force myself to laugh at its ugliness. Lawrence can't.

"Maybe we shouldn't," he murmurs.

"What did you expect? The Hardy Boys?"

"But I care about him," he says, confused.

"There'll be others."

"I don't think you understand the way I feel. I don't think you could understand it."

"No," I say. "Probably not. It's too subtle for me." And I begin to think how they tried to make me beautiful, how anything attractive in my face was put there by the doctors. They really wrestled it out of me, extracted it, but at such high cost and such great pain.

"I want to understand," I tell Lawrence.

*   *   *

They laid me on the table and gave me two rubber balls to squeeze. They were chewed up with nail marks. I rotated them slowly.

A German nurse with soft blonde hair dried her hands of sterilizing liquid. She directed my father, "Will you please hold your son's legs."

I felt his hands loosely holding my ankles. He looked at me, miserable. My mother stood small in the doorway.

The nurse lowered a bright light over my face. I looked into it. At first there was nothing but whiteness. Then I saw an eyeball floating between two lights.

"This is a magnifying lamp," the nurse explained. I saw the eye blink on the other side.

I imagined what she was seeing: the cores of blackheads, a violent chemistry in the cyst, here and there a black whisker shockingly cutting its way through the thick skin.

I saw the doctor enter through the glow of the light, radiant, drawing a rubber glove over one hand. In the other he held a needle. He pushed the sweaty hair off my forehead and began pressing the cysts along my cheek.

He worked silently.

Finally he said, "This will hurt. But when you're well, you will thank me." I saw the nurse nodding, reverent.

With the first prick, blood flashed across the dull green wall. My nails sank into the red balls. I felt his fingers pressing down the boil.

"It is the problem of evil," I thought I heard the doctor say.

I remembered the video we all had to watch in the crowded lobby. The doctor's only child born with cystic acne all over its innocent body. The German doctor mournfully narrated, "My wife and I wept when our child was born to us with cystic acne. He screamed constantly as an infant, unable to lie in one position for very long."

Hundreds of before-and-after photos of patients were flashed on the screen while the doctor talked his theory of enzymic reactions, pustules, scarring. Everyone was standing around the TV with their arms folded over their chests; they were secretly looking at the faces of the others, measuring the severity of their problem against everyone else's condition.

I remember staring constantly at a mirror. For me, the mirror was like skin, always healing itself, always getting better. Though I wanted nothing but the truth about my face, the mirror could never reflect it accurately; I saw only the desperate effort to heal.

My eyes were searching the doctor's. He was the only one who saw my condition the way I did, and he was punishing me for it. I saw my blood arc across his coat. He did not stop at my weeping. He did not hear my screaming. If he heard it, it was a tiny scream; I sounded like an infant to him. He would have strangled me if I didn't bear that resemblance to his son.

The nurse saw I was about to pass out. Perhaps she heard it in my breathing. If there was a soul in there, I physically forced it out.

The doctor peeled his glove off. As I slowly began to sit up on the table, an assistant entered the room and snapped a Polaroid.

There is a light drizzle, so we put the baby, swing and all, into a plastic garbage bag, and carry it to the house. I make Lawrence carry it, it's his gesture.

I stand up in the park, behind the oak tree where I'd first seen Ray's home. We both wear ski masks. Before Lawrence takes the baby down to the house, we look at each other, and it seems that for the first time we can really see each other, desperate eyes and faces sheathed in wool. The drizzle persists. I wish I could feel it on my face, but this mask lets nothing through.

I watch Lawrence furtively make his way up to the door, strip off the garbage bag, and hang the baby up under the porch light. It swings eerily and misshapen as Lawrence comes off the porch.

We stare at it from the park.

"Let's get out of here. Let's go to my studio."

When we enter his studio, he grabs both my hands. "Can you believe how that thing looked?" he asks excitedly.

"So beautiful," I assure him, "his beautiful little baby."

Lawrence puts up tea. While I sip it, I think about Lawrence staying here until he finds another place. It is small and smells like paint, and it's cold, but nothing a space heater couldn't improve. I would put him up too, if it comes to that.

Suddenly, there is an oppressive weight all around us, as though the walls of the studio are closing in, and I notice we are sitting, facing one another, our knees touching. Lawrence's face is twisted with confused sadness. Maybe it's our touching, our close proximity, that enables me to feel it, too.

"He'll know it was me?" he asks, as though everything had suddenly dawned on him.

I feel his tearful shaking rising up from my knees, like we are two old trees that have grown together.

"How will I ever explain it to him?" he asks, clutching me.

And though I know it will never suffice, I draw him close and forgive him.

ALLAN STEIN

The photo arrived in July during a warm spell, a time of year when the evening stays light until ten or ten-thirty. There is birdsong well into the night, a crazy, fluid, pitchless sound which persists even after dark. I feel as though I am hallucinating. The shallow light, then, gradually, darkness. The perplexing songs of the birds. At night I lie on cotton sheets with ice in a glass by the bed. My rooms face a park where the birds nest. The windows must be kept open, despite the awful noise. Together with the glaring heat of the afternoons, this twilight makes summer my least favorite season here. It is worse because I am a teacher. I have no work for three months.

The photo came in the mail, sent to me in error by a library in Connecticut. Inside a plastic sleeve, pasted on bent cardboard, was a picture of six people, among them the American writer Gertrude Stein. A tag affixed to the back of the cardboard told me the names and a date, 1905. I know little about Gertrude Stein. I know that she lived in Paris. In the photo she is standing with Michael and Leo and Sarah Stein. Another woman is not identified. It must be fall or winter. They are draped in tweed and corduroy. In winter I enjoy the sound of a closed window, cold to the touch, pelted by sleet and rain. The Stein faces were flat and hard like the cut ends of tree stumps. They were all staring, but in different directions. Gertrude resembles a crow. A boy, Allan Stein, stands in front of her.

Boys fascinate me.

Allan is chest-high to Gertrude. Dressed in a white sailor's shirt and knickers, he is wielding a stick. His eyes are dark flowers, barely opened. Gertrude has both hands on his shoulders, like the claws of a bird, a crow, about to devour him. My own family is dead, that is to say my parents are dead. I have no siblings and have never married. As I looked at the photo, Gertrude, Michael, Leo, and Sarah appeared and disappeared for me; one moment a family, then simply shapes, a wall of black. I touched the edge of Allan's white shirt, the hole he made in them by where he stood. His eyes were beguiling. They seemed to move forward, off the photo. Their contact was with me, not with the shadow of his family behind him. Caught (in fact dead), Allan appeared, nevertheless, to be thinking. He appeared to "regard" me. I pinned the photo to the wall beside my bed.

The posture, as much as the eyes, proclaimed his resistance. I hitched my belt up and tried slouching a little, feet slightly apart, eyes forward. I have read that saints gaze skyward because the exertion, the twisting of the eyes upward, releases chemicals in the brain. A kind of holiness comes over them, the physiological product of their upturned eyes. Allan's posture did the same to my body. A holiness descended into me, an ache or hollow like exhaustion. I took the mirror from the closet and propped it by the bed, near the photo of Allan. He watched me. When I was young I looked at no one. I cried when Robert Starr pinned me by the pool and stared into my eyes. I was twelve. He did nothing but hold me down and stare. His eyes were teeth, his look a tongue I felt all over me. It is impossible to know someone well. We can only use them, like a bucket or mirror.

At the library I learned that Allan was the son of Sarah and Michael, and that he lived in Paris from 1903, age eight, until 1951, when he died of "hypertension." I believe hypertension was a less usual condition in those days, a diagnosis given only to the rich. The poor were simply tired and needed sleep. Allan went to the hospital and died from it. It wasn't very clear what he actually did in life.

In one book I found Allan's portrait, painted by Picasso. It was from the same year as the photo. Allan is in profile, wearing a brown sweater. He is more dead than in the photo, but also more beautiful. There is no trace of thought in the portrait. He looks much older. I tore the painting from the book and pinned it to the wall at home, beside the photograph.

I have begun writing about Allan Stein.

Therese Ehrman, 1885–1972, was Allan's nanny and piano teacher at the beginning of the century. In her memoirs, dictated to Elise Haas in 1965, she recalls her first years with the Michael Steins, their journey to Paris, and the unusual life they led there.

"Among my parents' most intimate friends at the turn of the century were Michael and Sally Stein. I was a so-called child prodigy but hadn't a good piano. So it was arranged that I practiced on their Steinway every morning. Their little son, Allan, four or five years of age, began to study with me. And a celebrated musician of the time, Oscar Weil, heard him play and was so enthusiastic that he begged to give him theory and harmony lessons and congratulated his parents on choosing 'such a marvelous teacher,' etc. I didn't realize then what a compliment it was, but the Steins made up their minds that when they went to Europe they couldn't dream of going without me. Of course I was then all of about fifteen years old, fifteen or sixteen.

"This was my first trip to Europe. Actually I never expected to be able to get to Europe, certainly not at that age, and there was great excitement. I left with Mike and Sally Stein and their little boy in December 1903, and arrived at Cherbourg and was met by Mr. Stein's younger sister and brother, Leo and Gertrude Stein. No, Gertrude wasn't along; I'm mistaken there. It was just Leo. We actually arrived at Cherbourg about three o'clock in the morning, and I was thrilled and fascinated. I think I began to be . . . [a long silence] . . . from that moment of arriving in France. I knew no French but was absolutely charmed. Leo took us to the old hotel; oh dear, I've forgotten the name of it. The Hôtel Fayot. It was the famous hotel in the Latin Quarter, facing the Luxembourg Gardens, where the senators have their lunch; it was celebrated for its great restaurant. And that was an exciting night. I don't think anybody slept a wink.

"We found an apartment on the rue de Fleurus, 1 rue de Fleurus, which was the same street as Leo and Gertrude Stein, who lived at 27 rue de Fleurus. I remember ours was an apartment three flights up. There was no such thing as an elevator, and of course it had no bath. We had to go up the street to Gertrude's. They had a bath and were unique. I think in the whole street perhaps there was only one other bath. And the baths used to come around by cart. Pipes would be hoisted from the street into your apartment, the tin tub having been brought up ahead of time. And you 'bought' a bath, as it were. It was all very primitive and very exciting and very wonderful to me.

"Soon they moved to the rue Madame and part of my duties as an assistant in the household was to take the little boy to school. He went to a private school a few blocks away. And each morning I would meet Degas, the painter, who lived a block away, and each morning he'd ask how my little boy was. I was only ten years older than Allan by that time, but just the same, I never corrected him. I was very proud of him, this very handsome young boy. Degas was an interesting figure and must have been at the height of his painting career then. I was stupid enough to be really only interested in music. Well, it's hard to follow in detail. There's so much detail."

It is hot even at dawn in July. The air through the windows provides some relief. I can't help but wake up before six. Having no work, I keep the habit of walking for an hour before breakfast, then reading the paper with my toast and coffee. Recently I have added Allan to this regimen, spending several hours with books and my "word-sketches" each morning after breakfast. The park outside my window, where the birds nest, is empty when I walk.

At six the sun is still hidden (though it is light) and the grass is damp. The light bleeds evenly, like water blotted onto tissue. The city is much quieter then. I keep to the gravel paths and usually walk first around the perimeter of the park. It takes me a half hour. There is mist rising off the ponds. At night children swim in the ponds (although it is forbidden). I watch from my window. Sometimes I find them sleeping curled in blankets or without cover by the ponds in the morning. I've seen a crow take bread from the closed hand of a boy asleep on a bench by the swings. He did not wake up.

I am a teacher, but outside the school I have no responsibility for these children. They are not safe in this world, and I can do nothing to make them safe. This is not cruelty but honesty. One cannot argue with facts.

Allan Stein, who had just turned ten, woke up in the cold bedroom above the church at 58 rue Madame and listened for his parents. There was nothing. Birds, a very few, sang in the small garden beneath the tall window. The sky was still black. A broom could be heard, straw raking over stone, very near. Madame Vernot kept the steps so clean. Who could tell at what hour she would begin? Allan shivered in his bed, and saw that his fire was out. He reached toward the coal. If he stretched far enough, and kept one ankle pried beneath the brass rail for leverage, he could fill the stove and restart it without leaving his bed. He had asked Sally, his mother, if the bed could be moved closer, but she said it might catch fire and must be kept where it was.

Today is November 28, 1905. A very special day for Allan. He will meet his Aunt Gertrude at ten o'clock and travel across Paris to Montmartre. The painter Picasso will paint his portrait. It is a gift for his birthday, from his mother and father, who like paintings very much. Really it is a gift for themselves, like so much of what they give to Allan.

Allan got the fire started, then curled back into his blankets and listened to the birds. Why were there birds in late November? I don't know, but I myself have heard such birds in Paris in late November, and surely Allan, awake that cold early morning, could hear them too. They made a weak, diminished sound, a very sad bird sound. Allan felt the room grow warmer.

He had not eaten much at dinner, wanting to be slim for Picasso. He might pose without clothes, Aunty Gertrude told him, and that would be an honor. Sometimes, when he ate very much, his stomach stuck out like those of the cherubs in paintings he had seen. He wanted to look like a boxer, not a cherub. Allan felt the muscles of his chest and then his ribs. He ran his hands over them, stopping to push his finger into the shallow depression of his belly button. He flexed his stomach, and enjoyed the pressure against his fingertip. He raked his fingers through his hair and left them there, warm.

There was dim light in the sky. Today he would miss school. Paintings were not made in a moment, Sally had told him. Gertrude said Picasso did not need to see Allan to paint him. The sitting was a formality, a chance for conversation. She insisted on going with him. Picasso would be bored by a child. Under his tent of blankets, Allan pushed his closed fist hard against his stomach. Surely he and Picasso could discuss boxing.

The world, then, spun around his moment. The news was good, and the weather fine. That day the sky became startling and blue, cold as ice and clear. Paris around him shone like a gray pearl. In Europe, full of industry and peace, excitement reigned. Gossip and rumor crossed the ocean, and the war was still many years away. The globe spun like a prop in a newsreel film, and Allan alone sat awake in his bed in Paris, watching the glimmer of dawn light the sky.

When I say I am not responsible for the children outside of school, of course I am exaggerating the case. There are ways that I can help them, and I do. One boy, for example, whom I encountered near the ponds on a morning in June, asked if I had any money for food, and I brought him to my apartment and fed him. His name is of no importance. He was fifteen or sixteen years old and very dirty. All children seem, to me, either kept or abandoned, and this one was clearly abandoned. Most of the children at my school are kept-children. It is not an enviable condition, and is in some ways worse than being abandoned. A kept-child is the plaything of his parents. He is sheltered, fed, and clothed as a kind of annex, a decorative wing of the family that can be used to store that which will not fit elsewhere . . . innocence, for example, or joy. The unhappy parent requires a child, and requires that child to be happy. At least the abandoned are prepared for what they will encounter as adults. The children at my school are prepared for nothing.

The boy from the park had dark eyes and a filthy shock of brown hair. He smiled at me and made a habit of peeking out from behind his thick, dirty bangs. It is a mannerism he learned from magazines and films. I gave him a towel and told him he had to shower before I would feed him. This was in June, weeks before the photo arrived, and I had nothing to occupy my time except meals and waiting.

The boy undressed and left the bathroom door open while he showered. He thought I wanted to have sex with him, but that did not interest me. I fried eggs and potatoes, knowing he would be hungry. There was something I needed to ask him. When he came to the table he looked lost, disoriented by my failure to carry out the scenario.

"How can you sleep there?" I asked. "In the park?" He filled his plate with potatoes and drank the coffee.

"It's not a problem," he said. "No one bothers me there." I enjoyed his company. The table felt balanced, comfortable, because he was sitting across from me.

"I don't mean other people. I just wonder how you can sleep with all the noise, you know, birds, the traffic and such." His wet brown hair and the glimpse of his chest where he'd left his shirt unbuttoned gave me pleasure.

"The birds don't make noise." He smiled because my worry amused him. "Traffic's not so bad. It's kind of like a river, if you listen to it that way." I stared at him for a while. He poured more coffee.

"I hear them all night, through the window."

Aunty Gertrude and I catch the omnibus at Place d'Odéon. I am very hungry. I am nervous thinking of Picasso. He has asked if I will pose without my clothes. I would like that very much. Today I am missing school to pose for Picasso. The Louvre looks gray and awful, but Gertrude tells me to admire its mass and care-lessness. The river is very high. It is nice to look up it and down. Blaise is in the hospital with the grippe. If Picasso is done with us by three P.M., Aunty Gertrude says we may visit him. She tells me the Opera is "the nineteenth century, all of it, in stone." It is 11:32 now. I think the Opera looks like a great mint hat on a box. Aunty Gertrude says Picasso lives in Montmartre because it is higher up so he can see more. Everyone else lives in Montparnasse because everyone else lives in Montparnasse. The train tracks from the Gare du Nord are very broad. I will take an overnight train with Micky and Sally this spring. And if not with them, Gertrude says I may go with her to Aix, where it is warm. We get off at Place Blanche.

The door is closed at number 13 and no one answers when we call. I can call very loudly. Perhaps we are early, perhaps we are late. Picasso does not need to see me to paint me. Aunty Gertrude suggests we go to have a hot chocolate and wait. We go to La Dinette (leaving a note for Picasso). Aunty Gertrude tells me I am pale. I have not eaten last night or today, wanting to be slim when I stand without my clothes. Sometimes when I have eaten my stomach protrudes like the women of Rubens, which Micky has shown me and likes very much. Today my stomach is flat and very fetching. I have looked at it in the mirror this morning. I ask for a glass of gas water and Aunty Gertrude has *l'épinard* with cheese and a *porc grillé*, which she says is very good. Madame Rossi is very kind to me and brings a *crème caramel* when Gertrude is in the toilet, but I don't want to eat it. I tell her I have the grippe and the doctor will not let me eat. She takes it away.

It is two P.M. and Picasso is home now. He kisses me and kisses Gertrude and holds her hand when we walk to his studio. It is very cold. Gertrude and Picasso are laughing. My pants feel loose on my waist and this pleases me. His studio is full of junk.

Gertrude sits in a large stuffed chair and I go to stand near the stove. There are boxes set on a cloth by the stove, and Picasso points there and tells me to undress. Gertrude asks for some tea. I pull my undershirt off and become entangled. Picasso helps me pull it from my arms and he says that my belly is perfect. I am glad I have not eaten. He tells me I can stay near the stove. I lean against a tall box, then for a while I stand with my arms relaxed at my sides. Picasso touches me when he wants me to move or not move. His eyes are very strong, I think, always looking at me. He talks to Gertrude while he works. My zizi is standing, very much, but they don't notice. My feet are tired. After some silence, and the fire collapsing a little in the stove, Picasso asks me, "Allan, what is it that you love?" And I tell him, "I love horses."

The boy I fed has been sleeping in the library. I saw him first by the microfilm readers. I needed the machine, but it was taken by this boy. He was bundled in a thick jacket and had his head down on the machine. When I disturbed him he looked up but did not remember me. His cheeks were flushed from sleep, and his mouth was soft and unformed. He might have been only twelve, now that I saw him sleeping.

"Are you all right?" I asked. He squinted at me and then his face hardened and he left without speaking. It was so hot out, the jacket made him look sick, like a man with tuberculosis, or a junkie. He looked smaller than before.

The library obtained microfilm of the Steins' letters from an archive in Baltimore. Whole books of maps and photographs of Paris fill three shelves in the library's basement, where it is coolest. I can see no clock from the floor where I sit by the shelves.

I have begun to dream of Allan. Last night in my dream I was a child, seven or eight years old, obliged to ride a horse far bigger than any I had ever seen. There was the problem of mounting him. No equipment was provided and I faced the unadorned horse, coming barely to its knee. Allan was with me and he climbed the foreleg, took hold of the knobby knee, shinnied up to the mane, and swung himself onto the horse. Then he rode away. I was left by myself with no horse.

I saw Allan naked in a painting by Picasso called *Boy Leading a Horse*. I am convinced it is him. Allan stands, with his usual attitude, gesturing toward a powerful horse. Perhaps Picasso made sketches of the boy, standing nude, during the days Allan sat for his portrait. The painting was begun then, and completed the next spring. The boy's body is warm and mottled, like the ground where he stands. But the face and his organ are painted on like masks. The face mimics the more famous mask Picasso painted on the portrait of Gertrude. It is a boy where she is a woman. Of course they are *both* Picasso. The organ is equally a mask, painted in a uniform, darker tone as an image that both covers and conjures the ineffable, the unreducible reality beneath.

The heat kept me from sleeping, from even relaxing a little. The ice in the glass was melted and I dipped my fingers in the water. The wet fingers felt good on my face. There was music in the park, from somebody's radio. I could see them through the window from my bed. They might have been on drugs, or very tired. Three of them lay on the ground. Two others stumbled near the bushes, dancing. In daytime, on a stone terrace, bands played to an audience which danced in the shade of the trees. Brass bands were usual. Once a year the full symphony played from a stage at night and there were fireworks.

The dancers fell into the brush and were motionless. I sat up in bed and looked at them through binoculars. They were obscured by shadows. The three prone by the radio could be seen and they were sleeping. The birdsong was diminished, seemingly patternless except for a call and answer. I had heard this same pair on my morning walks, meaning it must be early already, or rather, it was already very late. The sky above the city was orange, dull and soft like cotton. It was impossible to sleep.

It wasn't too early to begin my walk. Outside, the air was cool. I felt it drifting, as though a freezer door had been propped open somewhere, and chilled air spilled from it like a cloud. The noise of the gravel underfoot seemed amplified. The cool air sank onto the paths (a wonder it had never reached my windows). I was near to the radio and the sleepers. A dancer rose from the brush, undressing. He stared at me, undoing his heavy jacket. It was him again, the boy I had fed. Our city is small and I should not have been surprised. This park was his home. I'd seen him here a dozen times.

Again he didn't recognize me. He pulled his shirt and pants off and walked across the gravel path.

"Hello," I said, because he was now just a few feet from me.

"Hey." He was unsteady on his feet. He looked at me but was unfocused. I don't think he really saw me.

"Doesn't the gravel hurt?" He laughed and wobbled some, then looked at the gravel. His underpants were torn. The elastic was unraveled and turned under at the waist. His skin there interested me and I thought about sex with him. Probably he was dirty. It was light behind the trees to the east. "Going for a swim?" I asked him. He smiled and coughed, then looked back into the brush where his friends were sleeping.

"Sure," he said.

"I can't swim," I told him. "I don't really like the water anyway." He swayed but kept his feet steady against the ground. I think he was afraid of falling. I nodded toward the pond and gestured with my hand. He looked that way. "No point waiting for your friends," I said. Around his hips and belly he was really quite beautiful. But it was hard to focus there. His face was absent, from the drugs, I guess, and his legs were too skinny.

His friends were awake now, and I went into the shadow of the trees and sat on a bench near the pond. They turned the radio from station to station. The boy stepped forward, into the water, then hesitated with his arms drawn up around his ribs. It was light above the trees. The birds began to sing. The boy took water in his hands and washed himself, gently, moving both hands in circles over his belly and chest. I heard steps and watched his friends with the radio. The boy looked into the trees and stretched his arms above his head. Four runners came toward us along the path. I saw the boy splashing, then he moved forward and disappeared under the surface. There was nothing, just a series of rings expanding outward. The runners passed. Still nothing, no disturbance, no last air.

"Hey," I called toward the pond, but of course he couldn't hear me. "Hey." The word echoed. His friends had found a station and they were dancing. I rose from the bench and walked to the shore. The water was tepid and greasy. I took my shoes off and stepped forward. The bottom of the pond was uneven and soft like a gum, toothless, and it sucked at my feet when I tried to move farther and get to him. I cannot swim; I think I've already told you that. I fell under and searched with my hands. I kept my eyes closed because the water made them sting. There was rotten wood and stones, swaths of carpet and bottles, plants like vines that had died and lay tangled at the bottom, plastic pipes and concrete broken into chunks. The water got in my throat and made me sick. His friends were by the shore now, shouting. One ran away down the path. I touched the boy's arm then lost it. A pale glimpse through

ALLAN STEIN

the water, a ghost, his back, a swath of white like Allan's shirt. Sometimes I wish I was a father. A boy can be so fragile. I grabbed an ankle, his foot. I witness boys as a teacher, but a father is allowed more intimacy. The boy hugs him and cries. His arms wrapped convulsively around my body. When the night becomes frightening he might sleep in his father's bed. I pulled him up to get air.

His body was warm and pliant. I felt his nipples, hard under my hands, and the brittle ribs. His belly was taut, and the elastic of his underpants floated loose from his waist. I got to shallow water and put my mouth over his to make him breathe. His friends tried to pull him from me, but I would not let them.

It was odd how quickly morning came, once the sky became light. I carried the boy onto the grass. He was pale like soap. Policemen drove down the path with lights and sirens. A man in a suit pushed me away and cleared junk from the boy's throat. I grabbed at his suit and vomited. The boy was naked. I had torn his underpants when I pulled him from the water. A policeman tackled me to keep me from the boy. An ambulance came. I lay by the bench and was sick. A medic gave me shots and a blanket.

Joggers and businessmen walking to work gathered around the pond, kept back by yellow tape the policemen strung. Firemen dragged the pond with nets and rakes, but there was nothing more to be found. The day stayed cool, even after the sun came up, and I was able to sleep.

The boy survived, and I felt sad about him. He seemed doomed, despite surviving. Childhood is a terminal condition, always pointed toward ending. It need not end suddenly or savagely, but all children are doomed. It is a part of their charm. They are marked for death. This fact powers the engine of longing adults feel whenever they look at a child. Childhood can only be seen by those for whom it has ended. It is conjured into existence, it becomes visible, only by its disappearance.

When it *is* finally seen, childhood has a trajectory: the trajectory of a countdown, aimed toward zero. This is the sickness of nostalgia.

POSTERITY

After a light lunch fixed by Maria — watercress salad, an omelet, and a glass of red wine — Whale watches *As the World Turns* on television, then goes to his bedroom for a nap. It is a safe, dreamless sleep. He wakes up clearheaded, his headache diminished.

He occupies the next hour preparing himself for afternoon tea and his visitor. He changes his shirt twice and tries a necktie before deciding on a blue polka-dot bow. He spends a long time studying his face in the mirror over the dresser. He lifts his chin for a manly, military pose, then stretches his long upper lip for a look of aristocratic inscrutability. He can pass for sixty, can't he? Even fifty-nine or fifty-eight? One of the nurses said he reminded her of the Duke of Windsor, but Whale believes he has a younger, more sensuous mouth than the lovelorn abdicator. Twenty-five years ago, David said he looked like that paragon of male sexuality, the Arrow Shirt Man. No more. He needs the tan he lost in the hospital to hide the deep lines etched around his eyes, the furrows scored down either side of his mouth. He gives his white hair a few final licks with his monogrammed, silver-backed brushes.

He knows he has no business going to such fuss, but it's been so long since he entertained a guest. There had been a letter among the four or five get-well cards waiting for him when he returned from the hospital.

Dear. Mr. Whale, sir,

I am a student of cinema at the University of Southern California. I have always been a great admirer of the movies you directed, not only the horror ones but also the original *Show Boat.* Would it be possible for me to interview you for a paper I hope to write? You must have a very full and busy schedule, but I will do my best to work around it. I am trained in shorthand and will be able to record every precious word you have to share.

Sincerely yours, Edmund Kay

This was interesting. He was touched a stranger even knew who he was. Once you stopped working and were of no use to people, even friends in the industry forgot your existence. The last time anybody sought him out was a year ago, when a brash young television producer from New York came to ask, not that he direct something for TV — a prospect Whale considered with both hope and alarm — but that he appear as a contestant on a game show called *I've Got a Secret.* "Your secret could be something like, 'I created Frankenstein.'" Whale politely yet firmly said no. He would not give up his privacy for the sake of five minutes of notoriety, a funny old coot in a sideshow.

But this letter was different, personal and intriguing. A young man wanted to sit and talk with him at length. On the morning his doctor let him discharge the day nurse, he had Maria telephone Edmund Kay and set a date for afternoon tea. It might have seemed a little desperate if Whale made the call himself. "Just a boy. Very young," Maria reported with a shrug after her conversation with him.

"There is iced tea, Maria?" Whale asks when he comes from his bedroom. "The cucumber sandwiches?"

"Yes, sir, Mr. Jimmy."

The sandwiches might be excessive, but they are what a young American would expect at a proper English tea. Whale goes to the hutch and selects two weighty Havanas from the shallow mahogany box. Allowed only one cigar a day, he takes an extra in case Mr. Kay partakes. He runs a smoothly foliated, spicy cylinder beneath his nose before slipping both cigars into the inside pocket of his jacket.

The doorbell rings and Whale goes to his club chair, settling in while Maria answers the door. He opens a maroon-bound book left on the end table — the Dickens he put aside last week when he found he couldn't read anything denser than a newspaper. He waits until Maria ushers the fellow into the room before he looks up.

"Mr. Kay, sir," Maria announces.

"Yes?" He feigns surprise that he has a visitor.

A slim boy in a V-necked sweater stands by his fireplace, staring. Short black hair hangs in a Roman fringe on his forehead. He rests his weight on one slouched hip, his boneless arms nervously twined behind him. Whale certainly didn't expect a football player or fraternity rowdy, but he's mildly disappointed that Edmund Kay is so clearly a baby poof.

"Ah. Mr. Kay. I'd almost forgotten. My guest for tea." He stands and holds out his hand.

"Mr. Whale? Mr. Whale," Kay repeats more confidently. He untangles his arms to shake hands. His voice is froggy, like a hoarse child's, his handshake as light as a feather.

He also appears to be Jewish, although that's of no matter to Whale. He has no romantic notions about Jews, negative or otherwise, not in this city. Even David was born David Levy.

"This is such an honor. You're one of my favorite all-time directors," Kay blurts out with a grin. "I can't believe I'm meeting you."

"No. I expect you can't," Whale says gently, intending to be both teasing and self-deprecating.

But the boy is too excited to catch the mockery. "And this is your house. Wow. Double wow. The house of Frankenstein." He looks around, maintaining his smile. "More housey than I expected," he admits. "I thought you'd live in a big old mansion or villa."

"One likes to live simply."

Maria stands solemnly by, wrinkling her implacable face at Kay, glancing suspiciously at Whale.

"Oh yeah. And I know people's movies aren't their lives." The boy suddenly leans in and growls, "Love dead. Hate living." He laughs, a high, girlish giggle.

Whale fights a cringe with a polite smile.

"That's my favorite line in my favorite movie of yours, Mr. Whale. *Bride of Frankenstein.*"

"Is it, now? I made so many pictures, I can't remember them all."

"Surely you remember your horror films? They're the greatest."

"Maria?" says Whale. "I think we'll take our tea down by the swimming pool. Will that be good for you, Mr. Kay?"

"Sure. And the interview. I can interview you, can't I?"

"If you like. Although I'm afraid you'll find me an old stick as a raconteur."

He had originally intended to give Kay a tour of the house, but the boy's gush and fervor will seem less loud outdoors.

"After you, Mr. Kay," says Whale as he opens the back door. Inspecting the boy from behind, he notices his wide hips and plump posterior. No, not his physical type, but an amusing character.

The yardman is gone, but the sweet smell of mown grass lingers on the sloping lawn. Kay chatters away on the path to the pool. All initial shyness in the presence of "the great director" has vanished. "I love the great horror films. Not like this new junk at the drive-ins. The science-fiction horror junk? Creatures from outer space and black lagoons. And giant insects. Lots of giant insects. I saw one last month about giant snails in the Imperial Valley. But the old ones? The movies made by you and Tod Browning and Robert Florey — "

Whale winces at the company he's been given.

"But yours are the best, Mr. Whale. The Frankenstein movies. *The Old Dark House. The Invisible Man.* They look great and have style. And funny! God, audiences back then must've flipped their wigs at the stuff you were doing. Like that 'love death, hate living' line. When Dr. Pretorius meets the Monster in the crypt and the Monster holds the skull that's going to be his bride? And then Pretorius says" — Kay's deadpan murmur is perfect, even if his English accent isn't — " 'You are wise in your generation.' "

"This," says Whale, pointing ahead, "is the studio where I now paint. A hobby. Mine and Winston Churchill's."

"Nice," says Kay. He refuses to be sidetracked. "And your lighting and camera angles. You got to go back to German silent movies to find anything like it. Did you know any of the great German silent directors, Mr. Whale? Pabst and Lang? Murnau? Was F. W. Murnau an influence on your work?"

Finally the boy has mentioned someone Whale doesn't despise. "No, I met Mr. Murnau very briefly, when I first came here. Shortly before his death. A great director. But no, I can't say he influenced my work in any way."

"You know how he died, don't you?"

Whale frowns. "I've heard tales. Here, please be seated." He gestures at the white cast-iron chairs around the table beside the pool. The umbrella overhead has been cranked open and casts a cool oblong shadow. "Our refreshments will be down shortly."

Kay sits and flips open his steno pad while Whale adjusts his bones against the iron scrollwork. "So. When were you born?"

Whale smiles again, but his smiles are growing less indulgent. "Mr. Kay. We'll talk. You may interview me. But we must take this slowly."

"Yes. Sorry. Right," says Kay, grimacing at himself. "It's just I'm so excited to meet you I can't control myself. I mean, I wasn't even sure you were alive until your secretary called."

There's no malice in that. There appears to be no guile or ulterior motives at all in the boy, and his dancing on Whale's toes is nothing more than the headlong rush of youth. Lucky child, Whale thinks. He could never afford to be so thoughtless and carefree. If only he had been born an American.

"Let's get better acquainted, Mr. Kay." The name has taken on a sinister, alphabetical sound. "You said you were a student at the university?"

"USC, yes, sir."

"And you study . . . motion pictures?"

"Oh yeah. Film history."

"As one might study ancient history or Elizabethan drama? Curious. I had no idea it might be an academic field. At Oxford in my day, people studied only what had been dead and gone for a hundred years at least."

"You're English, right?"

"Ah, you've guessed my little secret."

Maria comes down the path with a tray loaded with finger sandwiches, a pitcher of iced tea, and a plate of sponge cakes.

"Thank you, Maria. Very nice."

She makes a highly audible sigh and starts back up the hill.

"I confess I've acquired the American fondness for iced tea," he tells Kay. "What's lost in flavor is more than compensated for by a refreshing piquancy. Uh, cucumbers," he explains when Kay makes a face after a bite of sandwich. "Sliced very thin."

Kay opens his sandwich to peek inside. "Righto," he laughs.

"I presume you want to make pictures, Mr. Kay?"

"Not me. I just like to watch them. And write about them. The old ones. New movies stink. Jerry Lewis and Doris Day? *The Ten Commandments*?" He rolls his eyes. "I hate color, don't you? All that bright, flat lighting. They don't make them like they used to, that's for sure."

Whale wants to be flattered — recent movies are as cold and shiny as the newest automobiles — but he can't help feeling like a quaint Victorian sideboard discovered by a chatty little antiques dealer. Kay is only a boy, but he has an old queen's love of the past. The old is good because it's old and has no teeth. One hopes to keep a contemporary bite, as the Old Masters do. Whale has to remind himself that they are only talking about horror pictures.

"Shall we begin?" he asks. "What did you want to know?"

Kay wipes his hand on a napkin. "Everything. Whatever you want to tell me." He picks up his steno pad and ballpoint pen. "When were you born?"

"The twenty-second of July. In 1896."

He waits to see if Kay writes that down.

"The only son of a divine who was a master at Harrow. The family was full of divines. And military officers. Grandfather was a bishop — Church of England, of course." Whale shifts his gaze out toward the ocean, relaxing into the role. "I was a bit of a rascal when young. In and out of scrapes. I attended Eton — it wouldn't do for a master's son to attend where his father taught. I was to go up to Oxford the year war broke out. The Great War, you know. You had a Good War, but we had a great one."

He glances to see if the boy smiles at the quip, but Kay only continues to write.

"I never did make it to university. I enlisted. After serving as a lieutenant, and spending a year in a prisoner-of-war camp, school seemed redundant." When Whale first came to Hollywood he told people he had actually attended Oxford, until one day a smart-ass screenwriter asked which college.

He pauses so Kay can ask about his experience as a prisoner of war — it wouldn't do to draw too much attention to that oneself. The boy only nods and says, "Go on. I'll catch up."

"It was a source of great shame to the family when I went into the theater after the Armistice. People from good families didn't, you know."

Inventing this life used to give Whale such strange pleasure. As the lies were refined and repeated over the years, he could almost believe that this was his past. But the lies feel different today. Maybe it is the ease with which Kay swallows them, or the fact that Whale has not repeated this fairy tale in such a long time. Perhaps it's an effect of the stroke, unplugging his facility for make-believe. But this pretty story, made from the odds and ends of people he's known and books he's read, doesn't feel as convincing as it once did. It hangs on him like a suit of clothes he's too thin to wear anymore. The truth stands closer to him now, peering over his shoulder.

"You went into the theater," says Kay.

"Yes. I developed a taste for it as a prisoner of war. We had so much time on our hands we engaged in amateur theatricals. The Boche encouraged us, expecting we'd do *Hamlet* or *The Tempest*. The old Germans were very keen on Shakespeare, you know. They were sorely disappointed when our first program was *Charley's Aunt*. Our chaps loved it, but the Huns in the front rows just sat there, Prussian and stone-faced over our silly little farce about an Oxford student in women's clothing."

Again, not so much as a nibble from the boy. Whale skips the war as a lost cause.

"So when I returned" — he loudly clears his throat — "I had been bitten by the theater bug. I wanted to be part of that world. Footlights and make-believe. I began as an actor. I had the looks and made up in eagerness for what I lacked in talent. I joined a small troupe doing the theatrical circuit in the provinces. Leeds, Newcastle, Birmingham, Dudley. A wretched grind of drafty houses, moth-eaten costumes, and equally moth-eaten plays. A slightly desperate, seat-of-your-pants sort of life." He has let the truth into his story, but it doesn't embarrass him as it once did. "It was good for me. A valuable experience. You learn to live with the fickleness of the public, the vicissitudes of fate. You learn to go with the punches. And I met people important to me later in life, including Mr. Ernest Thesiger. He played your Dr. Pretorius in *Bride*, you know. He was Mr. Femm in *The Old Dark House* as well."

Kay's pen scribbles more excitedly.

"Ernest came from a background very different — I mean, similar to my own. Good family, service in the trenches, a spit-in-the-wind attitude about life. Quite a nasty fellow at times, in a droll, withering sort of way. Much like Dr. Pretorius himself. And utterly unashamed about his, uh, eccentricities." No, he won't talk about that, especially since the boy tilts that way himself. "For example, in the theater and later on the movie set, this former company commander would relax by sitting in a corner with needle and thread and quietly embroider."

"What did he embroider?"

"Oh, I don't know. Scarves and such."

"When did he die?"

"He hasn't. At least not that I've heard." The thought that Thesiger may be dead is oddly disturbing to Whale.

"He seems awfully old in your movies."

"Thesiger was born old and desiccated, a bit of a fossil. No, Thesiger will never die."

"Karloff is still alive."

"Yes. I suspect he is."

"But Colin Clive is dead."

"Quite dead." This is a distressing line of talk; Whale irritably pushes past it. "But so I returned to London, a wiser, more seasoned trouper. Roughly around, oh, 1925."

Kay resumes writing, less eagerly than before.

"I continued to perform but understood my limitations. Oh, I was pretty enough. I could play juvenile leads for a few more years, but my days were numbered. Luckily, I had a knack with pencil and paper, an idle hobby in school. I began to design sets, often for the very plays I performed in. It was a gypsy time in London theater, quite slapdash and bohemian. I met Elsa Lanchester then — "

"The Bride!"

"Yes, the Bride. But at that time a cabaret artist. She had danced as a child with — a famous dancer. That American woman. But when I met Elsa, she and a friend ran a little cabaret café called the Cave of Harmony. Just a hole off an alleyway in Soho, but quite charming, quite bohemian. Elsa used to perform there, old comic songs. There was one in particular called" — he smiles as he remembers — "'I Just Danced with a Man Who Danced with the Girl Who Danced with the Prince of Wales.'" He can almost hear Elsa singing, her schoolgirl mouth curling comically above her gums as she mimes the character's ludicrous delirium; he suddenly smells sickly-sweet perfumes and smoking paraffin — the place had been illuminated by candles stuck in wine bottles. "You can't imagine what life was like back then, for someone who'd been through — so much. So much." The rush of emotion takes him by surprise. He hasn't thought about the Cave of Harmony in years. "The twenties in London were like one long bank holiday, a break from everything dour and respectable. The Bright Young Things were out and about. Mitfords and Sitwells and that novelist fellow, Evelyn Waugh. He once came to the café. But all of us, high and low, were happily splashing about. Your latest batch of bohemians, these poets with their bongos and beards, have nothing on us. We had booze and jazz. I never especially liked jazz, but I loved the attitude that came with it. Do what you will and the devil take fuck all." He laughs at the obscenity he let slip. "And Dora. Dora Zinkiesen."

"Is that a name I should know?"

"No. Just a friend. A lovely Scotswoman with whom I danced the tango. At the Cave of Harmony." He remembers in his shoulder muscles the stop-and-go energy of the tango, he and tall Dora darting from pose to pose like two wind-up flamingos. He had loved to dance with Dora, so much that he mistook the tango for love and proposed marriage, which Dora was wise enough to refuse. "But we were all so young. Beautiful, careless, and young. Except for Charles. Gloomy old Charles. Charles Laughton, you know, before he and Elsa were married. He took an immediate dislike to me. I thought it was my vulgar past that made him uncomfortable — he was awfully hoity-toity for someone whose people ran a seaside hotel in Yorkshire. But no, years later, when we'd all gone Hollywood, I understood we had something else in common."

"A friend told me a story about Laughton," Kay offers, with a sly wiggle of eyebrows.

"Yes, there are several young men in this city with stories to tell." Whale frowns to signal that he does not need to hear another. "I was his son in a play called *The Man with Red Hair*, whose set I designed. I was the stage manager too. Difficult man to act with. You never knew what he was going to do next. Which can be marvelous for a real actor, keeping you on your toes, but I'd come to the conclusion I was not a real actor. I did less acting after that, more designing, and finally a little directing. I was hired to design the set for a play called *Journey's End*. Nobody expected much of it. The thing had been written by an insurance clerk, Bob Sherriff, a sweet if oblivious fellow. He had the broadest shoulders and smallest derriere of any man I've known. He was a rowing chap, one of those sports who mess about in boats, and lived happily with his mother. Still does, last I heard. But Bob wrote the play for his rowing club to perform to raise funds for new boats. They wouldn't touch it. It was too morbid, too sad. The whole thing took place in a dugout in the trenches. No singing, no dancing, no roles for pretty girls. I thought it a beautiful play. Every experienced director they approached turned it down. Not commercial, too much work for too little reward. I offered myself, bullying and begging that I could do it. And I did. *Journey's End*, to the surprise of everyone, myself included, was a huge success. It made the careers of all who were associated with it."

"I've never heard of it."

"That doesn't surprise me. Although it was also my first motion picture, you know."

"How much longer before we get to *Frankenstein?*"

The bored whine of the question startles Whale. He glances at the steno pad to see what the boy has written. He cannot read shorthand, but Kay seems to have recorded little since Whale last looked. "Sheriff is spelled double *r*, double *f*."

But even with Whale watching him, Kay doesn't write; he hasn't included Bob at all.

"Am I correct in assuming, Mr. Kay, that it's not me you're interested in, but only my horror pictures?"

The boy becomes flustered. "Oh no, I want to hear everything. I just didn't think most of that important enough to write down."

"I see."

He took such joy in remembering his London days that it hurts to think it was all idle chatter to his interviewer. What had he expected? The interest of posterity in a child with bangs? Someone who'd be as eager to hear about his life as David was when they first met? He has not told anyone his whole true story since he shared it with David.

"You must understand, Mr. Kay. The horror pictures were trifles. Entertainments. Grand guignol for the masses. The film I am proud of is *Show Boat*. With Paul Robeson and Helen Morgan."

Kay looks shocked. "*Show Boat* is great. But . . . you can't really believe that, Mr. Whale. Your horror films are classics. Everybody knows them."

When people praise his horror pictures, Whale fears they are being condescending. When they dismiss them as trash, however, he feels hurt and insulted. "Yes. They certainly have a life of their own. They've gone on without me."

"But you should be remembered too. I remember you. That's why I'm here. I want to hear about the man who made *Frankenstein*."

"Who did other things with his life as well."

"Sure. But it's the horror movies you'll be remembered for."

Whale's change of mood, the anger and resentment following his joy, is so abrupt it feels insane. "I am not dead, Mr. Kay."

"No. I never said you were. Or will be soon," he adds, without conviction.

Whale feels an inexplicable hatred for the boy. He fights it by concentrating on his youth, his delicate hands, his turned-up nose. Not beautiful, but not unattractive. Years ago in London, meeting such a fellow backstage or at the Cave of Harmony, Whale would overcome his feelings of resentment and challenge by going to bed with him. Sex was a great equalizer, if only for ten to thirty minutes. But sex has remained off in the distance since his return from the hospital. The idea of feeling lust for this boy is like glimpsing something at the bottom of a well.

"But *Journey's End*," Kay asks. "You were going to tell about making it as your first movie." He leans over the steno pad, determined to be more worthy.

"I have a proposal, Mr. Kay. This mode of question and answer is getting old, don't you think?"

"I don't mind."

"I do. I need to make it more interesting. And it'll enable you to distinguish between what you find necessary and what you find trivial. I will truthfully answer any question you ask. But in return, for each answer, you must remove one article of clothing."

Kay's little mouth pops open. He laughs, not his girlish giggle but a single guffaw that catches on itself like a cough. "That's funny, Mr. Whale."

"It is, isn't it?" Whale agrees. "My life in a game of strip poker. A biographical striptease." He feels better already. "Shall we play?"

"You're serious."

"Quite."

Kay glances around, needing a witness to confirm that the old man really proposed this. He peers at Whale from the corner of his eye. "Then the rumors are true?"

"What rumors might those be, Mr. Kay?"

"That you were forced to retire because, uh — a sex scandal."

"A homosexual scandal, you mean? I think we can call a spade a spade, now that we understand each other. But for me to answer a question of that magnitude, you'll have to remove both your shoes and your socks."

Kay just sits there, squinting and smirking. Whale wonders if he will pass on this question and try another, or simply end the interview. There's a screech as Kay pushes the cast-iron chair across the flagstones. "You're a dirty old man," he declares with a grin, and bends over to remove his argyle socks. He's already kicked off his penny loafers.

"You are kind to indulge your elders in their vices," Whale declares. "As I indulge the young in theirs."

Two pale feet with neatly trimmed nails emerge; the big toe of his right foot fidgets and flicks against the second toe.

Whale has leaned forward to examine them. He leans back again. "No. There was no scandal." And he reaches into his coat for a cigar, letting the boy stew in the possibility that this is all he will say on the matter.

Kay waits, nervously covering one foot with the other.

Whale slices a neat hole at the base of the cigar with his penknife, then lights the cigar with a wooden match, sucking and rotating until the tip is roundly lit. Clouds of blue smoke drift out across the swimming pool.

"Ah. My only other vice," he explains, and smiles at Kay. "I suppose you'd like a fuller answer to your question?"

Kay nods.

"I was bored." He perches an elbow on the back of his chair and holds the cigar at a rakish angle. "That's why I quit. Nothing more. I was bored with my assignments. Which were nothing but tripe. I'd made enemies at the studio, and they punished me by handing down worse and worse assignments. Until finally, in the middle of a loathsome picture titled *They Dare Not Love* — and no, my dear Kay, it had nothing to do with the love that dare not speak its name — I walked. I packed it in. I'd been saving up my berries for quite some time and didn't need to suffer their drear routine another single day."

"Did you make enemies because of your, uh, private life?"

"Because I was a pansy? Not at all. A full answer to that question, Mr. Kay, will cost you your sweater. I do hope you're wearing a vest today. If not, we'll break the bank very soon."

Kay hesitates a moment, then sets his pen aside to pull his sweater up over his head. "Too warm for a sweater," he claims. His sleeveless T-shirt displays a pattern of freckles across his shoulders. He brushes his hair forward before he takes up his pen again.

"You must understand how Hollywood was twenty years ago. Nobody cared a tinker's cuss who slept with whom, so long as you kept it out of the papers. And that was true only for the stars. A character actor? A writer? A director? To care about our behavior would have been like worrying over the morals of a plumber before letting him mend your pipes. Outside of Hollywood, who knows who George Cukor is, much less gives two spits about what he does with those boys his pals bring home from the malt shops along Santa Monica? We directors, we artistic types, were already looked upon as freaks. Nothing we did surprised the people in the front office."

Kay is staring at him in disbelief. "George Cukor? Who made *A Star Is Born*? You mean — "

"As gay as a goose," says Whale, always happy to take another swipe at Cukor. "A close friend of mine was his associate producer on *Camille*. Two of a kind, and nobody batted an eye. And when you toss Garbo into the soup as well . . ."

Kay is still too stunned by the first revelation even to hear the second one. "George Cukor! I never guessed."

"We are new to the life, aren't we, Mr. Kay? You haven't heard about George's notorious Sunday brunches? Gatherings of trade. Eating the leftovers from his oh-so-proper Saturday dinner parties. His pals regularly bring him fresh bodies, since Georgie-Porgie can't seem to keep a boyfriend."

But Kay doesn't laugh or sneer in disgust. He only nods to himself, amazed by his discovery.

"If a goat like that can continue about his business, my more domestic arrangement could've raised very few eyebrows." Whale fears his envy has peeked out; he won't say another word about Cukor. "This same close friend insists things are different now. David was always a puritan, but attitudes do seem changed since the war. Along with McCarthy and the Red Scare a few years back, there was a kind of Lavender Scare. Masculinity is all the rage now, not just in actors but in the people who work with them. You can't have a fellow like Alan Ladd being directed by a fairy. We'll spoil his red-blooded manliness. The fact is, there's nobody like a fairy for distinguishing real masculinity from the wooden variety now in vogue. But in 1941, when I walked, my hint of mint was not an issue."

"Then why did you have enemies at the studio?"

He thinks a moment. "Maybe it wasn't so much the presence of enemies as an absence of friends. I was lucky my first years at Universal. The Laemmles, father and son, Carl and Junior, indulged me. They gave me full approval on scripts, they let me improvise on the set, they stayed out of my hair. In return I gave them pictures that made heaps of money. The fact is, they didn't know the first thing about moviemaking. Laemmle Senior was a

short, sweet, chatty German Jew whom everyone called Uncle
Carl. Universal *was* a family affair. Uncle Carl filled the lot with
relatives from the Old Country, most of whom could barely speak
English. Junior could be the dullest fellow on earth, but he understood that I knew more than he did, so we worked well together.
All went smoothly, until they lost the studio. Uncle Carl had ne-
gotiated a loan with a bank back east. If a certain sum weren't
repaid by a certain date, then the bank could buy the Laemmles
out. The old fox thought this bank wouldn't be able to raise the
money for the purchase, but, for the first time in his life, he was
wrong."

He has not thought about the Laemmles in years; he suddenly
misses them, and not just because of the turn of his career.

"There was a rumor," he admits, "that they needed the money
because I'd gone over budget on *Show Boat*. Utter nonsense. They
were hard up because that prima donna of prestige pictures, John
Stahl, made a royal balls-up of *Magnificent Obsession*, shooting
hours of film with no end in sight. But suddenly, the Laemmles
were gone, replaced by people who knew just as little, but who
had no inkling how little they knew. They let me have my way for
another picture or two, until we made one called *The Road Back*.
Do you know it?"

Kay shakes his head.

"Do you know the novel? Sequel to *All Quiet on the Western
Front* by Erich Remarque."

Again Kay shakes his head.

Whale is so involved in explaining himself that he's forgotten
their game. "Take off your vest and I'll tell a story."

Kay nervously plucks at it, glancing toward the house.

"Don't be shy. There's time to stop before you go too far."

"Oh. I guess." Kay peels the shirt up, from the neck, and tosses
it on his shoes and sweater. His pouter pigeon chest is covered in

freckles, with two brown nipples and not a trace of hair. "Was *The Road Back* a horror movie?" he asks hopefully.

"Not at all. Horror pictures were a thing of the past by now. I'd done *Show Boat*. Major success. Great box office. But now I was to do something important, an indictment of the Great War and what it did to Germany. A remarkable story with remarkable people involved. I brought Bob Sherriff back over to write the script. It was my masterpiece, better than *Western Front*, better than anything Cukor ever did." Had it been a masterpiece? Whale wants to believe it was but knows he cannot be sure.

"Why haven't I heard of it?" asks Kay.

"Because the studio, or rather, the bank that now called itself a studio, butchered it." His headache, always present, flickers with sparks and splinters brought on by anger. "They cut away the guts and brought in another director to add slapstick, for fear the truth might depress the public. And they were afraid they'd lose their German market. The Boche consul in Los Angeles had been making a fuss ever since work began on the picture. Remarque's novels had been banned by the Nazis, publicly burned in their literary bonfires. They certainly didn't want this story seen by moviegoers around the world. And the bankers, those foolish, petty money people, caved in. They let the Nazis have their way, claiming the changes would improve the box office. And it still laid an egg. A great expensive bomb. For which I was blamed. After that, nothing went right for me at Universal. Nothing."

"You couldn't have gone to another studio?"

"I could. I did. Loaned out for this picture or that. But I'd stopped caring. I'd given them my best and it was rejected. All I wanted was to gather up my berries and spend my time making pictures alone — painted pictures. Like Winston Churchill."

"You stayed here during the war? You didn't go home?"

Whale has always hated this question, whether it came from

countrymen or Americans. It is especially infuriating coming from this child. A tightening of muscles behind his eyes increases his headache. "Take off your trousers," he tells Kay.

Kay smiles, lowers his head, and says, "Never mind. I'm saving these for something I really want to know."

"Ah, the stakes have become higher. You have to be more selective in the cards you play." But Whale needs to explain why he stayed. "There was no reason to go home. What could I do? Offer myself to the RAF? Man an antiaircraft gun during the Blitz? No, I'd have been just another potential casualty. I had offered myself as a casualty to Mother England for one war. I felt perfectly justified in sitting out the next."

Kay takes a deep, bored breath. "Can we talk about the horror movies now?"

The slightest irritation tightens the threads and knots of pain in his skull. He desperately needs his guest to distract him from this hurt. "Certainly, Mr. Kay. Is there anything in particular you want to know? So badly that we'll be able to get you out of your britches?"

"You really want to go on with this?"

"Of course. Don't feel shy if your linen isn't clean. Although I understand women in this country tell their daughters they must always wear clean underwear, because you never know if you'll be hit by a car. The same should be true for curious boys who visit lonely old movie directors." He draws a hot mouthful from his cigar for dramatic effect, then opens his jaw and sets the smoke free, watching the small cloud slowly somersault from the shadow of the umbrella into the sunlight, curling and scrolling upon itself in elaborate arabesques — like the pinching convolutions of his own brain. He has to close his eyes so he won't feel sick.

"Will you tell me everything you remember about making *Frankenstein*?" asks Kay. "Can that count as one question?"

"Perhaps," says Whale, opening his eyes and seeing Kay. "Oh, of course. Why not?" He'll still have the *Bride* to get the boy out of his knickers.

"I can't believe I'm doing this. But —" Kay stands to unbuckle his belt, glancing around the yard again. His freckles are mixed with little matte goose bumps. "I do this all the time at the dorm or gym. It's doing it in front of somebody famous that makes it creepy." But he has already unzipped and is stepping out of the sharply creased flannel legs. His thighs are pale and skinny; white BVDs swaddle his hips like a bandage. "Just like I'm going to go swimming, isn't it?" he mutters as he lowers the trousers on top of his other clothes. A whey-colored eye peeks through a hole in his seat as he bends over.

"Maybe you would like a swim when we're through?" Whale gently suggests. He suddenly regrets putting the boy through this, especially since seeing Kay in scanties gives him so little pleasure.

Kay sits down again, scrapes his chair up to the table, and leans forward. His shoulders bunch behind him like vulture wings. "Okay. *Frankenstein*. Tell me everything." Undressing has made him arrogant and demanding.

"Righto. *Frankenstein*. Yes. Let me see." But returning to his thoughts brings Whale back into his headache. It is as though a nail has been driven into the base of his skull, one intense pain echoed by a chorus of smaller pains. "*Dracula*, you know. Universal had a big success with *Dracula*. They wanted another project for La—? Lou? Lay—?"

"Lugosi?"

"Of course, Bela Lugosi." He's angry he couldn't remember something so simple. "They conceived the project for him, and somebody else was to direct. That frog. Florey. Yes, Robert Florey began it. But the studio wanted me for another story, and wanted me so baldly — I mean badly, not baldly. I was given the pick of stories being developed. And I picked that one, snatching it from under that silly frog's nose."

"You stole somebody else's idea?"

He hadn't meant to tell Kay that, but the headache leaves him no room to say anything except the truth. "Happens all the time in the studios. Florey would have made a hash of it. He shot tests. Looked ridiculous. Lugosi with a ton of clay packed around his head. Like that children's doll with a potato for a head."

"Mr. Potato Head?"

"He was supposed to be a golem but looked instead like Mr. Potato Head." Whale finds it more difficult to feel his way to the words he needs. "And then La-la-la-gosi" — he hopes that sounds like a joke and not a speech impediment — "refused to do the part. No more monsters. That's what he said. And he did not want to play a monster who couldn't t-t-talk. So I was free to pick my own monster. And I picked a contract player named Karloff."

Kay is writing quickly, eagerly, paying no attention to the sputters and erratic tones of Whale's speech.

"You may have heard of him." A bit of sarcasm should disguise his condition. "English. Real name — Pratt? I don't know who called him Karloff instead. He was playing mostly gangsters when I cast him."

"Who came up with his makeup and look?"

"My idea. Muchly. My sketches. Big heavy brow. Head flat on top so they could take out the old brain and put in the new, like tinned beef." How he longs to do that with his own. "And the makeup artist. Terrific man, very clever. Jack? Jack Pierce. He did good stuff. Brilliantly good. The electrodes on the neck? Those were his. We couldn't decide what to do with the eyes. Karloff's eyes were soulful, but intelligent. Too intelligent. Finally we melted wax on the eyelids, for a heavy, imbecilic look. Heavy shoes with foot-high soles. Padding. Heaps of padding. So much, poor Boris couldn't sit between takes. Someone rigged a plank he could lean against. With armrests. We used to prop the Monster there between takes and give him his tea. Which he had to sip very daintily so as not to spoil his scars."

"He's one of the great images of the twentieth century," Kay declares. "As important as the Mona Lisa."

"You think so? That's very kind of you." Stumbling through the briers and barbed wire of the headache, Whale catches up with what the boy just said. "Oh no. Don't be ridiculous. Just makeup and padding and a large actor. Hardly the Mona Lisa."

"But it's as familiar now, as famous."

"So is Adolf Hitler. So is M-m-mickey Mouse." He has to become angry to get the name out. "Definitely not the — "

His hand is suddenly empty. He clutches at the air, twice, and remembers he'd been holding a cigar. He looks down and sees it on the flagstones, flakes of ash crumbled open like petals around the ember.

"Colin Clive as the doctor. Where did you find him?"

Whale bends down to retrieve his cigar — and the change of gravity drives the spike through his skull.

For a split second, as if in a flash of light, everything else disappears. There is only a sensation so intense it can't register as pain until the shock of it passes. He freezes, stunned by the first shock, terrified there will be another, slowly understanding that he's still in great pain and that it feels like peace only in comparison to what preceded it. Is this death? He wants death to save him from the next bolt of lightning, the next artillery shell screaming toward him, until he remembers what death means and thinks: No, not yet, not yet.

"Colin Clive, Mr. Whale. How did you cast him?"

Whale turns his head toward the froggy voice, and sees the boy sitting at the table in BVDs. "Take them off," he whispers. "Quickly."

"No! We haven't finished *Frankenstein*."

"Please. Now." He fears he will lose consciousness, will black out and never be conscious again. It seems fitting that the last thing he'll ever see should be a naked man, even one who's not his type. Which is ridiculous. He cannot die. Not yet. "Never — ," he whispers. "Excuse me. I must go lie — " He forces himself up with one hand pushing against a cast-iron arm.

Kay bounces his chair back, ready to run if the old man pounces. But then he sees Whale's face, the colorless lips, the desperate eyes. "Mr. Whale? You all right?"

"I just need to — lie down. Studio. Daybed in the studio." He feels his way around the table, breathing deeply, straining to exhale the pain and save himself from death.

A scrawny angel with a pigeon chest and no wings stands two yards away, frightened of him. Not until Whale lurches from the table does Kay jump forward, catching him under an arm.

"Oh my God. What's wrong, Mr. Whale? Is it your heart?"

"Head. Not right. Not right." There is an instant of comfort when he feels another body against his side, but it's a small body, a weak one. He's afraid to rest his full weight against it. "In the studio. Help me there. Please."

The single blast of pain has left him weak and helpless. The memory of it nauseates him. He is afraid he will vomit on the boy or forget his bowels and soil himself. "Forgive me," he whispers. "Forgive me."

Kay steers them through the door into the cool darkness of the studio. He sits Whale on the sticky leather of the daybed and eases his head against a bolster. He follows Whale's pointed finger to the intercom and presses the buzzer.

"Yes, Mr. Jimmy?" The voice is full of static.

"An emergency! Mr. Whale's had an attack! Call an ambulance! Call the doctor!"

"No bloody doctor!" Whale snarls. "Tell her to bring my pills. My painkillers." The thought of a doctor and ambulance sickens him more than the idea of death. He refuses to go back to hospital. He cannot return to that white hell so soon after he escaped it.

The boy rapidly relays the instructions, his cheek pressed against the intercom.

The pain grows more familiar, less terrifying. It continues to sicken him but no longer feels like death.

"Nothing," says Whale when Kay kneels by the daybed. "This is nothing. Sorry to panic you. Only a headache. A terrible megrim." He lies with his head on the bolster, both feet on the floor. Kay moves to raise the feet. "Don't! Blood to my head. Blood makes it worse."

The boy stands back, wrapping his arms around his chest and rubbing them, as if to rub away the touch of sickness.

Gravel scatters outside as Maria comes running down the path. She swings open the screen door — and freezes when she sees Kay. Her little frown tightens. She catches sight of Whale on the daybed and snaps back to life. "Water," she tells Kay. "Glasses at the sink." She goes to Whale, scooping different bottles from the pocket of her apron. "Which one? I bring them all. This one, yes?" She holds the prescription up for Whale to read. He nods and she empties two capsules into her palm. Whale tilts them into his mouth and takes the glass of water Kay passes over her shoulder. The water is cool in his mouth, painful in the throat, nauseating in his stomach. The capsules won't take effect for several minutes, but to know that pain will pass makes pain bearable.

He lies there, catching his breath after the exertion of swallowing. Maria has recovered from her panic and stands above him, stiff and censorious. With her round face, tight hair, and imperious little chins, she looks like Queen Victoria. The guest for afternoon tea peers around her in his underpants.

"Mr. Kay," Whale declares in feigned surprise. "You're not dressed."

"Oh! I was — we were — " Kay frantically crosses arms over his chest and middle, blushing pinkly from his forehead down to his nipples. "I was going to swim!" he tells Maria.

Maria cuts her eyes at her employer.

"Yes, I suggested a swim," Whale declares. "I'm sorry I spoiled it for you, Mr. Kay. You should probably go home."

"Yes. Right. I'm going." Kay hurries outside to where he left his clothes.

And Whale feels better, as if the boy's presence had created this pain, although he understands that what lifted was merely his shame over Kay witnessing his helplessness.

Maria bends down to undo Whale's bow tie. She makes no attempt to be gentle.

"You must think I'm terrible, Maria."

"I do not think you anything anymore, Mr. Jimmy." Then she adds, "I think you are a crazy. Just back from the hospital and already you are chasing after boys."

"All we did was talk. We were having a little talking game. My attack had nothing to do with him. It might have happened if I were watching television."

"Hmmmph." She has lifted his shoulders to pull his jacket off. "How is your head? We should get you uphill before the pills knock you cold. Maybe your boy can help?"

Whale winces. "No. We should send him home. He's seen enough for one day."

"Don't be ridiculous. I cannot get you up the hill alone. You are not ashamed of your monkey business, but you are too proud to let this boy see you sick?"

"You're right, Maria. Always right," he says with a sigh. "Let me lie here a moment longer. Ask him to give you a hand." There is still pain, seams of ache beneath his scalp growing smudged and indistinct as the barbiturates take effect. In another minute the shame of having the boy see his helplessness will be smoothed away as well.

"Boy! Oh, boy!" he hears Maria call as she steps outside and goes to Kay. They speak softly out there. Whale cannot make out the words.

Portions of consciousness wink out as the pills take effect, his hard emotions first, then the gentler ones. Whale remembers feeling great pleasure at one point this afternoon. Over what? The Cave of Harmony. But more than his nostalgia for that, there was a feeling that he has whole worlds inside him, forgotten worlds that would die with him. He would die, wouldn't he? Death is the only alternative he can imagine to such pain and helplessness. The narcotic stillness stealing over him isn't peace. But he doesn't want death either. Not yet. Not yet. Only what does he need before this "yet" becomes acceptable? Fame and recognition? Late wisdom over the meaning of it all? The chance to see one more naked man? Only the last item is likely, but all seem poor trades for oblivion.

"Ups-a-daisy, Mr. Jimmy. We go now."

"I got him on this side. You okay, Mr. Whale?"

A boy and a woman stand on either side and lead him toward the door. The light ahead is shockingly bright. He closes his eyes and walks in slow motion through a red landscape without trees or grass, only mud that reduces his walk to a drunken stumble over a featherbed.

"When you're better, Mr. Whale, can we finish the interview?"

"Quite," Whale mumbles in answer to a half-heard question

about an inner-view. What is an inner-view? Another new invention like tele-vision?

The long, dreamlike walk up the hill is interminable. He grows impatient with the diminutive fellows propping him on either side. He is afraid they won't reach their lines before nightfall. He longs for someone large and strong to do the job quickly, someone who can cradle him in his arms and take him home, an athlete of death who'd carry him as easily as his monster once carried Mae Clarke off into the night.

ARSON

From the moment I learned about come-as-you-are parties, I wanted to throw one. Birthday parties, picnics, and costume balls paled in comparison. I couldn't shake the image of people — relatives, teachers, friends from junior high — converging on my house in candid states of dress. I pictured them coming from all directions, from apartments and parks and places of business, drawn from every type of routine. One person lifted a cold forkful of dinner to his lips. Another raised a flyswatter, though a fly was nowhere in sight. The vain cashier from Woolworth's wore curlers. The authoritarian crossing guard was wrapped in a baby-blue bath towel. Propriety, modesty, and just plain embarrassment made them move as slowly as sleepwalkers, and still they came, some of them grumbling, some of them pointing with glee at one another, a dowdy battalion in underwear and housecoats who forged through the city streets toward my door.

The image of this party was so vivid and gratifying that several times a day, I imagined picking up the telephone and dialing prospective guests. "Hello," I'd intone, as though nothing were out of the ordinary. And then I'd blurt the startling news, "I'm having a come-as-you-are party!" I suppose it was a kind of egotism or wishfulness to assume that people, regardless of their outfit or grooming, would drop what they were doing and appear in public, shedding their inhibitions just for me.

In retrospect, I can't help but see this obsession as the odd blossom of my loneliness. My mother was preoccupied with housework, my father with the practice of law. Most of the neighborhood kids were on vacation or attending summer school. The light that summer was direct and unrelenting, the afternoons vast. Left to my own devices, steeped in a restless imagination, my solitude was nearly constant.

The come-as-you-are feeling often welled up in me as I was getting ready for bed, brushing my teeth or staring at my naked body in the bathroom mirror. What, I wondered, were other people doing or feeling at that moment? Were they mesmerized by the weight of their limbs, by the heat of their skin, by the sight of their wrinkled genitalia? Why did my particular mind exist in my particular body? It was difficult to believe that anyone else beheld themselves with such abject and melancholy astonishment. In the bright isolation of the bathroom, as the neighborhood around me settled into the anonymity and silence of the night, I most desperately wanted a glimpse into the privacy of others.

That summer I began making regular visits to the model homes of Los Feliz Estates, a nearby tract in the Hollywood Hills. None of the real estate agents seemed to notice or mind a thirteen-year-old wandering through the rooms. Sometimes there would be a lull in the number of prospective buyers and I would find myself virtually alone, able to part the drapes or furtively flush a toilet. But no act thrilled me as much as coaxing open a desk or bureau drawer. I knew these houses didn't belong to anyone real. I understood that the rooms were furnished to give the illusion of home. Yet every time I opened a drawer — heart

racing, breath held in check — I expected to find some contra-
band, some evidence of a stranger's life: a rubber, a Tampax, a
diary, money stuffed in a sock. What I found instead was emptiness and the faint, escaping scent of wood.

In the bottom drawer of the built-in bureau in my bedroom, I
kept hidden a small collection of pornography, magazines with
almost apologetically innocent names like *Pony Boys!* and *Buddies*.
The young men between the covers, with their glistening pecto-
rals, backs, and thighs, appeared to have been marinated in oil.
One sunned on a rock. Another sprawled on a plaid couch, his
nakedness accentuated by the banality of his surroundings. A few
studio shots featured moody lighting and classical props — a plaster column, a Grecian urn — and in case there remained any
question of artistic intent, each model's crotch was sheathed in a
loincloth. Only rarely were two men shown in the same photograph, and even then they never touched; any heated contact between them was something the viewer inferred. For the most part,
each man waited for admiration on his solitary page. Arms tensed,
stomachs sucked in, they invited the camera's scrutiny. Their bra-
zenness excited me as much as their physiques.

Not a day went by without my fretting that the magazines, and
therefore my desire for men, might be discovered. Finding a fool-
proof hiding place became nothing short of a criminal pursuit,
and before I'd finally decided on the bottom drawer of the built-
in bureau, my illicit library had been wedged beneath the mattress
and stashed in an old Monopoly box. No sooner would I find a
new hiding place than I'd picture that place being violated. Suppose my mother decided to air the mattress one day? Suppose
my father got the urge to play Monopoly? The dread of being
discovered seeped into my dreams; I'd be blithely chatting with
a policeman, say, when I'd realize to my horror that instead

of wearing my usual clothes, I was wearing the pages of *Pony Boys!*.

Eventually, even the drawer of the built-in bureau seemed like a risky hiding place, and I thought it might be safer to keep the magazines *behind* the drawer. I took hold of the brass knobs and slid the drawer out with the stealth of a burglar, nervous that my mother, puttering in the kitchen directly below, might hear me and become suspicious. It's entirely possible that I took further precautions, like locking my bedroom door or turning on the transistor radio, so thoroughly did the fear of exposure control me like a marionette in those days. My anticipation mounted as the lowest drawer inched toward me on its tracks. When it finally popped out of the wall and landed with a muffled thud on the carpet, it left behind a rectangular hole. I bent down, peered inside. It was as if I'd pulled back the skin of the house and could glimpse the bones and organs within. Two-by-fours and rolls of tar paper lined the floor. Here and there, drips of plaster and paint were preserved in a secret museum. Dry rot had turned patches of wood velvety and uneven. The surface of a pipe a few feet away glinted in the sudden flood of sunlight, and from it issued the sound of water like a sudden rush of breath.

From then on, every time I removed the drawer and reached for my cache of naked men, I saw the darkness at the core of our house and suddenly doubted the white walls, the tidy rooms in which I lived.

To be homosexual was to invite ostracism and ridicule, and I would have done just about anything to escape my need to masturbate to images of men. I bargained with myself, made promises not to, devised equations of abstinence and reward. *Today is Monday; if you don't touch yourself till Saturday, you can go to Woolworth's and buy that model of a sixty-five Corvette.* But no sooner would I muster my resolve than I'd find myself in a haze of amnesia, a couple of magazines spread before me, opened to my favorite pages. Sometimes it seemed that the only antidote for constant shame was the forgetfulness of orgasm, my body crumpled in a fit of overflowing, every sensation obliterated except for pleasure.

In an effort to control once and for all my helplessness in the face of lust, I retrieved from the same bureau where I stashed the magazines a pair of plastic handcuffs I hadn't played with in years. Somehow, I got the idea to hook them to my wrists whenever the impulse to masturbate was about to overwhelm me. The reasoning that followed my literal self-restraint went something like this: *OK. You've done everything you possibly can to prevent it. If it happens, it happens, and you can't blame yourself.* And then I went at it while wearing the handcuffs. In this way I policed my own desire, kept guilt and shame at bay with a toy, and stroked myself with impunity. But it wasn't long before this ritual lost its power to ease my conscience, and soon I started to feel absurd, as though I were wearing a set of matching bracelets, and the plastic links seemed pitiful and weak, and I imagined someone barging in my room and finding a boy, bound by the wrists, unable to resist himself.

I bought the pornography at a store that sold candy, key chains, batteries, dusty artificial flowers, and tabloids in foreign languages. I discovered it by accident one afternoon while walking up and down Western Avenue in search of a Mother's Day card. The place was run by a woman whose eyes, magnified by thick glasses, seemed to follow you wherever you went like the gaze in certain portraits. Her eyes were deceptive, though, because she never seemed to care what happened in her store. Perched atop a stool behind the counter, she rarely moved except to sigh, her posture wilted by boredom. There were times I thought it would be a breeze to sneak past her into the alcove that contained the pornography and simply steal the magazines I wanted. That way

I wouldn't have to endure the humiliation of having to buy them, terrified she might ask my age, my hands shaking as I counted out change. Instead, I tried to ignore her, to act nonchalant as I strode toward the shelf where women licked their lips and played with their nipples. My habit was to peruse at least one or two of the girlie magazines before I moved on. I flipped through a blur of bleached hair, arched backs, and breasts rising from frothy lace bras. I probably even convinced myself that, blood humming from sheer fright, I was actually kind of excited by women, but drawn to men just a little more. Once I'd looked at girlie magazines long enough to give the impression — to whom, I wonder, since there was rarely another customer in sight — of genuine interest, I'd drift toward the rack where I invariably wanted the first magazine I laid eyes on. Whoever was on the cover — a man washing his car in the nude, sweat beading on his tattooed chest, soapy water dripping down the fenders — he was too beautiful a vision to contain. I couldn't look for long before my mouth went dry and my skin began to itch.

The mechanics of the sale were clouded by panic. But the last thing I saw before I left the store were the big omniscient eyes of the proprietress, like the eyes of God, brilliant with judgment, peering from a mortal's head.

Back in the silence and privacy of my room, I noticed that one corner of the brown paper bag that held my purchase was moist and soft from the sweat from my palm, as though it had turned to suede. Only then would it occur to me how ferociously I must have hugged, gripped, shifted the package from hand to hand as I hurried home, frightened the bag might rip wide open, afraid I'd run into someone I knew. Sitting cross-legged on the floor, I extracted the magazine from its wrapping and turned the pages, only a little more calmly than I had in the store. Once I'd gained an overall sense of the contents — how many men were featured, were they smooth or hirsute, husky or thin, was there some sort of story or theme involved? — I began again from the first page. This time I went more slowly, evaluating, savoring, finally choosing the most beautiful man as though I were holding a harem. By then I couldn't stand more excitement and, faint from the whole clandestine ordeal, peeled off my pants. Climax came quickly, and the instant it did, the mass and shadow of the model's physique seemed to bloom into three dimensions, and my own body, in a fever-dream of want, became more real along with his.

After masturbation there was room for remorse; it flooded in to take the place of satisfaction. Every time I so much as glanced at one of those magazines my appetite for men was confirmed, and it stung me to think that the price I'd have to pay was the world's condemnation. How could such an awful penalty result from such exquisite sensation? I can't, to this day, imagine what childhood would have been like without the need for secrecy, and the constant vigilance secrecy requires. The elaborate strategies, psychic acrobatics. You ache for a way to make sense of your nature. You dive headlong into the well of yourself. And no matter what plans you hatch, promises you make, no matter what you do to erase your desire, you feel incorrigible and aberrant before you even know the meaning of the words. Every day you await disgrace. You look for an ally and do not find one, because to find one would mean you had told. You pretend to be a person you are not, then worry that your pretense is obvious, as vulnerable to taunts as the secret itself. In a desperate attempt at self-protection, you shrink yourself down to nearly nothing, and still you are there, closed as a stone.

One Saturday toward the end of summer, a few days before school started, my parents were invited to a brunch in Orange County. My mother baked a chicken breast and left it in the refrigerator in case I got hungry while they were gone. My father cleaned out the car and checked the yard a couple of times to make sure he'd turned off the sprinklers. They departed with an unusual amount of ceremony, telling me they might not be back till late, asking me if I'd be OK. This show of concern might have been what made their leaving seem especially momentous. And opportune. Seconds after the Oldsmobile pulled out of the driveway, it occurred to me that I could purge my life of tempting possessions. Start from scratch in the eighth grade. Wipe clean the slate of longing.

Most of the bonfires I'd seen were from beach blanket movies, teenagers doing the twist and the watusi while flames raged and crackled on the sand. A bonfire seemed as effective a way as any to do the job; heat would scorch the photographs, turn the pages to flecks of ash. My first thought was to set the fire in the middle of the backyard, away from the plump hibiscus bushes and wooden lawn chairs. But the grass was still wet from the sprinklers and I figured the flames wouldn't take. I could grill each magazine on the barbecue, then pour the ashes into a trash can. But suppose a neighbor poked his head above the fence to see what curious meat was cooking. The whole outdoors seemed too . . . overt. I needed a more protected place.

The garage made sense mostly because my father's car was no longer in it, and it seemed logical — if a boy's tormented, over-eager inspiration could be called logical — to take advantage of the Oldsmobile's absence. The floor of the garage was cement, after all, and wouldn't burn. I could close the heavy wooden doors, yet still see what I was doing because of the two small windows on opposite walls. Except for my father's workbench and the Kenmore freezer my mother no longer used, the high-ceilinged garage was practically empty.

Match; magazines; empty garage! I waited fifteen or twenty

minutes to make sure my parents were good and gone. As I walked from room to room, the house seemed huge and plush with quiet — and I grew more resolute with every step.

When the moment was right, I dashed upstairs with a grocery bag and yanked the drawer out with such force it slammed into my knees. I groped around, grabbed the seven or eight magazines I owned, and crammed them into the bag. Should someone see me in my journey across the narrow breezeway that separated the house from the garage, I could tell them I was taking out the trash. On my way to the back door, I stopped at the kitchen cabinet where my mother kept a veritable gallery of ashtrays — weird shapes like glass taffy — and several boxes of wooden matches. I snatched an entire box, but made a mental note of its exact position on the shelf so that I could replace it without causing suspicion. How proud I was of my foresight, glad that my knack for deception had finally come in handy.

Standing inside the garage, facing outward to pull closed the double doors, I could see the crest of the Hollywood Hills rising against the horizon. In the midday sun, the windows of distant houses glowed like yellow embers. As soon as the doors were shut, the cavernous room grew sheltered and cool. I waited for my eyes to adjust, and then my renewal was under way. I piled the magazines in the middle of the room where puddles of oil, left by the Oldsmobile, stained the floor; in the dim light, they looked deep and primeval as pools of tar. I paused a moment to contemplate how best to start the fire, and it was then I noticed the men at my feet, their bodies seductive, tight, exciting. But I'd gone too far to stop what I was doing. When I struck the match on the side of the box, the rasp and stench of sulfur made me shudder.

For the first second, everything went according to plan. Touching a match to the first magazine, I felt a sense of profound relief that I wouldn't know again until years later when I actually touched a man. The *s* at the end of *Pony Boys!* caught fire and flared, igniting in turn another magazine on which a sailor wore only bell-bottom trousers. I thought he too would go up in flames, but instead, a trail of smoke curled lazily and disappeared. The fire went out before it had begun, and I had to rethink my approach.

On his cluttered workbench, my father stored the can of lighter fluid he used to start the barbecue charcoal; I found it without the slightest trouble, as though some prodding, superior force had placed it smack in my path. I removed the cap, aimed the metal spout toward the pile of pornography (which seemed to grow larger the longer it took to destroy) and squeezed a thin jet of fuel on top, saturating every page. Vapors assailed me, and with them came associations of afternoons in our backyard, Mother molding the hamburger patties my aproned father would flip with aplomb, his aluminum spatula catching the light. What a disappointment to return to my senses in a dank garage, the doors shut tight against prying eyes, the most incriminating objects I owned heaped in an acrid, sopping pile.

This time I stood back and tossed the lit match, having wits enough to understand that unless I kept my distance, my eyebrows and hair were in danger. But nothing could have prepared me for the whoosh that followed, a whisper of swift consumption. I recoiled from the blast of heat, walls around me tinted red. Flames shot several feet into the air, some of them as tall as I. From their flickering tips coiled strands of black smoke that streamed toward the ceiling and spread across it, ominous as thunderheads. Even if the fire eliminated my collection of men, what if there remained a thick black telltale smudge on the ceiling of my parents' garage? I floundered by firelight, plucked from the realm of possibility a dozen useless excuses, *a can of insecticide had exploded; I had tried one of Mother's cigarettes,* and while I was at it, the puddles of oil began to burn, and my bonfire reached its peak.

The first scrap of anatomy was a man's arm. It fluttered down like a molted feather, part of a picture singed at the edges. Legs and shoulders and buttocks came next. The magazines were burning to pieces, and the pieces, lifted on sudden updrafts, were raining everywhere. I swiped at the stifling air, trying to catch a couple of muscles. When it finally dawned on me that things were getting worse instead of better, I leapt in and out of the fire in a sorry effort to stomp it out. In the periphery of my vision, I saw my shadow loom up on the walls, all wavering agitation. I slapped at my smoldering shoelace, plucked at the cinders landing in my hair. The more I stomped on the hot spots, the more the bodies multiplied, a flurry of glowing male flesh. And just before I managed to smother the fire, in a single wracking spasm of guilt, I imagined my picture on the evening news and the blackened rubble of our former home.

Even after the flames had been extinguished, there was smoke to contend with. The garage was hazy, unbreathable. Throwing open the double doors, I half expected to see fire trucks arriving, or the neighbors lined up in a bucket brigade. I was stunned to realize that it was still a Saturday afternoon, the sky clear, the hills unsinged. Smoke billowed over my head and drifted into the placid air. I ran to the edge of our driveway and breathed deeply, as though I were preparing to dive into water, then ran back inside. I flung open the two small windows and used the grocery bag to fan away the remaining smoke. Coughing, eyes watering, I came out for air once more, turned on the spigot and wrestled the garden hose around the side of the house and into the garage. Though fairly certain the fire was out, I doused the mound of burnt magazines.

Getting rid of the smoke was a cinch compared to the bits of men's bodies. My dread of the magazines being discovered in my bedroom was nothing compared to the dread that I'd never locate all the fragments of anatomy lurking who-knows-where in the garage. A handsome head had landed near a jar of nails on my father's workbench. A naked gladiator, nearly complete, wedged himself in a terra-cotta pot. I imagined my parents pulling up in the Oldsmobile, quizzically sniffing the stale air, and finding pieces of male physique inexplicably stuck to their shoes. My hands were black by the time I finished scrutinizing every square inch of the garage, groping behind the freezer, hoisting myself up on a stepladder to check the high shelves of the workbench. I scooped every stray appendage into the grocery bag, which I stuffed at the bottom of the garbage can. Examining the ceiling with a flashlight, I convinced myself that my father wouldn't notice the vague gray shadow that, if pressed, I could blame on car exhaust. I considered spraying the garage with the can of air freshener my mother kept in the guest bathroom, but wouldn't lilac smell as suspicious as smoke? I swept the wet ashes into a dustpan. Then I had to scour the dustpan. Then I had to wash the bristles of the broom. Then I had to bleach the kitchen sink.

My clothes were permeated with smoke and smudged with soot, and I decided to stuff them behind the drawer where I'd hidden the pornography until I could figure out how to clean them without risking my mother's questions. My tennis shoes required an entirely different, but equally anxious, set of ablutions, and after I cleaned them I wadded the paper towels in such a way that the black smears were concealed. Even the washrag with which I cleaned my face had to be examined for traces of soot. It was as if I were leaking a dark persistent misery, as if I tainted everything I touched. For the rest of the afternoon and into the evening, every time I closed my eyes I saw a phantom of the con-flagration, as if I'd been branded by its afterimage. Trying to divert myself with records and books, I would periodically stop what I was doing and, as though jarred awake by a bad dream, sniff the clothes into which I'd changed, or search my skin for particles of ash, seized by the apprehension that I hadn't covered my tracks.

My parents were oblivious to the crisis when they returned home after dark. They must have had a couple of drinks at dinner; my mother's cheeks were flushed, and my father blinked slowly as he told me what they ate. I listened intently, asked several questions. Who else was there? Did they play any games? I wanted to distract them from my act of arson, but I was also soothed by the details of their party, a tale of mingling, ease, and indulgence.

That night, while getting ready for bed, it became clear to me that attempts to reform myself would prove every bit as disastrous as staying the same. The ruined clothes behind the drawer; the grocery bag at the bottom of a trash can — now I had even more to hide.

The guest list for my party consisted of Jack Perlstein and Richard Levine, two boys I knew from synagogue and junior high. Though unrelated, Jack and Richard might have been mistaken for brothers; they both possessed alert brown eyes and wavy hair. They also lived in the same stucco apartment house. Athletic and friendly, Jack and Richard were slow to exploit their physical power. We sometimes ate lunch together in the school cafeteria or walked home in a raucous trio. Jack and Richard shared a repertoire of phrases. "Yes, Mother dear," one of them would drone whenever the other offered advice. "Pip pip," in an arch English accent, greeted any pretentious remark. They both called me Cooper instead of Bernard, this formality having the paradoxical effect of tenderness.

Because we'd once studied Hebrew together in preparation for our bar mitzvas, Jack and Richard considered me, in the broader context of the junior high, an equal member of our ethnic subset, though I was nothing like them in temperament or strength. They teased me good naturedly about my tendency to daydream and equivocate — "Earth to Cooper, come in Cooper" — and for the first time my reticence seemed like an eccentricity rather than a flaw. A boy, for once, among boys, I relied on their attentions — back slaps, mock blows, gross jokes — for a taste of normalcy, attentions made especially tenuous and sweet because I suspected that Jack and Richard, like everyone else, would turn their backs if my secret were revealed.

I'd hardly seen either of them that summer. They'd been working together as counselors at a camp for Jewish youth outside Los Angeles. Figuring they'd be home by now, I dialed Richard first. "Uh-huh," he answered the phone, as though it were the middle, and not the beginning, of a conversation. We caught up on news of the summer with the halting, blasé phone persona of adolescent boys. And then, unable to restrain myself, I sprang my surprise. "A what?" asked Richard. After I explained the premise of the party, he told me that he was wearing shorts and a T-shirt. In my zeal to get the party under way, it somehow slipped my mind that, if I wanted to have the guests arrive in compromising clothes, it would be pointless to call them at two in the afternoon. I had to improvise, to bend the rules, and in what Richard himself might have called "a save," I asked him to come to my house the next day, but to wear what he wore to bed that night. "Whatever," he said. Then I phoned Jack and asked the same.

The sheer intensity of my anticipation embarrassed me long before the guests showed up. The day of the party, dressed in a pair of powder blue pajamas, I set up my hi-fi in the living room and recruited my mother to make a platter of sandwiches, aware that the outfit made my fuss seem all the more fruity. Circling the living room, I searched for something to touch or rearrange that would make the prospect of fun more likely. Wax apples were adjusted, pillows plumped. I chalked my excitement up to the fact that this was the first party I'd given on my own, and not to the fact that two boys I idolized were due to arrive at my house any minute, looking like they just rolled out of bed. Over and over, I imagined the hilarity that would ensue once the doorbell rang, Jack in his underwear, Richard in his bathrobe. Even if I couldn't have put it into words, the metaphysics of the party weren't lost on me: wrenched out of context, together in our bedclothes, we would be more alike than ever before.

The sound of the bell made my heart pound, and I had to take a moment to compose myself before opening the door. Standing side by side, the Hollywood Hills rising behind them, Jack and Richard wore the same chinos, short-sleeved shirts, and scruffy Keds they wore to school. The effect was as jarring as a bride in a bikini. "Did we wake you?" asked Jack, the two of them doubling over with laughter. I forced myself not to show any signs of anger or disappointment. "Very funny," I said, ushering them inside. They made a beeline for the sandwiches. Hot with shame, I raced upstairs to change. "Cooper," Richard shouted after me. "We came as we are."

"Yeah," I yelled back, "a couple of jerks."

"Honey," I heard my mother call from the kitchen, "I think your friends are here."

Jack and Richard's snickering was muffled by mouthfuls of tuna.

The few seconds I'd spent in their presence were almost as bad as the dream in which I wore the pages of *Pony Boys!*, proof I was skewed, forever out of synch. I threw on my school clothes, but the change seemed futile, like dressing a chimpanzee in a suit to make him look human. Returning to the living room, I berated myself for going through with such a stupid idea in the first place, and wished I'd never opened the door. Could I make them think it was all a bad joke? What I'd wanted all along, it occurred to me too late, was a girl's party, with lots of gossip, dancing practice, and lolling about in pretty pajamas. Worried that the slightest sound or movement might give away my girlish urges, I sat on the sofa and turned to stone. Ten minutes into the festivities and it was already obvious that laughter and astonishment weren't likely to materialize. The sandwiches were almost gone. The prospect of fun had deflated like a balloon. The wheels of the party spun in a rut.

Jack and Richard asked what we were going to do besides listen to records. Every so often one of us would throw out an idea that the others would instantly veto. No, I protested a little too loudly, when one of them said, "Monopoly?" Our indecision lumbered on and on, and I thought I could see, through the picture window, the deepening light of afternoon. It was one of those still and smoggy summer days. We finally decided to venture outside, snatched a pack of my mother's cigarettes, and left the house.

Refugees from a defunct party, we roamed the neighborhood. The heat made us too listless to accomplish anything more than petty mischief. Jack threw a rock and chipped the flank of a plaster deer. Richard flipped up the red flags on a few mailboxes. I showed them how you can squeeze the buds of drooping fuchsias to make them pop like cap guns. After a while we sat down on the grassy bank of someone's front yard, beneath the shade of a carob tree. The three of us lit cigarettes and pretended to smoke like veterans. Richard blew loose, short-lived smoke rings. Jack picked flecks of tobacco off his tongue and flicked them into the air. I took a long, labored drag, then held up my cigarette. "Filter tips," I said in a disgruntled baritone, "you could get a hernia from the draw." This was something I'd heard on TV, but Jack and Richard laughed in approval, and I felt the remark had restored me to their graces. Soon our cigarettes collapsed into ash. Dizzy from smoke, unable to speak, the three of us lay back on the lawn and stared at sunlight swimming through the leaves. Pressed against the turning earth, I felt dry grass crackle behind my ears. My friends breathed deeply on either side, two strapping, affable boys.

Life in the eighth grade was not very different from life in the seventh. Jack and Richard and I stuck together at school, yet no matter how well we got along, agreed on pop tunes, or copied homework, my secret remained a threat to our allegiance. My parents began to seem like people whose love I'd lose if they really knew me, and I viewed their habits — Mother washing dishes in the kitchen, Father rushing off to work — with a premature nostalgia. In the absence of pornography, I could ferret out the male flesh in *Reader's Digest, Look,* and *Life:* ads for after-shave, Vapo-Rub, vacations in Bermuda.

I no longer thought about throwing a come-as-you-are party, but my wish to see into private lives, to witness what the world kept hidden, would not disappear. The more fiercely I guarded my inner life, the more I loved transparency and revelation. I wanted the power to read people's minds. Radar hearing. X-ray eyes. I pored over a book at school that showed layers of anatomy — tissue and organs and skeleton — lifted away as the pages were turned. Pat Collins, the "Hip Hypnotist," was my favorite act on TV; she persuaded her subjects to shed their inhibitions, and they bawled like babies, barked like dogs. Charles Atlas, maker of he-men from weaklings, flexed his muscles in comic books, and there were times I stared with such fixity I could see the tiny dots of the printing, as if I were glimpsing the man's very atoms.

THE SPANKING

I ran away from home the first time when I was four years old. My family lived in a small town in the middle of Missouri, the Heart of America. It was 1960. My older sisters and big brother got to go to school during the day. Dad went to work. I wanted to be able to go somewhere, too, but I didn't know where. One warm September day I took off for the school to see what my brother and sisters were doing. It was just a few blocks away, but it seemed like miles to me. When I got there someone found me wandering around the halls and took me to my oldest sister. Susan told me to turn around and get home before I got a spanking. Instead of going home I walked about five more blocks to the small downtown square. I went into the drugstore and looked at their children's books. I asked the man behind the counter if I could have the Pinocchio book. He said no, I'd have to buy it. Instead he gave me a little notepad. I left the store and was standing outside on the sidewalk when my father's secretary came driving up. She jumped out of the car and ran up to me. There you are! Do you realize the whole town is looking for you?

She drove me home, and my mother called my father to tell

him I was okay. When he came home from work that night he pulled down my pants, pulled off his belt and whipped me with it on my butt. He spanked me in front of my brothers and sisters so we would all know not to ever run away again. I didn't even realize I'd run away. As far as I was concerned, I'd gone out for a walk.

My family moved around a lot. When I was in grade school we never stayed in the same house for longer than two years. No matter where we lived, I always managed to find a place to get away from my parents, three sisters and two brothers. I loved to walk along the railroad tracks or in nearby woods. I took my little black half-dachshund dog, Sneezy, on hikes with me. She was my constant companion. I found places where no one could see me. Where I could be alone to explore and daydream.

The next time I ran away from home was ten years later. I was fourteen and a freshman in high school. My dad had been promoted to the district manager of the public utilities company. We moved from a small Missouri college town into a modern ranch-style home in the last subdivision of the farthest suburb east of Kansas City. We were half an hour's drive to the middle of the city and ten minutes from rolling farmland covered with wheat, corn and grazing cattle. Dad became very active with the Chamber of Commerce and the Kiwanis Club. He did a lot of work toward bettering our community and became well respected. His picture was in the weekly newspaper a lot. Adults were always telling me how lucky I was to have him for a father.

I was mad at my parents because they made me go to bed at nine-thirty every night when my friend Steve Holley could stay out all night if he wanted to. Most of my friends got to stay up until at least eleven. Summertime was the hardest because my younger brother and sister and I had to be in bed before the sun had gone completely down. It was still light out and we could hear the other neighborhood kids outside playing. If we weren't in bed on time we were in big trouble. In the summer I went barefoot as much as possible. I prided myself in having tough, leathery skin on the bottom of my feet. When Dad was around he wouldn't let me go barefoot. He said as hard as he worked, he didn't want people to think he couldn't afford shoes for his kids.

My little brother, Jimmy, and I shared a bedroom. Even though we slept next to each other in identical Early American–style twin beds, we hardly spoke. Our beds were like islands, miles apart. Late at night I would tune my transistor radio into a Little Rock station that only came in at night. There was a show called "Bleecker Street" that played underground music like David Bowie, Dan Hicks and the Hot Licks, and Joni Mitchell, among others. I heard "Take a Walk on the Wild Side" by Lou Reed for the first time on that station and was sure he was singing to me. I also had a lamp above my bed and would read until Mom or Dad came by our closed door and yelled for me to turn the light off.

I hated my dad most of the time. I hated him with more than just an adolescent's hatred of his parents. He treated his kids like we were slaves. He used all of us as work horses and used my sisters for sex as well. We had to constantly be working around the house or out in our enormous backyard. When he wasn't home Mom would lighten up on the workload, but we all knew there were certain jobs that had to be done by the time Dad got home, or else.

Dad used to search through my room when I wasn't around. I had a pen pal that I met on a weekend church retreat. She lived in St. Louis. I kept her letters in a shoe box next to my bed. One afternoon I noticed that the box had been moved and the letters were out of order. I realized that Dad had gone through and read them. He knew my personal secrets with my pen pal. That scared me.

I used to sneak into Mom and Dad's room and steal *Playboy* and

Penthouse magazines from a stack on the top shelf of Dad's closet. I'd hide them under my mattress and late at night would scour every page looking for dirty stories and, hopefully, if I was lucky, pictures of naked men. The magazines would obviously be missing, but no one ever said anything to me about it. After I'd jacked off enough and was tired of them I would creep into my parents' room when the coast was clear and put them back.

Sometimes when Dad was taking a nap, I'd sneak up to his bedroom door just to look at him. He always kept the door open about six inches unless he'd called one of my sisters in there. Then he was sure to keep the door shut. He slept in his underwear and was big and hairy. I stared mesmerized at his body. I had to be sure the rest of the family was either preoccupied or out of the house when I did this. As soon as I heard him snoring and was certain he was sound asleep, I would tiptoe down the hardwood-floor hallway. I knew which boards squeaked, so I'd be careful not to step on them. The bathroom was right next to my parents' room, so if anyone did come I could just act like I was going in there. I would lurk near the bedroom door and lean forward just barely enough to peek in. My heart beat fast. I was ready to run like a deer at the drop of a hat, but I stood there frozen, looking at his body for as long as I could. I always thought Dad looked like a cross between Elvis and Rock Hudson in his wedding picture. Mom looked like Lauren Bacall. Now he looked like fat Elvis minus the sideburns. I was terrified of him catching me, but deep down inside part of me hoped that he would. I wanted Dad to call me into his room and have me shut the door the way he did with my sisters. I wanted him to do to me what he did with them. I don't think I would have minded it as much as they did.

Many nights after dinner Dad would make one of my sisters sit on his lap while the family watched TV. He would do this right in front of me like I wasn't even there. He'd whisper in their ears and rub their thighs and was always trying to feel them up. They'd push his hand away and say, "Daddy!" and try to be cheery because if they were mad about it he'd turn mean. We always had to be in a good mood. We had to walk on eggshells around him.

Dad was in love with my older sister Liz. I don't even know what all that was about. So much of it happened for years behind closed doors. Once I heard him tell her, "If I could marry you, I would." I don't know how far he got with her. I can only assume all the way. He rarely let us go out with our friends, especially not her. But then he would take her everywhere. To movies, for drives, out to eat in restaurants. I think Mom started to get jealous. Liz was mad at Mom. I could never figure out how Liz could be mad at her. Dad was the maniac. Now I think she was angry because Mom wouldn't stop Dad. At the time I didn't think Mom was doing anything wrong. I thought she had it worse than anyone because all this shit was happening to her and her kids and she had no way to stop it.

For fun I used to shoplift things that I knew my parents would never buy me . . . dirty books, candy and especially cans of Pam, the nonstick vegetable coating spray. You could get high from inhaling Pam and I did. I hid the cans in a box in my bedroom closet. Late at night when my little brother Jimmy was asleep, I'd get it out and spray it in a paper bag and inhale it over and over until I was completely stoned out of my mind. It had a warm, metallic smell. I could "hear" a flashing brown dot up to the right of my head, just behind me a little and out of sight. I had tried sniffing model-car glue before, but it didn't work as well. Sometimes I thought I'd hear someone outside my bedroom door or maybe see shadows of feet. I could never tell if I was being paranoid or if there really was someone out there. I'm surprised my parents didn't hear the paper bag rattling as I inhaled in and out, in and out. In his searches through my room Dad must have found the cans. But no one ever came in to see what I was doing. At least when I was sniffing Pam I didn't have to hear the bed springs squeaking through my sisters' bedroom wall from one of Dad's visits.

When Liz was a senior, one evening a month or so before graduating from high school, she went to a shopping mall with some friends. Dad came home early from work and was extremely pissed at Mom for letting her go. Liz was seventeen years old. He stomped back and forth, cursing, swearing, looking at his watch. He was accusing Mom of letting Liz go shopping like it was such a big crime. Liz got home around eight-thirty or nine. Dad was so angry that he took her into his room and pulled down her pants, put her over his lap and started spanking her.

I flipped out. It was so fucking humiliating. I was in my bedroom. I think I'd been told to go there. But I heard everything. When I heard the slaps against her butt and her squeal I lost it completely. I started screaming, "STOP IT! STOP IT! YOU'RE CRAZY!! STOP IT!!" Dad rushed into my room to see what was going on with me. I was sitting up on my bed screaming at him, out of my mind. I was fourteen. He came at me from around my brother's bed and slapped me across the side of the face so hard that my head went up in the air and then down on my bed. I blacked out for a moment. Liz yelped at the impact. I saw her standing in the doorway wide-eyed with a hand over her mouth. Her hair that usually flipped perfectly at her shoulders was all messed up. I got back up and started at him. I hit him in the chest, which made him laugh. I swung again. He grabbed me by the wrists and held onto me while I was struggling to get at him. He was too strong. I kept screaming, "YOU'RE CRAZY! YOU'RE CRAZY!" and he said for me to "shut up, you barefoot boy." He kept calling me "Barefoot Boy" over and over and laughing at me. He smelled like cigars and Old Spice aftershave lotion. Finally he left and went out in the hall or the living room or his bedroom. I just lay on my bed sobbing. Jimmy started to cry, too. He usually didn't seem to notice anything, but this time he couldn't help it.

Mom came in a little while later and stood by my bed. She rubbed my back as I shook all over and said, "Now, Joey, your father is NOT crazy. He is not crazy." Like she was trying to convince herself. I muttered angrily, "He is too!" She couldn't console me.

The next morning I didn't have to go to school because there was a big red handprint on the side of my face. When Dad came home from work for lunch he was in a jovial mood and tried to cheer me up. The following day I went back to school, and Karen Porter was shocked when she asked me what happened to my face and I told her Dad slapped me. She couldn't believe anyone's father would slap them that hard.

I had seen made-for-TV movies about runaways so I knew there were crash pads in cities where teenagers could go if they left home. Two movies, *Maybe I'll Come Home in the Spring*, starring Sally Field, and *Go Ask Alice*, were my inspiration. Sally Field ran away from a lovely upper-middle-class suburban home and fell in love with a hippie guy. She realized her mistake and returned home, but her boyfriend followed her. She was torn between her life on the street and her parents' love for her. She sadly decided to stay home and sent him away. *Go Ask Alice* was about a fifteen-year-old girl who ran away to San Francisco and got a job in a clothing boutique. She got mixed up with drugs and turned into a strung-out mess. These movies were supposed to scare kids from leaving home, but to me they were signs that if I left I would be okay. The movies told me there was a better life out there somewhere. I wasn't alone.

After Liz's spanking I decided it was time for me to go. It was the middle of May. School was almost out. I was finishing ninth grade. After dinner I went to the pool hall in our small downtown looking for Steve Holley. He would know where I could stay. He wasn't there. I walked all the way across town, through strange subdivisions filled with split-level homes and over dirt fields, soon to be more subdivisions, to Pappy's Pizza Parlour. He wasn't there either. I only had a jean jacket on to keep me warm and it was getting chilly out. I shivered, half from the cold and half from nerves. My friend Jerry McDaniels drove me back to the pool hall to see if Steve had shown up. He hadn't, and I didn't know what to do next. I was sitting in the back watching some guys shoot a game of pool when I saw my dad drive by in the family station wagon. Liz was with him. They slowed down as Dad searched the pool hall for me with angry eyes. He spotted me. We had eye contact. In the time it took them to find a parking place I ran out the back door and down a couple of side streets into an old residential neighborhood. I hid in some bushes until I was sure it was safe. My friend Sherry lived nearby, so I went to her house. She said I couldn't stay there but maybe I could stay with her friend Jacquie Smithson. Jacquie lived three blocks from my parents. We went over there and she said I couldn't stay with her either but she'd ask her next-door neighbor David, who was a grade ahead of us. We used to play kickball together in the bowling alley parking lot. He asked his mom if it was okay, and she said yes.

I was scared. I wanted to walk up the street to 50-Highway and stick out my thumb and catch a ride into Kansas City to get as far away as I could. But I had no idea where I would go once I got there. Plus, I was afraid my dad would drive by again. I decided to wait until the morning before going into the city. I slept in David's room in his family's refinished basement lined with light brown wood paneling. That night I had a dream where a voice, loud and clear, told me to go back home. It was my mother. When

I woke up I felt sick to my stomach and didn't want to get out of bed. The song "Me and You and a Dog Named Boo" was playing on the radio in the kitchen. "Travelin' and livin' off the land. Me and you and a dog named Boo. How I love bein' a free man." It was about hitchhiking. It was my call. Only there was no "you" or no "Boo." Just me. I thought about Sally Field and drugged-out Alice. I went back home. I was grounded for a month, which meant I couldn't go anywhere, not even leave our yard, unless I was with my parents. I wasn't allowed to see my friends. I was under house arrest.

GOING AWAY

E nough of this slow stuff. Take off your shirt."
Michael stands at the foot of the bed. He hesitates, looks down at his fully clothed body.

"Go ahead. I put up with this cold room for long enough. You can stand having your chest bare awhile."

He slips his hand to the bottom edge of his chamois shirt, fingers the soft and fraying fabric.

"Grab your nipples. Dig your fingernails into the skin. Twist them hard while you walk over to my closet."

Michael's feet stay planted on the wide pine floorboards. His shirt is still on, buttoned to the neck.

He steps forward and slams down his hand, smothering the stop button with too many fingers. The portable recorder crushes an image of itself into the down pillow it was propped against. Michael presses eject and removes the tape, holding it with just his fingertips as if it were one of the hummingbirds he finds sometimes, dead outside the kitchen's bay window.

As he walks across the bedroom he is shaking, his throat weak the way it gets just before vomiting. He sits down at the huge maple desk, Scott's desk, the one Scott built when they first moved into the farmhouse. The gray toolbox, stained with streaks of motor oil, sits in the center of the polished slab of wood. The top is tipped back like the lid of a casket open for display.

Without looking at the rest of the contents, Michael carefully replaces the cassette and shuts the box. He flips the metal latches on both sides and pushes it away, making room for his head, which he leans forward and rests on the desk. He feels the tears gather in the sacs below his tired eyes. A bubble of grief rises in his throat, chokes him for an instant. How could Scott ask this of him? Why did he always have to push things so far?

This morning, after Scott's parents and closest friends had been notified, after an hour of hugs and tears, after the hearse had come and taken the body to the funeral home, Michael asked everybody to leave. He forwarded his calls to Carrie, who as they had arranged long ago would handle the funeral's logistics. He locked the door, turned off most of the lights, and walked into the empty bedroom.

The smell was the first thing, so familiar by now, but at the same time painfully unexpected. That odd mix of antiseptic freshness with fermenting body odors: sweat-soaked sheets, the diapers filled with black ooze still resting in the bottom of the trashcan. Michael bit his cheek to keep from gagging.

The room was strangely dark, even with the new windows Scott had knocked into the wall just before he got sick the first time. The October Vermont light snuck in grainy, at too low an angle, stippling everything with a black-and-white photo's bleak contrasts. Nothing had been taken yet. Like a minyan huddling to pray, the oxygen tanks still clustered in the corner. The IV drip stood watch over the bed, its plastic tube dangling like a rope from the gallows. A half-empty can of Sustacal waited on the night table, ready to be poured. Michael imagined it as one of his own meticulous still lifes: "Recent AIDS Death, 1993."

Michael stared at the bed, certain he could make out the indentations in the mattress from Scott's shoulder blades. Then he reached underneath, where he'd seen Scott stash the box dozens of times. It was heavier than he had imagined, as if still filled with socket wrenches, pliers, vise grips. He hoisted the box and carried it to the big desk.

First he ran his fingers over the cool metal, the rounded edges and hinged black handle. He noticed the slight change in temperature when his fingers reached the strip of masking tape. He traced the tape's smooth length, the ragged ends where it had been torn from the roll. Then he read the words written carefully in red magic marker: WHEN I GO.

When I go. *When.* Michael had always wanted it to be *if*, wanted to hold out for the possibility of some miracle. But Scott had been realistic, practical-minded. When he knew he wouldn't be driving any more and sold the S-10, Scott had emptied the box of the auto repair kit that had been a high school graduation present from his grandfather. He'd given the tools to a kid down the road who had his own jacked-up pickup, but kept the box and marked its new function with his crude masking tape label.

For all these months, Michael had not been allowed to look into the box. He hadn't wanted to know what was in there anyway. But he had given his word that when Scott died, he would open the box that very same day. Scott always made him repeat that part of the promise. It was a strange request, to start looking through his lover's mementos before the funeral had even taken place, but Michael would do anything to put Scott at ease.

He unclipped the latches and opened the box warily, as if it were a magician's trick box and a snake might leap out at his face.

On the very top of the pile was a handwritten note on Scott's personal stationery.

Michael:

Just when you thought it was safe . . .

Sorry. I know how much it bugs you when I'm not being serious enough. How are you doing so far? Make sure to take time for yourself. Let Carrie deal with my parents, and you do that sit-and-shiver thing — whatever it's called — that your people do. (Just don't cover the mirrors; what would all the queens at the reception do without a place to check their hair?)

Listen. Darling. I don't know how to say this without sounding like an Ann Landers column, or worse yet the Cliff Notes to Kübler-Ross. But you have to move on. Promise me you will. That doesn't mean you should forget me. (You better not, kiddo, 'cause I'm watching your ass.) But you know my thing about restriction. If I thought after everything I was the one holding you back, I would just die. (Get it?)

Well, this is getting as long as the basketball season. Here's the deal. Most of what's in the box can wait. Some sentimental stuff. Letters to Milton, Sandra, and a couple other friends. An extra copy of the will. But the tape on top is for now. Right now. Use the portable box we usually take to the beach, prop it up on the pillow on my bed, and press play. Remember, you promised. Do it for me.

All my love, always,

Scott

Michael opens the box again now and unfolds the letter. It's quintessential Scott: full of jokes, as if nothing's a big deal. But if the smallest demand was violated, look out! And that line about "restriction."

Michael studies Scott's slanted lefty scrawl. It's even messier than usual in this note, as if he wanted to make sure Michael would be the only one capable of deciphering it. He thinks back six years ago to when they were at B.U., Scott a junior and he a senior, and they went shopping together for the first time. At one point Scott had stopped the cart and stood there, examining the grocery list he had written. "Let's see," he muttered to himself. "What's next? I can barely read my own writing." Michael ripped the paper out of Scott's hands and read aloud: "Raisins. Chocolate chips. Vanilla ice cream." Scott stared at him, amazed, then kissed him full on the lips, right there in the frozen foods aisle of the Stop & Shop. "Wow," he said. "I think I just might have to marry you."

Michael places the letter back in the box and stares at the cassette. It's old and a little scratched; Scott must have recycled it from the used tapes pile. Yankee frugality, he'd probably claim. Just plain cheap was the truth. But cheap and lovable. Michael picks up the cassette. The plastic is cold in his hands, weighs almost nothing. The exposed ribbon of brown magnetic tape is fragile as a strand of hair. Could this be all he has left?

He takes the tape and stands up, walks back to the bed. He has to. He gave Scott his word.

Michael snaps the tape into the player and hits rewind before fear might allow him to hesitate. The recorder whirs, clicks twice as the auto-reverse activates, and then the room fills with Scott's voice.

"He's baaack! Hi, Michael. It's me. The recently deceased. And you thought you'd gotten rid of me.

"I know you'll think I'm doing my Marlene impression, but this is just the way my voice is these days. You'll have to bear with me."

Judging from the throatiness, the frequency of pauses for

breath, Michael figures Scott must have recorded this two or three weeks ago, just as the last bout of pneumonia was setting in. He pictures Scott with the tubes in his nose, the mucus caking on his lip, green like mold. He blinks hard, tries to shake the image.

"Listen, I know you have trouble following instructions. You always have to do things your own way. The rebel artiste. Well, this time, you have to go my way, kiddo. You wouldn't want to disobey the dead."

Michael can't help cracking a smile. He thinks of the way Scott said he imagined heaven, as one eternal taping of "The Gong Show." All the dead sit at a long table, watching over the earth. Whenever one of the living does something disrespectful, the dead person who's been blasphemed gets to stand up and smash the giant gong, which Scott said manifested in the offending earthling as a splitting sinus headache.

"Now, I want you to stand at the foot of the bed. Stand there like you would some Saturday mornings when you'd come back to the bedroom after painting for a couple of hours. I wake up and you're just standing there, reeking of turpentine, watching me with that distant look in your eyes. You don't make a move, you just stand there. Even when I pull down the sheets and show you my chest, you just watch. I can't tell you how horny that always made me.

"Rub your hands through your hair. Lightly, just barely touch it. Imagine it's my tongue, tickling your scalp. It's my tongue nibbling at the wave of your widow's peak, biting your neck, around to your Adam's apple, leaving a trail of miniature hickies."

Michael moves his hand absentmindedly to the back of his head, grabs a handful of short bristles. He hasn't showered in three days. The hair is slick and soft with oil. He is thinking about when Scott discovered the first spot of KS as he was buttoning his collar one morning. They'd had fierce, acrobatic sex the night

before, and Scott thought the lesion was just a hickie. He teased
Michael about it, saying that was the problem with painters: They
always had to make their feelings visible before they believed they
were real. Michael remembers wanting to tackle Scott then and
bite him hard on the hickie, to draw blood and say, *"That's* how I
feel." What instinct had held him back?

"Move your hand down, slowly. Let it linger on your chest.
Then go farther, circle past your crotch, trail your fingers down
your thigh. Go ahead and grab if you want, squeeze the muscle.
Think about when I first discovered your leg thing."

The first time through, Michael hadn't been able to touch himself. He'd stood frozen, resisting the memory. He didn't want to
let Scott manipulate him the way he so often did, as if his emotions were wires Scott could connect and disconnect as easily as
those in the pickup truck engines he customized.

Now, as he listens to the same words again, Michael's fingers
rub softly on the loose fabric of his khaki pants. He glances at the
small wooden table next to the bed — "the shrine," Scott always
called it. Photographs of both their parents, Scott's namesake
nephew, and, front and center, the happy couple in their favorite
spot, the bleachers at Fenway. It was the first picture ever taken
of the two of them together. They stand just barely balanced on
their seats, blue caps cocked at crazy angles, their giant K signs
held in the air in tribute to Roger Clemens's copious strikeouts.
They're beaming because the Red Sox have won and because
they're about to have the best sex either of them has ever had.

Michael moves his hand lower, forcing himself to comply with
Scott's disembodied voice.

"I think it was the third or fourth date. At your place after the
Sox beat the Tigers in extra innings. Remember? I made you lie
down on the bed and promise to let go of all your muscles, like a
puppet. Then I gave you a tongue bath even though you still had

all your clothes on, starting at your sneakers and working my way up. I sucked on your ankles, letting my spit soak through the cotton socks, then your calves, turning the blue jeans black with wetness. When I got to your knee you flinched the way you do when a doctor tests you with that little hammer. I darted my tongue back to the same spot and you flinched again and tried to twist away. I had to punish you for breaking the rules. I had to hold you down and nibble at the underside of your knee. I'd never seen anybody writhe like that before. Even through your jeans, it made you shout so loud the upstairs neighbor banged on the floor. That's when I first fantasized about tying you to the bed, face down, and keeping you that way all night. Go ahead now. Touch the back of your knee."

Michael's hand is already there, ahead of the tape, his index finger flicking back and forth at his most sensitive spot. His eyes are rolled to the ceiling and he's not seeing anything, just feeling the tingle in his nerves.

"Touch the other knee. Back and forth, the way I always tortured you. All right. Enough of this slow stuff. Take off your shirt."

This time he does. He unhooks the buttons two at a time, rushing to keep up with the tape.

"Go ahead. I put up with this cold room for long enough. You can stand having your chest bare awhile."

Michael tosses the chamois shirt to the floor. It does seem cold in the room. He starts to feel guilty until he remembers it was Scott who refused the space heater, saying the electric bill would be too high. His nipples stiffen, turn crimson with the infusion of blood. His chest pricks with goosebumps, each separate follicle buzzing, alive. It's been so long since his chest has been touched this way. He always forgets to when he masturbates, concentrating instead on the quick route to satisfaction between his legs. Now he reaches a hand to the right nipple, presses the stiff bump between his thumb and forefinger.

"Grab your nipples. Dig your fingernails into the skin. Twist them hard while you walk over to my closet."

They kept separate closets. Scott's hasn't been opened in weeks because he couldn't get out of bed, let alone get dressed. Michael pulls the sliding wooden door and he is overwhelmed with the smell of Scott: the old Scott, Scott before the sickness. It's the smell of wet leaves, deep inside a raked-up pile. The smell of a wool jacket draped over a chair near the smoking woodstove. More pungent, personal odors as well: old boot liners, urine-stained boxer shorts. Michael breathes in as deeply as he can, the way he used to suck the air around Scott's underarms.

"The leather jacket is on the far left. Get it. Put it on."

The stiff leather creaks as he pulls it from the hanger. The jacket is heavy, feels almost solid. Michael slips his arms into the sleeves, then hunches fully into the jacket and his chest juts forward, a reflex against the cold animal skin.

"I bet that leather feels good on your bare chest. Think of it as a little piece of me on top of you. Think of what I would do if I was there."

He imagines Scott coming in after a morning of splitting firewood, surprising him from behind with his raw, icy hands. Scott would hold them there, palms pressed against Michael's sensitive spine, until finally they warmed to normal body temperature. Then, just when Michael had adjusted and let down his guard, Scott would flip them, nuzzle the still-freezing backs of his hands into Michael's armpits.

A chill shakes him, collects in his groin. He never thought he would let himself go this far.

"Walk back to the bed. Climb onto it and kneel at the foot, facing down where I would be. Yeah, I can see you. Just kneel there, arch your back, feel the leather rubbing against your skin. Reach in and touch your nipples again."

Michael is on the bed. He is kneeling, his feet tucked under him, leaning back against the cold brass rail. With both hands he kneads his chest, squeezing chunks of flesh. He slaps one flat palm over his heart, leaving a stinging red handprint. He flicks the left nipple with the back of his fingernail, then again, and again until it is purple.

"Now unzip your pants and pull them down. Not too far! Pull back the underwear, just a little. Pretend you're putting on a show. You love that. You always act shy, like you don't want me to see. But I know you do. You want to sit on me. Right?"

Michael unveils his stiff penis and shakes it seductively in the direction where Scott's face would be. He always did like to show it off, liked to get it from on top so he could watch Scott's eyes, riveted to every move.

"Go ahead." Scott's breathing is deeper now, more labored. "Go ahead and pump it."

Michael's right hand tugs quickly, pushing blood to the tip. He jerks himself with the head pointed down, almost touching his thigh, the way Scott liked to see it.

There is a knocking as the headboard hits against the wall. Over and over, the hollow plaster answering each thrust of Michael's hips. It's a comforting sound, familiar as his own heartbeat. The photos on the night table shake and threaten to topple, but he knows from experience that they won't. He thinks of all the times they had sex on this bed. The first time, with all their clothes on. Three days later, when he finally stayed the night. Then he remembers the time in the truck. He hasn't thought of this in months.

It was when they were moving from Boston up to Vermont. They had hired a Mayflower crew with a huge semi, and they were supposed to follow behind in the old Subaru. But just past Spring-field the Subaru blew a rod. They had to abandon it on the side of the highway and ride the rest of the way in the back of the moving truck.

It was pitch-dark and cold, the air thick with dust from the blankets draped over their belongings. The bed was against one wall, piled with boxes of clothes. There was just enough room for Michael to lie down with Scott on top of him.

As the truck whined through the gears and came up to speed on I-91, Scott readied Michael with a spit-covered finger, skip-ping the usual foreplay. Then he jerked himself hard, fumbled to get the condom on, and pushed against the tight opening. When he was all the way inside he just lay there on top of Michael, not moving at all, and not saying a word, letting the bump of the tires over each section of pavement be their rhythm. For fifteen mi-nutes they lay there, completely at the mercy of the road. Finally, they entered a construction area where the highway was grooved, waiting to be repaved. With the metal sides of the truck rattling as if they would pop their rivets, the rush of cars in the passing lane, the engine's hum pounding in their ears, they came within seconds of each other.

Michael picks up the speed of his jerking. He pulls his cock hard, yanks the skin until it folds in on itself and appears suddenly uncircumcised, like Scott's. He rams his hand down to the base, then jerks up again, then again, faster. He's getting close. He makes his cock look uncut again and imagines Scott's dick inside him the way it was that night in the truck. He leans back, listens for the voice. He wants to come to the sound of Scott's voice.

Suddenly he realizes there's nothing coming from the tape. He tries to remember the last thing Scott said, but he can't. He was so lost in his own pleasure that he didn't notice when it stopped. Now he pauses, listens again for the voice. He peers through the plastic window of the cassette player to see if the tape is still rolling. He can see the sprockets turning, but the only sound it emits is static.

Now he hears something, a faint noise. It could be the creaking of a bed, or a door slowly opening. No, it's a human voice. A single, high-pitched sob and then a painful gasp for air.

With one hand Michael reaches instinctively toward the cassette player, as if he could comfort Scott, run his fingers reassuringly through the soft blond hair. He realizes his other hand is still gripping his penis and he drops it like something poisonous, lets it fall limp against his thigh.

Michael starts to cry, the tears pooling in his eyelids until they sting and his eyelashes mat together. The recorder appears to him now as just a fuzzy black rectangle. He wants to punch it, to smash the plastic into a thousand pieces. How could he be doing this now, today? He never should have promised Scott he would listen to the tape.

He moves to slam it off but just as he does, the voice resumes.

"I'm sorry, Michael. Shit. I'm really sorry. Pull yourself together, Scottie.

"What was I thinking? This was supposed to be for you, not for me."

Michael hovers midway across the bed, his hand still reaching toward the tape player. He wants to stop it, but he's too terrified by the prospect of silence.

"I just couldn't let go of this fantasy, you know? That we'd come together, one last time. I was sure I could manage it.

"Leave it to a Red Sox fan, I guess. It's like I actually believed Yaz would hit a home run in the playoff game in '78, instead of popping up. I haven't even been able to get a hard-on in two months!

"Who knows? Maybe I'm getting worked up over nothing.

Maybe you've already shot your load all over the bed. Or maybe you got disgusted and turned off the tape ten minutes ago. How am I supposed to know? It's like having phone sex with somebody's answering machine."

Michael smiles just a crack, involuntarily, and the tears run in at the corners of his mouth. He licks the salt away.

"I guess this whole thing was dumb anyway. It could never work. But I just wanted to leave you with . . . I don't know. Something more than an empty room, a closet full of clothes, and that fucking photo shrine. I couldn't bear it if you became one of those dreadful AIDS widows.

"All right. I'll get off that trip. I know you've heard it all before. All I'm saying is, don't turn off any part of yourself on my account. And don't turn off any memories of me either, don't just think of me as the gorgeous young stud I was. Think of me like this, too. You know, the diapers, everything. It's all me. But don't forget to remember me how I was when I was fucking you. Yeah. I guess that's my last request. Think of me as sexy."

Michael flinches at the word, a silent sob shuddering through him. He makes himself hold it in, makes himself listen for anything else Scott might need to say. There is the sound of strained breathing, then the creak of the old bed, something metal shifting on the floor.

"Well, I'm exhausted. Need a shot of this oxygen. This has been a bit much for a man on his last legs, so to speak.

"I don't know what else to say, honey. I think this has really gone on long enough. I love you, Michael. I love you now and always. Take care of yourself."

His eyes are closed. He is still kneeling with his feet tucked under him but he can't feel his legs, can't feel the bed. He is in zero gravity, spinning through space. He hears background noise but it's as if both ears are covered with giant seashells. He hears an ocean that's not an ocean, a nonexistent wind.

Random snapshots of memory rush through Michael's mind: Scott bent over into the hood of the truck, the view of just his butt and legs, the single greasy handprint on his thigh; Scott and his nephew — the two Scotts, Scott squared — lying head to head on the living room rug over a game of Monopoly; Scott on his back in the bathtub, so far gone that you can see the outline of his spine just by looking at his stomach. Then Michael tries to remember what Scott was wearing the first time he ever saw him. He should know this, he has to, but he can't bring it to mind. Everything goes blank. He can't remember anything, not Scott's hair, not his eyes or his face. Just as quickly it all comes back, more vivid than ever. Michael is dizzy, confused by the tricks his brain is playing.

Now he is rocking. Back and forth with his whole body, like a Hasid davening in prayer. He is rocking, holding his stomach with both hands as if his intestines could spill out. The motion soothes him, makes his head feel light and good. It's a rhythm, something to hold onto.

The sound brings him back into the room. The high-pitched squeak of the bedsprings giving way, the steady knock-knock of the headboard against the plaster wall. He can't help it. He can't. The sound makes him remember.

He hasn't allowed himself to admit it until just now, but even at the very end, Scott never stopped turning him on. He had thought he knew every inch of Scott's body, but when that body started falling apart, started changing and doing unexpected things, it was like learning a new lover from scratch. He would turn Scott over to give him a warm sponge bath and he would explore every fold of rashy skin, every corner of bone. What could be more intimate then wiping the crud from somebody's ass, or picking the lint from between their toes? How could he ever be that close to another body?

He wishes things could be clean, could stay in their proper compartments. But he can't keep anything straight anymore. One second he sees Scott's emaciated chest, each rib poking through the skin like some picked-over carcass in a nature film, and the next he's remembering the smooth pearly foreskin that he loved to play with so much.

He thinks of the time Scott called him in from the studio over the intercom they'd set up. "Come quick. Come right away." Michael had panicked, dropped his palette paint-side down, assuming the IV had pulled loose again. When he got there Scott was propped up on his elbows, the sheets pulled midway down his thighs. "It's hard," he said, with a child's amazement. "It's hard." And together, with Michael's right hand on the bottom, Scott's left hand on top, they gently massaged the shaft, laughing, careful not to disturb the tubes that criss-crossed the bed, until Scott came in three small bursts.

Michael is startled by a sharp noise and the sound of a voice. It must be Carrie, or Scott's parents. But it seems early for them to have come with dinner. He listens closely and he realizes that it's his own voice. It's coming from the tape.

He opens his eyes, wipes the residue of tears so he can focus. He stares at the small black box from which he speaks to himself in his grandiose Prince Charles impression: "A quarter century. The silver plateau. It is, friends, a remarkable achievement." It's Scott's twenty-fifth birthday party, two years ago. He doesn't even remember that they taped the festivities. But they must have, and Scott must have recorded over the old tape by accident.

Scott's chimes in, doing Princess Di. The voice is different from the tape Michael's just been listening to: clearer, no rasp in the throat. "We thank our lovely husband the Prince, but remind him that our quarter century pales in comparison to his own abundant achievement of years." A group of people in the background howls with laughter. They were in top form, Michael thinks, their timing perfect as an old vaudeville act.

Then they're singing "Happy Birthday" in warbling falsettos, the whole group of them, everybody laughing, trying to spit out the words. Michael remembers feeling drunk even though he'd only had one glass of champagne, remembers falling against Scott's chest and pressing his ear to the solid rib cage, being tickled by the vibrations as Scott sang. And then the surreptitious hand that slipped into his jeans, Scott's fingers circling the base and tugging just a bit while the others sang on around them, oblivious.

Michael's entire body stirs with the memory. His knees grind into the firm mattress, making a tangle of the sheets. He should have stripped the bed this morning, but now he's glad he didn't. These are the sheets Scott slept in, the last thing that covered his living body. Michael grabs a handful of fabric and holds it to his nose. The smell gags him for an instant, sweat mixed with traces of shit and puke. But he holds the sheet to his face, inhales deeply again.

It all smells good to Michael right now. It all smells of Scott, of his body. Michael keeps the sheets in place with one hand and with the other, reaches down. His cock is already hard and wet with clear fluid gathering at the slit. The skin still tingles from being so close before. He knows it won't take long.

He wraps his fingers around the base just as Scott had at the birthday party and moves quickly in strong, even strokes. His eyes are open, looking to the head of the bed, and he can see Scott clearly. He sees the expression that would bloom on Scott's face when he was on the verge of orgasm: the lips curled back, the eyes closed to fluttering slits, a combination of strain and relief. It's the same expression, it occurs to him, that he found on Scott this morning.

Michael jerks one last time and releases, two spurts of fluid shooting over the dirty sheets, the rest dripping onto his hand, running between his fingers. He squeezes out a few more drops and then lets himself fall forward onto the bed. His head lands on the pillow, bumping against the cassette player's cold plastic.

On the tape they've moved on to the second part of the song. *How old are you now? How old are you now?* Michael hears his own voice rising above the others. And then Scott's voice. Competing divas. The other partygoers drop out and are silent as Michael and Scott slow to a grand finale. The two voices jar for a moment as they waver in and out of harmony, straining against each other. *Happy birthday to . . .* The voices soar up together on the last word, each man assuming the other would stay on the melody note, both instead singing the harmonic third, and Michael can't tell whose voice is whose.

AFTER THE CHANGE

State trooper Rita Benson smelled the doe as soon as she got out of her cruiser. It was a strong airborne river of shit and blood that she easily followed to a shallow ditch in front of a single-story Cape. The doe's breath was weak, then got stronger as Rita approached. The doe tried to get up. Only her front legs worked, clawing desperately at the ground, the lower half of her body stiff and useless. Broken back, Rita thought. Exhausted from the effort, the doe lowered her head and turned one fearful eye to Rita.

Through the kitchen window of the house Rita saw a man on the telephone. When their eyes met, he hung up the phone. He came out a moment later carrying a glass.

"Lemonade?" he offered.

"You call about the deer?"

"Bob Zeilinski."

He held out both his hands, the right with the glass. Rita instinctively offered her right, halting when she realized there was only his left to shake. Bob took her fingers and curled them over his palm, as if he were about to lead her somewhere, perhaps through a waltz. She dropped her hand and took the glass. In the following silence they could hear the doe's shallow breathing in the late August afternoon heat.

"She's on my property," Bob said. He pushed his cap back and scratched his round head. "But I didn't want to shoot her in case one of you boys happened by and saw me hunting out of season. That's the law, ain't it?"

"That's right, Mr. — "

"Call me Bob. Sergeant Shook send you? Pauly and I went to high school together. You must be new. Just start troopering?"

"I've been on the force for a year."

Rita caught Bob's eyes sliding down her front when she turned to look at a pickup and a Jeep slowing in front of the house.

The pickup pulled into Bob's driveway, followed by the badly rusted Willys. A thin man in jeans and a T-shirt, with a sharp pumpkin orange widow's peak slicing into his forehead, got out of the pickup. What looked like a bear got out of the Willys. The man's head and face were covered with thick black hair, his body round as a barrel. Rita saw Bob catch the men's eyes.

"Still breathing," the large man said after they formed a circle around the doe. The voice came out of his massive black beard without moving a hair. The doe started kicking again. "Still plenty of life," the thin man added. They watched as the doe tried to stand. When she gave up and lowered her head, the thin man said, "Me and Steen just dropped by to borrow your, ah — vegetable steamer, Bob."

Steen seemed to be smiling behind his beard, perhaps even laughing, it was hard to tell.

"Steen. Tom. This here's Trooper — " Bob looked at her name tag " — Benson. She's come to shoot this poor doe got hit by a car."

Steen pulled up his stomach with both hands, then slowly offered his right in Rita's direction. When she went to take it, he pulled it away in a continuous movement and scratched his beard. Tom quickly reached in and shook Rita's exposed hand.

She looked at Bob, then at the men, then at the deer. In her periphery Rita saw the men's eyes clicking like telegraphs.

"Yep. Gonna have to shoot her," Tom said.

"She's probably got young ones somewhere," Steen said. "Real young. Too bad."

"Too bad," Tom said.

"Shame," Bob said.

The three men walked back to the Willys and Steen handed out beers. They leaned against the jeep and eyed Rita's five-foot-four-inch frame, her short brown hair, cut Dutch boy in the back, her stiff spine and straight shoulders. Steen sniffed the air, then whispered, "Game makes me hard."

Rita took small sips of lemonade, her jaw jutting out and staying out after she lowered the glass. She heard what Steen had said. She concentrated on Tom. She could see he wasn't in on it, just going along, his eyes dropping when she caught him. Bob drank his beer and looked at his house. Only Steen looked directly at her.

"You got any boys?" he called to her. He didn't wait for an answer. "I got four. They all had the fear in 'em at first. But I got 'em cured. The youngest is seven, and I already got him on the scent. He's good in the woods. That's where I give 'em The Talk."

Rita took out her gun. She faced them with the pistol in one hand and the empty lemonade glass in the other.

"You know, The Talk," Steen offered as he encircled his stomach with one hand and pulled it up. "I give it to 'em on the trail. The birds and the bees and the little baby does." She couldn't see it, but she knew there was a leer behind the fur.

"You have that thing properly registered?" Rita asked Steen, looking at the ancient Willys.

"Yes, ma'am," Steen said. His tongue came out like a snake head and swabbed his beard. "She's my baby." He pounded the hood until it bounced up and down.

"You may have come here for the — vegetable steamer," Rita said, looking directly at each of them. She paused at Tom, knowing what he was going through, trying to be tough, one of the boys. She knew what he was feeling as if she was feeling it herself. She knew he was listening, and she addressed him, even though he wouldn't look at her. "But if I see you on the road, any of you, you'll get a Breathalyzer. Understood?"

After a pause, Steen said, putting a quiver in his voice, "Bob, can we stay over tonight? Watching a deer get shot point-blank, especially when it's looking at you, staring right at you with that big brown eye, always makes me a little upset. I might have to have more than one beer to calm me down. And I wouldn't want to drive after I've had more than one beer."

"I know what you mean," Bob said. "Of course you can."

Trooper Benson walked over to Bob, handed the empty glass to him, and said, "Stay here."

When they thought she was out of earshot, Bob whispered, "She's got a nice tight ass."

"Not enough of it. I like 'em big," Steen said.

"Big," Tom chimed in quietly.

Trooper Benson stood ten yards away from the deer, raised her revolver, aimed, and fired. After the echo faded and a small cloud of dust cleared, the doe was still breathing, the one terrified eye still looking at her. Steen said loudly, "I once shot a doe. Didn't get her clean, so I had to track her for three miles. When I found her, she was still alive. And wouldn't you know, I was out of cartridges."

"No!" Bob popped his eyes.

"So I had to slit her throat."

Rita fired again. Another explosion of dirt kicked up at the deer's head, missing. Two parallel drops of sweat rolled out of her hair at her temples.

"That must have been hard to do," Tom said. Rita could hear him talking to her, trying to soften it, make it easier for her. Then Steen answered, "Nah. It was easy."

A third report sounded. When Trooper Benson lowered her gun, the doe was still breathing.

Tom stepped into Rita's periphery, halted, letting her know he was in her field, then walked over to the deer. He made his hand into a pistol, his fingers tight as metal, and brought it close to the deer's head.

"You got to get close," Tom said. "Get right behind the ear. There'll be a little blood, but not too much." He moved back with the others.

Rita stepped forward and raised her revolver again. She used two hands to aim at a spot behind the doe's ear. She stepped a little closer. She fired. The report's echo faded into the hills, and the deer was dead. In the silence that followed, Steen giggled.

She knew her pants leg had been splattered, but she didn't look down. She didn't look at the men. She holstered her revolver.

"I'll call DPW to get it off your property, Mr. Zeilinski."

"I'd appreciate that, ma'am. Don't want to cross the law."

She slowly swept the men. She'd look forward to busting Steen some day. Bob and Sergeant Shook would probably have a good laugh. It was only Tom she wanted to say something to. Something like, You can change. Just walk away. She waited, but he wouldn't look at her.

"Gentlemen," she said, touching her hat. She walked back to the cruiser and checked in with the dispatcher, sat for a moment smelling the blood, then drove away.

As Rita drove back to the station she realized the sergeant had chosen her for this job. It's what rookies had to go through. But it wasn't being a rookie that momentarily filled her with regret.

She pulled off the side of the road and cut the engine. After taking a deep breath, she took out her wallet and pulled a photograph from a hidden pocket she had made in the leather. She studied the man in the picture — his sad, empty face, the expression of hopelessness, as if he was dying, as if he was a trapped animal. She looked at the photograph of herself, at the man she used to be.

If she were still a man, they would have laughed openly. If she still had her other body, their scorn would have been a begrudging sign of acceptance. She knew how they were. She thought about what the men had done to her, the way they mocked her, especially Steen. She crushed the photograph in her fist. They would never change, and it was too late for Tom. And she still wished, as she had when she was a little boy, unable to participate in the mob cruelty of little boys, that she could walk right up to things and kill them.

DISTORTION

A tree-lined lane, breeze rolling leaves as in film. Weeping willows rustle, rendered violet on the screen. The eye rolls slowly into and through the tunnel between trees, the path itself spattered with green sunlight. He'd thought of introducing the voice-over here, but his impulse now is to silence, not even canned wind or a dull background hum, but twisted silence as the eye rolls down the lane, imagining what's withheld from view. The spin across open fields, a hilltop cemetery shrouded by oak. Before we emerge from the lane, into the sky, the cut. To whatever, footage of George or Shawn or Bobby.

He pops out the tape, remotes CNN back onto the screen. George, probably, in shiny black pants and an open vest, revealing the compact musculature of his chest. He'll repeat the lane sequence seven times, each time going farther in and through, interspersed with footage of black men David's slept with. That's been done, sure, but his approach is more enlightened. He's using footage from *The Planet of the Apes*, the L.A. uprisings, basketball games, to pose questions about racial stereotypes and sexuality. Finally, in the distance, among the leaves, small shapes grow visible, squirming against the sky. These are small black dolls hanging by noosed strings, tossed by the wind in a way that suggests convulsions. This is an obvious reference to history, and David's using it to make a parade of images that excite him sexually pass as a political critique. As a closing shot he's considering the black slobbering head of a ravenous dog.

David's torn, usually. At an impressionable age he read an essay by that Susan Sontag woman, where she said Jews were guardians of the culture's moral sense and gay men of its aesthetics. He was obliged, therefore, to do both. While he's refined his sense of beauty, focused in on the particular beauty of African American males, he's created a distance between himself and his objects that he has a hard time justifying, since it buys into so many oppressive paradigms. He still manages to put personal ads in the weeklies: GJM, *36, lean, black hair, blue eyes, 8" cut, generous, seeks young black man to service*. The responses are always disappointing. He only found one film subject that way, Tony, a timid little English major he had to spice up with gangsta drag (baggy pants, hooded sweatshirt, baseball cap askew) so David could imagine he was being abused by some awesome young tough, straight outta the hood. In the film Tony emerges out of the mist, all in black, darkness itself against a textured stone wall.

On CNN a plane crash is being dissected for the zillionth time, the zillionth shot of pieces of the wreckage dredged from the ocean's floor. David could care less, but the news is like silence to him now, an empty background hum he often finds conducive to moments of artistic brilliance. That he's able at times to achieve such a heroic apathy toward the fate of the world and everyone in it, he considers a grand achievement approaching Zen enlightenment. He meditates every day, filling his mind with that emptiness where everything is shimmery potential, where nothing is good or evil. Images float past of pampered white children offering their backsides to men who look like Charles Barkley. Pampered white children abandoned in housing projects or prisons — dark passageways leading nowhere, metal gratings, concrete — the two settings are basically indistinguishable — tenderly raped by black men who've committed murders. David is one with the butt cheeks, tiny, soft, so white against the black hands which move them about.

He knows there's something essential missing from his film, it'll have to leap satori-like out of the psychic slime. On T.V., more grainy photos of the dead, passport, driver's license and high school yearbook, mostly. Touching accounts of some of the lives which were most filled with promise, most prematurely blunted. Artists, scholars, professionals, athletes. The dead are reverted to childhood, their mothers talk about their favorite cookie. The profound lack of virile black men involved in the tragedy makes it less conducive to blazes of illumination, so he remotes to MTV.

Reggie's been doing speed. Therefore, Los Angeles sucks. The public transportation is no good so if you want to get around, you have to find some guy with a car who wants to give you head. This one has an ugly apartment planted around a flat courtyard; it lets in all the neighbors' breakfast noises and salsa music and daytime television, but little, thank you, of the evil L.A. sunlight. It pens in two dogs whose frantic trajectories outline a space larger than the apartment itself, whose hair forms a thin woven layer over futon, clothes, lunch, dinner, carpet.

The guy spends an inordinate amount of time watching the five *Planet of the Apes* movies on his VCR, playing this computer game called "Lemmings" and wearing bizarre sunglasses. He's never divulged the source of his income, he doesn't seem to work, and Reggie could care less. He's too busy trying to keep his increasingly paranoid thought processes at bay, his conviction that the nourishment he's been receiving via dumpster diving contained a liberal assortment of cooked human parts, left there purposefully for him, styrofoam cartons just sitting there on top of the trash, that weird humanish taste no amount of sweet and sour sauce could hide. Oh, and that's just the beginning.

Why don't you take the dogs for a walk? the man suggests. He's looking at some pamphlet titled "Public Invited to Wind Its Way Through DNA." The reasons are many: the CIA, the Mexican Satanic Mafia and the cops, to name just three. But Reggie's obliged to make himself useful, the man obviously wants the apartment to himself to perform probably unspeakable acts, although come to think of it, is any act unspeakable? He's maybe going to pore over the tapes he's secretly made of their conversations, Reggie decides, or install equipment to scan Reggie's electromagnetic transmissions. Reason *numero cuatro*, the dogs themselves are evil.

Slobbering drooling snapping barking tangling leashes. In the cruisy part of Griffith Park, Reggie checks out the only youngish guy. My deal, he says, is I give a little head, but see my deal is, I collect. Yeah, yeah, who doesn't? Desperate people bore the shit out of Reggie, especially himself.

Back in the old days, psychiatrists always wanted to talk about his relationship with Dad, like the whole universe came down to that. Boring. Reggie was unhappy, a persistent drizzle on the other side of the psychiatrist's window, one of those views only available from inside correctional facilities: green and wet and dreamy, with a tiny gecko growing larger on the pane of glass. Inside, the human drone was like a trick to make the violence out there seem like relief. If it was true, as in the *Chhandogya Upanishad*, that the din of the dusty world and the locked-in-ness of human habitations are what human nature habitually abhors, while on the contrary, haze, mist and the haunting spirits of the mountains are what human nature seeks and yet can rarely find . . . then arson wasn't at all pathological, was it? And father fucking, who cares?

Reggie wasn't searching for a replacement. All sorts of people gave him hard ons, some reminded him of Dad, some didn't. The best way to escape society's sexual conditioning, he thought, is to branch out and turn sex into a whole range of things, right? Dad was a phase, Dad was over, he was worried about what was coming next, just around the corner, arson sex, cyborg sex, plant sex, not some mysterious reappearance of Dad.

Now, for twenty dollars, this unwholesome looking guy who smacks his lips when he talks is giving him a blow job in the bushes. The dogs are tied to a tree, unhappy. His dick is nowhere near hard. His head's throbbing and most of his life, until he can get some speed or some sleep, consists of pain. The light through the tree is green.

Black women are lined up, rhythmic bodies moving and weaving and snaking in harmony over the white nothingness of light only video can achieve. The bodies sometimes elongated, sometimes multiplied, the background sometimes fireworks, sometimes wild caged animals, sometimes live men with razors, sometimes the globe, sometimes pure radiating blue at accelerated speed. Back to the nothingness of white light. The lyrics: *my love said to me, a hero you'll be*, then some pop banality, with not only a feminist and black power subtext, but a hint of something way ugly at the very core of existence. David's reminded of the French symbolists, but can't put his finger on where or why. *Fear and loathing of the new* is rhymed with *funky dialects closing in on you.*

A picture of David's lover is perched on top of the television, because David feels it gives all his inspirational art and news a necessary subtext of death and decay. *Richard is one more dead gay man in a world*, the sentence goes, *that just doesn't care*. Fortunately, Richard was as indifferent to the world as the world was to him. Women, dolphins, oppressed Guatemalans, he didn't hold the world responsible. Additives, he said once, can accumulate in the body over time. I've put every imaginable chemical and body part inside mine, a virtual alchemical experiment. This is the end result of scientific inquiry. And I was hoping for illumination.

His skin was erupting with tiny pustules. He seemed to see death as impending relief. They'd been together two brilliant years, three tolerable ones, one total horror, half of a pretty good one and then three more excruciating, 365-day-long ones, as Richard broke out with the most loathsome infections, splotches and rashes and fevers, blisters around the anus, culminating in the short final explosion of AIDS dementia. He was awesome, cruel, honest, insane. David fell in love again, but had to move him to a hospice.

You believe, Richard told him, correctly, that everyone secretly wants to be raped by black men, and that's the basis of our entire cultural order.

A male nurse, ugly and blond, was giving him a sponge bath.

You think your own sexuality is the universe, Richard said. The nurse's eyes were empty, pretending, or actually, not listening to a word. David, Richard said, the fact that there are millions of black men locked up together in penal institutions out there doesn't excite me at all. I think of lice, body odor, ugly uniforms. I think of all those felons with bad skin and bad breath. Men who've never seen *Whatever Happened to Baby Jane*. Prisons are dull, David.

Nothing excited Richard at that point, except his own wit. When he wasn't in pain, he was obscenely content. Consciousness was manifesting itself as critic of Being. Being wanted to be so many things. Being wanted less to be a gangsta, David had decided, than to be a gangsta bitch. Gangstas were props, arranged accordingly. The women on the screen multiply again, five dancers into ten, into twenty, forty elongated women twisting in perfect harmony. If David could manifest himself, he'd be that. He glances at himself in the mirror, because beautiful black women remind him of his own looks, which pale in comparison. Not ugly, just boring. Boring could pass as cute when he was young, but now he's practically invisible. He's not much competition without money. Even the concept of "little white butt," inherently erotic, he's sure, to most black men, has lost its allure due to age.

One night, in a fit of lucidity, Richard was sad. Staring out the window at the eucalyptus, swaying *as if in film*, in an invisible breeze. *We have drifted apart lately, you and I* . . . His words began to turn against themselves, self-destruct, brilliant final sparks around the core of his waning selfishness and desire. Good-bye, good-bye. Staring, like a cat, at empty spaces. Going down now, taking all the microscopic life forms with him, the fungi and viral information, bacteria and spores. The last few T-cells giving up, calling it quits, submerging into the ocean of flux, the continual process of destruction, the world of Klee paintings, opposing armies of T-4s and macrophages and natural killer cells on one side, viral replicating machinery on the other, all going down with the ship. He lost consciousness, he died. David's first response was relief.

The day of Richard's funeral, David picked up Bobby in the park. My deal is, I give a little head, Bobby said, but see my deal is, I collect. Whatever. David didn't want a little head, he wanted to watch himself in his mirror being taken, he wanted his grief, his nostalgia, his whole life subdued under the fury of a black man's rage and lust. Bobby didn't do that. He would pose, however, one of his best sequences, Bobby wandering through the cottage in white boxers, picking up antiques, weird African artifacts, the kitschy vases that Richard collected, old pasty-faced dolls with horrific blue eyes. The white culture/black nature dualism was ridiculous, David knew, and not what this was about at all, he hoped.

When Bobby picked up a baroque mirror ringed with two stylized dragon figures, and contemplated his own image inside it, his face doubling at the same time that he started fondling his bulge, leaning backward in the most beautiful twisted motion and then dropping to one hand at the same time he let the mirror down on the bed, easily, perfectly . . . David had captured a physical movement so close to his own desire in time, *a subtle threat turned into an event of choreographed brilliance* . . . If he just let things happen in front of the camera, something obscure revealed itself in a way so enigmatic he could only name it mystery.

His mother called, to perform the social grace of consolation.

I'm with somebody, he said.

What do you mean you're with somebody?

For the first time in his life, he seemed to have thrown her off, and it was exquisite. She was prepared to offer her sympathy in a sophisticated way designed to let him know that this was the price he had to pay for the stupid life he'd chosen, for being gay.

I'm *with* somebody, he said. Call me back later.

He hung up the phone. She didn't call back for days, put it off on him, how *strange* he was being, and glided right on by with advice about how to get on with his life. He was already doing that, his first film had been accepted into the Gay and Lesbian Film Festival, thrown into a group of "multicultural shorts," sandwiched between a "stirring Filipino documentary on AIDS" and an "in-your-face exploration of the black lesbian experience." They'd classified the film as "multicultural" because the majority of the characters were played by beautiful mulattoes.

It was the life of Jesus, without words, motionless tableaus arranged among stylized, painted cardboard stage sets; a black Madonna holding the gorgeous infant, surrounded by the black wise men and the rough, half-naked shepherds; the boy Jesus with the elders, studying scrolls filled with symbols from Kabbala, Manicheanism, gnostic sects; and so on. David's best move was to go from a shot of Jesus on the cross to a shot of his mother, the black Madonna, on the cross, with Jesus staring into space beside her. This was his feminist moment. In the final shot, Jesus and the disciples were in a boat together, sailing away.

It was soft core porn, basically. Jesus stretched out on the cross in Hanes underwear, his groin thrust forward, his half-hard cock clearly visible through the cloth. He was played by an eighteen-year-old street kid named Donnie Ramirez, half black, half Jewish/Puerto Rican. In other scenes, a fan blew this sheer white sheet against his body, highlighting the slender muscles. He was straight and didn't sleep with David, although most of the disciples did. They were simply handsome, not mind-numbingly beautiful, so it was sort of required. The budget was low, but they were getting paid.

When Reggie returns, the guy's reviewing footage of these idealized landscapes that "always contain a certain note of the strange, but never descend to the exotic or the bizarre." There's a photo of a cheesy looking guy on top of the television. The face gives Reggie the weird impression it's vacationing in Hawaii. For lack of speed Reggie crashes under the blanket of dog hair.

Somewhere in there, the next few days, light is passing onto his skin, transforming it, and he, sprawled out in his underwear, is being recorded as light. Amazed at the brightness from above and his skin, which seems to be crawling with logos insects, with living information. At last he saw the angels: a vanilla moth landed on his shoulder, addressed the Earth, "Let us not be small-time little hoodlums all our lives, human beings. You wanted to be a cop. You wanted to make free U-turns in the street. You are a disaster, mankind, so weep. I can't believe you're standing there being a church that preaches love. Why not preach breathing air or something? Does it make sense?"

Somewhere shortly after, Reggie is presented with release forms, verifying he's at least eighteen and that he has no rights over the use of his own image. He barely registers all this in the brief flicker of a dream state. He wakes up for good Wednesday or Thursday, apparently, making it a two- or three-day crash, depending on his fucked up math, and there's the guy, sitting in a director's chair, loading the syringe.

In the background it's #4, *Conquest of the Planet of the Apes*, with the enslaved and ever more intelligent simians beginning their revolt against their human masters, led by the messianic offspring of the intelligent talking apes who arrived from the future — his own descendants actually, in this fucked up self-generating circle of time — in the original time traveling spaceship that Charlton Heston crashed into his own future with in the first movie. Charlton had been sliding ever since *Touch of Evil*, Reggie's favorite film ever. The apes, Roddy McDowell and Kim Hunter, escaped into the past just as Earth was finally being blown to bits by the mutant human descendants who lived *Beneath the Planet of the Apes* (Film #2). The man checks out Reggie's arm; he's got great veins, sticks the needle in.

Starts fiddling with Reggie's dick, nipples, chakras probably. His body's being transformed, from the inside this time, into a zillion tiny particles of light, warmth moving through him and totally opening him up. He trusts everyone completely, sees that humans are basically good, just a mess. He starts talking about his past.

This counselor, Xenobia, at the adolescent day treatment center, she always wanted to talk about Reggie's feelings of exclusion as a disadvantaged black youth. I'm not black, Reggie said, what does that have to do with anything? So she tried out the tragic mulatto routine, shunned by both sides, but Reggie wasn't exactly a mulatto either, what a falsely symmetrical word, half of one thing, half another, the synthesis of the dialectic . . . I hate Xenobia, and this smart hostile lesbian girl named Julie. With her primary colors, she needs to figure out her own problems. It was true that in her red and yellow sweaters Xenobia resembled a children's toy or a flag. It was true that she didn't understand young people at all. She was earnest and dumb. She never asked any of them if they were gay. The reason I feel most oppressed, Reggie told her, is that I'm color blind, so I can never be a fireman. Reggie didn't really believe in society. He believed in stupid people like Xenobia who filled up all these institutions from the bottom to the top and saw paragraphs from a book instead of confused, but basically intelligent humans.

Reggie lost his patience, grew careless sometimes. Mom? he'd say. Oh, she's going through menopause, she loves it, she says she's never felt freer in her life. She's cut down on her smoking, she's learning to be a ninja, I can never find her anymore.

That was a lie. Reggie's mother made him unbearably sad, the way she watched daytime television and washed the dishes when she was angry with people who'd stepped out of her life ten years before. She quit her ninja classes after three weeks, she cut her hair and looked like Glen Campbell as a woman. It was disturbing.

As for Xenobia, she didn't get poetry from a sixteen year old. She didn't understand that Reggie skipped his classes so he could get stoned and read William Faulkner in the bushes, masturbate in the sunshine and decorate his room with a collage of surrealist art cut out of library books. She declared him schizophrenic and had him committed to the adult ward in Redwood City. She came to see him there and said, You really are crazy. Do you wanna spend the rest of your life in your room, doing nothing? Her sweater was white with blue and red deer shapes.

So I've been thinking about words, says Reggie. David's face seems to convey nothing at all. They let us dress up our thoughts, says Reggie, with sound waves so we can communicate and manipulate each other and engage in discussions that let our thoughts merge and have thought babies kind of, just get weirder and freakier, which means they evolve really fast. The thoughts are alive, I think. We aren't. I know the sound waves are alive, too, but I'm not sure how the two relate. To think of yourself you have to neurally hook up all these different things that the two halves of the brain do. The planum temporale is bigger on most people's left side, you can even see the asymmetry in a fetus, it has to do with language centers. So, see, the left side is programmed to make certain kinds of speech, but the question is, programmed by who?

David likes to feel used, but secretly admired, by black men. He likes to feel that they're basically unfathomable to each other, but that they consider him to have soul, for a whitey. You try to stylize people to the point where they're some fantasy of, say, thoughtless aggression wrapped up in a super sensual body, and this sort of conversation happens. Fortunately, he's got Reggie down on film just how he wants him: beautiful and fucked up and silent.

Now, Reggie is pulsing with chemicals, which creates an effect that registers as an intense, spiritualized sexuality and David wants more of that. But Reggie can't stand people who say nothing at all, Reggie can't stand sitting in a room with nobody when energy is filling him out completely. He has his clothes on, he's out the door. David closes his eyes, dreaming of Reggie. The image proliferates, along with wars, famines, blasphemies. David reviews the footage.

GHOSTS, POCKETS, TRACES, NECESSARY CLOUDS

i.

From the kitchen, Mark heard the lock on his apartment door open with a sudden clunk. He turned a rubber band around four pieces of fan mail and put a kettle on the stove to boil. He heard the soft rustling of his lover's jacket as it was perched on the coat stand by the door.

It had been a few weeks since he last saw Jules; he could feel him slipping out of his grasp the last time he saw him, when Mark gave him a key to his apartment. Jules spent too much time talking about his wife. He said he really did not love her, but he was inviolably married too. Mark tolerated Jules's attempt at drawing pity and comfort from him, that was a minor drawback. To listen and maybe counsel was a small price to pay for a fairly consistent, unobtrusive affair.

They both wanted a sex life without the hassles. Mark in particular didn't want to spend all his money looking for sex anymore, but he wouldn't have told that to Jules. And Mark didn't want to put Jules on the spot by asking for some promise of security. It would be too much trouble to renegotiate their friendship.

Mark chose to put out the flags that said he wanted to be fucked, no strings attached, no romance involved, and he wouldn't change his tune now.

Maybe this would have Jules spend more time with him after all, having Mark's apartment as a pocket of abandon in a universe of heavy burdens and responsibility. And it was up to Mark to keep things light. Hence: the unshod feet, the T-shirt too thin and shrunken to fold into shorts too tight for pockets, the ginseng tea in sweltering weather. And he would try the it's too hot to wear a suit, why don't you put on some shorts? gambit.

Jules was just right. Sweet or aggressive at just the right times, independent but not cold. Jules wore the suit but not the attitude. Mild in public, wild in private. Certainly not a fan boy: Mark's past fame would mean nothing to him, if he knew about it, nor did he care for music. He was a regular guy who liked to have sex with men, Mark in particular. Just what Mark wanted, nobody militant, especially overtly so — a trustworthy man, straight-acting, for all the world innocent of secrets. That Jules liked to fall in love with men wasn't an issue when they met late one night at a very expensive, selective bar in the Upper East Side. A place named Indiscretions, the kind of place that has no sign or store-front, just word of mouth.

"Hi," Jules said. "Sorry I'm late."

"I'm starting to get accustomed to it," Mark said. "Would you like to take a seat? I'm making some tea."

"Thank you," Jules said, pulling out a chair from the breakfast nook. "Isn't it too hot for tea?"

"No time to brew and chill it. I could pour it over ice, if you like." Mark pulled down two mugs from the cupboard, conscious of how Jules was taking quick, interested glances at his legs, and chest, and privates. Mark almost stopped to pose for him to stare at, but that would be too funny. Just a casual tease, an obvious attempt to take Jules's attention, a flirt that Mark wouldn't allow himself in public — being so obvious, demonstrative. Mark placed small tea strainers on the mouth of each mug. "But it's ginseng tea, it's meant to be hot," Mark added. He then shook tea leaves, from a tiny tin box, into the strainers. "Wouldn't want to upset any Chinese gods."

Then Mark shot Jules a "what are you lookin' at?" eye, making Jules blush.

"Wouldn't want to do that," Jules said. Jules, fingering his tie loose under his collar, looked at the packet of letters. Mark felt urgently the need to take those letters away. He should have hidden them. And yet he couldn't stop Jules from undoing the rubber band.

"Fan letters," Mark said coldly. "Pretty juvenile."

"How am I not surprised that you get fan mail?"

"Before we met, I was a recording artist."

"Before the small home repairs thing?"

"During," Mark said, sitting down, the water burbling in the kettle. "It's interesting how some people write to you, still."

"You a musician?" Jules said. "Why didn't you tell me?"

"It's just something I did."

Jules began to unfold the flap of a beige envelope, addressed in purple ink. "Can I look?"

Mark quickly took the other letters from the table and tapped the tabletop with the hard paper edge of the envelopes. Jules stopped short of pulling out a page or two of typed, sticky erasable bond.

"I prefer you don't," Mark said softly.

"I'm just curious," Jules said. "I don't mean to intrude."

Mark stood up to take the whistling teakettle off the flame.

"Well, it isn't like I'm going to take over your life," Jules said.

"It isn't," Mark said. Mark brought over the mugs.

"It's not like I don't have a key to your place," Jules said.

"It's a privilege I give few."

Jules chuckled as Mark poured tea. "Mark, you can be so fuckin' imperious! If I've 'earned' your trust enough to let me in anytime I want to, you could at least feel comfortable."

Mark dipped the strainer in and out of the steaming cup with a slight shake of his wrist. "Would you want me to drop by your house?"

"No," Jules said. "Certainly that's not what we've agreed to."

"So don't read my mail," Mark said, removing the strainer and placing it on a paper napkin. "Sugar?"

"Yes. Why?"

"I don't need explanations," Mark said. "One or two spoons?"

"One," Jules said, with a finality to it.

They sipped the tea — Mark without sugar, as he knew it was supposed to be taken. If the ginseng had its desired revitalizing effect on the two, it would be the worst time for it. The silence was unbearable.

Mark felt shamed into turning his eyes. When he was busy with music, recording and tours, he never even read them. Some agency just mailed them a glossy of him and his keyboard, all ripped leather and spiky brush hair, and mirror shades, standing underneath a lonely streetlight near a pier, like a hustler.

"I'm sorry," Mark said, all of a sudden. "I can be very condescending."

"I thought you'd be different."

"How?"

"I'm probably not that gay, I'm not so hung up."

"It's just me, then."

"It's not just you, it's all of this," Jules said. "All this fuckin'

hide-and-seek. If you people weren't so full of shit, with your stupid lifestyle, and made it so hard for the rest of us, I'd probably
be with a guy now."

"I'm pretty ordinary."

"Not when I'm sticking it up your ass."

That flew by so quickly it made Mark shudder. Mark hadn't
seen that one coming. "It's a hard life," Mark said. "People won't
back off. That's why I don't make music anymore."

"Oh, yeah?"

"I can't understand why it's so important that they have to
know."

"I don't know either. . . . My wife and I were at a party last
week. She made all these fag jokes, as if she were talking to me in
front of these people. . . . It slips out when you least expect it, like
she's got evidence against me in her pocket. . . ."

"So you think she knows?"

"I think so," Jules said. "Anybody ever catch you?"

Mark stopped to consider what to reveal, and if he should.

"You don't have to if you don't want to," Jules said.

"There was this colleague of mine," Mark said. "Pretty open
about it; I didn't resent him for it. But he was so bent on dragging
people out in the open, I don't know why. We were at a bar, all
the record people and the band and me, and this guy just said,
in front of me, out loud for everyone to hear: 'Mark *has* to be
gay, someone who writes songs like that *has* to be gay.' He was
trying to provoke me. I almost punched his face in. I was just so
in love with him, and I was waiting for the right moment, for
when we would have privacy, for me to bring him home with me,
and show him who I really am. Because I found his openness so
attractive."

"You fall in love?"

"Not anymore," Mark said. "I'll never be open, especially if assholes like him get to feel good about themselves because I'm like them."

"I don't know," Jules said. "I don't get it with angry faggots. What did you say to him?"

"I said nothing, and somebody changed the subject quickly."

Mark noticed that Jules's cup was empty. Mark quietly offered him a refill by lifting his tea strainer. Jules nodded.

"I hate it," Mark said.

"This gay thing?"

"No. That I silenced myself into oblivion."

Mark refilled his cup.

"'Silenced myself into oblivion,'" Jules reiterated, sugaring his tea. "I like how that sounds."

"So do the people who write to me," Mark said. "Not exactly what I felt."

"So you were faking it?"

"I never really said anything to begin with."

It was so very uncomfortable. Mark wanted to keep things like this a closed issue. He never thought that his sex life — once anonymous, now more personable if discreet — would ever ask him to open up like this. He just wanted to be wanted for himself, not for what he felt or thought or did. And yet to acquiesce, to give full access to someone else seemed desirable, and even necessary, in moments when his heart was really in it — usually when he was meditating on it, while fixing a house, alone.

"Well . . . I didn't come here to talk," Jules said, taking Mark's forearm. "I'm not here to figure out my life, or figure out yours."

"Please. Continue."

"I'm sorry to have pushed it. I should have respected your privacy."

"Someone's got to push the envelope," Mark said.

Mark pushed the letters to Jules's side of the table, putting on a good, humbled face.

Jules just glanced at them, not really reading them, like glancing at a memo to see if it did have something to say to him. By the time Jules had sped through a few of them, Mark had cleared the table of his mug, rinsed the mug and the teakettle, and set them to dry on a wooden dish rack.

"So?" Mark said.

"These kids must not have much of a life," Jules said. "What kind of a freak would write something like this?"

"I was afraid you'd say that," Mark said.

"Why?"

Because I am like those kids.

"They're pretty weird," Mark said. "It's getting very hot in here . . . let me lend you a pair of shorts and a T-shirt."

"Okay," Jules said.

When Mark tried the shorts-and-T-shirt gambit on men he wasn't sure were in the mood, they never got a chance to try them on once they undressed.

It also worked this time.

ii.

Jan 6, 198-
Dear Mr. Mark Piper:

I hope my letter gets to you somehow.

I am a big fan of yours. When is your next record coming out? Will your old records be out on CD? (I just bought a used CD player. I've been buying most of my favorite stuff on CD since, wish is OK, since I don't have a lot of favore-ites.) I haven't found anything at the record store; they just have *Ghosts*, your first album (in cassette). I miss having new music from you. None of the other kids in school listen that much to you lately. You are too "wierd". I like "wierd" music, and "wierd" vidios. I guess I'm pretty "wierd".

I think I am your biggest fan. I have everything of yours. I say I "love" your music, like I would love someone. I listen to your music and I feel at home. I read the lirics on the sleeves and sometimes, when I hear the songs, they make me cry.

I have a hard time explaining how your songs feel to me. It's like you sing the songs of my life, like my life is a movie and your songs are the songs in the soundtrack album. (I'm wierd!) I once even dressed up for Halloween as you. You say things for me that I cannot say like you say them. Like when I love somebody, it's like your songs say. And when I'm sad or angry or confused I feel like you feel, and I don't know what that means, like your songs say. And when I hear your music I don't feel so wierd or lonely, because I think if you met me you would like me and understand me. Because I understand the ghosts in your music:

> *"Silenced into oblivion*
> *got too many things to hide*
> *pain that I've been given*
> *pain I've got inside*
> *ghosts inside my pockets*
> *shadow traces deep inside me*
> *necessary clouds inside me*
> *necessary clouds inside."*

Please make more records.
Sincerely,
Anthony French
Cincinnati, OH

iii.

Now it was as if he had jumped off the plane with all the thrill of the risk and the feeling of falling and the ground moving so fast toward him, and him ready to let his parachute unfurl, and let his feet touch the ground. But now, as soon as he jumped off the airplane, gravity stopped, and he just stayed still, in midair, with nowhere to go to, unable to land, desperate for that endless floating to be over, and to touch land, touch what was real, if there were only land underneath him —

Mark stretched on his back, his legs pulled tight to his chest, as Jules slowly entered him, the first feelings of penetration always uncomfortable, then that feeling of feeling full instead of empty, then, once in, Jules went in and out of him and the inarticulable ardor was not there. Just the discomfort, just the feeling of being perforated like tissue paper; it was like shitting backward, not a trace of that gut feeling of being loved and wanted and pleasured.

Mark looked above Jules's face, straining with sweat and effort, at the ceiling, and it was as if he were really up there, watching himself with a cold eye, a strange feeling of being disembodied, as if Jules were fucking his body but not him, as if he was letting his body be usurped, but his spirit was not here with him, his body was hollow, just meat without spirit.

And the strange thing was how Mark had initiated sex, as if he wanted it after all — as if he *should* want it. Because that was enough. Being fucked by someone less of a stranger was a consolation prize for not finding love, and certainly better than being fucked by a stranger. And yet did he not let him in, into the privacy of his home, even let him look at things that he'd rather keep private, things that it would hurt to reveal, did he not let him inside him?

There was something fundamentally wrong with this, and he

couldn't put his finger on it — wait, Jules was catching on that his heart wasn't in it; Mark moaned and begged to be fucked harder, even though Jules was going at it as he had in the past.

And in the past, hadn't it been pleasurable? That he'd found someone reasonably right for him, with a minimum of haranguing about it. The thrill of it, the first few months, it was immensely pleasurable to be overwhelmed by this man.

Now there was something missing that hadn't been missing before. Maybe it was missing before, but he didn't see it was missing.

And he could see Jules's face grimace and feel Jules's roar growing slowly inside him, and Mark remembered to fake it, to fake the pleasure, to stretch and moan and clench his jaws and his bowels in rhythm as if he too were coming from being fucked.

Even though he didn't feel anything but some uncomfortable physical sensations.

Jules came inside him. With a few thrusts, each one deeper and slower and more finally exhausting than the next, Jules became still, and leaned down to kiss Mark.

"You're *so* hot," Jules said.

"You're hot too," Mark said.

Mark still floated in the air, above ground masked by clouds that would not break. Mark breathed in silence for a few minutes while they cuddled, horrified by how easily he could deny himself, deny his feelings the dignity of their own truth, and pretend that their denial could erase any trace of what they revealed to him about himself, as if he could make their gravity seem not all that real, as if this lie was better than knowing in full, undeniable clarity what the shame and pain were all about. But the illusion that this man, that *any* man could really fulfill him through sex just couldn't be maintained any longer.

The clouds broke. Maybe he was truly the weird one, the one unable to live like everyone else, with their secrets, their hypocrisies, their lies, their distractions, their easy satisfactions, all because he was a man and engaged in this kind of sex. It was not the kind of sex, but the kind of love he wanted that disturbed him. The mere ghost of an idea, the idea of being a man and wanting to love and be loved by a man filled him with far more shame than just mere sex. And nothing could fulfill him in the face of such an unexplainable, impossible love. And mere sex, in the face of this unresolvable longing, was worse than mere loneliness.

The clouds broke, and he fell, and finally touched cold, hard ground.

RUNNING SHOES

I am a man who, having failed at business, marriage, and father-hood, lives in a mobile home with myself and my second and final wife, my Helen. She will stay, I know, because of time and because of Todd, my son, who is gone. I am clumsy with speech. Spoken words make me nervous, cautious. People expect them to make sense, to carry truth. When I speak I am startled by the chasm between what I think and the words that fumble from me. What I have written in my life have been letters either composed on a computer and printed out in tiny ink dots, or earlier, before the technology, drawn with red felt pens that rode along the edge of a ruler. This way the letters on the page would come out straight as soldiers, with flat, aborted bottoms, standing squarely against a blue line, and always on a legal pad. Near the end, when writing Todd, I'd slide the ruler aside, compose the letters in my own hand, and sign them, "Love, Dad," in a crooked red streak.

I became an adult when my own father chased me from the garage with an ax. I ran into the air force. Korea was on, it was 1952, I was 18. The armed forces seemed a safer place: posters vivid with camaraderie and patriotism, promises of home loans and tuition, clear and sanctioned enemies. Then there was college and the bank. I became a CPA and spent my days in front of led-gers, bowing my head to yellow fields of gray penciled numbers, able to add tall columns of figures at a running glance. This was never math to me, it was sense — balance, order. None of which would ever make sense to Todd. He dodged math in school, the way he did physical education, inventing ailments and excuses, forging notes in his mother's hand. I see these now not as signs of his weakness, but as the start of his strength. I could make sense of life by balancing numbers, I thought, everything coming out even in the end: no debits, no credits. He knew better, beyond much of this, even as a boy.

Watching men chase balls up and down a field, or back and forth across a court, also made sense of life to me. These games were, though are no longer, things I could love dearly and yet not dearly enough to fear or suffer their loss. Losing these games I watched other men play hurt me little. The thrill of seeing them won was short and shallow as well, beginning with whoops in an empty room, fists punching through the cigar smoke over my chair, ending with me brooding over the bottom of a bourbon.

On sports, like math, Todd drew only a blank. Which meant there was no plane on which our selves overlapped. He would stare at my TV, it full of a game, and by his very silence say, "What?" or once, audibly, when he was eight: "So many colors." He would then walk away, moving to where I left off, to the end of me, the beginning of himself. I would find him later, cloistered in his room, bent over his sketch pad, the faces he had drawn scat-tered over the floor.

I see now that Todd became a man at 18 as I had, when he ran away from home. We were behind the house, laying up a cord of wood for the winter, something we did every August in the high heat of summer. There was, he had told me, an art school in New

York that would take him, "That," I told him, "I cannot support. Paint if you want. A hobby or something. In your spare time. But first do something to support yourself."

We each stared down at the ax in my hand. Both of us knew the story, and in the morning when his car was gone, I knew I had chased him away. The irony was not lost, nor was it intentional. It was merely predictable.

I could not know then that his work would be considered brilliant in circles; that he would make money; that he would paint only at night and only when he was high; that his work would show in galleries, hanging from white, white walls in places I'd never heard of. Now, whenever I see something of his work, the only sense it makes to me is that it makes no sense at all; this, and that in his painting I see the light and the darkness moving together at once.

He didn't come home again until he was 28. Ten round years. I had lost my business, my house, Todd's mother to divorce, a lung to cancer, the habit of liquor. I had gained a wife who collects crystal people: tiny glass families that she houses in a curio cabinet near the front door so that they are the first thing she sees coming home. Sometimes, on her weekends — she is a nurse with odd days off — I will see her pulling them from the cabinet, spraying them with blue liquid and rubbing them in her palms, the way I imagine one would rub a stillborn puppy, hoping to massage a life into it. I also gained half her mobile home — looking at it from the street, I am reminded of a place where hurricanes hit, a target for an act of God. Often, it seems, in the spring and fall, we will see on TV a trailer park ripped to shrapnel by some riot of weather and Helen will turn to me, a hand against her cheek, her face dark with dread. I will look at her and say only, "Now, now." Helen was my nurse when I lost the lung, sturdy and firm, and intent on finding someone to fix. I was alone and lonely, having lost so much, and needed someone and something to gain. She takes care of me. Something I never knew how to do, alone or with anyone else. That was enough to make me love her then and still.

Todd stood at the door, the ten years and more between us, the red heat in his face from having run five miles. I had no idea who he was. I saw that his eyes were his mother's and that, until that moment, he had been only a product of my own ambition, my own imagination, my distance. He did not look like a son I would have. His hair was wild, big, a tumble of brown corkscrews reaching his shoulders. He had driven here — 2,000 miles — following a message I had left on his phone machine: "I guess it's been ten years. I have a new wife. This is your father. Not new anymore. Two years November. Maybe you would think about coming for Christmas." I then said something about bygones, and hung up, knowing that my words had fallen out of order, that I sounded like a man teetering between confession and absolution, not brave enough to offer or beg either. I felt a coward. He would know this, I thought, that I was an old man, toddling toward forgetfulness, forgiveness, bygones. He would know the smallness of my life, how petty my past, that the greatest thing I had done was fail at being his father. What I would know later was that he was gay and had been sick. And later still, after he had gone, I would think that to hear one's only son is at once gay and sick must be a sort of road-post toward the end of the world. I would tell myself I was being melodramatic, then not, just finally astute.

Todd sat in Helen's chair, his legs crossed, one foot kicking at the air. They were tattered, his shoes, the emblems fraying, an eruption of sock through a split in the seam where the sole and upper had been sewn together. I wondered at this. His car in the driveway would have cost more than this trailer. Helen was at the hospital, and from the TV came the scramble and crack of football helmets. Todd pulled a bandanna from his hair and wiped at the sweat on his forehead.

"Good run?" I said.

"Hard to breathe. The air here is so dry — brittle."

"You should see the summer."

"I should see a lot of summers."

From the TV came a whistle, and a flag was thrown. "Helen gets home usually around four. We eat early. You up, maybe, for a movie? A matinee?"

"Yeah, sure."

"We probably don't have the kinds of movies you're used to seeing in — "

He cut me off. For this I would have hit him ten years ago. "The world is one big cineplex now. Hollywood is everywhere, which is why it isn't there anymore and needn't be."

"Isn't where? What isn't where?" Used to be I would not ask such questions — the lost father too proud to pull into gas stations for directions. Todd's speech had often been riddle or drama to me. I used to ignore him. But now, sitting here, my newspaper in my lap, my game on the TV, my son in my wife's chair, I saw that Helen had taught me I could be safely lost.

"Hollywood. All that's left are the letters on the hill. The rest is history and myth." And, as if to end this pronouncement quickly, he hurled himself from the chair and toward the hall. "A movie," he said, "would be swell. You pick. I've seen nothing."

On the TV it was halftime, a band had taken the field, and the majorette's headdress had caught fire — apparently from her flaming baton. The plumage towering over her head whorled with fire; the band spread away from her; she struggled alone on the fifty-yard line, batting at the headdress, trying to topple it from her head. For this Todd stopped, looked back at the TV, threw his head back laughing. "Burn, girl!" he said.

"Todd!"

"Wait," he said. "Look. She got it off. Poor thing. Looks like she saved her hair, though." From the TV came roaring applause.

I picked a movie in which the father sickens and dies, leaving a son with an unresolved anger. This was an accident that embarrassed me. I wondered how I would later talk myself out of whatever entrapment or staging Todd must have imagined. At the climax of the film, when the son predictably bawls out his bottled rage, Todd abruptly went for popcorn, and I saw this as an act of revenge on his part, a statement of sorts.

It was still light when the movie let out, and I drove us to a park on the edge of town that is something like a forest of cacti. The day had gone suddenly cold, and the freeze in the air blued the sky. I told him what I had learned about the cacti. How slowly they grow. An inch a year, I thought. I pointed to the strange ways some of them reached to the sky, "like arms," I said.

"It's very lunar, here," he said.

"The man on the moon," I said.

"I was sick last year, Dad."

"Well, join the club."

"Mine you can't cut out."

"Your what?"

He looked into me, not at me or around me, but into me, for the first time since perhaps he was a child being taught to cross a busy street, as if to ask, "Why have you brought me to this dangerous place?"

"The big one. My blood." What I had always known, what had been voiceless and thoughtless and closeted in my head, became as clear to me as my own name, my own memory of my own life, the pulse of the clock in the dash. "You're telling me you're gay, aren't you?"

"That isn't really the point."

"It is *a* point." I pressed my fingers against my thighs, down toward my knees, grabbing them. "Are you sick now?"

"It never goes away, all the way. It's like a tide. It goes in and out, a little higher every time it comes in, and then you drown. I had pneumonia. I was in the hospital. I got better. This time. I'm back to running a little."

I noticed again his tattered running shoes. "Are you alone, I mean out there, in New York, Manhattan?"

Todd reached for the glove box. His hand was trembling. He fumbled with and then opened the latch and pulled out a map of the desert. "Yes," he whispered. The rest of him began to shake, and against the map fell the splatter of three tears. "I have friends," he said, "but I have no Helen."

"What about Nick?"

"He moved west. He died. That was '89. He was always only a friend. Not *only* a friend — *a* friend."

I wanted to touch him, but was afraid, not so much of him, but of my own hand, that it would impart no strength, that it would fail him again, or worse — as I hadn't touched him since he was a baby, or in violence as a boy — that it might shock him, feel to him like another blow. I thought of having no Helen, and began to know that Todd feared this aloneness more than this sickness, this tide rising inside him. When Todd was a boy, seven, he came to the table with a crayon behind each ear, and, sitting in his chair, his bread knife clutched like a weapon in his hand, said that Nick was his best friend in the whole world and didn't that mean he could spend the night, he in my sleeping bag, Nick in Todd's mother's.

"Yes," I said, "it could mean that, but wouldn't you rather I take you to a game?"

"No," he said, "not really. Sleeping over is better because that way when you wake up, he's still there and you can just start playing instantaneously." Instantaneously. I wondered where and when he had found this word.

On the day of the night Nick was to sleep in our house, Todd and I rolled the sleeping bags out on his bedroom floor. "They should be," he said, "next to each other in the middle of the room, so close they almost touch, but not quite." Nick showed up, small, silent and doe-eyed. I did not like him. He was shy and scared, prone with Todd to fits of giggling, which I would abruptly end when I entered Todd's room. "Now, now," I would say, putting out their laughter, "now, now."

By the time Todd turned nine, he was sleeping on the top of a set of bunk beds he had said was the only thing in the world he wanted for Christmas, the one and only thing. I rarely went into Todd's room, because, I think now, it did not seem like a son's room to me at all: it was against my imagination, or rather proved the presence of his, the absence of mine. The wall opposite the bunks was covered, littered, I thought, with his art — vague and brooding faces swimming from dark fields; huge sheets of paper covered with mottled blue sky, tricks of color and light I did not understand. One Thursday, having lost count of my bourbons playing poker the night before, I stayed home from the office, hung. Todd's mother was having her hair done. I stepped into Todd's room and saw first the wall of painted faces, then the ceramic nameplates Todd had obviously made and glued to each headboard over each bed: above the top bunk, written into clay with his finger, TODD, and another above the bottom bunk reading, NICK. There was a lurch in my stomach, a rush of saliva in my mouth, and I did not quite make it to the toilet in time.

When Todd came to dinner that night, I told him he must remove the plaques and promise never to glue anything to furniture again. "We paid good money," I said. When he protested I slapped him hard and once across the face. His mother looked away. Todd stared into my eyes, his tears defiant and silent, so silent they robbed all sound from the room, and I left the table, going early and hungry to bed. Two days later, Saturday, opening the door to Todd's room, I saw that the plaques were still on the bunks. Todd, sitting in the window and staring up the street into a rain that would later flood the state, turned to me, his face wet with the same defiant, silent tears. "Nicky's moving," he said, "to New Jersey." At this he pointed to a dot on a map tacked to the wall near his bed. "It's too far to visit. The time is different there. Three hours."

When Todd was fourteen, I replaced the bunk beds with a full bed. Before calling the Goodwill, I chiselled the plaques with the boys' names from the headboards. Their names split to shards. I helped the men load the bunks into an empty trunk, apologizing for the inexplicable scars on the wood, shaking my head and saying, "Boys. Boys."

At first, sitting in the car, surrounded by cacti, mountain, and failing light, and still, days later, surrounded by the Sunday paper, I did not know what to ask him, what to say. I knew only that he had been sick, had friends, but in a way that frightened him, was alone. Helen followed Todd, who carried her boxed Christmas tree from the storage shed, into the living room. While they assembled her tree, I shuttled from game to game on the TV, from section to section in the paper. The inky-green limbs rustled like skirts as Todd pulled them from a huge cardboard box and presented them to Helen, who screwed them into a thick dowel trunk.

"They're like bottle cleaners," Todd said.

"Like what?"

Todd reached a tree limb toward Helen. "Bottle cleaners. You know those brushes you use to wash bottles with."

Helen laughed. "Yes! Yes. Like for baby bottles."

"Bingo," Todd said.

Helen twisted a limb into the pocked, painted wood. Todd must have dragged his hand against a screw as he drew another limb from the box, because he winced and his hand came up bleeding. Helen, the nurse, reached for the wound.

"Don't," I said, dropping the remote control and lowering the footrest, "don't touch it."

They looked at me, first Helen, then Todd. The room sounded only of football. "*It?*" she said. "*It* doesn't *bite.*" Holding Todd's wrist in the air, she sailed him into the bathroom. I fell back to my paper, fumbled for the remote control, switched to San Diego at Denver. A man was down on the field, holding his groin, raising his knees toward his face, as if to kiss them.

"Yes, he's definitely down," one sportscaster said.

"Darned if he's not," said another.

"He's not, he's not crying, is he?" At this the camera zoomed in, trying to catch him crying behind his face mask.

"Can't really tell. No, must be sweat. You know, it hurts like childbirth." They both chuckled.

I had always marked the history of my life by what happened in these games. As they carried that man, grabbing himself, crying off the field, I marked the moment in my life when I knew that my wife and my son were braver than I.

Helen glided Todd back into the room by his wrist and presented his bandaged hand. "He's fixed," she said to me, and to him, "Now, *you* screw, *I'll* pluck."

After dinner Todd said he needed to use the phone. A few minutes later I heard his voice through the thinly paneled walls and over the noise of the TV. Helen was in the kitchen with dishes. I lowered the volume on the set and listened for Todd. "Nothing. Absolutely nothing . . . well, a little, I guess, a cactus, a tumbleweed . . . very Georgia O'Keeffe . . . no! none of that." At this he laughed and began whispering. I lowered the TV further, moved to a chair nearer the wall between us. "I swear to god . . . like the moon . . . some sort of lunar substation . . . very *Lost in Space* . . . yes . . . okay, so get a visual on this . . . no, nothing, nothing is real . . . yes, the tree too . . . what is Monsanto? . . . wait, I'll check . . . yes, even the bedspreads . . . *however*, it's fire retarded . . . right, *retardant*." At this I heard the rollicking, romping roll of his laughter, a laughter I had not heard in fifteen years, since he was 13 and I had barged into his bedroom, pulled the phone from his hand, said, "You are being a girl," and hung it up. At 28 my son was in the spare bedroom of my petroleum byproduct house, giggling like a girl, and imagining, I guessed, that I did not realize the fabrication of my own life, that I had fallen, failed at so much. That he found any of this, or even me, funny, bothered me little. What did bother me was this: How could he laugh so wildly, yet be more lonely than I, more dying than I? Helen and I rarely laughed together, though she would alone at the TV or on the phone with a friend, like Todd. My laughter, she said, sounded like a car that wouldn't turn over, a motor with a dead battery. I heard Todd hang up the phone and a moment later he was standing in the doorway, yawning.

"Where on earth did you learn to laugh like that?"

"You heard?"

"Only you laughing."

"From Mom, I guess. Yes, laughing, that would be a Mom part."

When I woke up the next morning Helen had already gone, and the notion of filling up a day for and with Todd frightened me. It was as if one day, with my son in it, represented an expanse of land and sky that I could neither walk nor see across. I could think only of meals, of where to get ourselves fed; or of movies, of where to sit in a dark cave, facing the pulse of a screen. I heard the aluminum door slam against its jamb, and, sitting up in bed, saw, through the frosted window, Todd in his running gear, cutting through the gravel drive in his tattered shoes. Then I saw him running toward the road. Long, loping, deliberate strides, his hands in gloves.

I don't move quickly, then or now. But on that morning I came close to leaping from my bed and running for the room where Todd had slept. He had brought, in addition to his running shoes, two other pairs: black boots with heavy buckles and a pair of rubber sandals. Both were size 11, 11-D. I dressed as quickly as I could and was out of the trailer and the park before Todd came home. I was, I think, giddy with the notion that I knew what to buy my grown son for Christmas.

They were the most colorful, highly technical, expensive shoes I had ever bought or seen. The logos on the shoes reminded me of Mercury's wings and I thought of Todd, in these shoes, running, running, running. In the three days before Christmas, I bought him books on running, running shorts, shirts, a journal. I bought him a book of runners' recipes. Running became the one thing I knew about him that was safe to ask, a thing for which doing homework brought no fear. He ran when the weather was not too bad, and on days he felt strong, days he felt his wind would not fail him. He ran around a reservoir, a battery, and a village — all in Manhattan. He had been in Vermont for October and had run through rains of falling leaves, a thing he had returned to New York to paint, the motion of falling leaves, "you and light passing through them," he said.

I see now that our zeal for his running, both his and mine, was also about fear. I feared Todd would stop running because he could run no longer, because he had fallen sick again, too sick to run. And Todd, I imagine, feared the same. I thought that to engage him in his running, to encourage him in it, might perpetuate the running, him.

I would be able to divine, perhaps because I am his father — no matter that I was inept or absent much of his life — Todd's reaction to my gift the moment the lid came off the box. Todd simply stared at the shoes, his face naked from discovery, his eyes pooling and blinking, and slowly plucked away the tissue paper.

"You got me shoes," he said.

"It looked like you needed some new ones."

"They fit," he said, pulling them on over his socks.

"I checked your others. While you were out. Running. I didn't mean to snoop. It was only your shoes."

He stood up, looked down at them on his feet, wiggled his toes in them. Helen offered that the shoes were cute, that she would love a pair like that for the hospital.

Todd looked at her. "I think the idea," he said, "is to keep them, and me, out of the hospital." Todd stared across the room at me, and said, I think, though I was never quite sure I heard him correctly, "You get it, don't you?"

"You look strong when you run," I said. "I mean, you seem to be a strong runner. Your form. Long, solid strides. As though you were built that way."

"Am," he said, just, "am." He then said thank you.

I do not remember what he gave me, only that when he handed it to me, he said, "You win. You tore the tape, crossed the line first." He looked down at his shoes. "I could never beat these." His jaw was trembling.

The looming regret I have about life is that there are stationary fronts, banks of cloud between fathers and sons, between men, between a man and himself. Because of these I had no idea how to touch him then, he in his new shoes, I sitting, staring lamely at a gift I cannot recall. Now that he is gone, I have no idea how to bear having failed at this, the knowledge of how to stand and hold on to my one son.

HOT LIGHTS

For long stretches of time a day I kept my body inside my clothes, but sometimes it broke out and made a fool out of "me," the me I wanted to represent to the outside world. Hungry for heat and light, my body rolled itself out of hiding at the snap of a klieg light, and this scared me. Certainly it ruined my chances for ever running for public office, and I suppose limited my options in other ways. For everything one's body does limits or directs the rest of one's future. I met Jig Johnson in the early seventies, when I was a college student, high as a kite but perpetually short on cash. Drugs were cheap then, so was liquor, but since I had only a job as a grocery clerk I was always on the make, trying to stay alive in New York. Four times a week I would sell my blood, traipsing from bank to blood bank all over midtown with a sprightly gait that tires me now just to think of it. A pal at school told me, *sotto voce*, of a man who paid students large sums for acting in porn loops. He said these loops, in primitive color, badly lit, could be seen in various raucous Times Square peep shows, where weirdos dropped a quarter in a slot and a lead shield shot up into the wall, unveiling a twist of naked limbs and cocks. At some random time, say, five minutes, the shield descended again implacably.

"Uh . . ." "Duh . . ." I weighed the pros and cons in my head like the figure of Libra on *Perry Mason*. Trying to figure out what would be right for me, but not thinking very clearly. I was naive to the nth degree. First of all, thanks to a steady diet of so-called "soft" porn, I didn't imagine that "acting" in porn would involve having sex in front of a camera. I had never actually seen a hard porn film. I had the suspicion that the actors might take off their clothes, might kiss, might pretend to have a kind of sex. Cynically I thought everything else was faked, as in Hollywood films. "Special effects." I remember, around that time, reading current discussions of gay representation in the media. I was taking "creative writing" at school, so I felt personally involved with the debate, and felt obliged to make all my gay characters positive images. Oh, amid what fog of delusion I walked Manhattan, straining my brains to think of ways to make everyone lovable. . . . How would my appearance in a porn film affect the representation of my tribe? I couldn't work it out. When I called Jig Johnson from a public phone in the lobby of school, the line was busy so I went to my French class. After 90 minutes of Rimbaud and Verlaine I tried the number again. Ring. Ring. "Hello?" That's when I started to panic. Luckily Johnson was businesslike and really together, as if to compensate for the stupid qualms of the guys who were probably always calling him up to feed their habits. He asked me if I was ready to play with the big boys. "Sure." He asked if I was free that evening for my audition. There was a bottle of Southern Comfort in my pocket. Secretively I downed some, then sifted my little pile of thoughts like Brian Wilson playing in that sandbox. "What time?" I said, nodding out.

In his apartment he held my cock in his hands and watched it swell up, like one of those time-lapse photography miracles on public TV. I stared down too, feeling the simultaneous pride and shame of an unbidden erection. Presently, when I was hard as a bone, Johnson slapped my cock, told me to get down on my hands and knees on the floor. "Head on the side of the bed," he called out from the other room, the room where my clothes were, I hoped. On the pinstriped gamy mattress, stained with a dozen men's come, I lay my head flat, praying I'd make it through my audition.

He dug a flash camera out of the hamper and dangled it close to my nose. God knows what I looked like, what distorted expression was frozen on my dumb face. Then the flash exploded and the chemical smell of the early Polaroid film filled the squalid room. As I remained there, stiff and blinking, he moved behind me to crouch down between my legs. I felt him trying to spread my knees, so I helped, trying to oblige. I don't know, did I do the right thing? I felt a wet hand slither down my butt, down its crack, and I wondered if he was going to screw me. I kept thinking, *I'm playing with the big boys now.*

But he told me he just wanted a picture of my asshole.

And there I was thinking, *What, no sex?* I remember being assaulted by my own thoughts and my feelings of unworthiness, while the Polaroid started to whirl. Presently he threw down two pictures in front of my face: grainy shots, in lurid color, of my demented face and my tight little red hole, like a bullet hole in the middle of what seemed an absurdly overstated butt.

"You'll be perfect," he said, and I wondered what perfection meant, if such banal evidences gave me so much pause. "You can dress now," he said, in a gentler tone. I covered my crotch with my hands as I walked out of the room. Like a little boy surprised. Suddenly I realized that porn acting involved actual sex captured on film. It just came to me in a revelation like Saint Paul on the way to Damascus — a blinding light. "Far out," I thought, for I was always ready to have sex with other guys, but at the same time the thought of film's perpetuity unnerved me. It's one thing to reflect that no matter how much of a mess she became, we can always think of Judy Garland as sweet sixteen singing in the corn-field; it was another to consider that, in a certain sense, I would always be a nineteen-year-old nitwit with a cock up my ass and a pot-induced glaze in my eyes. I found my clothes, undisturbed, and jammed them on willy-nilly. Johnson produced a bent card, with an address scribbled on the back. He tied my necktie for me, humming, helped me tuck in my shirt. He smelled of some lem-ony scent like the floor wax my mother used at home on her kitchen. He was indescribably dapper, everything I thought of when I thought of the words "New York." Even the points of his collar were perfect white triangles, stiff, formal, like watercress sandwiches cut in half. I felt like a slob in front of him, could hardly look him in the eye. If I had, oh dear, what pity or con-tempt would I have seen there? Or was I his mirror, his younger self, a self without a single social grace, no ease? I steeled up my courage and insisted that I wouldn't play an effeminate hysterical hairdresser in his loop, a type gay activists were deploring in the great debate. "You won't be playing any type," he said — probably baffled. "You'll just be yourself." Swell, except I didn't know who that self could be. In looks I resembled a slightly beefed-up ver-sion of the Disney actress Hayley Mills — very androgynous, in the spirit of the times — and my voice had hardly broken, so I was still prone to embarrassing squeaks that made me wish the floor would open up. So — so whatever . . .

At the front door another guy waited, in old army fatigues, and as if on a whim, Johnson had me unbutton the guy's pants and suck his cock for a minute. I thought about it for maybe ten sec-onds, then agreed, for auditioning had made me horny, and until this possibility of contact, I felt utterly unattractive. "Hi," the guy said. "Hmhhrw!" said I. He was my age, nineteen, or just about, with chalky white skin and hair dyed orange as Tropicana. I massaged his muscled thighs as I bobbed up and down in his lap. "That's fine," said Jig Johnson. "You can stop now." My co-star, whose name turned out to be Guy, shot a pitying glance at Johnson. "Where you recruiting now, Jig?" he said shakily. "Port Authority?" Johnson smiled and caressed Guy's orange sideburn in an absent, avuncular manner, while Guy yawned and gradually reeled his dick back in his khakis. "There'll be six of you tomorrow," Johnson said. "Meet us at ten o'clock, Kevin."

"Okay," I stuttered, "and thanks, Mr. Johnson."

Guy called after me, "You're too good for this son of a bitch." Right then I kind of fell in love a bit. I set my alarm over and over again, took a dozen showers.

Of the actual filming I recall very little. I mounted the stairs of a dilapidated building a block from Broadway — had the space once been a dance studio? Big quiet room, torn blinds drawn to the floor, a room scattered with the kind of furniture college students leave behind in their dorm rooms after they graduate. There was a steady roar in my head, a dull roar like a subway station, a roar which rose as I met my other co-stars and first saw the camera, a big box with a red light beaming underneath to show we were "on." Had they invented videotape back then? I don't think so. Here film itself was the precious, expensive thing, to be parceled out in stingy, dear bits. I asked for my script, to give me something to read, something to look at instead of all those distracting bodies sliding out of street clothes. I did notice that one guy had a shorter dick than mine, so I butched it up in all our scenes together. I'm no fool, I thought, *one less thing to obsess about . . .*

"Jig, Kevin wants to take a look at the script." First a blank look, then a laugh, then everyone laughed at my naivete. Guy, my co-star, patted my back consolingly, long white pats that brought the sweat dripping down into the crack of my ass. Nice guy. None of us had scripts *per se*, but there were scratch marks all over the carpet, drawn with chalk, I suppose, of where we would stand at various intervals, usually down on one knee. Mystifying marks like the arbitrary symbols in the Lascaux caves. Johnson told us to make up all our dialogue, since another gang of boys would dub us over in a different situation, probably a different city. Everyone was hard, stiff, unbelievably so, and when the hot lights bore down on my erection it gleamed like topaz, under a light coating of mineral oil, and I said to myself, *I'd* take that home with me! *I'd* pay money to see that! *Who's* attached to this rod of steel?

It — my rod of steel — twitched; and great shadows leapt and fell across Guy's startled, tiny face underneath: he resembled a still from some excellent Maya Deren film like *Meshes in the Afternoon*.

One guy, Charles, long blond hair like Fabio's, touch of a blond goatee at the base of his spine, spent hours bent over the back of a large sofa, getting fucked over and over, and his only line was "Mount me" — *that* stuck with me. In the morning his asshole was a thin slit, moist, exquisitely puckered, but by late afternoon it looked like a red rubber ball, torn in half, and pierced with blood, sunk deep within. Most of all I remember the heat of the lights, how huge lights two feet wide threatened to blow the fuses of the entire apartment building, and how when their shutters opened a giant click sound rocked the whole room. These white-hot domes, trained on one's skin, were like the great eyes of God the poet Jack Spicer wrote of in *Imaginary Elegies*. They see everything, even under the skin where your thoughts are. Your dirty little thoughts. You can take off all your clothes and pretend to be "naked," but you are still Kevin Killian from Smithtown, Long

Island, with all the petty details that denotes. And yet at the same time the heat made me feel languorous, forgetful, like Maria Montez at the top of some Aztec staircase — dangerous, as though there were nothing beyond the circle of white — no audience, no society, only oneself and the red or purple or black hard-on that floats magically to the level of one's lips. I suppose all actors must feel the same way in some part of being — that the camera's eye represents the eye of God, which at the same time judges all and, threateningly, withholds all judgment till time turns off.

We poured out onto the street at sunset, tired and spent, yakking it up. We would never be stars, I thought. No one would ever see this "loop." And I was glad, but sorry too. I asked if anyone knew the name of the picture. No one did. (Charlie said they should call it "Saddlesore.") It didn't really have a name, and as such, I thought, it had no real existence. Just six guys fucking and sucking. We said we would all meet in six months at a Times Square grindhouse for the premiere. *Auld* acquaintance. I tried visualizing our putative audience and words popped into my head: "a bunch of perverts" — shady men in black trenchcoats, visiting conventioneers touring the louche side of gay New York. Nobodies, in fact. "Bye, dudes." "Later." "Adios." I took away more money than I'd ever made in my life — a hundred dollars, except Johnson took back like three dollars because he bought us some lunch — beer and Kentucky Fried Chicken. At the same time I read some interview with Lou Reed: asked whether he thought homosexuality was increasing, he replied to the effect that, "It's a fad, but people will tire of it, because eventually you have to suck cock or get your ass fucked." I reflected that I had in one fell swoop ruined my chance to be President, earned $97.00, made a new boyfriend, kind of, solidified my connections with the entertainment world, had some great sex and still I felt utterly ashamed of my specularity, my need to see and be seen. I came onto the face and chest of a boy, and my semen seemed to spatter and fry before my eyes, as though his body were the very skillet of love, such was the wattage of those hot lights.

I remember walking around Columbus Circle looking for things to buy with my money, and feeling disappointed there were no stores there, only pretzel vendors and hot dog carts, so I bought a pretzel and a hot dog, and stood with one foot curled around the ironwork fence at Central Park South, watching the crowd. Wondering if anyone could "tell." My wallet felt fat, expansive, as though my money might grow to enormous size and eat the whole fucking city. I was so filled up with energy I thought I could walk all the way uptown to Guy's neighborhood, then just kind of drop in, rekindle our newfound intimacy, lick that dead-white skin from the nape of his neck to the puncture wounds inside his arm. . . . I slid into a bar on Sixth Avenue, pondering desire, Guy, money and guilt. Had I let down my tribe by playing a part which wasn't actually a part *per se*, but couldn't therefore be a "positive" one? Wish I could go back and console my younger self, rub his young shoulders, explicate latter-day porn theory to cheer him up. And also get him to cut back on all that drinking! At once the most and least ironic of art forms, pornography undercuts the performative authenticity of penetration with oh, just lashes of mad camp. Its greatest stars, like those of performance art, are the biggest dopes in the world; its most discerning fans those, like my present-day self, who feel ourselves beyond representation for one imaginary reason or another. I stepped into a liquor store on 82nd for a bottle of Seagrams 7, knowing I'd find an answer in its rich, musky depths. On the way out I saw a phone booth, and I called Guy, who had scrawled his number backwards up my thigh from the back of my knee to the juncture of my balls. "I know it's not six months yet," I said, "but I was thinking — "

"I can still taste your dick in my mouth," he said — an encouraging sign, or so I thought, but instead he hung up on me, and I felt a blush rise right up to my temples. I thought everyone was staring at the dumb boy on the dumb phone who just got the brushoff. The glare of judgment burning me like lasers through my cool.

I kept thinking, I'm wearing way too many clothes! And I fled. Finally night fell and I looked up at the moon that shone over Morningside Heights, its white soft beam so limpid, full of the poetry of Shakespeare and the Caribbean and George Eliot — the antithesis, I suppose, of the hot lights I had grown to need. How relaxed, how relieved I now felt, in the white moonlight. Relieved of the chore of playing with the big boys. My clothes seemed to fit again, I became myself. The moon's fleecy lambency corralled my pieces and re-linked us, we joined "hands" as it were and sang and danced in a circle, very Joseph Campbell, "me" regnant, manhood ceremonial. Birth of the hero. I became Kevin Killian. Did I make a mistake?

CASSANDRA

1972 / Trancas's mother had left everything: a husband, petunia beds, a blue-shuttered house on Zoe's street. She'd taken Trancas to live with her in drunken renunciation until she found the hard kernel of nothing from which she could start again. She was drinking her way to it, smoking Chesterfields two at a time. She was watching television, waiting for the day she'd wasted so many hours that the hours themselves would be ground down, the days indistinguishable from the nights, and she'd be able to look for a different self among the wreckage. She wanted to drop acid with her daughter, but Trancas claimed she didn't know where to get any.

"So long, girls," Trancas's mother called cheerfully from the colored twilight. Television light changed and changed in her glass of Scotch. She'd decided to think of herself and Trancas as sisters, two young criminal girls with everything ahead of them.

Zoe understood about Trancas's mother. She'd left the curtains and the shelf paper, gone to live in the wild. She wanted to look at her human life through an animal's eyes, to see where the mistakes were buried.

"Fuck off," Trancas muttered.

Zoe pinched Trancas's arm, which was hard and fat as a sausage. Zoe loved Trancas's mother. She respected her exhausted and ironic hope for rebirth.

"Have fun," Trancas's mother said. She looked at the television screen through her Scotch. It would have looked like a kaleidoscope, Zoe thought. Trancas's mother was skinny and precise as an ancient ballerina, grandly slovenly as an insane queen. She wore an Indian blouse embroidered with flowers and furtive glintings of mirror. She put out a wan, unsteady light that matched the light of the television. She could have been a figure from the television, projected into the room.

"Good night, Mrs. Harris," Zoe said. Trancas pushed her out the door, closed it as if she were shutting in deadly radiation. Trancas pitied and feared her mother with an ardor more potent than romance.

"Fuck off," Trancas said again, louder, to the scarred, thickly painted wood of the door.

"Don't be so hard on her," Zoe said.

"You're not her daughter," Trancas answered. "You go back to Garden City tomorrow."

"You hate Garden City."

"She burned up a chair last night," Trancas said. "With one of her cigarettes. I came out of my bedroom and there she was, fast asleep, with smoke all over the place and this little lick of fire right next to her ass."

"She should be more careful," Zoe said, but she understood even the desire to burn. Trancas' mother had probably dreamed about sitting on a chair of fire, going up with the smoke and looking down at the old business of the world.

"Damn right," Trancas said. "If she wants to kill herself, okay. Just don't take me and half the building along with her."

"She's depressed."

"She's a fucking lunatic, is what she is. Come on, let's get out of here."

Trancas and Zoe walked down Jane Street together, under the night shimmer of the trees. Trancas had been Zoe's best friend since they were both nine years old, and now Trancas had left the old world of rules and girlish hungers. Zoe visited on weekends. She kept other clothes in Trancas's closet: a black miniskirt, a translucent blouse the color of strong coffee. In New York, some men treated her as if she were beautiful.

"Tomorrow," Trancas said, "I want to go look at a motorcycle."

"What kind of motorcycle?"

Trancas pulled a scrap of newspaper from her back pocket. "Somebody on West Tenth is selling an old Harley for three hundred dollars," she said.

"You don't have three hundred dollars. You don't have any money at all."

"If I like this bike well enough, I'll get the three hundred."

Trancas was trying out a new heedlessness, a big mean-spirited freedom that never worried. She was planning her own escape. Lately she'd been packing on weight, pushing her jaw out to make her face look squarer and less kind. She talked about buying a motorcycle, a leather jacket, a pearl-handled knife. Zoe was still her best friend and, in some obscure new way, the bride of her new ideas. They walked the streets like lovers.

"Where could you get three hundred dollars?" Zoe asked.

"You can do it," Trancas said. "There are ways."

She was cultivating secrets. When she and Zoe met, Trancas had been tall and intelligent, clumsy, undesired. She'd lived in bulky, slow-moving confusion among her own chaos of mistakes and hopes. Now she was taking on size. She was talking about California.

"Maybe your mother would buy it for you," Zoe said.

"Right," Trancas answered.

"You could ask her."

"She doesn't have any money."

"Your father must send her some."

"She won't cash his checks. She wiped her ass with the last one and sent it back to him."

Trancas had fallen in love with her mother's bad behavior. Some of the stories were true.

"Why don't you ask your father, then?" Zoe said.

"For money for a motorcycle? He wants to buy me ballet shoes. He keeps telling me it's not too late to start."

Zoe took her friend's hand as they crossed Hudson Street. The night sky was filled with tight little fists of cloud, bright gray against the red-black.

They went to one of the bars Trancas liked, over in the East Village. The bar burned a damp blue light inside its own stale darkness. Men danced in leather cowboy clothes, and no one ever seemed to notice or care that Zoe and Trancas were sixteen. It was the kind of bar you could walk into with a snake draped over your shoulders. On the jukebox, James Brown sang "Super Bad."

Trancas and Zoe sat on the broken sofa at the back, near the pool table and the reek of the bathrooms. Trancas lit up a joint, passed it to Zoe.

"Crowded in here tonight," Trancas said.

"Mm-hm."

"Look at that guy with the tattoos."

"Where?"

"Right there. Playing pool."

A sinewy, feline-faced man leaned into the puddle of brighter light that fell onto the pool table, took aim at the seven ball. His arms swarmed with hearts and daggers and grinning skulls, the snaky bodies and alert, hungry faces of dragons.

"Cool," Trancas said.

"Mm-hm."

"I'm getting a tattoo."

"What kind?"

"Maybe a rose," Trancas said. "On my ass."

"You'd have it forever," Zoe told her.

"I'd like to know I was going to have something forever. Wouldn't you?"

"Well. Yes, I guess I would."

They smoked the joint, listened to the music. Time didn't pass in the bar, there was just music and different kinds of dark. Zoe was afraid and she liked it. She liked night in the city in bars like this, all the little dangers and promises. It was like going to live in the woods. Back in Garden City, all the food stood on the shelves in alphabetical order.

"Maybe a lightning bolt," Trancas said.

"What?" Zoe was getting stoned. She could feel the music moving in her. She could see that the worn brown plush of the sofa arm was a world unto itself.

"A lightning bolt instead of a rose," Trancas said. "I think maybe a rose'd be too, you know. A *rose*."

"I like roses," Zoe said.

"Then you should get one."

"Maybe I will."

"You can get a rose, and I'll get a lightning bolt. Or a dragon. I like the one dragon that guy's got on his arm."

"You can get a lightning bolt *and* a dragon," Zoe said.

"I will. I just have to decide which I want first."

Trancas took out another joint and then a man was sitting on the arm of the sofa. Zoe hadn't seen him sit down. She wondered if he'd been there all along. No, a few minutes ago she'd been staring at the bare brown plush.

"Hey," the man said. He smiled. He was haloed with hair. He had a brittle storm of black hair on his head and he had prickly black sideburns and an electric little V of beard. He was dark and blurred, like a tattoo.

"Hi," Zoe said. She got a buzz from him right away, this compact smiling man ablaze with hair. Dope made her languid and prone to sex.

"What's up?"

"Nothing. Sitting here."

She offered him the joint and he took a hit. His face pulled in cartoonishly around the joint, eyes squeezed shut and lips puckered. Zoe laughed.

"What's so funny?" he asked, handing back the joint.

She shook her head, took another hit. There was something sexy about this sweet little cartoon man. There was something alert and lost, canine. He wore black motorcycle boots, a black velvet shirt. He could have been a figure who popped out of a black cuckoo clock to announce the hour.

"You're very pretty," he said. "Do you mind me telling you that?"

"I'm not really pretty," she said. "I wish I was."

"You are."

"No. Maybe I look pretty in this light because I want to, I mean you're probably not seeing *me*, you're just seeing how much I'd like to be a pretty girl sitting on a sofa in a bar."

She laughed again. It was good dope.

"What was that?" he said.

"I don't know. I don't have any idea what I just said."

"You're a weird girl, huh?"

"Yes. I'm a weird girl."

"That's good. I like weird. You're a girl, ain't you?"

"What?"

"You're not a boy."

"No. I'm not a boy."

"Good," he said. "Hey, I like boys, but I like to know what's what. You understand what I'm saying?"

"I guess so. No. Not really."

"A lot of the girls who come in this place ain't really girls."

"I know that," she said. Did she know? She was losing track.

"I can tell you are, though. You've got this thing they can't fake, it's like a glow. You know what I'm saying?"

"You're saying I glow."

"Uh-huh. My name is Ted."

"Hi, Ted. I'm Zoe. This is my friend Trancas."

"Pleased to meet you. Listen, you two want to do a few lines?" he asked.

"Okay. Sure."

"I got a gram or two up at my place. I live right across the street there, how'd you two like to run over there with me and do a few quick lines?"

Zoe looked at Trancas, who shrugged. Trancas refused to say no. She wasn't turning into the kind of person who'd use that word.

"Okay," Zoe said.

"Come on."

The man stood up and Zoe and Trancas were standing up, too, when a voice said, "Girls, don't go with that one."

Zoe saw his shoes first, red sling-back pumps with a five-inch heel. She thought, My mother has a pair like that, but not so high. The rest of him was army fatigues, a ruffled off-the-shoulder blouse, a platinum wig that fell with a bright chemical crackle to his shoulders. He stood with his hands on his hips, emitting a faint, powdery light. His face was sharp and narrow, full of brash indignant complications.

"Fuck off, Cassandra," Ted said.

"That one is bad news, ladies," the man in the wig said. "Don't mess with him unless you like it rough and I mean *rough*."

"Fuck you."

"He had a girl in the hospital last month, and I told him if he started working this bar again I would hound his ass. You think I was bluffing, Nick, honey?"

"Actually, his name is Ted," Zoe said.

The man said to Zoe and Trancas, "This bar pulls scum in off the street like shit pulls in flies. Come on."

"Up to you, ladies," the man in the wig said. "As long as you know what you're getting yourselves into."

Zoe paused, half standing. She knew Trancas wouldn't change her mind. She couldn't; any show of fear or common sense would push her backward toward the tall unloved nervous girl she'd resolved to stop being. Zoe looked at the cartoon man, scowling now, and she looked at the man in the wig, who stood like a crazy goddess of propriety and delusion, his sharp face jutting out from between the silver curtains of his wig and piles of colored bracelets winking on his arms. Zoe thought of Alice on the far side of the looking glass, an innocent and sensible girl. What Alice brought to Wonderland was her calm good sense, her Englishness. She saved herself by being correct, by listening seriously to talking animals and crazy people.

Zoe decided. She said to Ted or Nick, "Maybe we'll just stay here." To Trancas she added, "Unless you want to go."

Trancas, relieved, shook her head. "I'll stay with you," she said. "Hey, girl, I can't leave you alone in a place like this."

The man said, "You're going to let yourselves get scared off by this sleazeball? You're joking. You're playing a joke on me, right?"

"No," Zoe said. "We're going to stay. Thanks, anyway."

His face puckered in on itself. He might have been trying to make his head smaller. "Right," he said. "Listen to bag ladies, listen to bums, they know what they're talking about. Listen to drag queens that were locked up in Bellevue a week ago."

"Not true," the wigged man said to Zoe. His voice was full of a dowager's conviction, a drawling and leisurely grandness. "I've never been to Bellevue or any other institution for the criminally insane. I don't deny that I've done a little time for shoplifting, but, honey, it didn't in any way compromise my ability to know a pervert when I see one."

"A pervert," the man said. "Right. You're calling me a pervert."

"A pervert," said the man in the wig, "is somebody who does things to other people they don't want done to them. Period."

"Come on," the leather man said to Zoe. "I don't want to look at this fucker's ugly face anymore."

"We're not going," Zoe told him. "Really."

He shook his head. "Stupid bitch," he said.

The man in the wig raised his hands and waggled his fingers. "Be gone," he said. "You have no power here."

And Nick or Ted was gone, whispering insults, scattering them like little poison roses.

"You made the right choice, girls," the man in the wig said. "Believe me."

Zoe was filled with gratitude and fear, a slippery respect. She'd seen drag queens in the bar before but it had never occurred to her that she was visible to them.

"My name is Trancas," Trancas said eagerly, "and this is my friend Zoe. What's your name?" Trancas wanted to live a bar life, to know all the drag queens by their names.

"Cassandra," the man said. "Charmed, I'm sure." Now that the leather man had gone, Cassandra appeared to have lost interest.

He glanced around, preparing to leave. He glittered in the heavy air like a school of fish.

"I like your earrings," Zoe said. One of Cassandra's earrings was a silver rocket ship, the other a copper moon with an irritable, unsettled face.

Trancas said, "Yeah, they're great."

Cassandra touched his earrings. "Oh, the rocket and the moon," he said. "Fabulous, aren't they? You want 'em?"

"Oh, no," Zoe said.

"I insist." Cassandra pulled the moon out of his ear. Its tiny copper face darkened in the bar light.

"No, really, please," Zoe said. "I couldn't."

"Is it a question of sanitation?" Cassandra asked.

"*No.* I just —"

"Let's split them," he said. "You take the moon, I'll keep the rocket." He dangled the moon, the size of a penny, before her face.

"Really?" Zoe said. "I mean, you don't know me."

"Honey," Cassandra told her, "I am a Christmas tree. I drop a little tinsel here, a little there. There is always, always more stuff. Trust me. It's a great big world and it is just *made* of stuff. Besides, I stole this trash, I can always steal more."

Zoe reached for the earring. Trancas helped her run the post through her earlobe. "This is a great little thing," Trancas said. "This is a treasure, here."

"Now we're earring sisters," Cassandra said. "Bound together for life."

"Thank you," Zoe said.

"You're welcome," Cassandra said. "Now excuse me, will you, girls?" He walked away, expert in his heels. His platinum wig sizzled with artificial light.

"Wow," Trancas said. "Now *that's* a character."

"I wonder if he saved our lives," Zoe said.

"Probably. He's our fairy fucking godmother, is what he is."

Trancas and Zoe went back to smoking dope on the sofa, but now only less could happen. They finished the joint and left the bar. They went to a few other places, smoked another joint, danced together and watched the men. When they got back to Trancas's apartment they found her mother snoring in front of the television. Zoe checked for the first stirrings of fire. Trancas put her finger to her mother's sleeping head. She said, "Bang." Her mother smiled over a dream, and did not awaken.

Momma said, "I wish you'd stay home this weekend. What's so endlessly fascinating about New York?"

"Trancas is lonely up there," Zoe said. "She needs me to come."

Momma wore red tennis shoes. She put her shadow over the tiny beans and lettuces, the darker, more confident unfurling of the squash. Momma stood in a swarm of little hungers. When the beans were ready she'd pull them off the vines, toss them in boiling water.

"Trancas," she said, "can probably manage on her own for a weekend or two."

"I miss her," Zoe said. "I'm lonely here, too."

She wore Cassandra's copper moon in her ear. She wore the clothes of her household life, patched jeans and a tie-dyed T-shirt. She squatted among the labeled rows, pulling weeds. The dirt threw up its own shade, something cool and slumbering it pulled from deep inside.

"Let her go, Mary," Poppa said. He carried a flat of marigolds so bright it seemed they must put out heat. Poppa himself had a hot brightness, a sorrow keen as fire.

"I just think it's getting to be a bit much," Momma said. "Every single weekend."

Poppa came and stood beside Zoe. He touched her hair. When they were in the garden together, he defended her right to do everything she wanted. Outside the garden, he lost track of her. His love still held but he couldn't hold onto the idea of her without a language of roots and topsoil; the shared, legible ambition to encourage growth.

"This is her best friend," he said. "And hey, it ain't like there's much happening here on Long Island on a Saturday night. Am I right, Zo?"

Zoe shrugged. There was a lot happening everywhere. But she had some kind of business in New York. She wasn't after fame and the victory of self-destruction like Trancas was. She wanted something else, something more like what Alice must have had after she'd gone to Wonderland and then returned to the world of gardens and schoolbooks and laundry on the line. She wanted to feel larger inside herself.

"Fine," Momma said, and her voice took on a gratified bitterness. She loved defeat with a sour, grudging appetite, the way she loved food. "Do whatever you like."

She went back into the house, stepping on the grass in red canvas shoes. Poppa stood over Zoe, still touching her hair with one hand and holding the flat of marigolds in the other. The smell of the flowers cascaded down, rank and sweet. Marigolds collapsed helplessly inside their own odor. They were just smell and color, no rude vegetable integrity.

"Let's get these planted," Poppa said tenderly. "And I'll take you to the twelve-thirty train."

"Thanks," she said. "I'm sorry I go away so much."

"It's okay," he told her, and she knew he was telling the truth. Susan's absence punched a hole in the house, and Billy's did, too. Susan took a piece of the future with her when she went; Billy took the mistakes of the past and made them permanent. Her own departure had a different kind of logic. It was part of her job to leave.

Sometimes Cassandra was in the bar. Sometimes he wasn't. Zoe found that she waited all week for the nights she went out to the bar with Trancas, and when Cassandra wasn't there Zoe felt dejected and diminished, as if a promise had not been kept. When Cassandra was there Zoe said hello to him with a swell of anxious hope, the way she'd speak to a boy she loved. Cassandra always said, 'Hello, honey,' and moved on. Zoe wasn't in love with Cassandra but she wanted something from him. She couldn't tell what it was.

Trancas started turning tricks to earn the money for a motorcycle. She told the first story as an accomplishment.

"I hung around in front of this video place on Forty-second," she said to Zoe in a coffee shop on Waverly. "I was so scared, I was like, what if nobody wants me? What if nobody even knows what I'm doing?"

Trancas's face was bright and homely, red with an exaltation that resembled rage. She dumped five spoonfuls of sugar into her coffee. She wore her gray denim jacket and a Grateful Dead T-shirt, a skeleton crowned with roses.

She said, "I told myself I'd stand there, like, fifteen minutes, and if nothing happened, I'd go home. So, like, about fourteen and a half minutes go by and suddenly this guy comes up to me, just a regular guy about fifty. He didn't look rich but he didn't look like a creep either, he was just all polyester, one of those *guys*, you know, just a guy, probably worked in an office and did something all day and then went home again. Anyway, he comes up to me and at first I thought, he's a friend of my father's. Then I thought, no, he's gonna tell me something like the bus stop is down at the corner or give me some kind of Jesus pamphlet or something. But no. He walks right up to me and says, 'Hi.' I say hello back, and he says, 'Can we make a deal?' And my heart is pounding and I'm so scared but my voice comes out like I've done this a thousand times before, like I'm an old hand at it. I look at him a minute and then I say, 'Maybe.' And it was *weird*, Zo. It was like I knew exactly what to do and what to say and how to be. He asks, 'What do you charge?' and I say, 'Depends on what you want.' I was so *cool*, I don't know where it came from."

"What did *he* say?" Zoe asked. She leaned forward over the scarred, speckled surface of the table. In the kitchen of the coffee shop, a man with an accent sang, "Hang down, Sloopy, Sloopy, hang down."

Trancas said, "He said, 'I want to get blown, and I want a little affection.' And you know what I said?"

"What?"

"I said, 'A blow job costs thirty dollars, and I don't do affection.'"

"I don't believe you."

"It's true. I was cool, Zo. I was playing a part and I was perfect at it."

"Then what happened?"

"He said, 'How's about twenty-five?' And I just *looked* at him, like, stop wasting my time, jerk. And he sort of laughed, this big old haw-haw-haw with his big teeth showing, and he said okay, thirty it is. Then I thought, shit, what happens now? Am I supposed to know a hotel for us to go to? But he said to come with him, and we went, like, a few blocks over to this hotel he was staying in, the Edison or something. Yeah, the Edison. And we went up to his room and I said, 'Before we go any farther, how about my thirty bucks?' He did that haw-haw-haw thing again, and he gave me the money. Man. His teeth were as big as dice.

He didn't ask me any questions. He didn't even ask how old I was. He just took his clothes off and he wasn't a pretty sight but he wasn't the worst thing I've ever seen either and I took my clothes off and blew the motherfucker right there on the bed and then I put my clothes back on and got the hell out."

"That's it?" Zoe asked.

"That's it. Thirty bucks."

"You really did it?"

"Only way to get the money."

"Weren't you scared?"

"Zoe, I *told* you I was scared."

"I mean, of him."

"No. He was nothing to be scared of, you'd know that if you'd seen him."

Zoe sipped her coffee, looked out the steamed window at Waverly Place. An obese man walked a gleeful-looking yellow dog he had dressed in a white blouse and a plaid skirt. There was a new world with no rules and there was the old world with too many. She didn't know how to live in either place. Her mother was the guardian spirit of the old world. Her mother was proud and offended and she warned Zoe: Never let a boy talk you into losing control, boys want to ruin everything you prize.

Cassandra was the guardian spirit of the new world. He believed in sex but he believed in safety, too. He cautioned girls against going off with men who secretly worshipped harm.

Zoe said to Trancas, "I don't know if you should be doing this."

Trancas's face held its rapt, furious light. She was already gone.

"Thirty dollars, Zo," she said. "For, like, twenty minutes' work. Nine more guys, and I can get myself that Harley."

"It's prostitution, though."

"Man. So is being a waitress or secretary. This just pays better."

Zoe looked at Trancas and tried to know. Was she setting herself free, or was she beginning the long work of killing herself? How could you be sure of the difference between emancipation and suicide?

"If you're going to keep doing it, be careful," Zoe said.

"Right," Trancas answered, and Zoe could see her dead. She could see her blue-white skin and the faint smile she'd wear, having beaten her mother, having gotten first to the wildest, most remote place of all. Having won.

Cassandra stood at the bar that night in an old prom dress, a chaos of emerald satin and lime-green chiffon. Zoe waited until Trancas had gone to the bathroom and went quickly up to Cassandra. Cassandra held a drink in his hand, talked to a tall black man in a velvet cloak and a canary-colored pillbox hat.

Zoe said, "Hello, Cassandra."

Cassandra's face was clever and squashed-looking under his pancake makeup, his lipstick and eyelashes. Cosmetics and the intricate cross-purposes of being a man and being a woman seemed to impel him forward, and he could look, at times, as if he were pressing his face against a pane of glass, speaking distinctly and a little too loud to someone on the other side.

"Why, hello, baby," he said. "How are you?"

"I'm all right. Actually, I wondered if I could talk to you for a minute."

"Honey, you can talk all you want. Start at the beginning and just work your way straight through to the end."

"Maybe, alone? It will just take a minute."

"There's nothing in this world that could possibly shock Miss Cinnamon here," Cassandra said.

"You got that right," Miss Cinnamon said. A scrap of yellow veil quivered like insect wings over his shining brow.

Zoe paused nervously. "Well," she said. "You know Trancas, my friend?"

"Sure I do."

Zoe paused. She wanted to bury her face in Cassandra's gaudy dress, the slick, livid sheen of it. She wanted to sit on Cassandra's skinny lap, to whisper secrets in his ear and be told that a terrible safety waited beyond the dangers of the ordinary world.

"Speak up, honey," Cassandra said. Her voice was hard and sure as a nail sinking into wood.

Zoe said, "She's started turning tricks."

"Well, I'm sure that's very profitable."

Miss Cinnamon put a huge hand on Zoe's arm. "Does she have herself a can of Mace, honey?"

"I'm worried about her," Zoe said.

"She should carry Mace and a knife," Miss Cinnamon said. "She can get herself a cute little knife, it doesn't have to be any big old thing. She can slip it right down inside her boot."

"Why are you worried?" Cassandra asked.

"I'm afraid she'll get hurt."

"That's why you need Mace and a knife, honey. Listen to what I'm telling you."

"People do get hurt," Cassandra said. "Terrible things happen."

"I know," Zoe said.

"You girls are so *young*. Don't you have parents, or something? Who takes care of you?"

"Trancas and her mother live here in the city. I come up on weekends, I live with my family out on Long Island."

"Another planet," Cassandra said.

"Terrible things happen there, too," Zoe told her.

"Honey, I can imagine. Oh, look, here comes your friend."

Trancas was back from the bathroom. She saw Zoe talking to

Cassandra and came over, full of her own greedy happiness, her love of trials and ruin. Zoe thought of her folding money into her pocket before sucking off a man with teeth the size of dice.

"Hey, Cassandra," Trancas said in her big-voiced, ranch-hand style. To Miss Cinnamon she added, "Great hat."

"Thank you, baby," Miss Cinnamon said demurely. Zoe saw that Miss Cinnamon had once been a little boy going to church with his mother. He had sat before an altar, under the suffering wooden eyes of Christ, as a chorus of velvets and brocades and crinolines sighed around him.

Cassandra said, "We were just discussing the ins and outs of the business."

Trancas glanced at Zoe. Trancas's face was clouded with embarrassment and a defiant anger that resembled pride but was not pride.

"Right," she said. "The business."

"My only advice to you, dear," Cassandra said, "is don't undersell. Not at your age. You could get twenty dollars for taking off your *shirt*, don't suck cock for less than fifty. If somebody tries to tell you he can get a blow job for half that much up the block, he's talking about getting it from some tired old thing who can barely walk unassisted and who needs her glasses to find a hard-on. Tell him to go right ahead and get himself a bargain, if that's what he's after. Now, if you're willing to fuck 'em, charge a hundred, at least. Don't flinch when you name your price. Don't bargain. And if you *do* fuck, make them all wear condoms. You don't know *where* some of those cocks have been."

"Okay," Trancas said.

"And, baby," Miss Cinnamon said, "I was telling your friend here, carry protection. You get yourself some Mace, and a pretty little knife you can slip down in your boot."

"Right," Trancas said.

"We're the voices of experience, dear," Cassandra said. "Listen to your aunts."

"Okay," Trancas said, and her face briefly shed its habitual expression of ardent mistrust.

They stood for a moment in silence, the four of them. Zoe was filled with a queasy mixture of love and fear unlike any emotion she could remember. She felt herself leaving her old life, the dinners and furniture, the calm green emptiness of the back yard. As a little girl she'd imagined living in the woods, but she knew she couldn't do that, not really. She couldn't build a nest in a tree, eat mushrooms and berries. Even if she'd had the courage to try it, someone would have come for her. She'd have been sent to one of the places that received girls who believed they could escape a life of rooms, and kept there until she'd renounced her wishes.

These were woods no one could stop her from living in. This was a destiny a girl was allowed to make for herself, this immense promiscuous city that harbored the strangest children.

She said to Cassandra, "Could I take you to tea sometime?"

Cassandra blinked, started to smile. "Excuse me? Tea?"

"Or, you know. A cup of coffee. I'd just like to talk to you. You're my aunt, right?"

Cassandra paused, considering. She smiled at Miss Cinnamon. Zoe felt as if she were talking to two wealthy, celebrated women. They had that private entitlement. They had that lofty, sneering grace.

"Tea," he said to Miss Cinnamon, and he pronounced the word as if it was both funny and frightening. Then he got a pen from the bartender and wrote his number on a napkin.

"You should know," he said as he handed the napkin to Zoe, "that your Aunt Cassandra will kill you if you ever, under any circumstances, call this number before three in the afternoon. Do you understand me?"

"Yes," Zoe said. "I understand."

Miss Cinnamon said, "There is nothing more evil than a drag queen getting woken up before she's ready. Believe me, baby, you don't want to mess with *that.*"

Contributors

EDMUND WHITE is the author of *Forgetting Elena, Nocturnes for the King of Naples, States of Desire: Travels in Gay America, A Boy's Own Story, Caracole, The Beautiful Room Is Empty, Genet: A Biography* (awarded the National Book Critics Circle Award and the Lambda Literary Award), *Skinned Alive,* and *My Paris.* In 1993 he was made a Chevalier de l'Ordre des Arts et Lettres.

JIM PROVENZANO's fiction is featured in *Waves, Queer View Mirror, Hey Paisan, Rainbow Sword,* and *Whispering Campaign.* He has received an N.E.A. grant and a fellowship from the New Jersey and Pennsylvania State arts councils. Born in Queens and raised in Ohio, he lives in San Francisco, where he's a member of the Golden Gate Wrestling Club.

R. S. JONES is the author of *Force of Gravity* and *Walking on Air.* The recipient of a Whiting Writer's Award, he lives in New York City.

JASON K. FRIEDMAN was born in Savannah, Georgia, and teaches in the University of Washington English Department. His short fiction has appeared in *Men on Men 6, His,* the *South Carolina Review, Asylum,* and the *Baltimore City Paper,* and his essay "'Am Am witness to its authenticity': Goth Style in Postmodern Southern Writing" appears in the forthcoming volume *Goth:*

Ethnographies of a Postpunk Subculture. He is the author of *Phantom Trucker* (Random House), a novel for children, and *The Creek Is Gone*, a novel for adults that was the finalist in the Associated Writing Programs 1992 Award Series in the Novel. He is currently working on a new novel for grown-ups.

SCOTT HEIM lived four fifths of his life in Kansas, but now resides in New York City. He is the author of *Mysterious Skin*, a novel, and *Saved from Drowning*, a book of poems. HarperCollins will publish his second novel, *In Awe*, in 1997.

DICK SCANLAN's stories and articles have appeared in *The New Yorker*, the *Village Voice*, the *New York Times*, *Vanity Fair*, the *Advocate*, *Christopher Street*, and other magazines. He lives in New York City with his two dogs. *Does Freddy Dance* is his first book.

ROBERT GLÜCK has recently published two novels, *Margery Kempe* and *Jack the Modernist*, both from High Risk Books/Serpent's Tail. Other books include *Reader*, poems and short prose, *Elements of a Coffee Service*, a book of stories, as well as a number of poetry chapbooks. Glück's work has appeared in *The Faber Book of Gay Short Fiction*, *Discontents*, *Poetics Journal*, *Men on Men* 1 and 4, *City Lights Journal*, *Semiotext(e) USA Anthology*, and elsewhere. The *1994 Dictionary of Literary Biography* listed Glück as one of the ten best postmodern writers in North America. He lives "high on a hill" in San Francisco with his lover, Chris Komater.

ERNESTO MESTRE was born in Guantánamo, Cuba, and is working on a novel set in Cuba during the two decades following the triumph of the Castro revolution. An excerpt from the novel was published in *The James White Review*. He lives in New York City.

JIM GRIMSLEY, author of *Dream Boy*, is the award-winning playwright-in-residence at Atlanta's 7 Stages Theatre. His first novel, *Winter Birds*, was a PEN/Hemingway Award finalist and winner of the Sue Kaufman Prize for First Fiction from the American Academy of Arts and Letters.

ADAM KLEIN studied creative writing at the University of Iowa and San Francisco State University. His work has appeared in *Re/ Mapping the Occident*, *Men on Men 5*, and *BOMB* magazine. He lives in New York City.

MATTHEW STADLER has written three novels, *Landscape: Memory*, *The Dissolution of Nicholas Dee*, and *The Sex Offender*. His forthcoming novel, *Allan Stein*, will be published by HarperCollins next spring. He is the recipient of a Guggenheim Fellowship and a Whiting Writer's Award. He lives and works in Seattle.

CHRISTOPHER BRAM grew up in Virginia and lives in New York City. He is the author of five novels, including *Hold Tight* and *Almost History*. A new novel, *Gossip*, is forthcoming from Dutton.

A native of Los Angeles, BERNARD COOPER is the author of *Maps to Anywhere* and *A Year of Rhymes* (both from Penguin). "Arson" is from *Truth Serum*, a collection of memoirs published by Houghton Mifflin. Parts of *Truth Serum* have appeared in several publications, including *Harper's* magazine, the *Paris Review*, the *Los Angeles Times Magazine*, and *The Best American Essays of 1995*.

JOE WESTMORELAND has been published in loads of queerzines, including *My Comrade*, *Straight to Hell*, *Whispering Campaign*, *Mirage/Period(ical)*, *Hissy Fit*, *Geraldine*, and his own *joezine*, as well as *Discontents*, *The New Fuck You (Adventures in Lesbian*

Reading), and *XXX Fruit*. He lives in New York City and is completing his first novel.

MICHAEL LOWENTHAL'S short stories and essays appear in more than a dozen books, including *Men on Men 5*, *Wrestling with the Angel*, *Friends and Lovers*, and the *Flesh and the Word* series, which he edits. He received a 1995–96 New Hampshire State Council on the Arts fellowship based on the first chapter of his recently completed novel, *In the Shadow of His Wings*. He lives in Boston.

JL SCHNEIDER lives in upstate New York, where he teaches composition, poetry, and fiction at a small community college. His work has recently appeared in *Studies in Contemporary Satire*, *Onion River Review*, and *Aphrodite Gone Berserk*. He is currently working on a novel about his high school experience.

STEPHEN BEACHY is the author of a novel, *The Whistling Song* (Norton, 1991). He has published fiction in *High Risk 2*, as well as *BOMB* and *Men's Style*. He lives in San Francisco, where he is completing his second novel, *Distortion*.

ALDO ALVAREZ is a Clifford D. Clark Fellow at Binghamton University, where he pursues a doctorate in English with a creative dissertation. Columbia University of the City of New York awarded him an M.F.A. in creative writing. His short fiction has been featured in *Christopher Street*, *Amelia*, *Blue Penny Quarterly*, *Pen & Sword*, *Merica*, and other magazines.

RICK BARRETT holds down a day job as a graphic designer in San Francisco. His work has been published in *Christopher Street*.

KEVIN KILLIAN is a San Francisco poet, playwright, novelist, and critic. For six years he has been writing, with Lew Ellingham, a biography of the American poet Jack Spicer. His new books are a collection of stories, *Little Men* (Hard Press), and, with Leslie Scalapino, a play, *Stone Marmalade* (Singing Horse Press).

MICHAEL CUNNINGHAM is the author of *A Home at the End of the World* and *Flesh and Blood*. He lives and writes in New York City.

Honorable Mention

Copyright Acknowledgments

Copyright Acknowledgments